THE JUNIOR BACHELOR SOCIETY

By John A. Williams

MOTHERSILL AND THE FOXES

MINORITIES IN THE CITY

FLASHBACKS

CAPTAIN BLACKMAN

THE KING GOD DIDN'T SAVE
AMISTAD I/AMISTAD II (Coeditor)
THE MOST NATIVE OF SONS

SONS OF DARKNESS, SONS OF LIGHT

THE MAN WHO CRIED I AM
BEYOND THE ANGRY BLACK (Editor)
THIS IS MY COUNTRY TOO

THE PROTECTORS

AFRICA, HER HISTORY, LANDS AND PEOPLE

SISSIE

THE ANGRY BLACK (Editor)

NIGHT SONG

ONE FOR NEW YORK/THE ANGRY ONES

JOHN A. WILLIAMS

The Junior
Bachelor Society

1976

Doubleday & Company, Inc., Garden City, New York

All the characters in this book are fictitious, and any resemblance
to actual persons, living or dead, is purely coincidental.

Library of Congress Cataloging in Publication Data

Williams, John Alfred, 1925–
The Junior Bachelor Society.

I.   Title.
PZ4.W72624Ju [PS3573.I4495]   813'.5'4
ISBN 0-385-09455-8
Library of Congress Catalog Card Number 75-32297

To my mother

Ola Mae Jones Williams Page, who didn't know a football from a hockey puck or a touchdown from a home run, but who knew much more.

I thought this: A organization is a organization and if I don't mean nothin by joinin it, I ought to keep my ass out of it.

Ned Cobb (Nate Shaw) 1885–1973

THE JUNIOR BACHELOR SOCIETY

ONE

Dressed in slacks, shirt, and sweater, Bubbles Wiggins placed his package of freshly laundered work clothes on the avocado kitchen table. Over the years he'd learned that this was the way to remember them. You got to the plant anticipating the feel and smell of clean clothes and then—goddamnit—you'd forgotten them and had to wear the sweaty, gritty, oily stuff another day. But if you put the clean ones on the table, you didn't forget them.

His coffee was ready and the toast had popped up. As he removed the cream from the refrigerator—it too, like the table and stove, was avocado—he also took his lunch and placed it atop his work clothes. There'd been a time when he took his lunch in the plant cafeteria, but no more, not for a long time. He'd been younger then, and half an hour seemed like enough time, even though you spent about fifteen minutes of it on line.

Slurping his coffee, Bubbles gazed about the kitchen, just as he did every morning, for it, like everything else in the house, was an extension of himself, his moods, his aspirations. Rows of dark, proud walnut cupboards, a spotless, waxed yellow floor. His glance moved to the windows, framed in yellow curtains, and outward to the explosion of color this early October. Maples —soft, hard, royal, and Japanese—flared yellow and red against the clear sky; poplars, golden now, angled like spearheads, stood unbending and slender in contrast to the great, twisting oaks. He missed the chestnut trees, their acrid smell and broad-veined leaves. Blight, they said, had killed them all.

Through Bubbles' scrotum there now flowed a quick sense of pleasure. Fall. Football season. God, how he'd loved football! He still remembered that game against Western, when he was in high school; still remembered being a third-string right halfback in a double-wing system. The A-team was so far ahead of Western that the coach put in the third stringers, a few at a time.

When Bubbles got in, Buonfiglio, the quarterback, called the play in which he faked giving Bubbles the ball, kept it himself, and hit the center, Bubbles remembered, some thirty years away from it now, how he pulled at the count of two, charged around faking receipt of the ball and kept on driving around the left side where he had five steps easy on Western's end, forget the tackle. And at least two on the linebacker. Oh! If I'd had that ball, I'da scored, man. *I was gone!* I'da played more after that. Buonfiglio went for no gain.

The kitchen was still, as if listening to his thoughts. *My life could've been different*, Bubbles thought.

He almost smiled to himself, ruefully. Why do I keep thinking about it? Here I've got a boy in college, playin football, first string. Great ballplayer, and I'm still thinking about *that* game.

He glanced at his watch. Wow! As he got up, hurriedly, his wife, Onetha, came into the kitchen. "Coffee's ready, baby. I forgot the toast. I'm runnin late."

"Okay. Sure am glad it's Friday. That hospital got to me this week."

He grabbed up his clothes and lunch. "Yeah, well I got to work tomorrow on this thing for Chappie, so don't count on me to shop with you."

"I know, I know," she said with a wave of her hand. "All these other lazy darkies Chappie helped, you'd think——"

Hand on the door, Bubbles paused, "That's the way it is, Neet."

"I know it. But they can always count on Bubbles Wiggins."

"Got to go. See you."

In the garage he slid between his car and Onetha's. Behind the wheel, he turned on the ignition and the garage exploded with the sound of 400 horsepower. Bubbles liked the sound. Power, man. He caressed the accelerator and slipped the gear into reverse. With steady pressure he backed into the street. At this hour it was quiet, the rows of Tudor, Federal, Colonial, and pseudo-Wright homes were still curtained. The Wigginses had been here four years but only knew *of* their neighbors who were big-time social workers or college professors or special consultants to banks or government housing programs. If there was another factory worker in the neighborhood, Bubbles didn't know him.

Cruising slowly down the street, Bubbles knew that his neighbors wouldn't be up and into their cars until nine or nine-thirty, rushing out along their privet-hedged walks in dark, well-cut suits and white shirts and ties, black faces set in the same grimaces of anxiety he'd seen on the faces of whites in similar neighborhoods in the movies, on television, in the newsclips. It was six-thirty now; Bubbles' job began at seven.

A good morning to be alive. Pretty, he thought, and wondered if his wife ever thought about such things when she was driving to work at Mohawk Hills Hospital where she was an assistant dietician. She never talked about it.

Bubbles turned into Athens Boulevard. What *did* they talk about these days, anyway? Rick, faking cornerbacks out of their jockstraps? Allison out there in New Mexico who any day now could be calling to say they were going to be grandparents? Rick, Allison. He laughed to himself. Talk about high-class names. Well, setting goals, or something like that.

On the boulevard he recognized Cudjo Evers' hog and raced to catch up with him. Lemme race that turkey, Bubbles thought, and as he came up on Cudjo's rear, he blew his horn, swerved to the left, and mashed down on the gas. The car bounded forward with screeching wheels. At the same time Cudjo saw him, Bubbles saw his body vibrate as he too stomped down on the gas. For a minute and a half they raced at seventy down the four-lane road, then Bubbles backed off as they approached the narrowing down to two lanes. Give that sucker a real race one of these days.

A few minutes later both cars wheeled off the boulevard into the parking lot of Obanoga Foundry. Cudjo jumped out of his car, the fat on his big body shaking. "Git you a car, chump."

"I just let you slide, man," Bubbles said. "That hog ain't nothin. I'ma blow you off the road one of these days."

"Sheeet, Bubbles. Caddie's the best car goin. Somebody done tole you a lie, Brother."

"We gonna see. Don't forget that meetin tomorrow."

"That thing for Chappie?"

"Yeah. Right after the ball game, hear?"

"Okay, Bubbles, I'ma try to make it." Cudjo waddled into the building in front of Bubbles. When he changed clothes, Bubbles knew, he'd expose arms as thin and stringy as rope. Twenty-five years of molding in the foundry did that for a man. Lifting seventy pounds of sand and steel five times an hour for eight hours. The wonder was that Cudjo hadn't lost weight anywhere else.

The long hallway, for as long as Bubbles had worked at Obanoga, was a dirty, silver gray, even when freshly painted. After punching their cards, they headed back into the foundry where the blast furnaces were roaring; they'd been started at three in the morning by men, all large, it seemed to Bubbles, who moved with infinite care and patience before their blazing openings. Now the furnaces were ready; the pourers, leaning on their ladles, gathered near, drinking coffee. The foundry opened out before Bubbles, alone now, since Cudjo had peeled off to go to the front dressing room. Cranes and hooks hung overhead; the tracks of the rollers were now empty, but in a matter of hours they'd be filled with molds, encased and locked, ready to receive the liquid brass or aluminum. One or two floor molders carefully laid out their patterns and wires, while their shakeout men turned over with shovels the treated mounds of sand and soil to make sure they'd dried out thoroughly from the day before.

Bubbles entered the core room and heard the giant mixer already growling in the corner where sand and oil were being prepared. Soon the entire core room would be filled with a blue haze and a stink of burned sand. The sand cores made here would be baked, then sent to the foundry where the molders would fit them into their molds, shoveling and packing the earth tightly around them. When the molten metals hardened, they'd have the shape of the cores that came from this room.

The belt was moving; some of the bench coremakers were already at work. Once Bubbles wanted to become a benchman, but those jobs seemed to be for whites only, and older whites at that. Bubbles had it figured now: when the white guys couldn't make their quotas working on the line, they were shifted to the benches where life was easier and a little cleaner. It was a source of pride to Bubbles that after twenty-five years he was still on the line; all the others, McMahon, Scalese, Roberts, Pete (never did know his last name), Scanlon, Martinelli—all of them, gone to the benches.

Bubbles moved briskly to the core room washroom, opened his locker and began to undress. From here he could hear the hoses hissing. Guys cleaning out their boxes. He never hosed his box the first thing in the morning. Water built up in the air hoses overnight and your first few cores stuck or cracked or both. PhhhnnnnnaaaAH! PhnnnAH! Vibrators being tested. The washroom was never filled this time in the morning except with black guys. They always wore street clothes and changed on the job. For twenty-five years. The white guys wore their clothes home. No style, Cudjo often said. The mixer ground to a stop; within minutes the young kids would be pushing wheelbarrows up and down the line dumping sand before the coreboxes; the platemen were already to work, clank, clank, clank, stacking the steel plates slowly; they were heavy. Bubbles would have to count his stack so he'd know at the end of the day just how many cores he'd made. The plates were perforated steel rectangles, fourteen by twenty-four inches, and weighed about fifteen pounds each; you snatched them from the stack by jamming your finger into a hole and swinging it just so it landed, your other hand helping, atop your corebox to hold in the sand when you flipped it over. It was the plate the finished core rested on after you clamped it onto the box.

Over the years Bubbles' right forefinger had built up an ugly gray callus, from the fingernail down past the first joint, from handling the plates. For years, in some social situations, he'd hidden that finger, jamming the hand it was on into his pocket. One day it didn't seem to matter anymore; the callus was as much a part of him now as a muscle.

I feel good, Bubbles thought, swinging out of the washroom, pausing to get coffee and a doughnut from the cart. He always felt good on the final day of the week. Always on this day he was tempted to try to set a new record in numbers of cores made. But why? Today, like all other Fridays going back for years, he successfully squelched the urge.

He leaned against his wooden sandbox with its large funnel-shaped top. This contained still another kind of sand, which went into the corebox after you'd powdered it. Automatically Bubbles ran his hand through the sand. If it was too cold, it was likely to run moist and stick in the box; too warm, it would run fine and the sand fins of the core would crumble in the box. This morning the sand felt just right.

Finished with his doughnut, he took a stub of a pencil from the drawer and counted the plates beside the bench. Fifty, correct. Once, when he was younger, the best coremaker in the plant bar none, he'd demanded seventy-five, and got them until the stack, falling over one day, narrowly missed crushing him against his machine.

He attacked his sifter with his steel brush, although he couldn't see one grain of sand stuck in the mesh; he cleaned it yesterday, as always, along with his brass scraper and pounder, which gleamed like fittings on a preplastic sloop. Clean tools saved time; clogged ones stole it, and time was the thing when doing piecework. Within time and using perfect equipment, you could knock off four hundred fifty 6602 General Motors cylinder-head cores a day, or at least Bubbles did, working on the cope; with the drag, for there was an extra motion required, you could get about four hundred 6601s.

Bubbles powdered his box while drawing on a cigarette. It was almost time. The handlers were gathered around the end of the belt, aprons and gloves already on. They'd take the cores from the belt and roll them on a wheeled carrier into the baking pens. Down the line now the other coremakers were checking their plates, shovels, and other tools. The plate carriers, sand carriers, and the bosses, sitting in their glass-enclosed office on the other side of the belt, all paused or lit up and waited, their eyes on the dozen men who manned the coreboxes on the line.

Bubbles Wiggins saw this every morning, or felt it; these minutes before the bell rang, signaling the start of the workday, had become precious to him. The helpers had spent hours getting the principals ready for the curtain; now the principals were poised to step off, twelve bodies moving through a variety of motions, over and over and over again, pausing only to count additional plates. He still enjoyed being watched by the handlers; they'd gather behind his sandbox, three or four, analyzing his every motion; it was a little like playing ball.

The first few moments each day were like the first few moments when he'd started the job a quarter of a century ago. Every tool was where his hand flashed, every motion leading smoothly to the next, from sandbox to corebox to belt and back again. Sand in the sifter; sift into the box; jolt. Two shovels of floor sand, jolt twice; hand smooth and pound; scrape level and plate. Fasten, flip the box, vibrate the core down, swing the box back over, quickly but softly—a bump would crack the core— snatch up the oil and treat the fins in one motion, then lift the whole business, forty pounds to the belt, and start all over again.

As he moved, Bubbles wondered how all the others were spending their mornings at this very hour. There were so many to try to get back for the big dinner for Chappie. Bubbles wanted a big turnout, from City Hall on down, and this'd been hinted at. The old days were past when City Hall didn't give a damn about the Ward. True, the Ward no longer existed, but the blacks still did, and had increased enough to become an even more powerful political force than before, able to carry the edge in several different wards now instead of just one.

Maybe after they all came for the Chappie thing, it wouldn't be so awkward to look up some of the cats in the City when he went down to watch Rick play. As far as he knew, Bubbles had the only kid playing Ivy League ball.

Jesus, he thought, shaking his head. So much time gone, just *gone*. I coulda had a different life if Buonfiglio'd given me that goddamn ball. *Man, I was gone*.

Well, it was done. He'd made a life, pounded it out of this sand and steel. In those first days he'd grabbed hold of the job the way he grabbed anything else, in full stride and hard. The white guys on the line were upset about blacks breaking in any- way, but when he was running three hundred cores a day, that was too much.

"Hey, kid," they said. Scalese and McMahon. "Look, kid, don't kill the job, whaddayasay? Take ya time. Run two hundred seventy-five, punch out and pick up an hour'nahalf day rate. Don't kill the job, okay?"

There he was, with Ralph, Snake, Clarie, Dart, and Chops off to college, Moon moving to New York to do what nobody knew then, and Shurley and Diane making a baby every year. Too late to be sorry about not using the GI Bill, just like not getting the ball from Buonfiglio that time.

TWO

The next day, Saturday, Bubbles reached over and raised the shade and the blinds and the sun leaned in, a great golden square. Blue, Bubbles thought, that sky is so blue.

Onetha was already up and the smell of pork sausages, freshly made coffee, and hot buckwheat cakes nudged into the room. Bubbles stretched luxuriously; they'd made love just before dawn broke, moving in semisleep, and after, he'd slept through her shower. He sat on the edge of the bed now, feeling at peace. Better get up from here, he thought, and trudged toward the bathroom, trying to fix the day's schedule in his mind.

First, he'd rake the leaves, then have a light lunch. He'd have to get that for himself. Onetha would be gone to the hairdresser and to a dozen other places. Shopping for food would be her last task.

Bubbles almost laughed. Some schedule he had. Raking the leaves and playing ball. After his lunch he'd take down his cleats and sweat sox for the usual Saturday game over in Jefferson Park. Take a pad and pencil along, too; start getting the guys together for that dinner for Chappie. After that, he thought, dressing now, stop by ol' Chef's and pick up a messa chitlins and potato salad for dinner. Have it warmed up by the time ol' Neet gets home.

"Bubbles!"

"Comin!"

He rushed into the kitchen rubbing his hands. "Sure does smell good in here!" He kissed her cheek as he brushed by to take his place at the table. He still felt gallant and delighted when her eyes sparkled the way they now did. It'd been good this morning. Once, whenever they did it, it was good, but then, without their even noticing it, sometimes it wasn't.

"Saturday mornin smell, I love it baby," he said.

Bubbles slashed butter between his stack of cakes and poured syrup over them. He cut a sausage with his fork. God he loved these Saturday and Sunday morning breakfasts! Miss the kids, though. If they were here, the platter'd be running over with sausage!

"C'mon, sit down," he said.

"Soon's I get mine, be right there."

"Good sausage," he said.

She said, "You say that *every* Saturday and Sunday."

"And you say that, too. You mean we're so old, we can't find anything new to say?"

"Oh, Bubbles, hush."

"And nothin new to do," he said, grinning. "But you sure socked it to ol Poppa this mornin, Momma. Wheeoo."

"You was doin some wailin yourself Mr. Bubbles." She smiled. "Done yourself proud."

They broke out laughing.

"When the kids are here they treat us like we done hung up the rubbers, hey?"

Onetha, her long, sculpted face bunching up now, almost choked on her coffee, and they were off again, laughing.

"Hey, you want some chitlins tonight?" Bubbles asked.

Onetha stopped chewing. "That'd be pork twice in one day, baby. Not good, the doctor, he say."

"Yeah. I forgot all about that. What you want me to pick up from Chef's?"

"That greasy old place—don't bother. I'll whip up some spaghetti—with just a little piece of hot sausage in the sauce, okay?"

"Okay. And some Italian bread, right?"

"I know; I know."

There'd always been a Jefferson Park. When Bubbles was a boy they had to chase the goats off it before they could play ball. The goats belonged to one of the Italian families that then lived across the street from the park. Four tennis courts and two swimming pools had been cut into it along with one baseball diamond, which also served as the football field. In winter the field was flooded for ice skating. Italians, Jews, and blacks had ringed the park over the years. Now the Italians and Jews were gone

THE JUNIOR BACHELOR SOCIETY

and the blacks were poor, a generation out of the South or at the most two. Like the Italians and the Jews, the native blacks had also moved away, perhaps not as far, but out of shouting distance of Jefferson.

Walking through the park gates now, feeling springy in his cleats, Bubbles remembered so clearly that it shocked him and made him pause, those Sunday games the Little Harlem Grill team played with other sandlot teams around the city. Whenever they fell behind, which was often, Chappie Davis would pull out one of the backs and, behind a bush if no dressing room was available, take the boy's equipment, pants, shoulder pads, helmet, and cleats, and rush into the line up. But Chappie was a small man; his raging desire to win, his sparks of grit, simply were not enough; Little Harlem Grill seemed to fall even farther behind when Chappie entered a game. Bubbles wondered if Chappie remembered all those times.

He broke out of his reverie and started loping across the field. "Hey, let's have it!" he called. He'd seen Shurley Walker with the football. Shurley wore gold-striped green sweats; he was a Packers fan. Shurley faded, his white cleats flashing in the sun. Bubbles was conscious of all the eyes on him, the youngbloods, half of whom he never recognized off the field, and he knew they were smirking, thinking: *Them ol jocks never quit, man. Out here every Saturday trying t' do they thing, whatever they think that is.* Bubbles shortened his stride and headfaked right, bodyfaked left, put on a burst of speed, which he hoped was dazzling, and charged straight ahead. Shurley still threw line drives; he'd busted more fingers than Bart Starr in his day. The ball was a little high; Bubbles could swear it was humming, but he reached up, coming off the ground in a picture pose, felt the ball slap his hands and he pulled it in. He hit the ground even faster than he'd gone up, then slowed, cut in a wide, graceful circle and trotted back to Shurley.

"You lookin like Warfield out there, man," Shurley said, grinning. "Let's hope you can catch two or three like that during the game."

"If you throw em right, I'll get em," Bubbles said, spiraling the ball up between them. "Hey, here comes Cudjo."

"Bout time."

They watched Cudjo trotting in through the gates, his old man's Afro thin and strange above his great, wide face.

"What say there, Brothers?" they heard him call out as he passed clots of youngsters. "Mornin, Brother. How you doin, Brother?" Trotting all the while like one of those great pro tackles, Buck Buchanan coming back on the field to start the second half. Seeing them, Cudjo veered to his right and shouted, "Let's see it, let's see it!"

Bubbles gripped the ball and lofted a soft pass in Cudjo's direction. It was behind him and Cudjo, after sticking out an arm at it, continued on in his trot. "Put em over the plate, Brother Bubbles."

"Aw, man," Bubbles complained while Shurley laughed. "You didn't try to get it."

Cudjo wheezed up. "Well I ain't whatchucall a scatback."

"Sure ain't," Bubbles agreed, reaching up to catch the ball thrown in by one of the youngsters. He looked around to check the number of warm bodies. Then he glanced toward the car parked outside the park. He, like Shurley and Cudjo, had passed it without bothering to glance at the driver. Swoop. Just sitting there watching. And hoping, maybe, Bubbles thought. He said, "Hey, wanna use Swoop?"

"Fuck im," Shurley said quickly.

"No way in hell," Cudjo said. "Who wants to be playin with a cop?"

"Shit, he played some ball after we got out," Bubbles reminded them.

"Maybe so, but he was always salty cause we didn't let him in the JBS," Cudjo said.

"He was younger than us. Then five years made a big difference," Shurley said. "Anyway, we were just about to break up."

"I didn't like the pea-pickin motherfucker then," Cudjo said angrily, "and when he gave me that ticket before he went plainclothes, I swore I'd like him never. Fuck a Swoop Ferguson. Les play some ball."

"Hey!" Shurley called to a group of teen-agers in gray sweats. "Wanna play? Give us five men; that'll make it eight apiece, okay?"

Cudjo laughed. He knew they'd send over their worst players, but it didn't matter. "That little cat, Tucker, they send to play with us all the time—he can *move*, baby."

"You damn right," Shurley said. "Ain't no biggern Walter Roberts right now; he'll get bigger. Wonder how come they never keep him?"

Bubbles scraped his cleats in the ground. "Cliques, gangs, groups. Just like we were. Guess he ain't in solid. Or maybe they fraida him."

"C'mon, c'mon, let's go," Shurley called. Bubbles knew he wanted to get the game over so he could return home and go back to sleep. He'd tended bar at the Ebenos until three. You'd think that after all these years of bartending he'd be used to this Saturday noon game and not worry about his sleep. But it was the same thing every week.

"Hey, Shurl," Bubbles said. "You know we got to talk about that dinner for Chappie, man, so don't plan on runnin home right away."

"Yeah," Cudjo said. "Let's drink some suds at my crib when we're through."

"How long's it gonna take?" Shurley asked.

Bubbles said, "Oh, man, half hour or something like that. Okay?"

"Cool." To the kids, he shouted, "Let's go."

The first play of the game Bubbles, taking the ball and fading back to look for the Tucker kid, sidestepped first one, then another defender, who'd got by Cudjo, Shurley, and the rest of the line. He saw Tucker and another kid making their cuts, and just as he stepped forward to throw the ball, one of the kids he'd sidestepped came back, snatched it from his hand with a laugh, and ran the few yards for a touchdown.

Mortified, Bubbles watched the other team slapping palms. They brayed, "Hey, grampa, baby, that sure was cool!"

"Now that's what you call a real Statue of Liberty play," Cudjo said breathing heavily.

Shurley took a look at Bubbles and decided to say nothing at all.

"Okay, okay," Bubbles said. "We get the ball again." He walked around in small circles kicking the sod until the ball was thrown, at him, he was glad to see, and he felt the adrenalin pumping and flashes of what he might have been flicked before him. They figured me for a patsy all day, he thought, then was off, running at half-speed behind Shurley and the Tucker kid; they'd already left Cudjo behind. He saw the defenders running toward his blockers in a smooth flow, as though they were pieces of metal being drawn to a magnet. Gauging their speed and positions, Bubbles cut sharply at a left angle and drove across the field, aiming for that point at which he could go straight downfield. He rose on his toes and began to pump; he felt wind on his face and saw by the eyes of the kids that he was going to make it. Shurley and Cudjo and the kids on his side were shouting. Bubbles came up on the last man between himself and the goal and strove for more speed; he pumped, the kid pumped, while eying each other, their cleats throwing up sprays of earth and grass. Bubbles leaned away from the outstretched hand and then was past it. He crossed the goal line with a long stride, cradling the ball on his hip.

Although gasping to catch his breath, Bubbles trotted nonchalantly back up the field. "Grampa's doin the best he can!" he shouted at the other side, while Cudjo, joining him in his trot, whispered, "Take your time for the next few plays, Bubbles."

"Don't you worry bout that, baby," he puffed. He dropped the ball and bent over, his hands on his knees.

"That was a great run, Bubbles," the Tucker kid said. The other kids ran by and slapped him on the shoulder. He wished Rick could have seen it. His breath was coming more evenly now and he took his place for the throwoff. Quickly he scanned the sky. Still a great day and he'd already got his touchdown.

By the time they quit the field for Cudjo's, he'd scored two more touchdowns and was exuberant. He drank the cold beer with a smile, savored its sting upon the buds of his tongue. Joyfully, he mashed his palms against his forehead to wipe away the sweat. Once again he watched himself driving over the field for each of those touchdowns, saw each of his moves as clearly as if they'd been filmed and halted frame after frame. He'd beat time out on that field, whipped his ass good.

Hey! he thought. Maybe—and he spoke. "If we can get all the guys here and the weather's good, maybe we can play the kids. The Junior Bachelor Society against the hippy-dips, whaddaya say?"

"We'd have nine men," Shurley said without opening his eyes.

"Man, we ain't askin these Brothers to come just for no touch football game," Cudjo said testily. "We want em for the testimonial dinner."

"Just a thought," Bubbles said, still thinking about how much like the old days it'd be. "Anyway, I got the letterhead and the envelopes, and, Cudjo, you reserved the hotel dining room for the——"

"——thirtieth of November. The tickets'll be ready next week."

Bubbles nudged Shurley who opened his eyes. "Is Diane gonna be able to work with Onetha and Evelyn on the tickets and the letters? We got to fill up the place, man. Fill it up."

"Yeah, man. Just have Neet call her when she's ready."

"Evelyn been ready," Cudjo said of his wife, who'd brought them the beer and vanished.

"I was in Buonfiglio's and ordered the plaque," Bubbles said, "so that's all set. He didn't take no deposit, cause he remembers us from school."

"You get that list from Snake?" Cudjo asked Bubbles.

"He's gonna call me this week."

"How's he sound?" Shurley asked.

Bubbles shrugged. "Okay to me."

In the pause that followed they thought of Snake Dumpson, or, as he was now called, Housing Commissioner Dumpson. He lived in the suburbs and they never saw him, only his pictures in the paper. But the city was so big now that you didn't see half the people you used to.

"Funny," Shurley said, opening his eyes for good now, and shifting in his seat.

"What?"

"About Snake. I mean, you'd think he'd come around more."

"He's got a different kind of life now," Bubbles said. "You know, a cat grows up, he changes."

"What Shurley means, man," Cudjo said, "is that he's here in town. It's not like with Ralph or Clarie or Chops or D'Artagnan. Some of them cats been all over the world and done fantastic things. Snake, shit, he just moved to the suburbs. He ain't gone nowhere."

"——well, anyway," Bubbles broke in. "He's gonna get all the addresses for me, you know. Like where the cats are? All except Moon. And he told me the mayor's office was helping out and that the mayor and a few others from City Hall would be at our thing. The mayor, in fact, would like to say a few words."

"What the fuck for?" Shurley asked indignantly. "It ain't no election year."

"No, let the sucker go," Cudjo said. "Let him say a few, but we got to give our own tribute. He can speak after, and, Bubbles, since you was president when we had the Bachelors, I think you ought to do the tribute, you know, and introduce our guys, y' know, for their *brief* testimonials."

"Yeah," Shurley laughed. "You always was the take-charge guy."

"You mean the fall guy," Bubbles said, remembering.

"Maybe then we thought that," Cudjo said. "We know better now."

THREE

"What'd you say, Mr. Dumpson?"

"Nothing," Kenneth Dumpson said. "I just grunted. This part of the city's certainly changed a lot."

"Yes, it has, Commissioner."

Dumpson glanced at his driver and wondered what kind of a life he'd had. He took it for granted that the drivers assigned to him resented him because he was black and they were all white, but that no longer bothered him; he found it amusing most times. Leaning back, his hand on the car phone, he said, "You know, Mike, I used to work out here. At Obanoga."

"You're kidding, Commissioner!"

Dumpson saw the driver's eyes flash at him in the mirror.

"Sure did," Dumpson said. He smiled inwardly. He knew what was going through the driver's mind. All these goddamn pecker-woods running around talking about black folks pulling them-selves up by their own bootstraps, like their people'd done. They never believed it when it happened. Let this hunkie know he wasn't any cream puff, that he'd done his time, paid his dues. Let him worry about how it happened that he, Snake Dumpson, had been in a foundry and escaped, and he, the driver, white and all that, was still nothing but a flunky. Worry 'bout it, baby.

They slowed to turn into the Obanoga driveway. Dumpson clutched his sandwiches, feeling a rising excitement; he'd not been back to this place since he left it, twenty-three years ago.

"They've got a cafeteria inside," Dumpson said. "Or you can find some lunch down the road at one of the stands. Whichever, I'll meet you back here in the lot in about thirty-five minutes. They only have a half hour here." As he climbed out of the car Dumpson knew the driver would choose to go down the road. None of the drivers liked to hang around with him in public. He could've had a black driver, but he much preferred to sit behind a white one, breaking the pattern of the way a lot of people thought it should be. Let them go home and talk about having driven the spade to such and such a place; cool. Just be on the damned job at eight in the morning.

Run, he thought, as he stood watching the driver wheel back to the road. Dumpson inhaled the acrid smell of burning sand and heated metal, and through the opened windows, he heard the grinders at work on their machines, smoothing off the rough edges of the brass and aluminum castings.

He entered the building. Everything was the same: the silvery walls with their coat of soot, the time clock on his left, the lunch line already forming. He got on line just as the whistle blew, and shuffled with it to the coffee bar, nodding and waving to the black men. He was looking for Cudjo, but didn't see him.

Benny Grimm pulled at his arm. "Kenny—Commissioner—Dumpson, is that you?" Benny was one of the owners of the plant.

"Hey, Benny," Dumpson said, smiling, shaking his hand. Boy, he thought, is he gray, and fat. "How are you, man?"

"I'm just fine, Commissioner, but what brings you out here unannounced?"

"Came to see Bubbles. Say, Benny, will you hand me one of those Seven-Ups? Thanks." They turned out of the line.

"City Hall agrees with you, Kenny."

Dumpson said, "No complaints, Ben." Grimm still wore that harassed look. "You're lookin good."

"Yeah, yeah. When you finish with Bubbles, if you've got the time, stop in the office. Always nice to talk to the old guys."

"Thanks, Benny. I'll try to stop in."

"Okay." Benny Grimm moved off.

Now, under the smoke-blackened ceilings, the rigs and pulleys, passing already exhausted shakeout men nibbling bags of salted peanuts, because today was payday, with the checks coming later, and they were out of money, he wondered how it'd got away, that closeness he'd had with Bubbles. It'd been so long since he'd seen him that he was almost afraid to go to his home; the foundry was a neutral place. They both had that in common twenty-three years ago.

Somewhere back there they'd hit a fork in the road. The goals became different along with their styles and thoughts. Ole Bubble.

Bubbles was the only guy, the only guy who hadn't laughed at him when, as kids playing with the Little Harlem Grill team in brand-new green-and-white jerseys, he, ole Snake, had blasted through for a touchdown from five out and in the process had his jersey ripped from his back. He had cried. Just sat down on the goal line and cried, and all the Little Harlem guys and the other team, too, surprised at the big dummy, laughed. Not Bubbles, who'd come over and tried to pull the shreds back together. "We're gonna get you another one, Snake, for scorin that touchdown."

And just about here, Dumpson thought, it happened. He slowed for a moment in the lunchtime stillness. It'd been summer and for him a summer job with Saturday overtime, shaking out here in the foundry. Bubbles'd been in the core room picking up some overtime on his own.

At the coffee break, Dumpson went to chat with a pressure tester, a guy who ran liquid chemicals into large hollow castings to see if they were completely sealed. Bubbles was on the other side of the room. The tester ran some smelly brown fluid into the casting and suddenly the casting cracked, sounding like a gong being hit, and the chemical, breaking out of pressure, squirted into Dumpson's eyes. He screamed, not so much from pain or shock, but at the vision of no more days on the gridiron or court. Bubbles must've heard him, and he heard Bubbles shouting, crashing across the floor toward him. Later Dumpson discovered that Bubbles charged like a bull, stepping into, knocking over moldings it'd taken a number of floormen two hours to put together. "Snake! Snake! What is it, man? Where'd you get it? Don't rub; don't rub!"

Benny Grimm ran out and within minutes, with Bubbles and a plant official beside him, he was hurried into a car and to a doctor.

Dumpson heaved a sigh. He'd been lucky. The skin on his face peeled away for weeks, but there was not one iota of eye damage. He'd probably closed them just fractions of seconds before the fluid hit. Bubble, he thought. My main man.

For years Bubbles Wiggins had staked out a corner of the core room where old cores, phased out or modified, stood on racks, no longer in use. The sand underfoot here was all dry, baked. Very little smoke from the main room reached this corner with its fluorescent lights and wide windows. No one else'd ever used the corner for lunch.

Without a wasted motion, Dumpson turned away from the main core room and sought out Bubbles' corner; if he found him, that would reflect a certain continuity and they could go from that.

Bubbles looked up at the intruder, scowling, then his face broke into a smile. "Hey, man, Snake! Damn, baby, what're you doin here?" He remained seated, but switched his sandwich to his left hand and extended his right, palm up. Dumpson smacked it with an exaggeration of force, his eyes searching Bubbles'.

"Bubble"—Bubbles noticed that when people wanted to say important things to him, they always dropped the "s"—"gotdamn, man, you looking *good*. How's ole Neet?"

"We gettin on groovy, Snake. You lookin good yourself. How much you weigh now?"

Dumpson patted his stomach. "Two yards even."

"Exercisin?"

"A little tennis, some golf," Dumpson said self-consciously. Tennis and golf he knew had always been upper-class sports and they sneered at them, when they were kids. "Hey," Dumpson said, recovering, "I've been readin about Rick, man. He's lookin very good."

Bubbles beamed. "Yeah. Next year he can tear that Ivy League apart. I mean, the Ivy League ain't where they play football."

"Oh, I don't know, Bubble. They turn a few bad cats outa there every now and again, and Rick's going to be one of em."

Pleased, Bubbles was suddenly afflicted with modesty. "Well— maybe." Then, changing the subject, he asked, "How's your wife?" He didn't know her name, and this, to Dumpson, for the moment, made that fork in the road even wider.

"Sandra. Call her Sandy. She's okay, you know. Some problems with the kids, but shit, that goes for everybody."

"Dig it," Bubbles said. They'd heard that Snake hadn't started

on kids until he was in his thirties, while the rest of them had
been knocking them out bam-a-lam from the time they got home
from the war. He watched Snake slip out of his jacket and hang
it on a bench. He sat down beside Bubbles and opened his sandwiches.

"You always was ready, Snake," Bubbles said with a chuckle.

They'd always had that flair for doing things. Snake'd come in
ready to impress all the way, with his sandwiches and soda, the
knowledge that he, Bubbles, would be sitting in the same old
corner. That, somehow, made the distance between them seem
smaller.

They chewed their sandwiches in silence until Dumpson said,
looking straight at Bubbles, "Well, it's been a long time."

They inspected their sandwiches. "Yeah," Bubbles said finally.

Dumpson said, "I thought I'd bring the shit instead of mailing
it."

Bubbles grinned. "I'm glad you did, Snake. But you could of
come by the house. We're in the phone book, and Onetha'd love
to see you."

"I'm going to. Just wanted to break some ice."

"Gotcha. Don't sweat it."

"Thanks," Dumpson said, smiling over his soda. Same ole
fuckin Bubbles. "We'll all come, me, Sandy, and the kids." He
was now watching Bubbles carefully.

"Sure didn't think you'd be comin by yourself." Bubbles had
managed to keep reproach from his tone.

They finished their sandwiches and leaned back. "Still on the
half-hour lunch, huh?" Dumpson asked.

"Shit," Bubbles said. "If it was left up to Benny, we wouldn't
have *no* time to eat."

"Say, Bubble. How's Neet goin to feel about Sandy?" He saw
bemusement rising in Bubbles' eyes and he hastened on: "I
mean, you know how the Sisters are these days with their black
man-white woman thing. . . ."

"Neet ain't into that, Snake," Bubbles said firmly. "If Sandy's
the babe for you, well then fuck them people, man." He faked a
punch to Dumpson's chin and said more softly, "I know my man
ain't gonna be ripped off by no lame shit like that."

Dumpson smiled and lowered his eyes. Then he said, "You know, I got a boy, big as a tank, and he couldn't care less about playin ball. Funny the way they turn out."

"Yeah. You can't tell, man."

"Look," Dumpson said, pulling some folded sheets from his pocket, opening them, and giving them to Bubbles. "I got the addresses: Chops, Clarie, Ralph, Dart." He smiled triumphantly as Bubbles flipped through the papers. "About Moon. I couldn't get any leads."

"I guess that's just as well," Bubbles said. "But this is great, Snake. We got the letterhead sittin up home. We'll get started tonight."

"If you need more help, just holler. We got lotsa secretaries around City Hall doin nuthin but givin away pussy," Dumpson said. "And the mayor wants to give Coach a citizenship citation. He'll do anything to help."

"Fill up the place," Bubbles said.

"He's already been after the Chamber of Commerce and the Junior League. He wants to keep this city cool as long's he's in office. I just hope the Brothers and Sisters show up; won't be too good if this turns out to be a mainly white thing."

"Don't worry. It's gonna be our thing all right."

Dumpson got up, brushing the seat of his pants. He slipped on his jacket. "Listen, call, Bubble, willya? For anything. Just to say 'kiss my ass' if you want, and let me know if there's anything else I can do. We gonna fall by one Sunday afternoon, okay?"

"Anytime," Bubbles said, as the whistle blew ending lunch hour.

"You know, you're pretty flat around the belly. Still playin ball?" Dumpson looked admiringly at Bubbles' waist.

"Yeah. Got me three a couple of weeks ago."

Dumpson extended his hand. "Take care of yourself, Bubbles. Be seein you."

The plant was coming alive with the pounding of heavy machinery, a hundred vibrators, mixing vats; the screech of carborundum grinding wheels against metal castings came from the grinding room; lifts were driven in and out of passageways in the foundry; platemen, leaning far forward, hauled stacks of plates to the benches of the coremakers.

All the way back to his office Dumpson was pensive. Seeing Bubbles again was like going back to a root. Try as he might, with due attention paid to that fork in their road, he could not decode to his satisfaction why he'd let Bubbles go. You could deal with the differences after the fact of there *being* differences. But the things they'd had together as youngsters was something else again.

He still thought of those days, whether in pride that he'd come so far from them or as a clue to himself, he didn't know. In many of their homes there'd not been electric lights, when they were three and four; they all went back that far, through Sunday school, their parents being friends, and living in the same area, going to the same schools. They'd had gas jets. Baths were in galvanized tin tubs, the big action on Saturday nights. Trains down the middle of the street.

Dumpson watched the city move past him with an unaccountable sinking feeling in his stomach, thinking now of Bloodfield and the stabbings, the fights, the screams, the sudden shriveling of soul and skin at the sounds of flesh striking flesh. He no longer recalled when the trek to Jewtown was made, but there were bathtubs there and electricity. There, still growing, they'd planned petty thefts as carefully and intricately as a price-fixing conference of corporation officials. They fought among themselves, sure, but remained bound to each other, a tribe, fatherless for the most part, seeking a reflection of manhood mainly from each other; they were sons who would not or could not bend to matriarchal will.

They found unity on the cinder track, and on the football field, the baseball diamond and the basketball court; in talking about girls and in copping pussy quickly in parks or damp cellars.

The Junior Bachelor Society only brought them closer. They held fried-chicken parties and drank Virginia Dare wine, traded records, borrowed each other's zoot suits and chains. But most of all they got it together playing ball, moving from sandlot to high school with an élan that startled the shit out of the white coaches and players. They talk about black ballplayers now, Dumpson thought, how any NBA team could start an all-black five—if it wanted to. *We had that back in high school!* At Overlook in his senior year, the first seven men on the team were black, and they'd cleaned up the city league, wiped them out with time enough to be cute.

The war had changed them, maybe, he thought. Some went into the Army, some into the Navy, but they all went; there were no 4-Fs in the Junior Bachelor Society. They'd had their drinking reunions at the war's end and separate-room, same-house fucking parties; they didn't go for the gang-bang the white boys in high school dug so much, as if afraid to go one-on-one. They always low-ranked their white teammates about that. They'd each recapitulated their parts in the war, proudly pronouncing the names of towns and villages in France, Germany, Italy, the Solomons, Carolines, Philippines, Marianas, and then drink some more, for it was summer then, when they got together again, and they were used to summer being a time between the time when things were done.

Some talked of going to college on the GI Bill. Before the war, everyone wanted to go and be a big football hero, like Brud Holland, Bernie Jefferson or Sidat-Singh. But some of them had seen too many things during the war, and held too little hope that hard study would pay off later; they wanted the payoff then. Bubbles talked of the good money he could make in a foundry. Moon had not said much of anything. No wonder. Cudjo, too, was ready to trade muscle for quick bread, and Shurley just wasn't going to be hurried in his decision-making. So, Clarie and Chops went away that fall to college, while D'Artagnan, Ralph and Snake went to the University.

Dumpson did better on the football field and the basketball court than he did in class, sliding through with a C. Even now he knew his succession of fairly good white collar jobs was due more to his athletic fame than his grades, although he had taken his master's in social work and another in city planning.

Living in the neighborhood during those undergraduate days, he was nonetheless apart from it, and only saw some JBS members on those weekend, off-season nights when he visited the local clubs with white teammates. The girls he'd grown up with called Dumpson and Ralph schoolboys, with a fine mix of pride and derison. But he rarely saw Ralph on the campus and never off it. All he knew then was that Ralph believed he was going to be a writer, and had worked for the *Express* later, when he was married to April.

Dart seemed to have vanished among the coeds and corridors of the Fine Arts building, from which he would sometimes be seen emerging with some fruity-looking people. Dumpson had heard that he'd married a European woman. Ralph, now Ralph had married that fine-looking April. Still a good-looking woman. He didn't know what'd happened; the talk was that April had not been too cool and Ralph had come home at the wrong time one night. Anyway, he'd married again. No kids, Dumpson guessed, or he'd have heard about them. Just the one girl, Raphaella. College now.

As for his own children, Dumpson had held off, waiting for security to edge around the corner, but the other guys had gone on ahead just the way all their parents had, pop-pop, poppity-pop! Wall-to-wall kids, but theirs were just about grown now, while his were in their teens.

Even as he moved from home into a dorm on campus, Dumpson had envied Bubbles, Cudjo, and Shurley their protective insulation that came with remaining in the Ward with its almost completely black population since the Jews moved away. His mother remained in the Ward. He graduated and moved into a white section of town.

Dumpson moved from his first job in the city public housing administration to urban renewal and city planning, in the process marrying Sandra Hancock. His isolation, he realized one night before their marriage, would be compounded, and his athletic triumphs notwithstanding, they'd give him grease in a minute with this white woman bearing his name. He'd moved then from being merely competent, to astute, daring. Snake Dumpson, he'd whispered to himself, from the three; Snake Dumpson on a quick-opener and going all the way.

But housing, as commonplace as prairie, as unthought of as the plumbing it contains, became a mushrooming political issue, tied to the fortunes of Afro-Americans who had so little of it. Grumbling from the Ward increased to a roar as the blacks began awakening from a long and troubled slumber, and spinning in panic, the white managers remembered that in the basement of City Hall itself there was a man with all the qualifications demanded by the residents of the Ward, to oversee fairness in housing demands. A black man, and they hauled him from cover, white wife, half-black children and all, and made him housing commissioner.

To be sure there were other things to do beside placating the blacks, and he did them well and thoroughly, while serving the black community in more ways than even it was aware. He oversaw rent controls, backed laws, and both cajoled and threatened builders and landlords on behalf of their unrestricted tenancy.

He had done it almost alone, unprotected, exposed.

FOUR

C'mon, c'mon, *c'mon!* Ezzard Jackson gripped the steering wheel tightly and his eyes snapped from the watch on his wrist to the inching traffic on the Rapidway. *Move!* Shit, he thought, these bastards gonna make ole Chops late. He stabbed his horn and viciously cut toward the inside lane. The drivers of cars near him blew back and gestured. He could see their mouths moving, but he kept nosing over from the outside lane into the middle, and finally a driver, afraid to challenge his desperation, halted and let him in. Wheeeeoooo, Jackson thought.

A quarter of a mile farther on, he made the exit and raced up the ramp with screeching wheels to a stop light. He glanced at his watch again and drummed on the steering wheel. At the yellow he mashed down, leaving a patch, and roared up the street, just barely making the next light. Five minutes later, still glancing at his watch, he wheeled into the parking lot and came to a rocking halt in his car slot.

Jumping out of the car, he looked nervously upward to the corner window of the fifth floor in the building across the street, where he saw the purple curtain moving ever so slightly. Jackson ran to the curb glancing up and down the street to gauge the speed of the on-rushing one-way traffic, and seeing a break in it, darted across and into the front door of the ancient gray building. A brass plate above the door which Jackson long ago stopped reading said, Lawrence Publishing Company.

The high-yellow receptionist watched his entrance with barely concealed amusement. Jackson pushed brusquely past Palmer, the janitor who, under orders from Mr. Lawrence, locked the door promptly at nine every morning. If you came in after that, Mr. Lawrence knew, and it wasn't a good thing to have him know how often you were late.

Torn between weariness and fury, Ezzard Jackson walked quickly over the worn purple rug to the elevator. Once inside he allowed himself one bitter, rebellious thought: forty-eight and still running for Josiah Malverne Lawrence, black genius, black consultant to presidents, overseer of Lawrence Plantations.

On the fourth floor he walked out briskly. "Hey, baby," he said to the new receptionist.

"Morning, Mr. Jackson," she said with a smile.

He found new life with this first greeting. He'd seen a succession of fourth-floor receptionists go and come during his twenty-five years here, but each'd been respectful and a little awed by him. Not like the main-floor receptionists who all tended to be older, yellow, well-built, and exuding something like former membership in the Club Georgia Peach chorus line. These, he suspected, had had some connection with Mr. Lawrence one time or another. But up here, the receptionists came young and hoped to move into Editorial; they had to be nice.

Jackson swung out into Editorial. He was medium height, but seemed shorter because he was running to fat, which he kept carefully packed behind his belt. His perfectly round head, upon which he disdained any attempt at an Afro, was cropped close, a part nickered in by the barber's scissors. He set a preoccupied expression on his face, and his steps gathered spring and authority as he walked. He liked striding down the center of the room between the rows of desks and partitions and wax plants set in teakwood veneer boxes.

In the open room with its cubicles hard against the walls, Jackson saw only two people at their desks, the new cat, Cutting, whom he didn't like, and the white girl, like Cutting, new, whom he did, Gail Peabody.

"Hey, man," Jackson said, cruising past, in high stride.

"Morning, Ezz," Cutting said, looking up from his typewriter.

Jackson waved at the girl and she smiled. He was upset that there was nothing special in that smile.

Up front at the window that overlooked the street, the other editors and secretaries were gathered. Jackson wondered if they'd been there watching him drive up and cross the street.

"Hey, Chops, c'mon, man," Griggs, the resident intellectual cried, waving him on. "Look at ole Perk. Quick, man!"

Jackson rushed to the window, noticing the space that opened respectfully for him between the mass of male and female bodies. He nodded at the greetings and returned them, patted this back, touched that elbow. Down in the parking lot, Willie B. Perkins, Editorial Director at Lawrence since its beginning, was hobbling hurriedly toward the curb across the street, the dust still settling from around his car now in its parking slot. Perkins' arms were filled with folders, and they could see anxiety growing in the aging, softly folded face, and, mounting that, the first gleam of terror in his eyes. At the last editorial meeting Mr. Lawrence had told Perk that if he couldn't get into the office on time, he could hand over his desk. After thirty-three years.

"C'mon, Perk," one speaker said through laughter. "*Hustle,* boy!"

"I bet ole Palmer's just about got his key in the door," another said to more laughter. Only the editors were talking; the secretaries and female editorial assistants merely made accompanying noises.

"Guess who's watching from five floor?" The voice was hushed, but there was muted laughter.

Down on the curb Willie B. Perkins' balding head swiveled back and forth, measuring the flow of traffic. Tentatively, he stepped down in the road.

"Yea, Perk! C'mon!" They began to wave to him, signaling for him to hurry across.

Jackson glanced behind him, saw Cutting and Gail Peabody still sitting at their desks at the other end of the room. That was what Jackson didn't like about Cutting; he didn't join in. He condemned them all by his refusal to join them. Gail was another matter; she was white. She wasn't supposed to join them.

Now Perkins edged out into the road.

"That spade is scared shitless!"

"Yeah, but if he ain't in here in thirty seconds, he's gonna be scared and out of a job, too!"

As if hearing them, Perkins started to run flat-footedly across the street. His somber tie unpinched itself from between his white shirt and dark gray jacket and flared back out over his shoulder. He shuffled quickly into the center of the street at precisely the same time one of the speeding cars pulled wide to pass another.

Upstairs the laughter died suddenly. One of the secretaries

said "Ooo!" at the same time she turned away, hands held to her face.

Cutting looked up, rose and hurried to the window.

Jackson's smile remained fixed.

At the last moment possible, Perkins, perhaps sensing rather than seeing the rushing car, jerked to a stop and stumbled backward.

Upstairs in the window through the streaking cars the viewers saw the sudden spraying in the air of manila folders and white sheets. Jackson closed his eyes quickly and tightly, and when he opened them, he saw Perkins back on the curb, holding his wrist and looking dazedly at the papers in the street now dancing in mad arcs with the passing of each car.

"He's all right," Jackson said roughly, trying to conceal the relief he felt. He turned to go to his cubicle, bumping into Cutting who'd come up, just as the nine o'clock buzzer rang.

"I better go give him a hand," Cutting said, with something like resignation or disgust in his voice. "He's a little shook up."

Jackson shrugged. The door to his cubicle was marked Assistant Editorial Director. From inside, minutes later, he saw Perk and Cutting stacking papers and folders. Perk looked beaten and ashamed, and Jackson knew from Cutting's demeanor that he was trying to give the older man back his pride. Jackson knew that, having witnessed the near tragedy from his office window, Mr. Lawrence would say nothing to Perk about it.

Jackson's phone rang and he waited until his secretary, sitting just outside his cubicle, buzzed him. "It's the publisher," she said.

"Hello, Ezzard," Mr. Lawrence began with a chuckle. Jackson was one of about three people Mr. Lawrence called by their first names.

"Hello, Mr. Lawrence," Jackson responded just as heartily. "How're you this morning, sir?"

Jackson, listening, nodded and burst into loud laughter. "It was somethin; it was somethin," he said. Somehow Mr. Lawrence could make the most tragic things comical. Like Perk's almost being killed. "You know, Mr. Lawrence, the white man says the Brothers can move, *if they have to.*"

Jackson gazed out on to the floor. Against the opposite wall sat Gail Peabody, about whom the publisher was now talking. "Fine, sir, she's doin just fine. Now I have some reservations about Cutting, as you know. It's a team thing, Mr. Lawrence. I just don't feel we can count on him when we need him. I don't believe he feels the same way the rest of us do about Lawrence Publishing. He strikes me as being a man on the way to somewhere else."

Jackson listened a while longer and then hung up when the conversation was finished. Mr. Lawrence himself had recruited Cutting, but with some reservations. Cutting had gone to a white school, and the publisher liked for his people to have gone to black schools, and most of them had. Jackson had gone to a black undergraduate school and a white graduate school, and this, he knew, Mr. Lawrence liked. More and more lately he had approached the idea, but never completely confronted it, that Mr. Lawrence felt that black schools inculcated their students with ideas, habits, and fears that he could shape to his own liking. People like Cutting, who went to white undergraduate schools, missed that indoctrination. Jackson didn't like to think about such things; he was too old now.

He heard Perk getting settled in the cubicle next to his. Jackson had nothing against the man; hell, he was doing more of Perk's work than Perk, despite the slight differences in titles. No, nothing at all against the man; he was a charity case.

At ten o'clock the buzzer sounded for the morning break and the editors, as they did every morning, rushed from their desks like stampeded steer, thudding and thumping over the carpeted floors to the company rec room. Neither Jackson nor Perk joined this daily rush for the cards, chessboard, or coffee; it would have been unseemly. They usually followed at a more leisurely pace.

This morning Perk preceded Jackson down when the rush had eased off, and Jackson found himself walking behind Cutting and Gail. Cutting, holding a piece of paper, was laughing.

"Yours in Blackness," Cutting read aloud, and burst into more laughter, choking it off as they saw Jackson coming up behind them.

"Hi," Cutting said, moving aside.

"Hello, Ezzard," the Peabody girl said.

Jackson nodded and rushed on, stunned, mortified, incredulous, for he had heard Cutting read those words, and he'd recognized them instantly as *his* words. He felt like a little boy who'd got caught being slick. The afternoon before he'd written and then slipped the Peabody girl a note declaiming in brief his love for her; it was something he'd done with other women a hundred times with better than 90 per cent success. And he'd signed it, just so she wouldn't think he was a traitor to the revolution, so she would understand that he was not one of those black men who sweated over white trim, *Yours in Blackness, Ezzard.*

Now the bitch was laughing at him and sharing her laughter with that motherfucker, Cutting. Past them, his rage was boundless, yet he knew there was nothing he could do for the moment. But in the end he'd see both of them in hell at the most, and at the very least, they wouldn't be around Lawrence much longer.

"Hit me, sucker!" Plap! The card game was going full blast already. Jackson drew his coffee and stood watching Griggs and Wheeler at the chessboard. As usual, Griggs was winning; Jackson could tell by the way Wheeler kept shaking his head. Perk held forth at the card table, his wrist encased in an Ace bandage. He chuckled while he dealt soft hands to Croft, Malone, Baker, and Fellows. The others smoked and talked in subdued voices, under the clinking of quarters on the table. Gail Peabody stood alone; Cutting stood on the far side of the room looking at everyone with an amused smile on his face.

I'm gonna get you, Jackson thought as their eyes met and slid past. You are a gone sumbitch, Cutting. He wondered if Cutting would tell others, use his note as entree into a club that so far refused him entrance.

Jackson left before the end of the coffee break and walked slowly down the nearly empty floor to his office. He felt the years attacking him again, hinting at a massive defeat of his spirit. He recognized the feeling, but this time it was compounded by a series of rejections: the Peabody girl handing his note over to Cutting, and his wife going to the hospital again. How could he have prevented these occurrences? He could not have.

His inability to control these personal events plunged him into depression, for they underlined his helplessness in other matters, matters that secretly terrorized him. Those matters centered on Lawrence Publications. There was no other place in the entire world for him to work now. Not only was he too old to make a

shift, he was, in habit and thought, too black to adapt to anything else. And even if he did move to a white publication,
would it be as assistant editorial director? No, not even close to
it.

Also, he'd made many enemies. If he'd been cruel, he now
thought, it was on the hinted orders of Mr. Lawrence. If he'd
been a bastard, it was to hold on to his job, move to the top of
the writhing heap, and provide security for his family. He knew
he was called an Uncle Tom as well as Mr. Lawrence's razor,
and he knew which people were probably responsible for the rumors. So: they talked about you when you got near the top of the
mountain; they wanted to slow you up, kick you back down. And
there'd be a new rumor now, the one about his chasing Gail
Peabody. Cutting, he supposed, wouldn't waste any time getting
that one started.

At his desk, Jackson carefully pulled papers into a neat, small
pile for the editorial meeting scheduled for after the coffee
break. It was going to be another long day, he thought, with a
sigh that escaped through clenched teeth. Christine going to the
hospital to have another cyst removed. Two, that'd be in the past
two and a half years.

That meant Mrs. Warren would be hanging around to take
care of the kids in the morning when they went to school and
later when they came home and on into the evening, while he
made his usual rounds, checking contacts and leads. Mrs. Warren
had said, in the manner of old people who have absolutely nothing to lose, that if she were married to Jackson, he'd have to keep
his behind home some nights, Mr. Lawrence or no. And Christine, speaking as if to an invalid, said, "Well, Ezzard's job is
twenty-four hours a day, Mrs. Warren. We're used to it."

"Both of you runnin so much the children don't hardly see
you," Mrs. Warren countered.

"TCB," Christine said with a laugh.

"Takin care of *funny* business," Jackson overheard, as he left
the apartment one night. He wondered about that emphasis on
funny.

Accepting his mail from his secretary, Jackson thought, Old
people sitting all day in front of television or at the windows,

watching neighbors and visitors coming and going. Who do they see? What do they see?

Jackson placed the mail on the desk without looking at it, and glanced at the papers he was taking to the conference. The top sheet was his selection of the ten most popular tunes of the week. The listing appeared together with a story on one of the groups in the body of the magazine—a coincidence Mr. Lawrence had noted without raising the question of payola. He'd merely said that he wanted personally to check the top ten every week. Jackson stopped writing the stories and the checks that came to his home from the grateful recipients of his publicity dwindled down to nothing. But things had become more peaceful between Jackson and Mr. Lawrence since Jackson had met with a fair degree of success in pushing to get an honorary doctorate for his boss. That looked good for next spring; in fact, it looked solid.

After the meeting, which, like all the others, was defined by Mr. Lawrence's credo, *I am in this business not to support or suggest causes, gentlemen, but to make money,* Jackson returned listlessly to his cubicle. Everyone was in business to make money; it was just that Mr. Lawrence never let you forget it. He was like a schoolteacher who believed he had thickheaded pupils; he did not believe you could support causes and make money at the same time; you did one or the other, and if you stayed with him, it was to make him money.

Jackson hefted then riffled through his mail. You got to the point where you opened your own; you could never tell what would come in, maybe a tip on a story; maybe even a check. Most of all, at Lawrence you simply did not let people get into your business, even if it was magazine business.

Invitations to speak, invitations to parties, blurbs about the openings of personalities, wine-tastings, auto-show openings. Yeah. They'd started doing big, annual spreads on the new car models and the advertising from Detroit had started to roll in. Jackson's idea. It'd gotten him a fifty-dollar raise.

He withdrew a letter from the stack. Personal. Handwritten address.

Richard Wiggins, the letter said, was the returnee. Richard

Wiggins, Jackson mused. He looked at the postmark. Bubbles!
He thought. Bubbles Wiggins!

Dear Chops:

I bet you're surprised to hear from me after all these
years, right? How are you? Christine? The kids? What
do you have, a boy and a girl? That's what I heard. Of
course, I see your name all the time up front in the
magazine. You've sure done yourself proud and back
here we're all proud of you.

As for us, Onetha is doing well. She's been at Mohawk now for a long time. Rick, as you know, because
your magazine did that story on him, is playing ball at
Columbia. Thanks. I'm still at the foundry, like Cudjo
Evers, doing our thing. My daughter, Allison, is in New
Mexico, married and just now checking with the doctor
to see if she's pregnant or not. Can you imagine? Me a
grandfather.

What I wanted to talk about Chops is Chappie Davis.
You know he's going to be 70 next month on Nov. 30.
All of us here decided we really ought to do something
for the old guy because he was so great with us when
we were growing up in the Boy Scouts, football, basketball and our advisor when we formed The Junior Bachelor Society. The way we see it in our old age (smile) is
that if it hadn't been for Chappie a lot of us, including
you guys who left and did so good, would've wound up
like some of the guys who didn't hang out with us.

So what we want is to have a big dinner for him.
Black tie and all (which means I'll have to rent one)
and give him a plaque, and each one can tell what the
old man meant to us personally. The JBS is sponsoring
the thing. Our committee here is Shurley Walker, Cudjo
Evers and me. Our wives are helping and Snake Dumpson, the housing commissioner (did you know about
that?), got all the addresses for us. Everyone but Moon.

We're writing to Ralph Joplin, D'Artagnan Foxx, and
Clarie Henderson. We'd really like you and Christine

and the kids to come. We can use $100 for the kitty, but the important thing is that you come. Let me know. You can stay with us or I'll make a hotel reservation. They don't look at us cross-eyed anymore, Chops. (Smile) Write soon or call the above number.

He was struggling through all that whiteness—snow. His terror (it'd always lived deeply within him) stretched his little fingers tightly around the hard wrist of his mother. She shook it off. *The bag, she said. Hold on to the bag. I cain't hold on to you and the bags, too, Ezzard. Now, you just try to walk like a man, y'hear?*

The snow had been piled into mounds so high they couldn't see across the streets except at corners. Under each street light they stopped while she set the bags down and glanced at the paper in her hand; the paper conformed now to the curve of the handle of the suitcase and the pressure of her hand.

Now and again they first heard, then saw a car clinking and clattering in its chains as it crept down the near silent streets. Then, two blocks away, the same time his mother, breathing heavily now, said, *Won't be long Ezzard,* he heard the shouts of boys at play, and wondered first at their silliness, then at their daring. The voices were lusty, challenging, splintering the frigid night.

The fort was built around the base of a street light, and as Jackson and his mother plodded and slid through the deepening snow, he could see the figures of the boys, rising like dark trolls from up behind the fortress walls of snow and ice to repel other dark, charging shapes, battle yells rending the stillness. Snowballs, like small comets, flashed through the air. Closer, Jackson perceived that the brash sounds and snarls were exploding from the throats of little black boys, scarved, booted, buckled, and bundled against the snow and cold.

Here, chilrens, she said, resting the bags in the snow once more. *Where live Miz Susie Jefferson?*

Right there. Upstairs.

Ezzard Jackson felt the eyes on him, measuring, then dismissing him as the war resumed and he and his mother slipped and puffed up the steps.

Mrs. Jefferson had a daughter.

"I'm off," Christine was saying over the phone. "And Mrs. Warren's here."

Both times she'd gone to the hospital—the same one—she had insisted on going alone. It was only for twenty-four hours and she'd be right back home, the cyst gone, and in another week it'd be just like always. "We can get back to takin care of business," Christine said. "I know you must be hurtin a little, baby, because I am."

"Talk that talk, Christine," Jackson said, trying to put humor into his tone. "Hey, got a letter from Bubbles Wiggins, your old flame."

There was a pause on her end of the line. "Bubbles Wiggins? Oh, from back *home*. Anything wrong?"

"No. Just wants us to come back for a testimonial for Chappie Davis next month. Let's do it."

"Okay by me. Didn't know Chappie was still alive. Listen, baby. I've got to go, but I'll call you tonight."

"When are they going to cut?"

"At two, they said, so I should be in fairly good shape tonight."

"Okay."

The battle shouts came to him muffled; he was already falling to sleep as his mother and the other woman undressed him for bed and slipped him beside another small, warm body—Christine—to which he snuggled close, relieved to be off the train, out of the snow and cold, and far, far away from whatever it was that had sent them rushing and reeling through another, southern night to this cold place. Through the closed bedroom door he heard his mother's voice floating soft and tired, filled with the inflections of gratitude, and Mrs. Jefferson's voice beating them back.

Oh, Miz Jefferson . . .
Now, Miz Jackson . . .

It'd been *their* town, Jackson reflected. He'd been an intruder, making them laugh at his accent, but they'd taken him in, finally, to share their games and homes and schoolrooms, and the five years in which his mother had got their own place was long enough for him to have become the regular shortstop on the Little Harlem Grill Junior softball team and a guard on the football team. It was long enough for him to have felt stirrings about Christine. It just seemed like a short time, when they got back on the train heading South.

He no longer remembered how long they stayed, remembered only some vague difference of spirit between the boys there and the boys in the North, and he was glad when they returned to Christine's town, even though the neighborhood had shifted from Bloodfield to Jewtown. But they were all there, Bubbles and Cudjo and Ralph and Clarie; still there D'Artagnan and Moon and Shurley and Snake; they'd merely transferred their hoops and howls from the battered houses along the railroad tracks to the alleys between bakeries, fish markets, and kosher delicatessens and butchers. And they'd been joined by still others whose faces now drifted past Jackson's inner eye, nameless, the grimaces and grins fixed in time, though many had since died.

The Boy Scouts with Chappie as scoutmaster, the hikes to Ram's Gulch, the two weeks at Camp Woodvale were about over, the fart festivals and ghost stories told before dying campfires on chilled nights bearing mixed scents of brook water, birch, aspen, maple, and coniferous trees were settling in another time, subservient now to covert-cloth suits, pork pie hats, oyster-colored, plaid-lined rain coats, and oxblood cordovan shoes. Chappie then was handing them over to the high school coaches and there were girls now, and uniforms, and cheers. All life was bound in the heat of late adolescence, was publicly physical and privately mental.

Jackson breathed easier there beneath the two-hundred-year-old arched maples; they seemed to shelter him from old, noxious memories. But, within himself he felt that something had been irrevocably bent, a bush always to the weatherside, without shelter, except there. It had been fit and proper in that time of learning of the body's awakening that he became aware of Christine, her body moving under soft cotton dresses, her pouting breasts, the wisdom and guile that could float from their hiding places in the corners of her eyes and come to rest smack in the middle of them, to stare out, daringly.

No amount of derring-do could turn her head from Bubbles to himself until that other girl, Onetha, came. Or was it that Bubbles had done with Christine?

Christine, April, Iris, Diane, Evelyn, Onetha—the names danced before him like a field of cornflowers in a soft wind. But, he felt always an outsider, huddled before a different wind. He married the first real warmth he'd ever known.

That had not come, however, until, once more, Jackson and his mother went back South to bury a relative. For some reason they stayed. His mother, who could be so strong at times, at others was weak of will, and took the line of least resistance. Yes, she admitted, it was expensive up North. And yes, the white folks were pretty much the same—down deep the same—as the white folks South. So, why didn't she stay home this time where she belonged? *You been tweakin at his roots too much, Miz Jackson; oughta be settlin down now.*

There, he behaved as though his audience was made up of the Junior Bachelor Society, formed just before he left. He played to the JBS 1,200 miles away from it, and ignored the cautions of the blacks, sneered at the startled whites. The war began, lumbered on distantly, but somehow managing to cause the disappearance from the corners and factories of countless black men, and although Jackson had lived in the South for a good part of his life, as he approached eighteen he decided that he would not be drafted there. He returned North alone, roomed with church people, worked after school and practice, while waiting to be called. There was no problem re-enrolling in school. The flow, like black lava, of Negro families to the North was constant and the white teachers were by now used to incomplete and inadequate records transferred up from Down Home.

By graduation Christine was his steady. When his mother came he told her he was going to marry Christine, and they were still arguing a month later when Jackson's draft papers came. He was going to marry her when he got leave, he shouted over and over to his mother, to drown out her solemn pronouncement: "Christine *used* to be a good girl, but she's too fast now." The pronouncement begged him to ask questions, but Jackson, deep in his terror, saw the trap and avoided it; he did not want to hear answers, therefore he would not ask questions.

Jackson and Christine married on his first leave from Drum and he, stronger by then, immediately dispatched her South to his mother saying she could begin college while he was in the Army.

Jackson fingered Bubble's letter. What would it be like? The town wasn't the same, that he knew from Christine's relatives. There might be a story in the reunion. Hell, yes, with Ralph Joplin and Snake (he wondered how many times the story would be told of the jersey being ripped off Snake's back and Snake crying) and maybe even Dart, if he could come all the way from Europe. And Clarie Henderson. Not much of a story with Bubbles and Cudjo in the foundry, or Shurley bartending. Maybe Chappie himself was the hook. There weren't enough stories on how people in the neighborhoods had always looked after their own. The kids coming up today, they think community-help programs started with them. There were a lot of Chappies. Nobody ever heard of them except the kids they kept out of jail. Surrogate father and all that. The only father I ever had, Jackson thought, reaching for his buzzing phone.

"Mr. Lawrence wants you in his office right away."

"He didn't say what he wanted?"

"No."

He never did, Jackson thought, stopping himself from banging down the phone. Ezzard Jackson was Mr. Lawrence's rubber ball. *Bounce,* man!

FIVE

The small apartment, with its heavy, dark 1930s furniture, the nondescript, gray, hand-me-down tapestries on the walls, the rotogravure photos in warping, grease-stained frames on the chests and tables, was silent except for the periodic electronized bellow of eighty thousand voices drowning out the monotones of the announcers.

Charles Chappie Davis waited for Sundays. On Saturdays he sometimes watched the good college football teams play, but Sunday was his day. He sat now in a soft, deep wing chair directly in front of the color television set. On a small table to his left rested his telephone and on another to his right was a pack of cigars, a half gallon of milk, and three quarters of a sweet potato pie. Patches of sunlight lay brightly against the furnishings of the room, highlighting the small glass case in which stood dulled, gold-plated small trophies, peeling and blackening.

Humph! the old man thought, his head, shoulders, and chest heaving and then dropping back into place. *That boy runs like he got a rudder up his ass. Cuts, zip, zap. Kiick can't do that. He runs more like Csonka, bam! right into people. Not ole Mercury. He's got a sense of survival along with everything else. That Csonka, if he had to run more than forty yards, heh! He couldn't make it. Runs like ole Snake used to, except Snake had the moves. Give you a leg and snatch it back. Snake was good. Damned good, but he could have been better if he hadn't been afraid. Not many people knew that.*

From Monday to Friday, Chappie walked to work and back, moving at a brisk clip, taking in with quick glances the unending and myriad changes in this city where he had been born and raised. He felt that it, like himself, was dying at an ever increasing rate of speed. Yes, he wore fashionable clothes, like the ones everyone was wearing now, but that did not retard the dying of his body; the city, too, had taken to modish garb, fluted with

speedways that curled around it, with its high-rise office buildings and apartment houses. But, beneath the streets there lay
buried in six inches of asphalt or concrete, the old bones, the
streetcar and train tracks and here and there between the brave
thrusts toward a vague and shifting modernity stood the red-
brick buildings of the nineteenth century. And the Remington
Hotel was an old building. It had been about fifty years old
when Chappie was a boy and swam in the Erie Canal. The canal
was now a boulevard.

Chappie felt at home in the basement of the Remington where
he oversaw the stock, the whiskey, beer, soda, and cigarettes and
general supplies. Merging into the shadows of his area—a table,
chair, and shelves against a wall—with his radio, he was completely at home amid the ancient smells of dank brick and mor-
tar.

He had two helpers, Jumbo Coles who worked full time, having been dropped from school because he was retarded, and the
Tucker kid, who worked part time after school or athletic practice. Often, while sitting in his corner, he'd watch the two boys
from the shadows, the big Jumbo doomed to listening to echoes
without source in his head, and the slender, quick Tucker kid,
patiently explaining things to him. For extra change, Jumbo and
the Tucker kid also ran whiskey to the whores and Johns who
worked out of the hotel. Once, it was said, the hotel had been so
grand that William Lloyd Garrison stayed in it.

Life was easy enough for Chappie; he earned a bill a week,
cash, and took down his social security for a nice enough bundle
for an old man. And when he had to, he tapped the account he'd
built up running numbers. He'd done that for twenty-five years,
until the people downtown got greedy and then, fifteen years ago
they'd smashed the numbers. The district attorney then was
mayor now. It was D'Amica who got Chappie off with a
suspended sentence and found the job at the Remington for him.
D'Amica had been around a long time himself; knew all the
ropes.

*See that? It's the same way those cracker schools play ball,
now they got some black players on their squads. Ole Morris ran
that ball all the way down to the five and they send for Kiick to
take it in. Peckerwoods!*

Yeh! That big ole honky Csonka runs just like Snake used to. Hummmm. Snake belonged to Moon. Moon could smell his fear. Moon was a good tackler because he didn't give a damn. Just drilled in there at practice and God help whoever had the ball. Don't suppose he'll be back. No, they don't teach them to tackle any more. It takes something to run full speed at a man coming toward you at full speed, a ball under his arm. You've got to get your feet together at the last minute, drive home that shoulder. The man who moves the fastest gets hurt the least.

Chappie reached for the milk container and drank directly from it. He'd always liked milk, and in the old days when he walked into a bar, they had the crème de menthe and milk set up before he could get his foot on the rail. Number-running days.

He'd been at the top of the heap then. Good clothes, fine women, and no problems, like so many of the men he grew up with were having. He thought of Big Ralph Joplin and shook his head. *We ought to get together, damn it. Grew up together, swam in the canal, remember all his bad luck with that Down Home girl, Sissie. Sissie, dead now. (They're dropping like flies, Chappie.) Me and Ralph been living here in the same town for damned near all our lives. Jesus, Little Ralph was one of my boys.*

They got the ball again? Do it, Mean Joe Greene! Tear his goddamn dick loose!

Often on Sundays Bubbles, Shurley, or Cudjo, or all together would keep him company during one of the games. But today they were working on the testimonial dinner they were giving him and he was alone. While Chappie enjoyed having company, he disliked it on a regular basis, so he was pleased to be alone now, working his way slowly through the sweet potato pie and his half gallon of milk.

They didn't know just yet who would be coming, but Chappie hoped all of them; it would be nice to have them all in one room again, if only for a little while. He glanced around. *I'll have to get this place cleaned up.* None of them wrote once they left town, but he'd heard about them from one source or another. This one broke up with his wife; that one went to Europe; one did this and the other that. In his mind they were fixed at age seventeen, half-boys, half-men. Even the dead, like Greek and

Redbones and Jake. Chappie remembered now how he'd gone to Crook-Eye over at Little Harlem Grill and got him to spring for the football and softball jerseys. *Man, they were proud of those jerseys!* That was before they went to high school and got real uniforms like the silk football pants.

Who'd they say they were trying to get? Soften them up Franco and let Frenchy carry it. That boy is big. They sure turn out some monsters these days. Great God in Glory!

Oh, yes. Trying to get Moon, Clarie, Dart—it'd be nice to see Dart again—back for the dinner. Haven't heard much about ole Dart. And Moon, supposed to be a bigtime pimp in Los Angeles. And Ralph. Little Ralph.

Chappie'd seen a road company performance of Ralph's very first play, *Shadows on the Sun.* He shook his head admiringly.

Never know what kids are thinking when they're going back and forth through a house. Big Ralph and ole Sissie, too, would've been proud if they'd seen it.

And who else? That boy married that fast little Jefferson girl, Ezzard—Chops—and Cudjo, Shurley, and Snake.

Snake never came around. Not once. Too high class now, I guess. But I remember all those kids with their snotty noses and patches in their pants, and their daddies had run off; remember those rubber welfare gloves the welfare used to hand out to them at Christmas. A pop fly to a kid wearing one of those gloves was an automatic single, cause the ball always bounced out. Ole Snake may be living out there in the suburbs with his white wife, but ole Chappie remembers other days.

GO ON FRANCO! GO! Chappie hunched forward in his chair, and leaned his body in the same direction as the scrambling player on the screen. *Pheww, that boy can run. First down. Now, don't throw it away, Bradshaw; don't hand them the goddamn ball, now.*

Bubbles, now he always comes around. You can count on ole Bubbles. He played without a lot of sparkle, but good and steady, like Buoniconti out there. Bubbles never got the breaks. Maybe he just never had his sights raised high enough. I know Cudjo didn't. He knew he didn't have but two more brains than Jumbo and just settled right in a groove. Couldn't ask for a more generous kid, though.

Then ole Chops, coming and going, going and coming. Nice-looking momma. Chops wasn't too big, but he moved good and had his moments. Good hitter, good shortstop—as long as the ball went to his right. If it went to his left, close your eyes and pray. Good pulling guard. Came out of his holes like Gangbusters and Superman combined, huffing and puffing and lookin mean. But he couldn't block right to save his soul. If he had to take a man out, he took him in; if he had to take him in, he took him out.

Chappie remembered the night he gave the Little Harlem Grill basketball team a spagetti dinner, a kind of thanks and good-by thing. The kids were all on the high school team then, and playing just once in a while for him. He had been crushed to discover that they thought more of their white coach than they did him. He'd had to tell them then that if it hadn't been for him none of them would have been able to pull on their jockstraps.

He remembered that Bubbles came to the party with Christine; Chops came alone, said little, and drank a lot. It was snowing that night, great wet, twisting drops, and the snowplows were already out. Chappie had helped Chops home, sliding the boy through the snow while trying to stay up himself. "You want that girl, Chops, you got to fight for her, boy. Gettin drunk and stayin quiet won't help."

"Chappie," the boy said, the wine talking, "if I had any sense, I wouldn't want her."

She was fast, that little Jefferson girl. I wonder if she's been good to Chops. Heard they killed his father down home. Chops never talked about it.

Shurley now, he's got a good wife, ole Diane. He's some boy. All his life he pretended to be sleepy and tired and no ac-count. Just didn't believe in letting people know his business or his feelings. He was like Warfield, just naturally good, but his mind was somewhere else, and he only played ball because everyone else did. Sure hated white people. Ooooweee. Why not?

Chappie'd cut through Guido's back lot that day, a yard grown over with weeds and sprayed with broken glass that glittered in the sun. Passing through, it was just by chance that he glanced over where Saslow's whitefish were being smoked, and saw Shurley laying on the ground. Moving nearer, he heard him crying. Shurley was about nine or ten at the time. Chappie fetched a dime up out of his pocket.

I thought there was nothing wrong that a ten-cent piece couldn't fix.

"Hey, Shurley, what's wrong?"

Knew it was bad from the way he was crying, and his face all swollen and lumped up.

It took a long time to get it out of the boy, so long that later Chappie had to run to his drops in the afternoon to make up for the time he'd lost with Shurley.

Damn whiteboys made ole Shurley suck their dicks.

Well, I fixed all of em real good. Kids didn't have fathers or big brothers. Somebody had to take their fights.

He'd been good then, fast, dazzling, and righteous. It'd been no match and the late Saturday night darkness closed down around Chappie standing over three forms on the ground.

Looked out for my boys.

Big boys like that. They should have been jerking off or getting some moochie from their own girls.

Ole Shurley, slow-moving Shurley. Black folks would fall out if they knew he'd owned the Ebenos for the past fifteen years. Yessir, bought out ole Papadapoulous, as soon as he could. "Coach, it's my secret and yours. I never planned to die working for no white man."

Now, nearly asleep as the announcers droned on, Chappie thought of D'Artagnan Foxx. He had had a long affair with Foxx's mother, which ended, but not before they discussed running away and taking the boy with them.

Yes, she had my nose really opened. I'd have done it.

But, loyalty to her husband prevailed. *Clumsiest footpad in the world. Couldn't do anything without getting caught. Had a record as long as my arm.*

Dart was a standout. Ralph had not had any special talent for writing plays then, and no one guessed that Snake would, or could, become adept at politics, and there'd been nothing about Chops that showed me he was going to become a journalist. But Dart was an early diamond.

Always had what they call presence and later, when the voice came, made me think of Robeson. Big, with that deep voice. And played some ball. Dart at tail. Snake at full. In high school it was Snake at full and Dart at left and behind him was Redbones and Bubbles was at right, second or third string. My boys stacked up.

Could make me cry when he sang "Ol' Man River" or "Motherless Child." I'd have some time keeping the water back, because I could hear things in his voice.

Always something a little soft about Dart. I think he knew it too, and wasn't going to let it show, so he became the chief headknocker. Chief.

The figures on the television screen were becoming blurs in motion.

And Clarie, Chappie thought. You talked different things with different boys; how to draw a cue ball or make it run, or how to smack the water in a racing dive, little extra things like that. For Clarie, the extra thing had been books, learning.

A prolonged burst of cheers made Chappie jerk up his head in time to see three or four players piled up, rolling across the goal line. One of them bounced to his feet holding the football up by the end, in triumph.

A soul Brother, Chappie thought, pleased, just before sleep overwhelmed him.

SIX

"We'd appreciate it if you would help us out on this one, Clarence."

Clarence Henderson's eyes bored back at the chairman of the Invitation Committee. "I bet you would," he said. But he knew there was nothing else he could do; nothing else he'd want to do given the situation. "Why was everyone so quick to say no when I first offered to be the contact with Moore? What's happened?"

The man standing before Henderson, sweating in his cheap brown suit, shrugged. "Clarence, I wish I knew. No one in the English department has *heard* of the man—or at least, that's what they say. It seems hard," he said, almost talking to himself, "to believe that's the case. They simply do not want to do anything for him over there."

"Billingsly knows about him. Billingsly was responsible for his coming," Henderson said accusingly.

"But Billingsly is on leave," the chairman said.

"In any case," Henderson said challengingly, "I don't *know* the man. I've only met him."

Quickly the man said, "But that gives you the edge on everyone else."

Almost shouting Henderson said, "You know I can't say no, but if you people were *serious* about black writers and black literature, this wouldn't be happening."

"It's not a racial thing——"

"Aw, Clyde, cut the crap. We both know better than that."

The chairman seemed to gaze momentarily at something beyond Henderson's shoulder, then his eyes dropped.

Henderson said, "Well. Look, where do we start? Does he have a hotel?"

"The Sunset."

"The Sunset. Hell, Clyde, that's a third-rate hotel and you know it. What's wrong with the Miramar or the Hutchinson? You know damned well that if John Updike or Norman Mailer came out here that is where you'd put them automatically."

"That's what they told me to do, Clarence——"

"Well, change it, Clyde!"

"I'll try."

"If you don't, forget about me, and I mean it."

The chairman heaved a great sigh. "I'll see what I can do."

"How's he going to get to the campus?"

"Rent a car, I guess. That's what everyone else does."

Henderson turned to leave the office, then pivoted back to the chairman again. "I'm going to pretend I didn't hear that. Every white man who visits here gets a university car, Clyde, and goddamn it, you *know* it. You *know* it."

It was jive, all jive, Henderson thought. If they didn't want the man there, why had they extended the invitation? Going through motions, rituals, as if they were still trying to appease the lusty, murderous spirits of 1967 and '68.

Was Barney Moore aware of the games that went down, *had* to go down each time he appeared on a college campus? What had he done to deserve them? The fact that Moore was an old friend of Ralph's was important, yes. But what they were doing to him as an artist counted for far more. Pretending there was no such thing when that art was done by a man who was black. Henderson was feeling all the resentment of a subject who's envoy was being discourteously treated in a foreign land. Recall him! They don't deserve the grace of his presence!

This was what happened to Ralph, too, he imagined, in this "new day" when black artists were invited to the campuses. Their relationship, Ralph's and Moore's, was still intertwined.

Clarence had read of those old days in the Village when Moore had helped Ralph mop the building in which Ralph lived and worked as a superintendent; how Moore had published his first novel before Ralph had had his first play produced; how Ralph had been the best man at Moore's wedding. And of those days when Moore had visited Langston and been kindly advised that there would be rough water ahead, white water.

Clarence liked to relate these incidents to his students, for they indicated a continuity they did not believe the black artist had. They stopped thinking about relationships after Hemingway got Fitzgerald into the ring.

Clarence was still staring at Clyde.

Doggedly the sweating man said, "I don't know anything, Clarence." His voice dropped an octave. "They gave me absolutely no budget for this man's visit." His eyes, fixed as in a plea, searched Clarence Henderson's face. "I went to Plotkin. He didn't want to disturb *his* budget."

"Then I guess I'll have to go to the chancellor, Clyde."

The man laughed. "Oh. I thought you knew. Didn't you know? I thought you did. Everything starts at the top, Clarence, whether here or anywhere else. And the top blames the bottom and the bottom can't do anything about it. And the chancellor knows who visits his school."

Henderson heard the muted clacking of typewriter keys somewhere on the floor, and the sound of bare feet thudding down the hall. He shook his head. "I understand. I just forgot. Let me use your phone, will you, Clyde?"

He stared out of the window while waiting for the phone to ring. He could see the ocean glistening between the campus buildings, and smell the eucalyptus trees; their odor reminded him of his armpits after exercising.

"Hey, Jesse. Yeah, this is Henderson. Yeah. Listen, can you call a meeting for this afternoon? The problem is that Barney Moore is coming in tomorrow. About three weeks. Trustees Lecturer, and nothing's been done. *Nothing's* been done." Henderson covered the phone and spoke to the man. "They haven't even heard about it." He spoke into the instrument again. "I've got a class this morning. Make it about two this afternoon." Henderson hung up.

The chairman of the invitation committee asked, "Was that Jesse Simpson?"

Henderson smiled at his tone. They didn't like Jesse Simpson. Simpson had faked them all out; had them believing he was the most militant black man to come down the pike since David Walker. "Yeah, that was Simpson. Maybe the Black Studies people can light some fire around this place." Henderson hoped he sounded threatening. Just being on speaking terms with Simpson perhaps made that appear so. But Simpson was militant only as long as it benefited him; if sucking ass moved him up or ahead, he was adept at that, too, only they didn't know it. Yet.

"Maybe they can," the chairman said. "Moore'll be in Plotkin's office at eleven tomorrow. How about giving us some help?"

"Okay, Clyde. Do they have an office ready for him at least?"

"Not sure. He'll be down the hall from you, I understand."

Henderson said, "Well, let's see what happens." He walked out of the chairman's office.

Passing the typists and clerks, Jesse Simpson's words came bellowing back over the phone: "Man, just who in the fuck is Barney Moore?" Henderson had answered, About three weeks. Inwardly he groaned now. It was going to be a long, hard, hot day. Too hot for this late in October, and too hard for him to bear at this stage of his life.

He stalked quickly over the grass to his classroom. He'd long ago given up walking on concrete, for the bicyclists never stayed in their marked paths; he'd been hit by them twice. In the Humanities Building he forced himself through the crush of students and entered his classroom. It was already filled.

He caught his breath while he lit his pipe and wondered how many had read Moore's most recent novel which he'd assigned last week. And there was the paper due on Ralph's first play, *Shadows on the Sun*. The course was Afro-American Literature, one of two he taught. The other was Comparative Modern European Literature. Although the semester was only a month old, he was already distressed to discover, as he did whenever he taught this course, that the interest of the white students far outstripped that of the black students. With but one or two exceptions the black students chased the rhetoric, chipped at authors' marriages and types of cars they were reputed to own, how much time they'd spent in Europe (while the revolution was going on), whether they were together.

Henderson glanced pointedly at Ashton who sat in the back row, the light from the windows reflecting wildly on his oversized shades. His big-brimmed hat (zoot suit shit was coming back fast now) was tilted at a crazy angle. Ashton was a star back on the football team, and catching hell from most of the black students because his girl was white. Black students who wore headgear in the classroom irritated Henderson, but he'd not said anything. Times had changed.

Besides, he was particularly vulnerable, in no position to create unnecessary hassles. He could not strike out when it suited him, and not even always when he was right. The replies uncoiled quickly, and they stung; they were always about his color —or lack of it.

"Okay," he said to the class. "Barney Moore will be on campus starting tomorrow for three weeks. I hope to have him visit the class, so if you've been slow reading his new book, get on it.

"Now I'll take the papers due in on Joplin's play." He took a deep draw on his pipe and waited for the rustle of papers, the shoving of book bags and murmuring. None of this came. He looked around the room and then took a few steps toward the front row.

Goddamn! he thought. Why do they insist on doing this to you, year after year? Nothing changes. They think the obligation flows from one direction only.

"No papers, huh?" He was still taking in those stolid, expressionless faces. Once they would have been self-conscious or sheepish; once there would have been three or four papers at least. Now there was nothing, just faces intensely scrutinizing his own, as if he were the object of an examination; as if he and not they were being put to a test that could not be measured in a classroom situation.

"Class dismissed," he said, turning to collect his papers and noticing that the collective, expressionless face had suddenly fractured into twenty-two different emotions. For he had, perhaps even more than he could have guessed, communicated to them his feeling that they were not worth teaching, that his time could better be spent with others or at least in some other place. He left the room, picked his way through the still crowded halls to the open campus.

"Professor Henderson, Professor Henderson!"

Henderson turned around without stopping. Of course it was Gerda Tolkien. "Yes?" he said when she'd caught up with him.

"I'm sorry about not getting my paper in."

"Me too."

The whirr and click of bikes and their gears surrounded them.

The riders were almost blurs coasting or pumping up and down the paths.

"I can leave it in your office this afternoon," Gerda said, thrusting her face around in front of him so he had to look at her.

"Stick it under the door. I won't be there."

"All right. Are there any special questions we should ask Mr. Moore?"

"Whatever you want to ask." Henderson knew that Gerda had read all of Moore's books.

"I'm really sorry about the paper, Clarence. I'd like to make it up to you."

They were approaching James Beckwourth Hall—something of an embarrassment to the state school system. Officials had not known Jim Beckwourth, who had discovered the northern passes into the state, was black but were elated that he was, particularly in these times.

"Just hand in the paper, Gerda, if you want a grade."

"Okay." She smiled and peeled away from him.

Some unlucky instructor was going to wind up marrying Gerda, Henderson thought. She liked professors, especially out of Black Studies and English; Black Studies for her militancy and English for her intellectualism. Big gun on campus, lots of notches in the handle, but Henderson was not one of them.

Henderson closed the door of his office and sat down beside his desk. Papers were in neat stacks on its top; old themes students never claimed, notices from the department chairmen, the various committee chairmen, the chancellor's office. In contrast, pencils and ball-point pens law strewn all about, and in the center of the desk stood a two-handled mug which bore the inscription: *Clarie*. Leaning against it was Bubbles Wiggins' letter and Henderson's Xeroxed reply.

Yes, he was going, with Pat, his wife. They'd found him, the JBS, and that had touched him; his life seemed without luster now; he was passing through it by rote. But, like a photographer with a telephoto lens on his camera, he'd watched from afar the progress of his former mates. He, on a lower level (he told himself), had eased through the cities and nations Dart and Ralph, for example, had lived in or visited. He'd tasted on those sabbaticals or summer vacations; they seemed to have feasted. No matter. No one could have thought that any of them would be capable of getting away.

But none had got away like him.

Clarie and Ralph sat in the coach of the darkened train glancing at their reflections in the windows. They'd already talked of the service they'd see in the Navy, of returning home on leave, uniformed and beribboned; they'd already seen themselves, sealeg-steady, walking across the decks of battleships and carriers. They walked into the recruiting office together, but came out separately, and when they met back home on boot leave, Henderson did not tell Ralph that he'd been sent to a white camp. "They sent me to Newport News," Henderson said. "Where'd you go?"

"Great Lakes."

Boot leave at home was a relief for Henderson, for during his eight weeks as a white sailor, he'd lived in fear that someone would reveal him as a Negro. Still, when he returned to his base and reported to the master-at-arms and told him he was colored, not white, as he had not done at the recruiting station, he instantly regretted it. While awaiting assignment to and attending specialists' school, he shared the routine duties with his black fellows, but not the weekends.

He still remembered the fear he felt when one of his barracks-mates recognized him on a bus in Boston. While the sailor was staring briefly at him, Henderson turned casually toward his white WAVE date. He hadn't been any good with her that night; he was too worried about what would happen when he returned to the barracks.

Nothing happened. The sailors had grinned knowingly; he'd been "swinging down the line." If that had happened today, Henderson told himself, he'd be torn from limb to limb. How time changes everything.

And now he laughed thinking about the high school basketball team made up of the JBS. The first five all black—except that the fans away from home took him to be the only white player and rooted for him, the girls, he thought, must've believed he was superbad to be good enough to play with a team full of spades. Toomer's line came to him: "And when I'd make a long clean shot, she'd clap. . . ."

Clarence Henderson had been, was still, but to a lesser extent and for different reasons, Dutilleul, the Walker-Through-Walls. Once it'd been breathtaking, marvelously heady, to sit in bars and restaurants where blacks could not go, to pick up women they feared to glance at.

He thought of Dart and Snake who had married white women. He had married black; fair, but black. He could easily have done what they had done. Henderson wanted to check them out; check out everyone, see what their lives had been like. Of course, he owed a special thing to Chappie.

"Stay in school and get that education. Don't get caught sitting back waiting. You get that schooling; there's not a man alive who can take it from you. Be ready, because when the chance comes, it won't wait like a train."

There was no one else to listen to. Father gone. Mother gone. He'd been raised by an uncle and aunt, on the black side, and they had not loved him. He'd taken Chappie's advice and after the war he went to Morris Brown on a football scholarship where they still talked of John "Big Train" Moody the way they talked of Motley, would talk of Brown, Hill, Harris, Brockington. The schools down there then required the taking of courses in Negro History and Negro Literature, courses the students tried to shun because they did not believe black people had either a history or a literature. They believed nothing then, but were forced to digest the courses anyway. How all that had changed! It didn't matter that whites still didn't believe, or wouldn't believe; the matter rested on the ability, the willingness, of blacks to believe, and they did; now it was just a matter of being used to believing, and that was coming, slowly. Chappie had been right.

Henderson rose and walked down the corridor to the supply room where the coffee maker sat. He saw the chairman's secretary. "Penny, you got an office ready for Barney Moore?"

You looked at Penny and you knew right away that when she first came to California, she planned to go into the movies. She never made it, but there was still something about her precisely applied make-up, her subdued movements and modulated voice that made Henderson think: actress.

She said, "He can have Appleton's office. He's on leave. I'll have it ready by tomorrow."

Henderson said, "He might like a typewriter, paper and pads and pencils."

"Will do. He's a friend of yours, I hear?"

"I've met him."

"Nice man?"

Henderson fingered his pipe. "Well, he's a friend of a friend. I imagine he's okay." He filled his cup and went back to his office. Nice man, he thought. Maybe they thought he'd do a tap dance with switchblades in both hands. Maybe they even thought that he, Dr. Clarence Henderson, with the onset of the full moon, pillaged and raped when not doing the Charleston.

He couldn't stop them from thinking. He had tenure and a full professorship; they could go to hell. But he knew he had 1967 and 1968 to thank for his security and position, even though he knew his field. He'd taught just about every known English and American literature course—literature from the Greek (as though there had been nothing before) to Iceberg Slim. But all of it had counted for less than his knowledge of "Afro-American" literature. They could say they'd always had such an authority in the department; there simply had not been a demand for his services in that area. Oh, they were slick, quick on their feet.

Now Henderson glanced at the rows of anthologies of black writing gleaming in their covers. Some were good, but most were not. Publishers had made money out of black student demands. Two years ago the anthologies had stopped coming; the polemicists, together with the writers, washed out. The waterfall had been cut off; now lessening down to a trickle. Somewhere back East someone had pressed a button and closed the gates. A few hung on, like Moore.

Ah, but he, Henderson, like his black colleagues the nation over, had benefited more from the street explosions than those who'd caused them. He had moved quickly through a couple of prestige schools on the shock waves, arriving here just before they subsided.

Perhaps because of his ability to walk through the walls of color, Henderson had learned much of both races, strengths, weaknesses, cunning, and those digested, and with a nimbleness he had used in sports, he sidestepped all efforts to place and confine him in Black Studies rather than English departments.

The former were politically precarious and often merely pasted together; they were expendable. But English departments, fulcrums of cultural education would remain, the Anglo-literature they propounded echoing more and more hollowly when other literatures, produced in the same times and places, were uncovered. No, English departments, with all their faults and failures, were for the time being, cultural blockhouses. From within he could spike their cannon, defuse their shells.

As for Black Studies, Henderson had observed a strange phenomenon; there seemed to be an abundance of non-American blacks in them, as if the colleges and universities were more interested in hiring the color than the relevant, Afro-American experience. Of one thing Henderson was positive. The academic powers were not serious, and never had been, about the permanence of the Black Thing. Black people themselves would have to see to that, and maybe, goddamnit, they would.

Jesse Simpson was an exception to the rule that many Black Studies departments were headed by West Indians or Africans. He was a big, slow-moving, slow-talking Afro-American, his height accentuated by his Afro.

Pushing up his shades and pulling together the front of his dungaree jacket, he was saying when Henderson entered the meeting and sat down, "Well, we're going to do all we can to help the Brother while he's here. All we can."

Phipps agreed. "That is the least we can do, the very least."

Henderson stared past them, out the window.

But Broadus' boyish voice cracked out at them, making them turn.

"But what is it we're gonna do? Who's gonna see about a car? We know Henderson's taking care of the office. Nobody's said anything about us getting together and having an affair for the Brother. Ain't nobody saying nothing about money or budget——"

Henderson started to smile. Broadus was bending back and forth as he spoke, reminding him of the old-time preachers or Jews dovening in some of the synagogues he'd visited as a kid back home. "——now, I'm not known for being jive," Broadus continued, "so I'm going to say right out that I haven't read any of the books the Brother has put together, okay? But Henderson says he's heavy and is due some courtesy—at least as much as some of these jive white boys running through here with their bitty-bop poetry. How're we gonna see to it? Who's putting what on the line?"

Simpson crossed his legs and said, "We'll go for a couple of jugs."

Incredulous, Broadus stared at him and almost whispered, "Jugs of what, wine?"

"Yeah," Simpson said defensively. "Look, man, you know we don't have a budget for this kind of thing."

"Oh," Broadus mocked. "If the school don't spring, nothin happens, is that it?"

They didn't like Broadus, Henderson knew; he wasn't like them. An ex-jock, Broadus had taken his MA in Physical Education at Indiana and then, finding a religion he'd perhaps never lost, returned to pure education and then Black Studies. He was an oddball in the department, quick to perceive where the shit lay, quicker to call attention to its presence. Where others saw Black Studies as being at once infinitely scholarly, Broadus saw them as picks, shovels, hoes—tools with which to start laying roads that would outlast those of the Roman Empire. And he was a young man, Henderson thought, thinking of his own almost fifty years.

"You are always jumping to conclusions, Milton," Phipps said. Phipps represented the West Indian wing of the Black Studies department.

O'Malley, the only white person in the department, certified black because he had been chased out of Rhodesia for advocating equal rights for the black majority, said, "It does seem to me that Milton has reached the only available conclusion. Racism, we know, does thrive on this campus, and we know that white guests of less stature than Professor Moore"—Henderson smiled. O'Malley gave title to everyone. In his own black Irish way, he was a most generous person—"have received far more in courtesies and honors. Professor Moore being a writer, is an English department person. The English department, Dr. Henderson tells us, will do nothing. Being black, Professor Moore is also a Black Studies department person. Milton asks, quite rightly, what we as a department, as a group of people who understand the ramifications of racism, will do to make known our dissatisfaction of the treatment of Professor Moore. And I also ask." He lifted his chin challengingly and looked about the room.

Henderson wondered why they were all so attentive when O'Malley spoke.

"Well, I got to go," Broadus said. "Whatever it is, count me in." He pulled on his red, green, and black knitted cap. "Clarie, put me and Geraldine down for a dinner party for the Brother. Just give us a day's notice when you want it." His voice grew louder as he left the room. "Messing around with these jive ole Negroes." He stopped and turned to face Henderson. "Clarie, you better steer the Brother clear of the Black Studies library."

Oh, shit, Henderson thought. "Why?"

Broadus' square football player's face melted into a sneer and he glanced at Simpson. "You say the Brother's written about ten books? Well, the Black Studies library doesn't have a one and the librarian's never heard of him." Broadus closed the door softly.

Henderson stood. He heard Simpson, Phipps, and O'Malley stirring. In the English department, he'd made a point to order for the main library every book by every black writer he'd read or heard about, and in his desk he had copies of a black bibliography that ran 125 pages typed. Criminal, he thought, eying Simpson who returned his gaze coolly. "Now I know why you never heard of him, Jesse. If Moore was like a couple of other black writers you're always talking about and teaching, you'd have had a budget for him."

"Yeah," Simpson said quickly, "and so would everyone else."

"I guess so," Henderson said, walking to the door.

"Dr. Henderson!" O'Malley cried.

"We're not through yet!" Phipps said.

Henderson walked out, closing the door as softly as Broadus had before him.

This would pass; Moore's three weeks would be a memory. He and Pat might talk about it while flying east for Chappie's dinner. He wished it were summer so he could take more time to look around, see maybe what the job situation was back there once again. For Henderson had concluded that there was something unreal about the West Coast. Something happened to its people, black and white, when they came jetting over the mountains or driving through the passes and were confronted with nothing before them but 10,000 miles of Pacific Ocean. Perhaps a quiet dying.

Poor Moore, Henderson thought, now driving off campus on the spit of land that speared into the mountains. Well, he'd do his best to shelter the man from the local idiocy. He remembered Moore as being a droll man, given to pork pie hats and even looking remarkably like Lester Young. Greek too, Henderson recalled, had looked like Pres and that, maybe, was what had sent him to the tenor sax. Dead now, Bubbles had said in his letter, like all of them might have been, if not for Chappie.

"Well, darling, I'm not sure I want to go. I'd much rather take off for Los Angeles or San Francisco."

"We can go to those places almost anytime," Henderson said, setting a forkful of food down. It wasn't good to eat while angry, and he was, suddenly, irrationally.

His wife, Pat, eyed him cautiously from her end of the table. She said, less offhandedly, "That's a long way, honey."

Henderson glared at her, then dropped his eyes to the table. The two of us. Just the two of us. No kids, no nothing. Just us. Marrying late and letting the good times roll.

"It's what I want to do," he snapped. That was another thing about Californians. Believed they lived in God's country and didn't want to get up off their asses to compare notes with the rest of the world. Might discover that they lived in Lucifer land, after all.

His manner told her that with or without her, he was going. She didn't know how she felt about that. She could swing through Vegas while he was away, or do Tiajuana, but she'd done those things before; too many times.

"I'd like for you to come," Henderson said in a more gentle tone.

Pat smiled and watched him pick up his fork again and chew slowly on his food.

Pat Artis Henderson came from a well-to-do family down in Los Angeles. Her father was in real estate, called himself a realtor, and was president of the Consolidated Realtors Board. The opening of new sections of Los Angeles to blacks during the boom of the 1950s had made her father rich. The area south of

Crenshaw Boulevard, Leimert Park, and Baldwin Hills had been the big targets back then, and now only Baldwin Hills remained mostly closed to blacks. Pat knew that her father dreamed of busting it wide open one of these days before he died, of surrounding the Crenshaw shopping area with black communities. He could top his fortune by breaking the Hills.

Pat was an only child and the recipient of all the wealth Mr. and Mrs. Artis could divert nowhere else. Theirs was a swimming-pool and lawn-party society, and Mrs. Artis an officer in the Links. And it was a brown-bag society which excluded from its loose membership people whose skins were darker than a plain, brown grocery bag. There were exceptions; Nat Cole was, of course, one, and Bill Walker, and Sammy Davis; also the occasionally black actor who was featured or starred in one film and then went into decline, like James Edwards.

Pat was not as fair as her husband. Both knew by now, or had guessed, that she had married him with her parents enthusiastic approval, because he was fair enough to pass, and this pulled her over the line; sometimes while traveling they had passed, laughing at night in bed, and later, the adventure seeming to have heightened their appetites, made love through half the night. Pat was a white woman who tanned well, was all. They'd both heard the comments on half a hundred beaches.

"Don't sulk. I'll go," Pat said. She had never believed that his childhood was as poor as he said it was. She could never picture him in a ghetto situation. Obviously, what he wished to do was to show her, and also, to show her off, to let his friends see how far he'd come. "But, can we go to New York going or coming?" she asked.

Henderson felt another surge of anger. Always bargaining; always altering plans. There'd never been a straight-ahead, uncomplicated deal. But, why not, he thought wearily? Why in the hell not? It was a great place to pass in.

And it was a great book town.

Inwardly Henderson relaxed and felt a warmth spreading through his body. When he finished dinner he would go into his study, a bedroom converted into a book-lined, cabineted vault, with his desk and chair placed against one wall like a throne, the desk lamp, like a spotlight, focused on his yellow pads and pencils, which themselves were centered on the desk top. He loved being in the room.

On Saturdays when he was a boy, he'd had to give over a part of his mornings to Miss Minding. Dusting and mopping her bookstore, polishing and straightening made him miss at least the first four innings during baseball season and the first quarter during football season.

It had been like going into a church. Emma Minding's Bookshop. The shop had been softly lighted and customers spoke in low tones. The noises of the traffic never seemed to have penetrated the interior, where shoppers passed from one shelf to the other, one table to the other, with noiseless tread. Even Miss Minding's voice, low and sweet, seemed to have emerged from between the pages of *Wuthering Heights*. It had been fitting to polish the shelves and tables to a glossy shine, the better to contain the quiet spirits of the philosophers, the novelists; the better to reflect Zola, whom he saw in the flesh as Paul Muni; the better to measure the stride of the Modern Library muse or the Borzoi hound. Heady stuff. He could talk of Hemingway and Wright and Fitzgerald and Dreiser and Hughes with the members of the JBS: a word here or there, while the umpire dusted off the plate, without ever having read them, although he hungered to. Hungered to hunker down in a corner, or beneath one of the colonial tables that breathed of newly applied lemon-scented furniture polish, and read the books of the authors who winked past his flying dustcloth. ("Whaddya say, kid?")

He no longer remembered when he had left Emma Minding's shop, but did remember returning to it, in uniform, those first ten days after his discharge, when the movies still had reduced rates for servicemen. Miss Minding had seemed to be much older, though he'd been gone only three years.

"Clarence," she had said, the voice the same. "I had to look twice. I thought you were someone else."

Henderson had smiled. A white person, no doubt.

"How wonderful you look, Clarence, and I'm so happy you're all right."

And for the first time she had touched him, tentatively, perhaps with some inner joy that some of the past remained intact. Miss Minding had fluttered, softly spinning about in her quiet shop, her fingers touching her pale lips in wonder. "I want you to have something, Clarence, but I don't know what. Pick something out, please."

And he had said, "Schopenhauer," and she stopped moving and looked at him. He looked back at her. "Ah, Schopenhauer," she said even more softly than usual, while Henderson thought of, but did not say, quoting the philosopher: *Succession is the form of the principle of sufficient reason in time, and succession is the whole nature of time.* "I didn't know you liked Schopenhauer."

"Yes," he said.

"Then here." She stretched, light, translucent, a moth preparing to fly, and picked up the Modern Library edition. *The Philosophy of Schopenhauer,* and handed it to him with a gesture that appeared to indicate that she was giving over a part of herself.

Henderson remembered how a spring within him tightened, a certain joy. That had been the first time. The spring had long since broken.

Now, as it had done for several years, the sight and feel of good books made his saliva glands run. First editions, culled from booklists or obscure bookdealers, of *Native Son,* of *Cane,* of *Black Reconstruction* made him feel weak. Yet, Clarence Henderson didn't know what it was he sought in his books; he was only conscious that he was indeed searching for something.

He raised his eyes from his food and looked across the table at his wife. He already saw himself alone, moving slowly down the Fourth Avenue stalls, or along Eighth Street or in Brentano's or the Gotham, poring over books. Pat would be shopping at the expensive women's shops, and he would be just another "white" man looking over books. "Good. Very good idea," he said, nodding his approval.

SEVEN

It was his turn this Saturday, and he stopped in Christ Papadapoulous' little store to get the Saltine crackers and the quarter pound of liverwurst. When he came out, his baseball glove strapped to his belt, D'Artagnan Foxx began to whistle. He trotted down the block slowly, like an outfielder taking the field, hurdled Christ's Fro-Joy ice cream sign, and whooped into Chevrolet Bob's garage. Bob was already in the grease pit under a car, banging and cursing.

Rounding the corner, Dart broke off his whistling to push against the door that led upstairs to Moon's house. The hallway was dim, but Dart was used to it. As he took the stairs two at a time, he hummed the baritone parts of "Sleepers Awake."

As usual, Moon was still in bed, but he sat up, smiling, then climbed out to go to the bathroom, thrusting his penis back inside his pajamas; he was the only one in the gang who wore them. Everyone else slept in their underwear.

They sat on the porch in the sun, eating. Bloodfield was quiet this time Saturday mornings. Great Fruehauf trailers were parked in the lot across the street, and Dart often wondered about the places where they'd been, where they would go again. For some Saturdays there were no trailers parked there at all. The others straggled up with gloves, and they sat on the porch bannisters or on the floor until Chappie, usually with bloodshot eyes and reeking breath, called from downstairs, the bag with the bats, balls, and catcher's equipment slung over his shoulder.

This, too, was a Saturday, and the November sun was hot through the glass door. It had seemed to Dart for a moment that it was the same old sun. But it wasn't. Like him, it was older and perhaps even a bit wiser. Besides, it was a Parisian sun, and that was Paris laid out before him, not Bloodfield with its parking lots, tired, gray houses and tin-roofed garages.

The man sitting at the other end of the glistening, contem-

porary white plastic table, set with cobalt blue dishes and nap-
kins, saw the momentary yearning in his friend's eyes, even in
the quick, unconscious tightening of his neck muscles as he inclined his head a fraction of a degree toward some daydream.

On the heels of these seconds, which stood out as time frozen,
Dart turned to him, a little smile playing on his wide, well-
shaped lips. He sighed and laughed now, his eyes sweeping back
down Rue Bayard to Cours Albert, and beyond the Seine to Quai
d'Orsay, as if frightened that it was all a mirage and would
disappear if he blinked his eyes. Raising his coffee cup to his
mouth, Dart twinkled his eyes at Michael. Michael knew he
liked being here.

"Will you be going then, Dart? Was that what you were just
thinking about?"

"Yes, to both questions. I've asked Katya to get hopping on it.
Maybe even get me a concert there." He winked at Michael.
"That's where I got my start, lover. I was the token black in Fine
Arts at the University. There was an old faggot named Klipstein,
my voice teacher, who used to chase me around trying to feel me
up. I spent more time running than singing."

They both laughed softly, then Michael said, arching his
brows until sections of pale white skin stretched from beneath
the Cannes tan, "Did you give him a break?"

"Who old Klipstein? No, God, Michael. I didn't until I was in
the Army. It was girls all the way until then."

"And now it's girls sometime."

"Yes," Dart teased. "I wouldn't want to miss out on anything."

Michael made a sucking noise through his teeth. "Swine.
Simone will go, too?"

"She's never been, and now's as good a time as any."

"Don't be apologetic," Michael said. "She's your wife."

Dart poured himself another cup of coffee and said, "Now
who's being a swine?" He turned to the glass doors again,
stretching his long legs in the sun. All his life he'd wanted to live
like this, luxuriously, but quietly, feeling or seeing richness at
every touch, forever in range of his eyes, but it had eluded him;
he owned none of it, but shared the wealth of others as a visitor
or a lover. In another few hours Dart would be back in his own

flat on the Keizersgracht in Amsterdam. It was a pleasant enough place, but stolid and colorless when compared to Michael's stylish duplex here on Avenue Montaigne.

"I'll see my parents there," Dart said. He continued to look out on the city for another moment, then turned to Michael.

"Oh, I see," Michael said. He knew Dart expected him to say something.

"I guess I'd look foolish if you were to make this *soirée* talk," Dart said.

Michael shrugged. "I don't suppose it would be of much interest to people to know that you've real parents in America instead of rich, white, adoptive ones in England." Few people had ever believed that story anyway, Michael knew. "I can't think of anything worse than having rich, wealthy parents who're forever traveling to Africa, India, Australia, or Canada." Whenever Dart had mentioned his fictitious parents, they were always on a trip.

Dart said, "I don't know how that started. I wanted to be different, *better* than other people, and once I was away from home, I just made up Lord and Lady Moorehead. They became quite real to me. He was a big, ruddy man, experienced in all things, familiar with all the world. And she was like Eleanor Roosevelt, only pretty.

"I'm afraid my parents are—well, no, they *weren't* average then. Maybe they are now." He mashed a corner of a *croissant* with his thumb. "My father was a thief. I still remember police cars quietly pulling up in front of our house and how the cops— who knew him—spoke to him. They called him Johnny. 'Well, Johnny, can't stay out of trouble.' I think he was a kleptomaniac. My mother used to slip around with the coach. I liked that. I hoped they'd run away and take me with them. Really did. Anyway, I think it'll be good for me to see them. They're not getting any younger and neither am I."

Michael got up and stood behind Dart, and gently squeezed the muscles in his shoulders. Dart relaxed. "I'm glad you told me," Michael said.

"Why?"

"I'm intimidated by people who aren't afraid to go home. I'm afraid something will happen there to make them different. But your telling me makes me think we'll stay close enough to share secrets."

Dart stood and stretched, his bulk filling the doorway. Michael punched him lightly in the side, but was smiling. He said, "What a vain person you are, Dart." He started to clear the table, but stopped to say, "I guess you have a right to be, though."

They had not talked driving through the city, but now, as they approached the route south, past Place d'Italie, on the way to Orly, Dart said, "Why so quiet, Michael? It's been a marvelous weekend."

"Oh, I know, but you won't be back until the middle of next month, if then. They may decide that they now love you in America, after you've been away from it for so long."

"It would be nice," Dart admitted, "if they did want me to stay and work. I'd love to have beacoup dollars. But there are so many younger and better people now, and blacks are having a certain vogue, the way they had in France after the First World War.

"Besides," Dart went on, glancing at Michael, whose gloved hands caressed rather than gripped the steering wheel of the Jaguar, "there's the Robeson image. It still clings. How in the hell could there be another Paul Robeson? Just one was too goddamn good for the world."

Michael shifted and the motor growled; they settled back as the car picked up more speed.

What irony, Dart thought. Here he was, three thousand miles from home, an outcast. Not only had he been hounded out of the States, he was being hounded, and had been hounded throughout Europe ever since he came. He could blame his mediocre success on being an imitation of Paul Robeson; that worked. But he had been chased not because of that but because of a woman he had not loved nor really cared for, but whom he'd made love to because she'd wanted it. Discovered, it was no good telling the husband, Wilbur Marcus, that he was just a big, black faggot, which he was, at least some of the time. Nor could he have told Marcus that he'd made love to his wife because he was afraid *not* to, afraid everything back then would have gone up in smoke.

Dart had held the hope for years that Wilbur Marcus would die, but he'd had to conclude that the rich, wherever they lived, moved through the years aging with grace, casually sidestepping the Reaper's scythe. They lived longer than the poor. That was one of the secrets of their power.

Even when they were not to the manor born, they quickly adopted the ways of the senior inhabitants. Marcus had been a friend of D'Amica, a saloonkeeper, bit-sized racketeer, and fight promoter. Suddenly he was no longer in town, no longer seen moving sure-footedly through the black section of Jewtown. The stories of his gambling with the blacks in a small room above Chevrolet Bob's ceased to come, and the years slipped by.

And when, once or twice a year, Mr. and Mrs. Marcus' photograph appeared on the first page of the society section of the morning and evening papers, in town from Hollywood, where he was a movie producer, to visit his parents, it seemed that Wilbur Marcus never had been the hustler who sold bad whiskey to the bums in his saloon. That Marcus seemed never to have existed. The papers made much of him for he was, saving Jackie Coogan and Bill Lundigan, the only people from the city who'd made it in Hollywood.

That spring had come early and the lilac bushes, which grew untended along some of the streets, scented the air, lent a perfecting touch to that Easter Sunday. The church was full—as it was on Mother's Day and Christmas, and as it had been a week before, on Palm Sunday. Lilies and a discreet array of potted plants lined the window sills above which, magnificently highlighted by the sun, the stained glass windows sparkled. The women and girls wore the brave Easter finery, the purples and lavenders, the yellows and whites. The men and boys, some clad in new two-pants Bond's suits, invariably had snow-white handkerchiefs in their breast pockets, their hair laid back with Nu-Nile or Dixie Peach. The smells came together that morning, so keenly in Dart's nostrils that he never thought of Easter without recalling them. Mum, slicked judiciously into the armpits, the tantalizing female scent of Tangee powder and lipstick, the Djierkiss perfume and the bay rum. There were these and the smell of freshly starched and ironed shirts and blouses and choir robes.

That Easter, Dart had looked out over the packed church, saw the members of the Junior Bachelor Society. In the rear row were the white people, visitors. Chappie had crept in at precisely the moment Dart was trying to recall the white man in the finely tailored suit; he looked familiar, and his wife (he'd assumed) looked like a movie star, a Claire Trevor, or an Evelyn Keyes. Dart saw Chappie's eyes quickly search the church for Dart's mother, then he'd slipped into a seat.

Iris Joplin had finished her solo and the pianist was playing his, Dart's, introduction. Standing, he sang:

"Were you there when they crucified my lord?
"Were you there when they crucified my lord? (This line
    rose, demanding, grief-stricken.)
"Oh, oh, *sin*ners! (He snapped the last word in the cellar
    of his diaphragm.)
"Sometimes, it causes me to tremble
                              tremble
                                  tremble—"

The women and girls started to cry softly, and one or two men, their white handkerchiefs moving rapidly across their faces, wiped their eyes.

Then he did not understand, nor could he really tell, when he had won over an audience. Why that sudden silence, deeper, far deeper than the usual silence, came was a mystery to him, but he felt that he was out there in spirit, moving among them, touching and comforting them. When he came to the final stanza

"Were you there when they laid him in the tomb?
"Were you there when they laid him in the tomb?
"Oh, oh, sinners, (This time he sang it tenderly, as if with
    desolation.)
"Sometimes, it causes me to wonder
                              wonder
                                  wonder—"

they were crying openly. He signaled the pianist for another chorus, which he hummed to settle them, then sat down in the silence that comes after a solo in church. He felt them working out from under the trance, and glanced back at the trimly dressed white man and then recognized him as Wilbur Marcus. That was the day when Marcus became his patron.

Years later, after the war, his voice lessons finished, his career in the hands of Marcus who was to make him another Paul Robeson, who promised that he, D'Artagnan Foxx, would make people forget Canada Lee, Dooley Wilson, and Bill Robinson, the promise ended; ended on the silk sheets of Wilbur Marcus' bed, in the arms and trapped between the thighs of Renee Marcus, on an afternoon moody with gray clouds and with the sound of a bulldozer rasping in the air; Beverly Drive was being extended to make room for new subdivisions for housing for the Hollywoodish rich.

Marcus was with one of these second-rate studios, Monogram or Republic, but was on his way to the class-A houses. He waited outside the bedroom while Renee cried and Dart nervously pulled on his clothes. He handed Dart a scotch on the rocks, and for a moment Dart had hoped fervently that Marcus was a queer; that Marcus would ask him to remain as he'd been, a house guest, and suggest that the next time Dart did it to his wife, he be told, so he could watch. They were after all in Hollywood.

Marcus waited until Dart, conscious of the bulldozer, gulped down the drink. Then Marcus reached for the glass and tossed it into the fireplace.

"Pack your things and go. I put money for your fare back East in your room. I want you to know that for you it all ends as of today. Don't dream anymore, boy. Because I'm going to see to it, for as long as I live, that you don't work as a singer. I don't care where you are. There'll be times when you'll forget this day and sit down and wonder why it is that nobody wants you. Then you'll remember what I'm saying now. There's no place on this earth where I don't know somebody; no place where I don't have influence. Out."

It'd all been said in a normal tone of voice, the blue eyes behind the thick glasses as calm as ever.

Marcus had been as good as his word for twenty-five years, a quarter of a century, Dart thought as they took the road into Orly. Wherever he'd gone, north, south, east, or west in the States, he'd had to make do with small, club-sponsored concerts. It'd been little better with the Atlantic Ocean between himself and Marcus, although for a time it seemed that Marcus had forgotten him. But just when he seemed much in demand in Germany, France, Sweden, and Holland, that demand mysteriously melted away, even most of the recordings.

Now, even if Marcus died, it was too late. The voice was almost gone, and he was at forty-nine running here and there to fill third-rate concert bookings to make ends meet, many of them coming from old friends who felt sorry for him. Like the one he'd just finished in Paris. Well, Michael would see to it that there were always Paris bookings. Dart reached into the back seat for his small bag as Michael came to a stop. Michael touched his hand. "Do have a good time, Dart. Drop me a card, if it's convenient."

Dart gripped him gently behind the neck. "See you."

An hour and a half later he emerged from the KLM Museumplein terminal; he would walk home from there. The distance was short. At the north end of the plein there stood the Rijkmuseum, as formidable as a Middle Ages castle. The Stedelijk museum, distinctly more modern, with its glassed roof, was at the southwest end. Directly across the street was a building he'd hoped for years to work in, the Concertgebouw. But he'd always been a spectator within its gray walls, never a performer.

Simone, hearing him on the threadbare, carpeted stairs, opened the door and looked down. "Hallo, darling," she said.

Dart smiled up at her. It was hard not to smile back at Simone, difficult not to respond in kind to her own cheery openness. "Simone," he said, breathing heavily, "how beautiful you look."

"And you," she said, kissing him lightly, "are a beauty, too."

The way she held him, he knew she wanted to make love; he also knew it from the bold way she looked at him through her smile. It was as if, sensing he'd made love to someone while away, it, the imagination of his doing it, had stoked her own appetites. These, Dart knew, could sometimes be monstrous.

"How did it go?" she asked, just as he was about to inquire after mail.

"Well enough," he said, starting to smile as she made her way across the living room to prepare him a drink. He watched her, full-hipped and all motion, striding across the floor and back, her very full breasts moving softly under her blouse. She handed him his drink, then sat on the floor beside him, her head resting against his knee. He eased his fingers into her long, black hair and tenderly stroked her scalp.

She never asked him about people. *How did it go* meant only the concert and the responses of the audience and the few critics. Long, long ago, at Spoleto she had angrily told him: "I cannot help what you do when you are away from me. If I could, I would, but I cannot. I am not one of your American women. I face the reality that you are a man."

Which meant, he realized some time after, that he had to face the realization that she was a woman, in all its myriad implications. If she ever thought he was bisexual, she never spoke of it. Yet he knew she knew.

He could still see the marble steps curving down from the music room of Yves Dormoy's house, the marble sparkling white beneath the red stair carpeting. Simone was walking down in front with Yves's wife, and he and Yves were behind them. Simone turned to say something to them at the precise moment when Yves's hand was moving slyly toward Dart's crotch. Yves was drunk, of course. A problem. Simone smiled, but a small horror seemed to have frozen her eyes which, nevertheless, flashing upward to Dart's face for verification, saw in his eyes the shock of her having seen. Who could measure such a moment, but it was all there, spoken in infinitely microcosmic, wordlessly plain language. Simone knew, then, and accepted.

"Hungry?" Simone asked, pressing her cheek more firmly against his thigh.

"A little." She remained motionless and he, glancing slowly around the flat, was once again moved by its comfortable atmosphere. Stolid, practically colorless, true. But one stepped into it, as visitors had often remarked, and were into something, a place, a mood that was completely familiar.

Simone bit him gently through the cloth of his pants and gathered her legs beneath her in order to get up. "Yes, mail," she said, standing now and brushing back her hair. "From Katya and Iris. Come." He took her hand and eased up out of the chair, following her into the kitchen. The letters lay unopened beside a place already set for him.

She detached the porcelain cap from the brown bottle of beer and set a mug beside his plate. Something about this particular beer and the way it was capped reminded Dart of his boyhood when his father used to make beer in the bathtub.

He opened Katya's letter first; hers, he knew, dealt with the future. Even when, years ago, he'd told her about Marcus, she'd vowed to get him back to the States in triumph. She never faced up to the fact this feat was impossible. Still, on her visits to Europe, she talked about the angles, the changes, the quick-openers that they might take advantage of, but somehow they never worked out. But now, with obvious excitement, she was relating in her letter, her signing him for a Black Arts Festival to be run by the Central City Arts and Fine Arts Association. It would put him on the night before the testimonial dinner to a Mr. Charles Davis, whom she understood used to be his coach. It would be a black tie affair. She was already into the process of inviting the top critics from New York, Boston, and Washington to attend his concert, and hoped that their interest would make it possible for him to do Lincoln Center before returning to Amsterdam. Perhaps they'd like him so much that he would not have to return. Finally, like all agents, she mentioned his fee, $3,500, which would more than pay for their fare and expenses. She had refused lesser amounts on the grounds that even though he was not that well-known in the States, he, Dart, was a concert singer of the first rank in Europe.

Dart smiled at Simone when he set down the letter. All its details were shit except the money; that was the only concrete item about the deal, perhaps worth ten years of banging Katya in hotel rooms around Europe.

"Good news, eh," Simone said, picking up the letter, while Dart ripped open the one from Iris Stapleton.

The infrequent letters from Iris made him nostalgic for home more than talking about it with her, more than hearing from someone back there. For both of them time had halted, almost, and they could remember Ransom's dark shop with the rain-spattered *Defenders* and *Vigilantes* in the racks outside, and Gideon's barbershop across the street. They recalled Alpert's Deli with its odors of herring and dill pickles, Volinsky and Bloom's with their trays of half-moon or black-and-white cookies and Guido's; Guido had remained, it was said, with all the Urban Renewal, until his death, and then his wife, Rose, and their sons, stayed on, Rose enshawled in black, still a queen, still soft of voice.

Iris and Dart's paths crossed only when on the road. Amsterdam was a jazz town, or had been. There were still hard-jazz buffs around who winced when jazz greats came to town echoing white rock in their backgrounds.

Not Iris, at least not when he'd seen her in town or they happened to be in some other city in Europe. Talking about Ralph brought them to neutral topics, those that steered clear of his mediocre successes or her constant triumphs. She was now as enshrined in Barcelona as Gaudi. Dart, on the other hand, recalled Barcelona dryly, a city he passed through going to Montserrat to sing a program of gospel music, perhaps in tribute to the Black Madonna there. . . .

Iris had heard from Ralph about a big dinner the JBS was putting on for Chappie and wondered if Dart would be going. Ralph expressed the hope that he would, and that he'd be going too, wouldn't miss it, not for ole Chappie.

She, Iris, who hadn't been back in a while, wanted a full report when he returned to Europe. Maybe he and Simone could visit her? She wanted to know if it was true that jazz music was coming back, that rock had run its course, that double and triple rhythms in black music had become a multiplicity of rhythms, and how it worked out; oh, Dart would know what she meant if he had a chance to listen to any of it. Would he give Ralph and her father all her love, if he saw them, and please think about coming to Barcelona? She hoped he'd find his own family well.

EIGHT

It looked like Moon was going to get his ass beat. Bad. Collins had that look in his eyes. And he was drunk. Maybe it was about that time, Moon thought, carefully watching the detective pacing up and down. He'd taken enough shit from that transplanted cracker; time to hitch his pants up for him. Good.

"Well, where is she, Moon?" Collins fixed Moon with his bloodshot eyes. Moon handed him the joint he'd just torched. Collins, a big man, moved swiftly across the space between them and slapped the cigarette to the rug. "Cocksucker," he said. "I could put your ass *under* the jail for that shit. I don't want grass; I want cunt, you pimp motherfucker."

Moon bent from the hooded chair, picked up the joint, and carefully wiped the spot where it had landed. He mashed out the joint and leaned back. "She's workin, man. You know she's workin."

He watched the cop stomp over to his bar and pour out half a tumbler of bourbon. Collins downed most of it in one gulp and said in a loud voice, "I don't know how you guys do it. I mean, *look* at you, you black bastard. Here's this beautiful blonde, a body like Marilyn Monroe. She could be in the movies, the *movies*, and here she is hauling her ass up and down Hollywood selling cock because she loves you. *You!*" Collins finished his drink and poured another. Moon looked at him in disgust. "Why is it you white guys always say cock instead of pussy? A cock hangs out. You got a cock; I got a cock. Don't you know the goddamn difference?"

"Damn it!" Collins said.

In the shadows of the hood of his chair Moon felt under the cushion for his own gun. When he touched it, he felt both reassured and frightened. It was bad when it got down to this. And on a warm November night with men and women out there doing what they'd always done. Some women did it for nothing or for love, which was about the same thing as far as Moon was concerned. He was in it for the money and perhaps for the power he seemed to hold over his women. He could have smiled. They fed all the pimps that line. They said they were in it for love of him, but any man who'd buy that was a fool. They were in it because they wanted to be. Shuck and jive all they wanted, but they were getting theirs and he was getting his: money.

He'd done well as a pimp in New York, Chicago, and now, Hollywood. The life was good when it was going right and the cops behaved and the chicks didn't run into Jack-the-Rippers. More and more as he approached the five-oh mark, he'd thought of quitting, cutting out with Dorrie, maybe down to Mexico. But he wanted to do it on his time, not someone else's.

Like this dumb Collins. Pay the sonofbitch off good; tip him even, with a case of Wild Turkey, since he claimed he couldn't afford nothin but Jim Beam. Set him up with Gail. Cheap motherfucker didn't want to be paid in trade. Both the pussy and the bread.

How was he to know the silly cracker would fall in love with her? Wife. Three kids. Still haven't finished doing Disneyland. In love with a Hollywood hooker. That's all right, too, but he oughta keep his dick outa the cash register.

Maybe this was the end, but Moon hoped it wasn't. It wasn't his time. But say it was? The girls would have to hang on until he set up a line for them. They'd understand. He'd have to make it for his stash back with Momma. All because of this—

But Collins had seen him feeling for his gun and whipped out his own.

"I wish you would, Moon. I wish you would. I'd blow your black ass to Catalina Island. Go for it."

Moon held out empty hands before him. "Man, I don't have nothin. You nervous or something? Put that thing down." Moon leaned out of the line of fire. "Hey," he said soothingly. "We can straighten all this out. Listen, take Gail down to Mexico for a week. On me, okay?"

Collins hesitated. Moon pursued.

"A week at Acapulco, man. Lay in the sun. Go first class. Pretty down there . . ." Shit, Moon was thinking, I let Gail go with this nut for a week, he'd either kill her there or try to run to the South Pole. "Just make it with her any time you want, Collins. She'll be all yours for a week."

"And then?" Collins said holding his gun lower now, closer to its holster.

"We got an arrangement," Moon pleaded. "You come on back. You got a family. Kids. And you know you got a nice piece of my action. Everything's fine except when you get to hurtin for Gail. C'mon, man, cool down. You know I just can't snatch her off the street. She's earning our bread. Dig it, now. I can turn you on to Dorrie in about an hour——"

"I don't want any black cock——"

"You chump," Moon shouted. "That's all you were wanting until you met Gail, and suppose I told you she wasn't white——"

"Bullshit! She's white and that's what I want."

"Gail's just *lookin* white, you turkey!" He stiffened as Collins rushed toward him.

"You pimp bastard," Collins shouted, thrusting forward his gun to spearhead his rush.

"Hold it!" Moon cried, backing up quickly, but Collins was upon him and he grabbed for the cop's gun hand, wrapped both hands around it and forced the gun straight up in the air. Moon was the bigger. He grimaced down at Collins who said, sullenly, "Let go. I'm putting it away."

"Why the fuck should I trust you?" Moon panted. "I'll just take the goddamn piece until you cool down." He wrenched the gun free and disdainfully jammed it into his back pocket.

"I'm gonna kill you, Moon," Collins said, grinding his teeth. His breath reeked with whiskey.

Moon made up his mind then. Most of the cops he'd ever dealt with treated him as though he was basically a faggot or something, when he knew he behaved the way he did because it was business. But he was tired of eating shit; he was fifty, or almost, and on the edge of the continent. Yes, eating shit and pretending he was slick, just taking care of business. But this was the last cracker motherfucker who was ever going to threaten him and walk away in one piece. The last one.

Moon pushed Collins hard in the chest, the way he'd seen cops push people around, and followed up on the push before Collins could regain his balance. "You gonna what? Man, you know we ain't never got down to *that* before." He pushed him again, as one would push away a sullied dog. Momentarily they studied each other in the tiny silences that came between their movements, and those silences filled up quickly with the muted sounds of traffic, Marvin Gaye's voice from someone's record player.

"Hey, cut it out," Collins said, still stumbling. He'd never seen Moon like this. Something had gone wrong with the evening. Collins stumbled over a table. Moon pushed him once more and snatched his blackjack and slid it down the front of his open-throated silk, red shirt. "I ought to whip your ass with this. You didn't know I used to play ball, did you, Collins? You didn't know I used to stomp motherfuckers like you just because they were in my way, did you, Collins? You didn't know cats used to drop the football rather than run by me, did you, Collins? You thought I was some kind of motherfuckin chump, didn't you, man?" Hissing, Moon kicked Collins in the ass. "Any man who'd blow his own game's got to be a fool, Mr. Law. Can you get that? Blow your shit, but not mine."

Moon saw Collins, still stumbling, make a small, swift move, and in desperation flung himself on the cop and wrestled the second, smaller gun, away from him. He tossed it into the chair behind him. "I heard that was the style these days. Ever since Watts. You motherfuckers runnin scared, ain't you?" Moon was breathing heavily now, but he felt good, better than he had in years. Shit, this was Moon, *Moon!* He said, "What you got left, chump, nothin? Wanna do these?" He help up his fists, luxuriating in the feel of tightened fingers. "Don't want you to think pimps're soft. Here."

He leaned toward Collins, his right fist six inches away from the cop's face, then hooking, he whipped it forward against Collins' chin. Collins' head snapped back and when he'd focused his eyes again, Moon saw that there was a different light in them.

"Two guns and a blackjack," Moon said. "I ought to break your goddamn kneecaps with this jack, tap, tap. Then you wouldn't have to go down on Gail. You'd be down already. Oh, yeah." Moon was answering the question in the cop's eyes. "She tell's me what your thing is. We keep files, too. In our heads. We in business, baby. You like to go in and tongue out everything everyone else done left behind. But thas all right," he said consolingly. We can dig it; different strokes and all that—here." He came up on Collins with a left that knocked him over. "Woo!" Moon said. "There went my EmBee, but it sho felt good. I guess that kick in the ass cost me my whole game, huh, Collins? But *that* felt good, too. Les do it again." This time Moon reared back and came forward like a punter. He grunted at the same time Collins did. The cop's hand floundered through air as if to ward off blows, and Moon thought of a photograph he'd seen of a man before a firing squad holding up his hands to try to ward off the bullets fired at him."You ain't so bad, now, is you champ?" Moon grabbed Collins by the hair and jerked his face around. "Know what? I ought to make you suck my black dick, you jive turkey. Tellin me you don't want no black pussy. I'ma do that." Moon fumbled with his fly, and carried away by his joyous malevolence, removed his eyes from the cop for a half second, seeking the catch.

Moon saw the movement too late. Collins had scissored his legs against Moon's, toppling him with a crash. With a roar Collins was up, lunging for the gun in the chair seat. Moon kicked over the chair and Collins' service revolver and his own .32 fell to the rug out of reach. Moon sprang up, his hand already snaking against the skin of his chest and belly. The blackjack felt just right in his hand. Collins on his knees drove up to meet Moon's charge.

Moon forgot that it was a sap in his hand. He swung in rage with all his might, catching Collins flush in the face, and felt teeth flying wetly out of his mouth. Collins slumped to the carpet, staining it red.

"Shit," Moon hissed. "Shit."

He retrieved the guns and replaced the chair and sat down in it. He smoked a cigarette and looked at the detective. He kicked him. "Just because you had to put your goddamn dick in the cash register. I mean your tongue, motherfucker."

Gonna be one messed-up cat in this town, Moon thought. Collins would close him down at the least and kill him at the most. Even if Collins said forgive and forget, Moon wasn't going to take his word. Collins liked to suck on that bourbon too much.

And how could he forget his face? Surely the nose was broken and the teeth gone and a cheekbone stove in. No. Hat time, Moon told himself.

He got up quickly, decisively, and began to pack. Make it on one of the red-eye specials to New York, then creep home for the stash Mom's been holding. They made more than one white carpet, more than one Mercedes-Benz, more than one a whole lotta things. But they didn't put together but one Moon. Just one. So it was hat time.

The cash he placed in a Mark Cross briefcase and put some newspapers on top. He pulled on a jacket then stepped in front of his mirror and tugged at his Afro. It came off and Moon Porter smiled at himself. You a slick motherfucker, he told himself, patting his bald head. He would drop it and the others into the incinerator on the way out. With his bags and briefcase and wigs, Moon left the apartment, dropping the wigs into the burner on the way to the parking lot.

He glanced up at his apartment when he was seated in his car. Collins was going to be hurting when he came to, and puking. Good time to be going. He took the time to cruise up and down the streets where the girls were working. He'd about given up when he saw Gail sitting with a trick through the window of a cafe on Vine. He cruised by slowly and parked down the street, waiting.

"Poppa, what's happenin? Why you here?"

Gail had slid in with a rustle of silk and a blast of perfume.

Moon handed her an inch-thick packet of bills. "Had some trouble with Collins, and I got to split. You be careful. Get them chicks and get on up to San Francisco. I'll call tomorrow night."

"Oh, shit," she said. "New York?"

"Yeah."

"He hurt bad?"

Moon smiled. She was asking him if Collins was dead. He turned to her and said, "He's pretty messed up."

"Made you come out from under that wig, must be pretty bad. You sending for us?"

"You know I am, otherwise I wouldn't have taken the time to hip you. Now get them chicks movin, 'cause Collins and his boys are going to be salty."

"Kiss?" She leaned toward him.

He kissed her. She slid out and walked away from the cafe.

"Wait," Moon called. "Get back in." When she was seated beside him once more, he said. "I'm making it to the airport. You drive this thing back and get the girls and drive up there. Save some bread. Maybe you can even drive to New York, if not, sell the sumbitch and get a good piece of bread for it. Okay?"

Gail nodded and settled back. Moon headed toward La Cienega and the Santa Monica Freeway.

Later, the half-empty plane powering through the night, Moon looked down at Las Vegas. There was the place to have people working, but that was a very heavy mob scene, and he didn't have any contacts. Didn't want to, either. Ah, well, Moon thought. With the stash back home and what he had with him, maybe it was time to make a decision about his future. But what would he do? He didn't know anything except hustling people, and he'd enjoyed that.

Enjoyed it the way he'd enjoyed playing ball. What would life have been like had he gone on to school the way his mother and Chappie wanted him to? He hadn't been a fool. They weren't breaking down your door then the way they were now to get you to go to college. And the pros—forget it. Bill Willis, Marion Motley, Buddy Young, and one or two others slipped through the almost closed door. And sports were all he'd been interested in. He liked to bust stars so that they saw stars. Big Bad Moon. Yeah, but those days were gone. Maybe he could write a book, like Iceberg Slim, about the days in the trade; maybe he could make a pile off it mentioning the big names, guys who liked his girls in New York, Chicago, and Los Angeles.

Yeah, and wake up with a mouthful of grave dirt!

Use a pen name, like some of the writers did? Maybe he should try to look up ole Ralph Joplin in New York and see what he thought of the idea. Ralph was a writer. He wrote plays, but maybe he'd know something about books, too.

Moon settled back again burrowing into his seat for the long sprint to New York. But the man pacing back and forth in the aisle drew his attention. Something vaguely familiar about him, about his shadowed face and the way he moved his body. Moon shifted. Probably one of those crackers hangs around Hollywood trying to get chicks to piss on him.

The name came suddenly to him. Clarie Henderson. *Clarie*. "Hey, Clarie," he whispered loudly.

The man stopped and peered into the shadows toward Moon. "Clarie," Moon said again. The man moved forward, passing under seat lights, and stopped at Moon's seat. Moon reached up and put on his light. "It's me, Moon."

Instantly he was sorry. He'd blown his cool as suddenly and quietly as *zink!* He felt fearful of the forces that had made him give himself away; he'd thought those demons dead.

Clarence Henderson moved carefully toward the man in the seat, the names *Clarie* and *Moon* causing immediate and unfamiliar vibrations within him. Clarie was already a dead giveaway; the only people who called him that were the ones he grew up with. And Moon. Moon? The light shone on the bald, unfamiliar head, the increasingly familiar face. Henderson was stunned. The shock was all the more intense in the nearly darkened interior of the plane which was rushing through the air at five hundred miles an hour, 37,000 feet in the air. That face, the calculating smile upon it, and Henderson recalling a Saturday afternoon when he had intercepted, cut for the sidelines, the high school crowd on its feet, and the October sun gleaming on Moon's helmet (no face guards then); the safety man angling over to pick them up, and Moon, the sun burnishing his helmet to gold, seeming to gather up, draw all his moving parts together, delivered himself like shot from a sling, low, perfectly low—not a running block, but a killing block—knee-high, and took out the safety with a sound heard all over the field, a sound accompanied by the dull crack heard only by the three of them. A shattered fibula, the safety sprawling with a scream, he and Moon trucking over the goal line. The face, full, strong, now padded with fat.

Still moving cautiously without moving his eyes from the big figure beneath the light, Henderson slid into the empty seat across the aisle.

"Damn," he whispered to himself.

The studying seemed hours long, framed by the sound of the engines, the hushed voices of the passengers who were still awake. Studying, the effect of the years, the clothes, the cut of them, as if they too held answers.

To Moon Clarie looked like a hip white man. His suit ran two hundred easy. Like that type, he wore his hair long, curling up at the back of the neck on the edge of the shirt collar. And he looked in good shape. His movements gave him away, a certain fluidity of motion one often detects in ex-athletes, and a muted, reckless cuteness perceived in the better Negro athletes.

And Henderson a second before he leaned across the aisle to embrace Moon (they would have considered that faggot stuff as kids, but it did seem that Americans were less self-conscious about touching each other now) set aside the pimp stories that had drifted to him; he knew nothing of that part of Moon's life; he had never met the Moon of rumor. He had put on some weight. His eyes still held that amused glint, that Fuck-Everything look which had secretly terrified most of the JBS. Yes, the expensive shoes—platforms. Pimp shoes, his kids called them. A California version of a Cardin-cut suit, a tie so expensive that even without light it gave off a soft, rich glow—

Then they were hugging, Moon rising out of his seat to meet Henderson's standing, open-armed invitation. Their fingers fell on slight layers of fat, which covered the definitions of muscles under their clothing, and each continued to measure the attrition of years.

"So you're going," Henderson said joyfully. It was good to think of people journeying great distances to honor Chappie. "Man, that's great and you're looking great."

"You, too, Clarie. Hey, sit down. Let's see if we can't get us a drink." Moon waved to the pair of stewardesses who were talking in a nearby bay. The movement, automatic, just short of being authoritarian, made Henderson feel a sensation of envy. One stewardess came over immediately, smiling.

"Clarie?"

"Scotch."

"Two," Moon said. "Hell, make it four." She wheeled away. Henderson watched Moon study her briefly, the way he might study the weave in a roll of suiting. They turned to each other, still studying.

"You lost it all," Henderson said, jerking his chin upward, indicating Moon's head.

"Yeah. Once it started to go, there was no stopping it." Moon noticed that Henderson was peering toward the section up ahead.

"My wife's up there sleeping. You'll have to meet her."

"Kids?"

"No, you?"

Moon chortled. "Here and there, I'm told, but probably not. What was that you said about going someplace?"

"The thing for Chappie, man. The banquet?"

"Coach? Chappie Davis?"

"Yeah. Didn't you get a letter from Bubbles?"

Moon jerked forward. "Bubbles Wiggins, ole Bubbles?" The names, riding a tidal wave of memories, were breaking upon him too fast.

Henderson now understood that this meeting was even more of a coincidence than he had imagined. "Bubbles wrote to all the JBS he could inviting us back for a banquet for Chappie. Dart is coming from Europe, I understand, Ralph, Chops; Cudjo and Shurley are there with Bubbles, you know, and Snake. Dart's gonna sing at a Black Arts Festival—its for this Friday and Saturday. Pat and I—that's my wife—want to stop in New York, shake California out of our clothes for a couple of days——"

"——that's right! You live out here, too." Moon's voice had risen. The coincidences were everywhere.

"Yeah, I teach at——"

Right, Moon thought, as the drinks came. Clarie's a college professor.

"——and I've been there about seven years."

"I remember reading about your wedding in *Jet*. Yeah. I'm in L.A. Hollywood." You *were* in Hollywood he told himself. "And you know what I do."

Henderson stared at him, but he saw Moon's eyes filling with amusement at his pretended ignorance. Finally Henderson said, "I heard, but you hear a lot of things."

"It's okay," Moon said. "Say"—a shifting in their seats a different pitch in their voices—"didn't I hear you made colored All-American at Morehouse?"

Henderson laughed. There was a lot of catching up to do. That'd been twenty-six years ago. "Morris Brown. You remember. The school where John 'Big Train' Moody went before the war. Same town. Atlanta. Yeah I did, in my senior year." He tapped Moon on the wrist. "And broke a couple of records in the 440."

"No shit," Moon said, grinning in admiration. He glanced away for a moment. "I should have gone on to college."

Henderson nodded. Yes, he should have. Moon was the best athlete in the JBS. Would have been a bitch in college.

"Didn't make much sense to me then," Moon said. "But now a blood can buy himself a whole lifetime just by the way he can juke on the field. I mean, the photographers and TV people have to work, man, to keep the Brothers *out* of pictures in every sport, man. Every sport but hockey, and I read the other day that one got signed."

Henderson heard Moon's voice trailing off, filled with hints of things that could have been. "Yeah," he said, as softly. Himself as Don Hutson, Moon as Bronko Nagurski, the guys in the *News* (or was it the *Mirror?*) in full color every Sunday of the then short football season.

"The big thing is," Henderson said, shattering the spell, "back in those days, and maybe even now, black colleges *played* some football, man. Wasn't no bullshit; it was pure headknocking, the kind of playing you didn't even see in the pros until the blacks got there." The scotch was making Henderson feel warm inside, good. The scotch and Moon. "Know why?" he went on.

Moon raised his eyebrows instead of saying No.

"Scholarships. Half the football team was on scholarships. Half-assed scholarships. No cars, no bread, no change for the folks back home. Just to be in school, Moon. A way up and maybe out. Nothing else happening but Hawk with oversized wings. I had the GI Bill, but the younger guys didn't have shit; didn't have the stink that goes with shit. And they'd do anything to keep from getting cut. Like slip a razor blade into your jockstrap."

Moon repressed a shudder. Clarie had been good with the JBS and in high school, but like nearly everyone else, he'd had his breaking point, the time when he stopped putting out one hundred per cent and went to faking. Yet he'd been an All-American. "But you did all right," Moon said.

Henderson laughed. "Yeah, I slipped on through." He had been listening to himself. It'd been a long time since he'd used the idiom. You didn't do it with students; they might think you were trying to be hip and fall out laughing. He and Pat almost never used it at home. He marveled at how alive, how vibrantly descriptive it was, and thought of what Emerson had written long ago about "low" language, the street language, jawing.

"Snake," Moon said. "I heard he was tearing them up back at the University."

Henderson settled deeper in his seat. "Yeah, he did all right, man. Basketball, football. Course, he wasn't no Brud Holland——"

"Brud was an end, Clarie you ought——" Moon had come forward in his seat ready to stomp his point.

Henderson said, laughing because Moon had risen to the bait, "I know it, but on that end-around, he ran like a fullback!"

Moon had burst into laughter too, and jigged his legs. "Hey, didn't he though!"

Laughter still pleasuring his being, Moon saw in his past his Uncle Jasper, Ralph Joplin's father, or Chappie taking them to the football games up on The Hill.

Depression time. The haves seated inside, their pennants flying, their innards warmed by booze or hot dogs with real meat in them or both. Outside, clutching the hands of their elders, they circled the stadium with the have-nots, wolf packs, trying to find an opening left by the police or ROTC students. Moon remembered times when carried forward by the momentum of the pack, they made it through the gates, pushing and punching cops and ROTCees alike, until whistles rent the air summoning reinforcements to push out the pack. All for a fucking game, a motherfucking game. Then they climbed Jumbo's Back. Up there they saw only half the action, but from up there the names sounded over the amplifiers like bronze gongs being struck: Vannie Albanese, Joe Minsavage, Hugh Daugherty, Indian Bill Geyer, Brud Holland, Al Blozis, Wilmeth Sidat-Singh, Marty Glickman, Leland Bunky Morris, Gene Berger.

And Snake Dumpson.

Moon wondered if by the time Snake played, there were other little boys with their elders who had to sit up on Jumbo's Back in the cold.

Henderson said, "Well, you are coming to the banquet?"

"Now that I know, I wouldn't miss it," Moon said. He was going to be in town anyway. Why not? A couple of days wouldn't hurt. Be good to see the guys once more. Strange, learning about the thing for Chappie this way; like it'd all been planned up in the space through which they were flying.

"Otherwise, this would just be a business trip?" Henderson asked. Belatedly, he listened to the echoing ramifications of his question. He glanced at Moon who didn't seem to be taking the words for anything more than what they meant when spoken.

"Yeah. Taking care of some loose ends in New York," Moon said.

"Your Uncle Jasper," Henderson said. "He still with us?"

"Naw. He went, oh, about ten years ago. We put him away nice. Momma's hanging in there, though. Moved out to Tipperary Hill." They both laughed. Tipperary Hill was where the Irish, with their connections at City Hall, had had the green light placed at the top of the traffic signal instead of in its usual place, at the bottom.

"I hear the place has changed a lot," Henderson said. "The Ward is gone." He thought he saw his wife moving out of the darkness down the aisle toward them, and he did not understand why he felt everything within him quickly tighten. He sensed that Moon had seen her before he had.

As kids, nearly all the JBS had had the fear that Moon, with nothing more than a smile, a cocking of his head, a fluttering of his eyelids, could have taken any of their girls. His relationships with their girls was a thing they walked around, their stomachs curdling each time Moon would say, "Oh, is that *your* girl? She's a good-looking chick, man, fine." The words conveyed innocence, the tone absolute guilt.

Henderson shook his head slightly, as if to clear it, and stood as Pat—it was Pat—approached them. He saw her with Moon's eyes. Statuesque, big hipped, full breasted, and foxed. But what was there for her to see in Moon? This Moon? His good looks were demeaned by his baldness; his face was padded with fat, and his waist was thick. But who could tell what about a man attracted a woman?

"Pat," Henderson said, "you'll never believe this, but——"

Dulled by lack of sleep and the movement through time zones, they landed in New York. There had already been the routine:

"Where are you staying?"

"We reserved at the Park Sheraton. You?"

"I don't have reservations, so——"

"Oh, they should have something at the Park," Pat said.

"Sure," Henderson had said with as much enthusiasm as he could gather. In the air, under the cover of darkness, it had seemed all right. Now it was daylight. And Moon was a pimp. Also into drugs? Other rackets? He had to get Pat aside and tell her.

Moon had sensed the change and the reasons for it. He could dig it. His way of making it did not draw applause. College professors and other respectable people were not likely to love pimps, although they might dig their women. Different worlds. He'd just go 'head and take care of business the way he'd planned. Call Dorrie and Gail. Call Momma, tell her he was on the way. Replace the wigs, see about some clothes, rent a car. He'd see Clarie and his ole lady at the Chappie thing. No sweat. "Maybe," he said to ease Henderson's dilemma, "I'll try the Hilton. Parks don't move me. Like California is a big park with cities set into it."

They had parted at the airport in different cabs.

In his room Moon placed the call to San Francisco. He recognized the caution in Dorrie's voice.

"Me," he said.

"Hi, Poppa. So glad—"

"Where's Gail?"

"Well—"

A sense of foreboding overtook Moon. "She split?"

"Yeah, with Elaine and Susan."

"Uh-huh," Moon said, knowing already the answers to the questions he was going to ask.

"Collins ain't doin too good, hey?"

Dorrie said, "Baby, that's one cop you never ever have to worry about again."

Moon sucked in his gut; air pushed of his nostrils. "I did him in?"

"Double did him in. You all right, Walter?"

She hardly ever called him that.

He felt his breath streaming long and hot into the mouthpiece. "Looks like that time, Momma. You there by yourself?"

"Yes. Just waitin on you."

"Yeah, but don't wait there, though, cause that California's seen the last of my rusty-dusty."

"Shall I come to you?"

"No. These goddamn vice cops got their own network. Worse than the FBI. Listen: I'm goin home and get my stash, see my momma and then——"

"What about me, Walter?" Her voice was suddenly plaintive and afraid.

Gently Moon said, "Lemme finish, Dorrie. I'll meet you in Montreal on Sunday. Got some bread?"

"Gail gave me some, and I put together a good bundle the last night out."

"Where'd they go, Mexico?"

"That's all them chicks know is Mexico."

"Okay. You remember that cat Rudy we met up there four years ago?"

"I remember. Him and his two hos and a half."

Moon laughed. Rudy was certainly one of the raggediest pimps he'd ever run across. And Rudy owed him for a couple of favors. Call him, too.

"I'll give him a call. You get to his crib and lay up until I get there."

"Poppa?"

"What?"

"I could go to Mexico, too. I mean, you just get in a car and drive south until you across the border. But—how do I get to Montreal? I never went anywhere without you."

In the silence Moon reflected. He wasn't a very good pimp,

maybe. But, she was right. They'd been together a long time. They were used to each other. "Honey, take a plane to Vancouver, then make a connection to Montreal, all right?"

"Got it."

"He's really wasted, huh?"

"Yes, lord."

"Well, I didn't mean to do it."

"I didn't think so. We going to live in Montreal?"

"Maybe. It's not a bad town."

"I'd work anywhere for you, Poppa."

"Don't want you to work anymore."

"What?"

"We through with that shit. I've been thinking."

"How are we goin to live?"

"We got time to think about that."

"Oh. Sunday, you said?"

"Yeah, but you leave right now, and Dorrie?"

"Yes?"

"Take care of yourself, hear?"

"For you, Walter, and don't let anything happen. Please."

When he hung up Moon stared at Manhattan. Get out today. They didn't know where he came from back home. The freak cops knew only New York, Chicago, and Hollywood. It had been a part of his game not to let folks know where his roots were. Doubling on past, like a fox. But the goddamn freak cops. The skin trade was too lucrative for them not to be efficient. And he was a cop killer on top of it.

But he'd cut back home. Never had a record there. Touch base a last time. He grinned. Clarie and his wife would shit when they saw him in the new wig he was going to buy this morning. He'd drive from home to the border. Three hours. And safe.

NINE

It felt odd being back home, looking down at the streets which, compared to New York at the same time of day, were nearly deserted. Ralph Joplin listened to his wife, Eve, humming in her bath. A good sound, comforting. He must get up, he told himself, and call his father. But he didn't move.

The hotel seemed almost too quiet. It had a new face. The interiors he had never seen, but he suspected that these too were new. As a kid this, the Centre Hotel, had been one of those places blacks never went except to sweep floors or empty spittoons in the barbershop or to shine shoes. A black kid scampering from the entrance on Wayne Street through to Salt had brought bellboys, clerks, managers, and their assistants shouting from a variety of nooks, crannies, and closets. The kids used to do it on dares—dart through the revolving doors, juking through groups of startled guests on their way to dinner or the bar. The past. The future had to take care of itself, and maybe—

He didn't want to think that hard. Not about the future.

Besides the past kept nudging in, shouldering, pushing, demanding attention. Yes, odd to be back at the heart of a situation once totally familiar, but now uneasily strange. He knew something of Dart's life, something about Chops's, of Clarie's (Barney Moore, just back from Clarie's school had filled him in on the latest), of Snake's. He didn't expect Moon. Having heard something about his life, too, he hadn't expected what you would call an all-out search for him. Cudjo, Shurley, and Bubbles—well, he imagined nothing much had changed for them. Maybe now they owned homes which had dens containing bars and television sets for the games. Was that change? Or a continuum? Could you transcend a quarter of a century, relate to the Depression, welfare, jockstraps, touchdowns, home runs, and baskets? Still, there was a cement to it all. Chappie. And quite probably more: the shared experience. They had all survived this city, to them the nation, the world, the universe. They had not really lived in it.

So, all that had happened here since he left was unreal. But here, here in this very city his mother Sissie, journeying three thousand miles by train in a casket, was buried. Buried beside his brother and a sister. His father, Big Ralph, survived still. His daughter, Raffy, like the kids of his contemporaries, had shoved early out into the world, climbing what one hoped was the ladder provided by education. And April, his first wife, still here, still bitter? If so, why?

All those who had remained in this gray, industrial city, now face-lifted with speedways and new buildings—would they, could they understand his furious sprint by car from New York City this morning? Why should they *want* to understand it?

Shandor. Just one more day of Shandor coming to him and saying: "Ralph, I think this line would play better if Henri maybe gave the black power salute—" Or, "Ralph, that line sounds a little too strong for the action; they're not compatible. Maybe you can cover the iron with a little velvet, baby? You know what I mean."

Nuance by nuance, beat by beat, Shandor was trying to change his play. Shandor, other directors, producers, and theater owners all seemed to be waiting for that moment when he would have to say, finally, "Play it the way I wrote it or don't do it." Then they would draw the curtain on him the way they had with a small host of black playwrights, sent them to teaching school or to moving out of town. Sent them, or they went in disgust? The point wasn't even debatable; they were gone. Broadway was the poorer, but didn't know it, and of course the people never even knew. What was left? Pimp-school productions, white image fittings.

The folks here would know of his fruitless sojourns in Hollywood. No. They'd know about the trips, but not that they were fruitless. Chops's stories were all upbeat: everybody making a million, everyone with twenty closets filled with clothes and shoes. They would know, the folks here, about his relationship to Henri Catroux, returning to Broadway after a long movie career, if that's what they wanted to call it, and they would know by now and perhaps forgotten that he had married Henri's former wife. That had been a long time ago, before Henri was summoned to challenge the Belafonte presence. And now poor Henri —and Belafonte and others, too—were being upstaged by a whole new generation of black film actors who wouldn't have lasted a minute on the stage. One moment they had been invisible, and the next, gigantic, fucking and fighting all over the screen, acting out the fantasies of white film company executives and perhaps from time to time nightmaring for many the dream first packaged by immigrants; immigrants who, out of their own sufferings, perceived the secret of the American heart, its fear and foolishness and gave it body, a *golem* in blackface, but made it a joke.

Where other playwrights' works went from Broadway to Hollywood, the works of black playwrights rarely got past the Henry Street Settlement House. Sometimes Joe Papp was nice to them. Where white actors could begin Off-Broadway, go Broadway and Hollywood, black actors walked boards which were planks into oblivion. Henri and a few others were exceptions; they had earned the right for their names to become prideful, household words: Henri, Harry, Sidney, Ossie, Ruby, Cicely, Al, etc.; it'd taken fifteen years for that to have happened. Yet, which among them could say, truthfully, that all was well?

Ralph had not liked his Hollywood sojourns. Had he been a younger man, maybe. Had he not had an ancient fear of things that seemed to be but really were not, he might have liked it, yes. Indeed, parts of it had not been hard to take. Defenseless, one could lose perspective before the onslaught of black front men and women, white double-talk about art, the heated swimming pools, the cringing crews of sycophants, the extraordinary homes and offices, the unrelenting exercise of power. But art in Hollywood, or the film business wherever it was, became something else; a piece of cloth dyed in bright colors to excite the natives. Film people went down on you and cut your throat at the same time, smiling all the while. They talked of art, certainly, but believed they were the only ones who should profit from it. They had made screwing the artist a fine art in itself. They made film the heaven to which those in the writing and performing arts looked for ultimate approval, and if they paid you enough you were knighted a great artist. And other artists thought you were too.

They were through with him, Ralph knew. He hadn't done things right. It felt odd being back home because for the second time in his life he was unsure of his future. The uncertainty was underlined now. It was here that he stumbled away from April, afraid, unsure, but then his will to write had been strong, an anthracite fire, slow-burning and hot. The fire was waning now. Over fifteen years of writing with one hand, and battling the system that would not acknowledge that it had produced him with the other, had not embittered as much as wearied him.

It was natural that he recalled, suddenly, a moment during the unwearied years, like the night at the Hemlock. He and April had never gone to it before because it was tucked in a corner of the Ward, a place where the whites conducted clandestine affairs, third-rate-ganster business, and catered to the white college clientele. The place was empty when they arrived and faced down the old, bleached blonde waitresses. They were grudgingly served. Ralph put a coin in the box. "La Vie en Rose" came up . . .

Louis Armstrong's soft bursts as he led April to the empty dance floor upon which they moved into a ballet, a mix of Lindy and whatever seemed right, anticipating each other's every move. ("Hold me close and hold me tight . . .") They had smiled at each other, pleased that they had found a new closeness in the music, in their movements. They'd never, never danced like that before, and perhaps never would again. Swirling, their shoes hissing against the floor, they were like shadows spinning and twisting without sound, seeming to hang in air like Nijinsky, finding beats between beats, like Jamieson; April with a smile of disdain for all who could not dance the way they were dancing, all in less than three minutes. Quite simply, that night they discovered another way to make love, just moving to perfect time, anticipating precisely, to music unsurpassed. They hardly noticed the waitresses and bartenders and barflies applauding. That was during the years when weariness was a shit thing, a white folks' concept.

He had had a second time of feeling that good when his first play opened on Broadway. Opening night, reading the reviews in his small apartment in the Village surrounded by a few friends, people in the company and the jackals. No. That night was different from the "La Vie en Rose" night. But they were both paragraphs in his life: the points in shooting where the director calls for new camera angles. Both were tight shots.

Another tight shot was in the works: portrait of a playwright with no stage to write for.

He'd trucked through that jungle composed of Kerr, Atkinson, Watts, Taubman, Tynan, Tallmer; had seen new jungles grow: Barnes, Simon, Bailey, Harris, et al. What would he do if he stopped writing plays? He'd been a playwright all his life, in thought and wish first, and in deed later. What did a black ex-playwright do at fifty? At only fifty! He had wrought "traditional" plays, "experimental" plays, "revolutionary" plays and now when he was peaking in power and vision (he believed), a power and insight that for the first time allowed him to overcome his heritage, all of it, there came Shandor, like a mid-Pacific tidal wave, silent as a snake, one hundred feet high— disaster. And if you threatened a play, in this case, *And Then a Long Darkness,* you threatened its author, his life.

Ralph Joplin turned on his stomach and for a moment listened to his wife still in the bathroom. Did she know? Could she perceive his crisis? His gaze drifted down to the street, five floors below. People were still people from there, not ants, as when Cross Damon sees them in *The Outsider.*

Which white playwright—his mind would not give him release —who had begun having his plays produced at the same time he did was in crisis now? Albee? Gelber? Friedman? Simon?

The man's walk was more familiar than someone remembered from a party, more distinctive than any among the people he currently knew; the gait drew all of Ralph's attention. The pace was like that of a big cat, tipping on concrete. The shoulders were rounded, the head bobbed like that of a fighter feinting; the heels seemed to touch the ground, but in fact, merely caressed it, the weight of the man against the sidewalk coming on the toes; the arms swung reluctantly, as if fearful of being surprised in a position of defenselessness.

Ralph smiled now, admiring the walk and all it seemed to

symbolize. And he recognized the man. It was his father, Big Ralph Joplin. Ralph continued to watch him, listening for sounds, feeling for things inside himself. But he felt and heard nothing. His relationship to his father was an allegiance to being, nothing more. Ralph could devise a semiwarmth on the rare occasions when he saw his father, but a certain honesty prevented him from doing more.

Big Ralph turned a corner and was out of sight. Wayne and Jellenick, Ralph guessed, where they used to line up in front of the Downeyflake shop window at night and wait for the manager to signal whether or not they would be given the leftover pastries from the day.

Ralph eased himself off the bed and went to the bathroom. "Guess what?" he said to Eve who was in soap bubbles up to her neck.

"What did you see, honey, leaning out the window?"

"My father."

Eve stopped moving the cloth around on her body. "Oh. Does he look good?" She smiled. She wondered what it would feel like, watching one of her parents walking some distance away, out of sound of voice. Then she said, "It's just as well you didn't call him. Probably on the way home right now."

Her husband spoke hollowly. "From up here he looked okay. You know, I walk a little like he does." His laugh was embarrassed, to cover, Eve imagined, a confusion of feelings.

"Is it a b-a-a-d walk?" she teased.

"Can't you tell?" Ralph remembered all those hours of practicing a b-a-a-d walk, until be believed he had one down, one that was distinctive, uniquely his. When had he lost it? Or had his father's way of walking always lingered, waiting for the unnatural one to wane? He had been studying what was visible of Eve's body. She winked at him. "Want some?"

"Will it make me feel better?" He took the soap and slid it around on the nipples of her breasts.

"Doesn't it always?"

Ralph plucked her thigh from the soap bubbles and kissed the inside of it. "I'm sorry to tell you, lady, but that doesn't quite solve all the problems."

"I wish it could. You have been one evil man lately."

"Menopause, maybe."

"You think you're kidding, don't you?"

"I am. My menopause is a combination of Shandor and *And Then a Long Darkness.*"

"Thought so, but you didn't seem to want to talk about it."

"Didn't want you to play Dr. Bluman's receptionist again."

"Oh, come on, baby. At this late date—that's what I mean, honey. . . ."

"Sorry. Listen. I'm going to find some booze before we go to the Ebenos for dinner. I'll call my father when I get back."

Coyly, Eve grasped his hand. "Sure I can't do anything for you raht now?"

"Raht now, sugah, keep it warm. Lots of things you can do a little later."

"I'm looking forward to it."

"Better."

The woman had just passed as Ralph stepped into the corridor. The way she looked from behind almost made him go right back to Eve. This woman was larger and although her body was thickening, her shape remained, and he supposed, the juices still flowed heavily. She knew it too, from the way she was trucking to the elevators.

"Hey, motherfucker, that's mine."

Ralph turned, startled at the sharp growl behind him, seeing as he did the woman turning too, surprised.

"Chops!" Ralph said. "Man, you caught me." He turned from Jackson to the woman, now recognizing her. "Christine!" The three embraced. Ralph kissed Christine Jackson.

"Jesus, Chris, time has blessed you." To Ezzard Jackson he said, taking in his rounding stomach, the soft jowls and eyes that seemed unable to rest easily upon his own, Ralph said, "Man you look about half as good as Chris."

"Shit," Jackson countered, "you're looking a little battered yourself, Ralph. Like they been whippin you to death."

"You know somethin? That's the way I feel too."

"Your wife with you?" Christine's question. They'd never met Eve.

"Yeah. She's taking a bath. When did you get in? Shurley and Bubbles put everybody up here?"

"Haven't seen anyone but you," Jackson said. "Guess we'll see everyone later, here or at the restaurant. Where you heading, man?"

"To get me some booze. Dull the nerve endings, being back home."

"That's how come we're here instead of with my folks," Christine said. "Folks is folks. Yeah."

They were walking toward the elevators. Jackson said when they got on, "I remember ole Clarie got caught in a revolving door running through the lobby of this joint, and some bellboy kicked his ass good."

"Almost got caught a couple of times myself," Ralph said. "Hey, I met your boss in a restaurant in Barcelona about three years ago."

"Oh, yeah," Jackson said. He flicked his eyes toward Ralph. "He told me."

How much, Ralph wondered? That he had had Julio's best table in the Reno and that he was anxious for dinner to be over (it had been obvious and Julio had not been pleased) so he could get back in bed with that big blonde he had with him? That he had flashed two watches, one with Barcelona time, the other with the office time back home so he could "know exactly what the jigaboos were supposed to be doing" because he didn't trust any of them?

"Where you going now?" Ralph asked.

"Leg-stretching. Drop into one of those bars we used to couldn't go into. Show Chris the Downeyflake where we used to beat each other's ass to get a place in line so that cat could give us bags of leftover cookies."

"I was just thinking about that myself," Ralph said. "You talk to Bubbles yet?"

"Yeah. He just got in from work. He'll meet us there. Shurley's manager of the joint. Didn't know that. And Snake'll be there——"

"He married a white gal, didn't he?" Christine interrupted.

"So I understand," Ralph said. "So did Dart. But you ain't gonna let a little thing like that mess up things, is ya, honey?"

They were walking through the lobby now and Chris shrugged. "It's really none of my business. I'm a little surprised you didn't get yourself one, Ralph."

Ralph said, "Next time around, maybe."

"I know Ezzard wishes he had one, don't you baby?" She laughed and Ralph thought it was dangerous and mocking.

Ezzard Jackson, fingering the note in his pocket, said mildly, "You all right with me sport." Sometime this weekend he would lay it on her. If he didn't become afraid. He knew the contents by heart now, and hated and feared every word.

> Dear Ezzard: Guess what's ten times bigger than a cyst? Guess who has not had a cyst removed twice? But something ten times bigger?
>
> A friend

They paused in the street. "It's strange," Jackson said. "We always thought only rich people stayed in hotels."

"Aren't we rich?" Chris teased.

Jackson studied his wife as he sucked his teeth. She was really turned out for this one. Looked scrumptious. She'd be dazzling somebody before this was all over. And I'ma dazzle her, he thought. "Ain't we rich?" he mimicked her and turned away.

"There's a jug shop," Ralph said.

"I guess I'll get me one, too," Jackson said.

Chris said, "Well, let me go and window-shop, while you two talk. I'll see you back upstairs."

Jackson grunted.

In the liquor store Ralph said, "Who's supposed to be here, everybody but Moon?"

"Guess so. That dude must be rollin in bread, playin in Hollywood."

"So, how's things goin, Chops?"

Jackson smiled, a little sadly Ralph thought. "They could always be better. Seems like I've only known two things in my whole life, now that I'm back: Chris and Mr. Lawrence, and I'm tired of both. Too late now."

Ralph peered more intently at the rows of scotch. He said, "Yeah, it's late, man." He looked up. "Aw, shit. It's a thing you go through at our age."

Jackson studied the bourbon shelves. "I've been going through it a long time. Knowing things you don't want to know. I guess I can't buy J. W. Dant. Big successful editor of Lawrence Publications ought to be able to afford a quart of Grandad or Turkey."

Ralph had been thinking the same thing. He couldn't truck out a bottle of cheap scotch. "How're your kids?"

Jackson growled, "Them monsters. About as bad as they momma. Cept one's a boy. He can't get pregnant."

Ralph became feverishly busy checking, double, and triple-checking the shelves. How many more innuendos from how many others would come before the weekend was over? Selecting his bottle and feeling suddenly ashamed of his feelings, he said to Jackson, "Hey, man. You didn't come all the way here to wish Chappie good luck with an attitude, did you?"

Jackson grimaced, picked up a bottle, and said, "It's gonna pass, man; it's gonna pass. Hear you got a new one in rehearsal."

"It may not ever get *out* of rehearsal, these people keep fuckin wid me."

"You too, huh?"

Laughing hard and clutching their bottles, they made their way to the cashier who smiled hesitantly at first one, then the other. When he finished ringing up their bills, the cashier said to Jackson, "Don't I know you?"

"Dunno. Name's Jackson."

"Yeah," the cashier said. "You played guard with Overlook, right? I played with Western——"

"Stosh Kwalick," Ralph said.

"Right!" the cashier said. "You remembered. I don't remember you," he said, looking at Ralph.

"I was in an out. A sub," Ralph said.

The cashier was smiling now. "And that tackle and fullback you had, Kee-rist! Lotsa good ballplayers. You guys cleaned up the conference for two or three years in a row."

"Yeah, we did pretty good," Jackson said. "This your shop?"

The cashier's voice dropped and perhaps his head took on a sudden droop. "Naw, I just work here. I dunno. Went to the war, tried three or four different things. Nothin worked. Wife, kids, and suddenly I'm gettin old without a pot to piss in. Time, it went so fuckin fast. . . ."

Ralph and Jackson nodded gently, sympathetically. The cashier snapped his head up abruptly and a great smile played across his face. "Just flashing on the past, fellas. It's good to know that some of the old crowd's doin okay. I can tell by the booze you've bought. Lissen, stop in again."

"Oh, we're in from outa town," Jackson said. "I'm in Kansas City, and Ralph's in New York."

"Yeah, no shit? Best thing, gettin outa this fuckin town. I wish I'd done it. That big fullback, he's a big deal in town, you know. Commissioner. You guys did all right. Good luck."

Settled in Jackson's room, each with a glass of whiskey, Jackson said, "That's the first gray boy I've met in years didn't get pissed because I drink better bourbon than he does. Know why he remembers me so well? I was his goddamn pigeon. That Polack did everything to me but chew me up and spit me out. If I'da been playin end or somethin out there in the open, everybody woulda seen that hunky walkin over me. Shit."

"He used to be into that zoot suit shit," Ralph said. "Dressed out like a spade. Chain, knobs, ten-gallon hat, and all. He hurt me a few times too."

They drank until Ralph said, "Haven't seen you in about—what, ten years?"

"Easy ten," Jackson said.

"But you been doin okay?"

"Yeah, but I should've got away from Mr. Lawrence a long time ago."

Ralph nodded. "The guys who did leave wonder why it took them so long. Cantwell told me that when he left he took a ream of good bond and a box of number two pencils, and ole Lawrence called the publisher of *The New Vision* about it. As though they'd fire him because he copped paper and pencils. I heard the man was chinchy, but he was spending bread in Barcelona like it was going out of style. Even so you must be in pretty good shape with pension plans and shit as long as you've been there."

"I dunno. I suppose when the time comes all that will turn out to be shit, too. That's to be expected. The point is, I never got to be my own man, the way a writer is."

"You don't think of yourself as a writer anymore?"

"Never did, really. I'm an editor. I kill writers. Murder them. Once it was a lot of fun, you know, fucking over stringers and shit, pretending that we were really going to become a black *Time* magazine."

"Chops, you gotta cheer up," Ralph said, rising. "I've got to go and call my old man."

"How's he doin?"

"He's all right. Saw him walkin down the street this afternoon. How's your mother comin on?"

"She's back down home, man. Seems to be making it okay. Hey, why don't we cab over to the restaurant together?"

"You're on. Knock when you're ready."

Big Ralph Joplin turned up the thermostat. He felt rich whenever he did. He listened to the furnace humming and thought of all the years when he had had to shovel coal into furnaces or other coal stoves, and of the shaking and sifting of the ashes to retrieve the good coals. A man spent so much of his life back then keeping warm during the winters.

And you didn't have to walk through nor sit in cold seats or on hills to watch football games anymore. You see it all on television, right in your own home. Sometimes he watched the games with his brother, Lewis. His sisters, Emma and Alice, had long since died, one of cheap whiskey and the other of overwork. There was left only Lewis and himself. Iris had been away so long and wrote so infrequently that under her name in his address book he had written "daughter." Ralph was not a regular visitor, but he could be, his father knew, counted on. His granddaughter, Raffy, he saw for hot minutes only when she was home from school. No, there was only Lewis and himself.

Now, slowly and proudly, the late afternoon sun cutting sharply through the brittle, cold air outside into his warm kitchen, he unfolded the evening paper and thumbed softly through it as though he did not wish to disturb the mood of the house. It would be there. It was in the morning paper, so it had to be in the evening *Express*. His son had worked for the *Express* once. . . . Big Ralph paused and raised his head so that his eyes fell not on the paper, but on the past. That had been a long time ago when Ralph worked on the paper. "Little Ralph" was now fifty.

There it was, the arrangement of photos vertical instead of horizontal like the morning paper had them.

The will to win which was infused over a quarter of a century ago in a group of local youngsters by a man who didn't know the meaning of defeat has paid off. His prodigal sons have returned to honor coach Charles Chappie Davis, a resident of the city. Mr. Davis is seventy years old.

"His boys" include City Housing Commissioner Kenneth Dumpson, former all-star athlete on the Hill; D'Artagnan Foxx, the concert singer who now lives in Amsterdam, The Netherlands, and who studied under the late University maestro, Stephan Klipstein. Mr. Foxx will be featured at the Black Arts Festival tomorrow night at the Civic Center Playhouse.

A scene from Ralph Joplin's first broadway success, *Shadows on the Sun,* will also make up a segment of the Festival. Mr. Joplin whose father, like Mr. Davis, is a long-time resident of the city, lives in New York City. He is a graduate of the University.

Ezzard Jackson, assistant editorial director of Lawrence Publications and a graduate of Wilberforce and Northwestern University's School of Journalism, now lives in Kansas City, Mo.

Once a black All-American end at Morris Brown College in Atlanta, Dr. Clarence Henderson, Professor of English at the University of California, Santa Maria, had also returned to honor Mr. Davis.

Excluding Commissioner Dumpson, the former teammates and friends who remained in the city are Cudjo Evers, Shurley Walker, and Richard Wiggins. They will host a welcoming dinner tonight at the popular West Side restaurant, The Ebenos, which is managed by Mr. Walker for Christ Papadapoulous. Mr. Evers and Mr. Wiggins are employed by Obanoga Foundries.

During their days at Overlook High, Mr. Davis' proteges, to whom he taught sandlot sports, won city-wide championships for the Big O in football, basketball, baseball and track for three years running, starting in 1940. All won All-City honors at one time or another during that period after which all saw service during World War II.

A banquet will be held in the Centre Hotel on Saturday night to conclude the honors to Mr. Davis. Mayor Hofstader will present him with the Citizenship Award.

Smiling, Big Ralph reached to answer the phone. "I knew it was you, son. I was just reading all about you boys and Chappie in the paper. How are you? When'll I see you?"

In his hotel room Ralph looked longingly at Eve's behind as she stood before the mirror putting on her last dollop of make-up. "Tomorrow," he said. "I thought the three of us might pick up some flowers and go to the cemetery——"

He saw Eve stop her movements. Their eyes met in the mirror and he knew she was thinking of his mother's death, his trip to California with his sister, after the storm broke in New York; and thinking too of the infrequent visits to this city to see his father who existed in the womb of his loneliness and seemed to like it. Ralph winked at her. "——and then have some lunch, talk, okay?"

Big Ralph nodded a couple of times before he caught himself. He rarely spoke on the phone to anyone except Lewis. "Sure. That'll be fine with me. You gonna pick me up?" He glanced at the paper, opened to the story and pictures. He nodded to the phone again. "Half-past eleven. Sure, that's all right. You boys have a good time tonight and give my best to Chappie, will you, son?"

TEN

Five hours earlier.

Shurley Walker had looked up from an unnecessary polishing of his glassware to greet with minimum civility the familiar figure entering the Ebenos. He set the glass down in its place and pressed the button, the same one he pressed whenever this man came.

"Sappening, Shurley?"

"Thing's cool, Swoop."

The place was empty save for the two men. The man Shurley called Swoop moved over softly creaking floors to the bar where Shurley stood and placed himself solidly in front of him.

"How's the old man, Shurley? Seems like he's turning more and more of the business over to you." Over his shoulder he surveyed the set table. "Read about the shindig tonight. All the ole boys done come home. The all-stars. The superjocks. The homeboys." He nodded in approval. "Looks like it's gonna be a groovy thing, Shurl."

"Yeah, we gonna try and do it up right," Shurley said. He feigned a distraction he did not feel. When Swoop Ferguson was in your joint, you'd better not be distracted. Then he said, "Well, the old man's all right. Gettin on like most of us, but faster."

Swoop grinned. He liked Shurley's sense of humor. "I sure hope he remembers that I want first crack at this joint when he quits."

"Oh, he knows," Shurley said laconically. Swoop was going to shit—just like a lot of other poeple, when he discovered that the place was his, Shurley's, down the line, and that Papadapoulous has been *his* front for years since they both knew that it was not easy for a black man to come by his liquor license unless his contacts were thick and deep. They also knew that whatever it cost a white bar owner under the table, it cost a black man five times more.

Shurley no longer knew precisely when the notion of buying the Ebenos occurred to him, but when it had and he'd gone to Papadapoulous, it'd been like talking to an old friend.

The old man was nothing else. Like everyone else in the Ward, Christ belonged there, a part of things. They first noticed him on warm, humid summer nights, his dappled-gray horse, head bent, blinders on, pulling his popcorn and ice cream wagon down the streets, a little steam whistle piping a steady note. Used real butter then, Shurley remembered, recalling the smell and taste of it, and the popcorn, and the alfalfa stuffed under the wagon for the horse.

Christ came and went, a husky man with thinning hair, even then, culling pennies, nickels, and dimes to take home to his black common-law wife. And later he had a store over near Moon's house. Located on a corner, light struck its dark interiors and gleamed on the rows of canned goods and the chrome-plated fittings of his meat case.

The old man liked to gamble and had been lucky. As soon as he learned how the numbers went, he put down 333 in the box every day with Chappie. But mostly he was lucky at poker up-stairs over Chevrolet Bob's garage, gambling with Sugar, D'Amica, Wilbur Marcus, Crook-Eye, Knock-em-Dead, and others. The story went that he won three or four big pots during the early years of the war and took the money and opened the Ebenos.

After the war the Ward began to break up. People moved to other parts of the city with the money earned in war plants or just because they were tired of the Ward and could find places they could rent without too much trouble. The Ebenos went downhill. Papadapoulous tried no music and then live jazz, and still couldn't draw. When Shurley approached him he was ready to sell and to pretend he still owned it. He was after all a poker player and after all his years in the Ward it seemed natural that he should sell to a black man, in effect, in that town anyway, another Greek.

Shurley passed up from under the bar the white envelope with the money. Swoop shoved it into his pocket.

"How come you never count it, Swoop?"

"Because I know Papadapoulous don't be fuckin with the

program, that's how come. Tell him thanks. I really appreciate not having any hassles. You all know how to take care of business. Now you take some the those bloods running them dives on the other side of town. They always be wafflin. A hassle to make things go smooth. So don't nobody get bruised. If a white cop had that section, they'd never complain, just go ahead and give up the bread. No, they fuck with me cause I'm a Brother."

"Yeah," Shurley said sympathetically. "Drink, Swoop?"

"No. I got to roll. See you later. Hope you guys have a good time tonight."

When he was gone Shurley called out the date and pressed another button on the tape recorder.

Now he was truly alone. Mickey Mouse had long since finished cleaning. He would be back later. Shurley liked these few solitary moments; patrons would have annoyed him. For he liked to savor his secret ownership of the place. He smiled at the smell of Mickey Mouse's cleaning deodorant, which was mixed with the odors of the food Sugar had left slow-cooking on the stove. Im-mac-u-late, Shurley thought, allowing himself to see the restaurant as a stranger walking in might see it. He'd spent so much of his life in half-kept, trifling bars and restaurants; places where women didn't dare to squat to pee, and places where men stood feet away from the urinals to avoid getting their shoes soaked by the pools of piss. And food, shit.

Nobody had to tell Shurley he ran a nice place. They didn't anyway; they told Papadapoulous. No matter. Clean bathrooms, good chairs and tables, great food, thanks to Sugar. And he had a good clientele, black and white. Whites from nearby since the Ward had been demolished in favor of high-rent apartments. Blacks from neighborhoods where the restaurants never served what they'd been used to. No more beer drinkers who switched to liquor on weekends and blew their bread at the expense of their families. Shurley didn't give a fuck what the sociologists said about that kind of behavior. He'd never done that and he didn't want people in his place who did. He wished for things to be nice and easy. Cool.

Sugar wheezed in. "Saw that pea-pickin Swoop Negro gettin in his car," he said, rubbing his hands together. Sugar never talked about the reasons for Swoop's stopping by so regularly.

But, Shurley guessed, he knew; Sugar'd been around too long not to know. And if he knew Shurley instead of the old man owned the place, he never let on.

"Yeah, he stopped in," Shurley said. Old Sugar. Got his name, the rumor went, because women found him so sweet when he was a young man. "How ya doin, Sug? That grease back there sure is sayin somethin."

"Oh, I'm awright this afternoon. Any reservations come in while I been gone?"

Shurley picked up a pad. "Two couples from the University. Sunday. You know that Professor Harris who's always praising your soul food?"

"That phony Brother with the fancy talk? Yeah."

Shurley said, "His money spends."

"What'd he ask for?"

"Chitlins."

"Chitlins! Goddamn, he might as well asked for a T-bone. Them gray cocksuckers done got holt of our food and boosted them prices, whoo-eeee!"

Sugar, a grayish-gold color, with the stump of a cigar in his mouth, took off his overcoat and jacket. "Why, man, white folks up North didn't know diddley-squat about no kinda collards and turnips and mustards and chitlins and hocks n shit until Negroes got up here. Now all that shit, it's in the supermarkets. Used t' throw away chitlins, and look up here now and see they cannin the motherfuckers, and hocks is nearly a gotdamn dollar a pound——"

Laughing, Shurley interrupted. Sugar always had his tirades about food and what it cost these days. "Sugar?"

"What?" Sugar said, chewing angrily on his cigar stump. "Fo you say anything, give me a taste of the J & B back there."

Shurley poured out half a glass and handed it to Sugar. "Order some chitlins, Sug. Some of the guys may want some."

Sugar finished the glass in a swallow. "Oh, man, you know I was gonna order em."

Shurley laughed again. "You just love to go through numbers, Sug." He poured another drink. "Listen. I really appreciate what you're doing, fixing the dinner and all." He placed the bottle back on the shelf and watched Sugar finish his second drink, which he did with a loud sigh.

"Shurley, all them Negroes—raggedy-assed little boys just like you—turned out to *be* somebody, but they ain't forgot ole Chappie. People likes to fergit who he'ped em. I'm glad to do it. Negroes ought to do more things like this, Shurley."

Shurley watched him shuffle to the kitchen, whistling. The man could burn. There wasn't any doubt about that. Best fucking cook in town, and maybe the whole world. Shurley filled a glass with ice and poured ginger ale over it. He glanced at his watch.

Well, he thought, pretty soon. Mickey Mouse would be back wearing a white shirt, bow tie, and service jacket for the bar. And Marvin and Clifford would be down from the Hill to wait the tables. Shurley recruited students and dressed them in tuxedos. No other black restaurant in town, and not many white ones, had tuxedoed waiters. The Ebenos, he knew, moved the student waiters to prideful service. The way dining-car waiters used to feel and be. The students seemed to know what he was doing and did their part to make the restaurant a class place. So Shurley had always hired them. They were people going someplace, not coming back from somewhere else, losers; waiting tables for them, therefore, was not the end of a line. Besides, there were not too many places in town where a black student could find regular employment. Providing sustenance for them, in one form or another, was a part of the tradition of the community. The old men like Chappie and Sug told stories about lost and lonely students back in the twenties who, unwelcome on the Hill, drifted down to Bloodfield and later Jewtown where they were made to feel at home, and where they understood that a bond existed between their unseen, unknown parents, themselves, and the folk here in town.

In summer, when the students were gone, Shurley and his wife Diane ran the Ebenos with as much help as they could get with their own kids, Mickey Mouse and Sug. They had five children: George, Grace, Gertrude, Gwendolyn, and Geoffry. But they weren't kids any longer. Maybe, but just barely, Gwen and Geoff. George had made the Army his career and had risen through the ranks to captain and was now stationed in Iran. George had made him a grandfather. Grace had married a slick-talking hip preacher and was in Lexington, Kentucky; Trudy was about to marry one of his former waiters who would be graduat-

ing from law school next June. Gwen would be off next year, and
Geoff the year after, and the house, which once bulged with people and their sounds and smells, was already falling silent and
odorless.

Boy, Shurley thought, it sure went fast! He smiled listening to
Sugar alternately cursing and whistling. But, shit, Shurley
thought again, I knew all along I was gonna make it!

He had thought long and hard about going to college when he
came home from the war. But the college men he'd met in the
372nd hadn't done any better than the other black men in the
regiment who hadn't finished high school. They might have been
noncoms and officers, second lieutenants mostly, but they took
the same shit from whitey as anyone else. No, he decided. He
could not afford to waste four years and maybe more. He could
turn out to be an educated bum.

He signed on at Hurricane as a floorman, a janitor. The pay
was good for the time, and no black man he knew had to exhaust
himself pushing a broom or gathering up the curls of aluminum
from the assembly lines where they put the air conditioners together. He made the days at Hurricane and six hours each afternoon into evening at Conley's department store, packing items
for delivery, knee-deep in excelsior. The two jobs brought him a
hundred bills a week, and on Saturdays he waxed office floors for
a growing clientele. That was a breeze. He swept the floors,
poured liquid wax into the mop water, and did two operations in
one. You had to find shortcuts.

He'd seen Snake and Ralph and sometimes Dart in the joints
once in a while, but he was more often with Cudjo and Bubbles;
their lives, like his, were in the present, not the future. Like
Ralph and April, he and Diane got married in church; church
weddings were in the air then, a departure from the marriages of
their parents in the church parlors or in City Hall.

Sing out to the world: We're married!

Shurley drew his thoughts back to the present. Next month his
liquor license would have to be renewed and, this time, his ownership of the Ebenos would be made public. If they gave him
trouble, he would truck on down to the State Investigating Commission with his tapes. But could he take on the whole police
force of the city? The cops could do anything. Set him up, burn

him down, close him up forever. Then what? They'd saved money, somehow, and Diane had always worked. Now she was making good bread as a receptionist for the county welfare department, and the kids were all just about on their own. They'd make out if the worst happened. A new life at fifty? What kind of life?

But he wouldn't take their shit. Ever since that day when the white boys made him—made him—*suck their dicks,* he'd known that he was going to fuck white people good, some day. If black people like Swoop got caught in the middle, that was too bad. Shouldn't have been there in the first place.

Later Swoop Ferguson dropped off the shares in the station, picked up his own shares from the other bag men and paused to study the bulletin board before heading home. His eyes quickly picked out the newest fliers; the paper was spanking white. The older notices, yellowed and frayed, no longer attracted anyone's attention, but no one bothered to remove them either. They were cases still unsolved, nagging reminders that burglars, rapists, muggers, murderers, and con men were still seeping unhindered through the public. The weekend killings, with the killers remorseful and hungover, were a part of the scene. But the unsolved murders, a big city disease once, were growing in number here.

When Swoop first became a police officer, the second black on the force, black wanteds were a minority. Now, some eighteen years later, they were the majority. Swoop never questioned the reverse in ratio. He did a job and would keep doing it until he retired in two and a half years.

The newest bulletin was an APB on a Walter "Moon" Porter, alleged to be a pimp, who was wanted for questioning in the murder of a Hollywood, California, police officer. Swoop deftly removed the notice and pocketed it. He did not look at it until he had driven some distance away from the station and parked.

Walter Porter, The Moon, baddest tackle in high school football history. All-City three years in a row. Swoop remembered the three-point stance in a photograph at the Center. Cocky grin mixed with what was meant to be an intimidating scowl. Swoop smiled triumphantly at the notice.

Swoop's family had moved from the migrant cabins outside town into the city at the end of the war. The older black residents scornfully called them, and other families like his, "beanpickers" or "peapickers," and hadn't had much to do with them. They were another class, a different breed. Swoop had been about sixteen then when Moon and the others returned home from the war.

During that summer when they were trying to decide what they wanted to do, they played ball in Jefferson Park. They called him beanpicker and peapicker still, and let him play only to even out the sides. And he had been a good ballplayer; made All-City twice himself. It was just that all the high school coaches measured every black athlete who came after them, against the guys in that club, The Junior Bachelor Society. Swoop had hated that; still hated it. Once when in uniform, he'd ticketed Cudjo and later, when he got on the vice squad, he'd almost put a collar on Chappie for gambling, but it hadn't stayed on. Chappie knew too many people and was, Swoop discovered soon enough, "protected."

Yeah, Swoop thought. Those old Negroes thought their shit didn't stink. Worse than white folks. Now lookit here. He smoothed out the notice again. The white cops wouldn't be knowing Moon came from here. Wouldn't be knowing or caring about it like me. To them, one splib is just like any other. What a collar! Swoop thought. He saw himself swooping down unheralded upon Moon as he had done to countless others so many times before, thus gaining his name, and snatching him out of the middle of some function the JBS was holding this weekend. And if Moon proved to be the perpetrator, maybe he, Swoop, would get promoted to detective first-class. Sure would help that retirement bread! Swoop glanced at his watch. He'd call his wife, then go back and stake out the Ebenos, just in case ole Moon was in town for that. He'd do it alone; fuck those cats at the station.

ELEVEN

Sandra Dumpson kissed her kids good night, though they tried to avoid a routine they now considered childish. Perhaps it was a childish thing; they were now fifteen and eighteen, the elder a freshman at the University. She rushed out of the house anticipating a look of annoyance on Ken's face when she arrived at the car. Instead, he was patiently waiting, holding the door for her. This was special tonight, she thought. Usually it was get in by yourself, kiddo, which was all right too.

Ken had not said much about this gathering of his boyhood club, and he had only mentioned in passing weeks ago that it would be nice to drop by and see an old friend, a member, one Sunday.

("Which friend?")

("Bubbles. You don't know him.")

Bubbles, she gathered, was not one of the illustrious JBS members. Ralph Joplin was, of course. They'd seen his plays in New York and a couple of road productions here in town. And Dart Foxx she knew about, but had never been able to find a recording of his. She remembered when Dart had been the University's Negro showpiece. Clarence Henderson and Ezzard Jackson. Like Dart, they had some prominence, had left town, traveled, and "done things."

"Bubbles," she said. "You don't hear nicknames like that anymore. He'll be there tonight?"

They eased out of the driveway onto the street.

"Bubbles, Shurley, and Cudjo, like it said in the papers. They stayed behind, like me."

Like me, Sandra thought. Not much sense in pointing out again that the similarities ended with skin coloring. Ken did not believe so, but that was exactly what they'd been telling him for years now. His people. He'd been cursed for his candor, punctuality, and effectiveness. They called him an Uncle Tom.

His back was bitten up and the politicians, ministers, militants, would-be leaders were still at him. They had betrayed him countless times without the batting of an eyelash. She had pretended not to hear, not to see, and Ken had kept up his end by pretending to be unashamed of their actions, casually dismissing a meeting, luncheon, or conference at which no one showed up nor even called. But they both knew. She was aware too of his delicate, convoluted maneuvering to keep her out of the line of fire, away from black males and females who were hostile to her as well as to him, and who often enough found their marriage the one overwhelming crime of his entire existence.

However, many of his people would have hated him anyway. For the risks he had taken while they found other things to do. They didn't know that he'd put his ass on the line time and time again, and probably wouldn't have cared. They wanted him to lose it. On both sides, though, they were slicing the life out of him. The whites were subtle; the blacks obvious. Her husband was a man in a vise.

"There's one guy who won't be there," Dumpson said. "Guy named Walter Porter. Moon."

"Moon?"

"His head's so big. Had to get a special helmet for him. Anyway, I couldn't locate him. Didn't try too hard, either," he finished grimly.

"Oh?"

"He's supposed to be a big-time pimp."

Sandra laughed. "He start here?"

"Not that anyone knows."

"But he was a success? You all were, you know. Even Bubbles. Not everyone wants to be on top. A lot of people simply want to reach the place where they can live quietly and comfortably."

"I know, baby."

"Ken?"

"Yeah?"

"Why didn't we go to see Bubbles?"

"It wasn't because I felt any kind of superior thing——"

"I know that, honey."

Dumpson said, "I thought about it. But what would we *talk* about when we finished with the kids, the city, and the Bachelors? I think he was just being nice. Reaching back for something good we had as kids. I didn't want it to be awkward. I don't know——"

Sandra turned in her seat toward him. "Silly. We should have gone. That's all most people who have anyone to talk to talk about—their kids, their cities——"

"I guess so. Maybe I just didn't want to do it. I'm tired of handling the past. The old-timers who remember me and my mother, who need a place to live—I just can't send them a letter. Sometimes I call personally. Or I ask them to come in. I can't refer them to the welfare department. I *know* them. Sandy, the past is starting to hurt a little bit. This thing tonight and the weekend, I'm ready for it. I've been getting ready for a month and I don't want to see anything but good times rolling. Got it?"

"Got it."

Sandra lit a cigarette and remembered to open the window. "The big reunion," she said softly. "You can go home again—for a couple of days." After a pause she said, "You know it's all so corny that it's nice? What kind of a man was Chappie?"

Dumpson laughed, throwing back his head. "Numbers runner. Gambler, hard-drinker, cocksman, uncle, father, friend, brother, egomaniac—thought he was another Jim Thorpe, but he wasn't. But he *was there* when no one else was or cared enough to be. And you know, there's some guy just like that in every black community, and there will always be one. So, we just sayin thanks. Bubbles' idea."

"What's Bubbles' real name?"

"You didn't read the papers carefully. Richard. We never called him Dick or Richie. Just Bubbles."

"You must've had some good times, lover. Maybe without even knowing it."

"They were all right, now that I look back. Jesus, Sandy. That seeming vacuum. Today white kids wear Hank Aaron T-shirts. For a long time there we didn't even know there were such things as black ballplayers. Chappie turned us around, hipped us to Cool Poppa Bell, Josh Gibson, and an army of folks. The cat must've done a lot of reading when he wasn't doing other things. The more I think about it, the more I marvel."

Sandra Dumpson watched the houses, lawns, and shrubs as

they passed by. Over the years she had done pretty well imagining a life like her husband's, although her own childhood had been just the opposite. No worries, the future bright and highly visible. This was communicated to her through her parents. She would marry a young college graduate who would become a junior and then, like her father, a senior partner in a prestigious law firm. There would be tennis, riding, trips abroad, work with the Junior League, children, volunteer work for the right politician. She herself had had to prepare for all that. So, off to college. The University here, a great and ancient Methodist institution, then bulging at the seams with returned GIs. Sandra had not been the brightest of high school students and other schools had rejected her applications. Not this one, which won grudging approval of her father, mostly because of its football team.

Ken Dumpson was the biggest thing in the University's history since Vannie Albanese, and there was that certain magic, but more properly a vast, billowing relief that the war was over and a new world, framed by the slogans of freedom and democracy, was about to begin. For Sandra more than a little portion of the magic was composed of her new freedom. She was away from home. No curfew. No casual, but thorough, examination of her dates by her parents. Free to come and go, to feel totally uninhibited with her new Margaret Sanger-issued diaphragm. She could sleep late alone or with someone, cut classes, if she wished.

They met in an American Literature survey course. Where hadn't they made love on that campus? On Jumbo's Back, where he used to go during the Depression to watch the football games. They now called it Mount Zeus. They made love in empty classrooms, day and night, and at least once under the great organ when the DKSs were not playing it to ring the chimes in the Tower. And after, when she stayed on for graduate work and Ken got his own apartment away from his mother, she would slink through the night, her collar pulled up, a hat scrunched down on her head, knowing that behind every curtain and drape in that neighborhood there lurked a busybody. It had been Ken's reputation—star athlete—that had formed a bubble of protection around them.

Quite simply, her parents had shit when she told them she and

Ken were getting married. They had never spoken of, or about, black people; they just didn't exist for them, not even the athletes her father cheered if they were on the team he was rooting for. Black people were as ghosts passing through a house that was temporarily haunted; they would go away in due course, faster if they were not discussed. But they shat. Quietly and in good taste. She had stayed with them that weekend in Huntington, just to be fair, to give them time to have their say, and to bid farewell to a life she did not then believe she would ever live again.

She remembered crying and not knowing why when they stopped in a motel outside Toronto on their honeymoon. Ken vacillated between anger and helplessness, threatening to send her back home in one breath, and trying to soothe her in the next. Maybe, at that particular moment, she had been as much a bigot as her parents, crying at the fix she'd got herself into. That was a long time ago.

Now she played tennis, rode horses, did volunteer work. They lived outside the city, near the Gorge, in a split level with a swimming pool. If people thought about their marriage, and she was sure they did, they no longer showed it the way they once did. Cut off from her parents for ten years, they had come back, filling the house, along with Ken's mother, to share the kids and the holidays. It was funny, and sometimes good, what time did to people.

It'd been some trip for them, passing through the valley, black on the one side, white on the other. But, the way Ken had put it long ago determined the direction they had taken: "In that game against Penn State for the Lambert Trophy, I carried the ball four times out of every five we had the ball. The guys were making the holes inside. I was the only one picking up lines, so I had to carry the ball. I didn't want to. I was whipped, and I didn't want to say no. I just carried the sumbitch until we scored and won. That was all. I had to do it and I did."

Thanks, Chappie, Sandra thought.

Ken Dumpson was slowing now, looking for a place to park. Sandra saw the restaurant sign in phony Greek letters. Glancing at Ken, she saw that he was relaxed, an expression of eagerness creeping over his face.

"Here we go," he said, pulling into a spot, the big car murmuring as he edged it smoothly to the curb.

From his car tucked in a corner of a parking lot at an angle and across the street from the Ebenos, Swoop Ferguson saw the Dumpsons. He said half-aloud, "There goes the Commissioner and his ole lady. He be shitting house keys when I walk in there and snatch Moon out." He drew on the cigarette that was cupped in his hand to hide its glow. Maybe Moon wasn't coming, but spose, just spose he does? Whooooeeeeeeee!

Freshly bathed and dressed, Cudjo Evers and his wife, Evelyn, headed cross-town to pick up Diane Walker. Cudjo pressed a button and the window of his Cadillac slid down. He took a deep breath. The end of November, the smell of December frosts in the air. He liked the smell. "You lookin good, baby."

"Thank you, Cudjo. You smellin like Wilt Chamberlain and Hank Aaron combined." Cudjo had started using Brut cologne when the two athletes advertised it in television commercials.

Evelyn, gone heavier and now firmed up with a girdle and long bra, sighed, then laughed. "Tell you the truth, honey, I did do the best I could with the material I've got to work with."

Cudjo laughed then. "We ain't what we used to be, Ev," and as he said it, he thought of the auditorium of the Center. Spring or fall, it would be, the place a tent of crepe-paper streamers, Duke's band on the record player, the speakers throwing his music across the hall and back, "Things Ain't What They Used to Be," and Cudjo and Evelyn, large even then, in a dark corner doing the Lindy, moving to the music as large people often do, lightly, gracefully—

—there's nothing that can match the grace
of a fat man's rolling, haughty pace—

Cudjo had written those lines in his attic one summer when the jibes about his weight had sent him into hiding and where, in hot, sweating silence he exercised diligently, without losing an ounce.

They had called him "Jelly."

And they had laughed at him when he turned out for Chappie's sandlot teams, but he had the weight for football; he was hard to move and for short distances he was vicious in his blocking. In high school he held down one tackle spot while Moon had the other. He hated the wind sprints, and the laps killed him. The exercises he could fake.

Sometimes, during a game, hungering for the cheers the backs and ends got, Cudjo, after making a spectacular tackle or block, would lay where he had fallen, listening, pleased, to the ref's whistle, and watch through a stricken face the trainer as he straddled him and pulled at his belt to give him air he did not need. And, just when the coach was about to send in a sub, Cudjo would bound to his feet, shaking his head as if to clear it, and signaling that he was all right. Then the cheers came.

He had been a good catcher and a solid hitter, although when the games were close, a pinch runner would have to come in for him.

They had stopped laughing at his size and stopped calling him "Jelly."

He and Evelyn seemed to have been ordained for each other. No one else had ever dated her, and when Cudjo dated other girls, there always came that time when they let him know, one way or the other, that they were just being kind to him. Cudjo and Evelyn did not have children of their own; they were godparents, extended parents of the children of their friends. They were well off, perhaps better off than their friends because of this situation, and, like Bubbles and Onetha, they had managed to acquire a home in a good neighborhood, own two cars, and have a little money in the bank.

Cudjo rested his hand on Evelyn's knee and thought, Couldn't have made it without ole Ev, though. But things were going to be different; maybe rougher. The foundry had just about killed him, and he'd hidden the fact from Evelyn as long as possible. From the first he'd not told her, perhaps from pride, maybe from fear. When he had the operation that fused three of his vertebrae ten years ago, he told Ev he was as good as new. When he'd been forced to wear the brace and take off from work on the average of five days per month, he told her it was because the doctor had advised him to take it a little easier. The doctor in fact had told him that a disc was badly herniated and that continued work in the foundry would leave him a cripple. Some days he got through on Seconal, moving through motions on memory. His shakeout man, a lean young black man just up from home, watched his every move, his every spasmodic jerk. You started as a shakeout man, then moved up to molder—when there was a vacancy. Cudjo knew that Bean was already tasting his job, looking forward to the long bread and to having his own shakeout man to dump the molds, tong out the castings, water the sand, and shovel it over. The shakeout man was the apprentice; the molder was the master.

Yeh. But just what the fuck could he do now that he was fifty? No one at Obanoga was making noises like he could be a boss. Hmmmmm. Maybe he ought to put it to them. Hadn't thought of it. Time they had some black bosses out there, instead of all those Italians and Poles. They were all right when he first started, right after the war; weren't too many Brothers out there then. Now, the foundry was full of them.

Cudjo thought ahead to Monday, saw his machine at the head of, and inside, a circle of rollers upon which he placed the finished molds, but he could not see himself at the machine. He looked, but all he could envision was Bean and a stranger shaking out for him. He'd talk to Ev about it on Sunday, after the JBS functions.

At a traffic light he shifted slightly in his seat. He saw Ev glance at the movement. She did that—glanced and saw everything, but said nothing. Waiting to put her foot down. Now, she reached across and pushed his plastic backrest into place; it had moved out of position when he shifted. She said nothing.

Cudjo drove on, reflecting how he had not been out to play ball on Saturday in three weeks. The games took too much out of him, hauling all his weight around, trying to cut and block, the juices from that eroding disc slipping, sloshing out, the muscles around it rallying to it, tightening and stiffening like a squad protecting a wounded captain.

He and Bubbles had never talked about it, but they were proud they had lasted so long. They'd seen others leave Obanoga with bad lungs, broken fingers, slipped discs, smashed feet, and how about Donelli upon whose head had fallen a truckload of castings? That smashed brain could order the body to do nothing. In the hospital where they visited him, he wore a sheet as a diaper, drooled, and from beneath his head bandages looked blankly at the world. How about Katuzak who had caught a ball of exploding molten brass right in the gut? But they had survived, he and Bubbles. Now there was going to be only Bubbles left. What would he do? Maybe like Ralph's father, he could get a job night-watching a used-car lot to make sure people didn't sneak in and strip the automobiles of everything.

Shit, he thought. He wasn't nearly as old as Ralph's father. Boss? Boss, yes. They wouldn't go for it, them hunkies, just like they hadn't gone for it in pro ball, football, or baseball. Not yet. Basketball was different; but then, Obanoga was a basketball team—nearly all black.

He saw himself Monday morning in Benny Grimm's office, Benny looking up, surprised to see him in street clothes on Monday. Lots of guys went in on Friday to pick up their checks. "What's up, Cudjo?"

And Cudjo throwing down his large envelope with the X-rays in it, all the doctors' reports and warnings, Benny picking them up, but not really seeing anything, Cudjo, taking a seat heavily, and saying, "Benny, can't cut it anymore. I'm looking for a boss job. I got the time in. Lots of bosses around here didn't start until ten years after me. I know the operation. More important, I know the men. Lots of black men out there in the shop—"

That's the way he would put it. If Benny said no— Well, there'd be something else and Obanoga could pay compensation while he did it.

Relieved and a little surprised that the decision had come at last, that he had passed over the hump almost without knowing it, Cudjo put his hand back upon his wife's knee. "Be good to see them cats again." He swung up into Shurley Walker's driveway.

As the headlights flared up on the sturdy, two-story frame house, Diane Walker emerged, walking quickly over the porch and down the steps. Evelyn Evers always envied her slimness; Diane was as slender as she was fat. Evelyn opened the door.

"I'll get in the back, girl," Diane said.

"You tryina say somethin about our size?" Cudjo said. "You better watch yo lip, woman."

"Cudjo, hush," Diane said, leaning from the back seat to kiss him and his wife in turn.

"You smell almost as good as Evelyn, baby. You chicks ain't smelled like this since year one. Ump!"

Cudjo backed out of the drive as Diane said, "Negro, you know I always smell just like this."

"How he supposed to know?" Evelyn asked quickly.

Cudjo laughed.

"See there, Cudjo. You tryna make Ev think we inta somethin. But you know I couldn't be carrying all that weight on top a me, don't you, girl?"

Now Evelyn laughed. "Sometimes it's even too much for me."

"You mean after you all through feelin good, dontcha?" Cudjo said.

The car filled with their repartee and laughter as it moved along the streets. Cudjo could not think of anyone else he and Ev ever joked with about their weight beside Diane and Shurley.

"That your new wig, Di?" Evelyn asked.

"Girl, you know that's my natural hair."

"Natural dynel from the wig shop. How do you like mine?"

"Ooo, my, that's a nice one, honey."

"Really like it?"

"It's a nice one, Ev. We be showin those folks from Europe, California, and Missouri that we inta somethin. They be thinkin we ain't nothin but hicks."

"Amen," Cudjo said, chucklin. "If I was from Europe, California, or Missouri, I'd sure be turned on by them wigs. Sho would."

"Aw, Cudjo, be quiet." Diane sighed. "Shurley's been at the joint just about all day, setting this thing up."

"I know it's gonna be boss," Cudjo said. "When Shurl puts his mind to something, that's the only way it can turn out."

"I wonder what Chris is like these days," Diane mused aloud.

Evelyn turned to face her directly. "You've been wondering too, huh?"

Cudjo said, "You chicks is a mess."

"I wonder if you'd say that if you were married to Chris," Diane said.

"Just drive, Cudjo," Evelyn said.

"I know ole Chops can handle things," he said.

"She sure was hustling after Bubbles," Diane said.

"Long time ago," Cudjo threw back. He slid his eyes toward his wife. "Diane, you know anything about Moon gettin word of this thing? We couldn't get in touch with him."

Cudjo knew, but Shurley didn't, that Moon had copped Diane's drawers a number of times before they, Shurley and Diane, got married.

"Don't know anything about it," she said testily.

Evelyn grinned in the darkness. Behind her, Diane fell silent.

After a while Cudjo said, "I wonder what Clarie's ole lady's like."

"Probably the same color as Dart's wife," Diane sniffed.

"Oooo, girl, what you said." Evelyn felt devilish.

Wearily Cudjo said, "Forget it."

"I don't know about Ev," Diane said. "But I'm only teasing, Cudjo. You know I couldn't care less about who married who. I'm just not as cool as you. I talk about things, but I don't mean any harm. You think I want to mess up all the work you, Bubbles, and Shurley've done? Yeah, big shot. Shurley tells me you haven't been out to play ball in three weeks. Getting old, baby."

Softly Cudjo said, "Well, Di, I tell you. I think you're right." Then Diane's voice reached him filled with the hollows of reflection, of thoughts never voiced: "Shurley said you were smarter than the rest. At fifty maybe it was time to stop being eighteen. Said maybe he'd quit those Saturday games, too."

They were silent for the length of several blocks. Cudjo began to hum and Evelyn and Diane joined him before he realized that the tune was "Things Ain't What They Used to Be."

Swoop Ferguson ducked quickly when the sweep of the headlights swung into, and past, the corner of the parking lot. The car backed out and he sat up, watching it. Ole Cudjo's Caddie. Cudjo and Evelyn must got over half a ton together. On the hoof. He watched them park and recognized Diane Walker as the third member of the group. Ferguson watched the women pull at and smooth their dresses, pat their hair. He felt, just for a second, a surge of envy that he and his wife were not at this very moment entering the Ebenos to renew old friendships; they did not have many friends. Everyone shunned cops except other cops. Then he shifted in his seat, glancing at the luminous dials on his watch.

Entering the Ebenos, his face changing, slipping into a grin, as he scanned the room, Cudjo nevertheless felt the eyes on his back and wondered what the hell Swoop's car was sitting in the parking lot for, with Swoop undoubtedly in it, so he could have an unobstructed view of the front of the restaurant.

TWELVE

Pat Henderson looked up at the new arrivals. She could have laughed. Mr. and *Mrs.* Five by Five, accompanied by Madame Thin. She smiled at them over her drink as her husband, Clarence, bopped (there was no other way to put it, really) toward them, his arms held stiffly at his sides, hunkering in his back, his feet coming clean up off the floor, shouting and hugging, joined by the man who was the commissioner—Snake? And Dart, Ralph, and the one called Chops.

It reminded Pat of a Methodist church dinner in Watts. She tried first to catch the eye of the European woman, Dart's wife, Simone. But she was involved in the drama at the door and her smile was warm, approving, and tender. Pat shifted her glance to the other white woman, Sandra; she too was taking it all in, with something like wonderment. Her eyes then moved to Eve Joplin and Pat was startled to discover that she was studying her. Without blinking, Pat Henderson looked again at the group. Mewing and cooing, Chops's wife had thrown herself into the melee. Sure was a frisky woman. Maybe too frisky.

And the old man, Mr. Davis, was in seventh heaven.

Simone's smile widened as the group approached her at the end of the table. Dart was saying, "Here's me, man. Simone. Honey, this is Cudjo and Evelyn Evers, and Diane is Shurley's wife." Cudjo ignored Simone's outstretched hand and bent to kiss her cheek. Straightening, he said, "Every gal gets some of this heavy sugar tonight."

"Cudjo, you been into vitamin E or Ginseng?"

Cudjo ignored Chris Jackson. "Eve. Mmmmm! How you manage to put up with Ralph all this time?"

"Sandra?" he said. "Well hello there. About time we got together." Kiss.

"Pat," he said, having read her, "you may not like this, but you gonna get a kiss anyway."

Eyes glinting, Pat laughed and placed a hand in a tender position against his head as he kissed her cheek.

When he raised he said, "Hey 'Netha, sappening?"

Finished with the wives of the newcomers, Cudjo reared back before the seat being held for him by one of the grinning young waiters, while Mickey Mouse hovered near waiting for his drink order. Flapping his arms like a monstrous, joyful bird, Cudjo said loudly: "Well how you cats doin anyway?"

He was drowned in a burst of laughter as he gave his order to Mickey Mouse.

"Same ole——"

"We were in Amsterdam in——"

"You looking good, man, Jesus——"

"Chris? Foxy, baby, foxy. You know——"

"——ole Shurley's still as cool as Dracula's freezer——"

"Clarie, my man, you 'bout as goddamn dap as ever——"

"——1966 I guess it was. Stayed on——"

"Swimming and jogging man——"

"——nowhere near seventy as far as I can see, Coach——"

"——yessir! Lookin just like one of these high-butted chippies——"

"——nice place, Shurl, really nice——"

"Lissen, Bubbles——"

"——and he's hittin it about 182 pounds——"

"——died and wanted to be buried here——"

"——Barney Moore, yeah, we go back a long way——"

"——*Monsters in Manhattan,* fantastic play, man——"

"——marvelous town, although, frankly, if I could afford it, we'd live in Paris because——"

"——Allison's just about to make us grands——"

"——Onetha——"

"——Juice get him a couplea hard shots when he's makin a cut like Sayres and it's——"

"Lissen, Bubble——"

"——expect too much from black writers——"

"——school like here or Penn State, good chance at All-American this year——"

"——Iran, Shurl? Isn't that a CIA outpost?"

"——seein him tomorrow. Going to the cemetery——"

"——format, bigger type, more space, fatter ads——"

"——on the *plane?* Moon on the plane?"

"——and said he was coming." Henderson's voice was suddenly alone and clear of the babble of voices, odd-ends of conversations.

Chappie Davis leaned forward. "What's that, Clarie? You saw Moon, and he's coming?"

"On the plane, Coach. Thought he was coming for this. When I told him, he said he'd come."

Sandra Dumpson glanced at her husband, then at her glass. "The cat is bald. Not a lick of hair."

Shurley asked the question. "Is it true?"

Henderson paused. "Yeah. He just about said so."

Chappie Davis leaned back in his chair and laughed. When these men were kids, their eyes shone when the local pimp walked by, dressed up, passing out dimes. "Pimps make good money. And money's what it's all about."

"He was turned out like money," Pat said.

Cudjo had by now managed to get Bubbles' eye. They sauntered toward the kitchen.

"Swoop's sittin out there in the parking lot," Cudjo said.

Bubbles looked at him carefully, seeking the full import of his words, and when they impacted, he said, "For Moon?"

Cudjo said, "Dunno, man. Must not be anybody else. He's the only one who hasn't come in. But I never heard about any papers on Moon. You?"

"No."

They stood at the entrance to the kitchen watching Sugar spin, wheel, settle and begin sharpening a knife.

"Whatsat, Sug?"

"You boys leave me alone now. Prime ribsa beef Aw Jews. Just get on back now. Tell Mickey Mouse he can open some of the wine now, and get it on the table." He looked at them and frowned. "An' you better eat, too."

"Wine?"

"Wine. Good, French wine."

"Shurl's *really*——"

"C'mon, OUT!"

"We goin, Sug."

They moved a few steps from the kitchen. "Lissen, Bubbles. Suppose Moon does show up tonight or tomorrow or at the banquet?"

"He's got the right," Bubbles said stubbornly. He looked at the table filled with merriment. "He's got the right," he said again. "But we got the right to expect him to be clean *here*."

Cudjo persisted. "But if Swoop's got some papers on him?"

Bubbles continued to survey the scene in front of him: Shurley making a show of inspecting the wine bottle labels, the heads bowed in a cluster around Chappie, as if he were the sun and his listeners the orbiting planets. The pleasure emanating from the table was palpable, the scene was good, warm. Black, white, men, women, the gang, with its additions, back together. He, Bubbles, with Shurley and Cudjo, with help from Snake, had reached into the far corners of places and gathered these people. Now he had to protect them. Fair was fair. He said to Cudjo without turning, "I don't know what we do. Let's start by calling his momma."

Moon had left New York that morning, driving slowly through Harlem first, noticing the changes: the expensive new high-risers thrusting north from 110th Street, the State Office Building in Harlem Square, the streets gray and nearly empty before the first tentative onslaughts of The Hawk. He cut to the West Side highway, his new wig resting easily upon his scalp, the other in his bag in the trunk of the car.

Eventually he found himself on the Thruway; it would lead, more directly than he wished, to his home. When he stopped for coffee he lined out a route on his map that would take him through the state's interior. Prettier than California, he'd always told people about upstate. Once he left the Thruway he was glad. Here were the single homes commanding acres of land, not developments nor fastways filled with cars. Here too were the sad little towns that would have to become Woodstocks or sink into nothingness between the hills.

Moon had seen them before but not paid attention until he saw the first car with a buck affixed to the top, then another. He began to glance at the cars which were filled with blue-jowled men dressed in red and gold caps and jackets. Hunting season. He'd almost forgotten his boyhood autumns, probably because of football, when the older men, sniffing the frost in the air, memories of the hunt in southern forests given voice, took down their rifles and shotguns, gave them cleanings they didn't need, and went for their hunting licenses; he'd not remembered the taste of fried squirrel or rabbit killed by Uncle Jasper and cooked by his mother.

Over music from the car radio, Moon laughed to himself, remembering Mr. Richard, one of those old men, who loved to relate the details of how he cooked navy beans with onions and piece of fatback, a pinch of Arm & Hammer baking soda. Mr. Richard liked to hunt coons at night with his mangy old dogs. Christ, they didn't make people like him any more; the quiet, lovable neighborhood drunk. He tipped his hat, gave kids nickels, when he had them, and minded his own business. He was just as available to run errands for Ransom, Gideon, or Saslow as to rescue people from a burning house. He went fishing one day and never came back. They found his half-empty bottle of gin and a good-sized bass on his line. Mr. Richard didn't know how to swim.

It was past noon when Moon's hunger took hold and he pulled into the parking lot of a batten-board-sided hotel. The sign said: THE BEAR AND BUCK *Hunters and Skiers Welcome.* He got out of his car and stood in the mountain silence. He saw, beyond the cars parked there, a lake reflecting the blue and gold of the sky, and a row of white cottages.

Nice, he thought.

A black man smiled at him from inside the entrance and pushed the door open for him.

Moon hesitated. The man's smile deepened, as if understanding.

"I'm looking for some lunch," Moon said.

"Right up the stairs here," the man said gesturing. "Red beans and rice and pork chops. These hunters get hungry, you know. Been out there all morning working up an appetite."

Moon stepped in past him and waited, for what he didn't know.

"My name's Heflin," he said, sticking out his hand.

Sounds and acts like he owns this joint, Moon thought, shaking hands. "Coles," he said. "This your store?"

Heflin had seen through Moon's attempt to conceal his curiosity. It never failed to surprise people, black and white, that a black man not only lived in these mountains, but owned a hotel too. And yet, Heflin had discovered, you never knew when a black housewife, kid, or husband was going to cross the main street of one of these towns; they crossed with the airs of people who've had roots here for generations.

"Yep. All mine. A hundred acres."

Moon glanced at Heflin with new eyes, a sudden sense of possibility startling him.

"C'mon," Heflin said. "I got to go up." He was a thin, spare man whose stride took the carpeted steps two at a time.

"How long you had the place?"

"Fifteen years."

Moon heard music and voices. Heflin explained: "The hunters get started before the crack of dawn. But there's nothin movin out there this time of day. They come in eat, drink, and get warmed up."

The hunters looked up from their tables, saw that Moon was not one of them, and returned to their food.

Oversized windows let stream in the bright daylight, and Moon, caught in the glare, the lake shimmering in the distance and beyond it framed by the leafless trees, an infinity of space, stopped and took a deep breath. He knew Heflin was waiting for a word of praise, but he said more to himself than to the man beside him, "Goddamn, it's nice."

Heflin chuckled modestly, leading Moon to a table at a window. Moon was still looking out when Heflin asked, "Where you from, Coles?"

"The City."

"Uh-huh," Heflin said, nodding his head slowly. "Yeah. Course most of my business comes from the folks down in the City and Jersey. Even these white boys."

Moon had the feeling that Heflin did not believe him.

"I used to work in the City," Heflin went on. "But it got to be too much. Want a drink?"

"Yeah——"

"How about a French 75 up here in the mountains?"

Moon searched Heflin's face for an expression and found none. "A French 75?" he asked knowing that it used to be a pimp's drink: gin, champagne, and trimmings. A stone dick-licker.

"Used to drink them all the time." Now Heflin's smile hinted. "Still do, once in a while."

"Just some scotch," Moon said. "And I'll have the red beans and rice and chops."

"Coming up."

Moon was glad for the respite. The man was smooth; he moved without shifting gears, and was always alert. Heflin bothered Moon. Even so, he was aware of a growing excitement as he looked at the scene outside. Shhhhhhh . . . t! Dorrie and *me*, like this in Canada!

He wondered if the fact that he was the only black in the restaurant was what made Heflin return to the table with a bottle. "They'll be out in a few minutes with your food, Coles." He poured with a long, soft sigh, held his glass aloft, and they drank. "Might as well catch up with the guests," he said. "Otherwise, by five or six o'clock I couldn't stand them."

"What'd you do in the City?" Moon thought he'd get to that before Heflin did.

Heflin laughed and swirled the fluid in his glass. "I guess you could say I was a pimp." He winked at Moon. "I got out, came up here. White folks gave me a hard time, but I had the bread; they couldn't stop me. They don't bother me too much now. And the State Troopers aren't like the City cops. They're overgrown farm boys with small-time hustles, like tie-ins with auto wreckers, things like that."

"I was in the recording business," Moon said. He wished he'd worn something else; he felt that Heflin had priced every article of clothing on his body—just the way he often did with people.

Heflin grimaced, impatiently, Moon thought. "Yeah, I hear that's rough."

"Well, I want to retire too."

"Everybody's gettin to that point, aren't they?" Heflin snorted.

"How do I get down like this?" Moon gestured toward the window, stretching back from the table so the waiter could set down his steaming plate of food, and upon which Heflin looked with pride.

"Where you want to get down?"

"Oh, just say any place."

Heflin shrugged. "Try to buy something that's already up. If not, you've got to buy the land and build. Near a lake, if you can. Or get right-of-way to one. Also, not far from ski and hunting areas. Give you year-around business, almost." Heflin poured them another drink. He glanced up at Moon, his brows arched. "You were playin Chelsea about twenty years ago, weren't you?"

Moon laughed to cover his alarm. That seedy block, south side of the street, Twenty-third Street, closer to Tenth Avenue than Ninth, overheated rooms filled with low-wattage bulbs, his girls operating out of them.

"I told you," he said. "I was in music. Recording."

"Okay, Coles. I guess I made a mistake."

"What's it take to get a start?"

Heflin rubbed his chin. No skin off his ass if the man wanted to be somebody else. "Forty, fifty thousand would give you some options. The more you got, or can *git*, the better off you are, like anything else."

Moon said, "I think I'll stay overnight. Got a cabin? I'd like to do some walking and looking and thinking."

"Sure, man, I got some space. And about seven tonight, we'll get a few country girls in. They drop around to drink with the hunters, you know." Heflin's look was open, innocent.

"A phone?"

"There's one in your cottage. Unless you want to use the booth; it's downstairs."

Later, in the Ebenos, Cudjo watched Bubbles' face as Bubbles hung up the phone. He saw there relief chased by doubt, chased by suspicion. "What?" he asked.

Sugar huffed by, holding high the huge platter of aromatic beef.

"She doesn't know anything about his coming." Bubbles was speaking rapidly, one eye on the table. "She hasn't heard from him in about three weeks." They started to move toward the table.

"Well, it's not something Clarie would lie about," Cudjo said. They started toward the table.

Anyone else they would have called a lying old bitch. Not Mrs. Porter. She had fed them in her restaurant for as long as she'd had it when they were kids; had pushed them pork chop and chicken sandwiches, sodas, candy bars; she had sprung for the movies on countless Sunday afternoons, for there was always someone who didn't have movie money. Mrs. Porter was all right. Even after she lost the restaurant because there was no business, she still gave. If she was protecting Moon, well, she was supposed to; couldn't blame her for that.

But, Bubbles thought, what about *us?*

Chappie felt a little ill at ease. Not with Shurley, Bubbles, and Cudjo, but with the others. How they had changed. How well they spoke. Sometimes when they spoke, even jokingly, they reminded him of the great black men whom he'd heard and seen on television. He felt, he told himself, the way the older Jewish people did about Abba Eban. Chappie was most at ease when they talked the way they used to. As Sugar came to the table, all broken-toothed smiles, with Mickey Mouse and Clifford and Marvin fluttering near, and everyone was oohing and ahing, Chappie looked at Shurley. Now was the time for Shurley to tell them. Tell em Shurley. Tell em the place is yours, that you've owned it for a long time. Go 'head. But Shurley was talking to Dumpson and Bubbles:

"It never bothered me. George was interested for a while, and you know, I'd take him to games and throw with him, and he made the teams and all, but he just up and quit. Maybe the kids don't need it anymore——"

"——my kid was just like that," Ezzard Jackson put in. "Except that he wasn't very good. Really. I didn't mind it. Kids have sense now. They don't want to be pulling through wind sprints and practice and stuff; they'd rather be out boppin on the corner——"

"——don't know why it bothers me so much," Dumpson said. "The kid's as big as a house."

"——doesn't mean that they're any less manly, because they don't want to play ball," Dart said.

Bubbles felt somewhat put upon. It wasn't his fault that Rick liked sports, especially football. Like the others, Bubbles had carried his kid to the games and played with him. Although Bubbles had made All-City in track, he wished he'd made it in football, to give him a better position in the conversation. He suspected that Chops, Snake, and maybe Shurley felt that a continuity had been broken, even betrayed.

Why Bubbles' kid, Dumpson wondered, and not mine or Shurley's or Snake's or Chops's. "What do you think, Chappie?" he asked.

"Don't think nothin about it. Some do, some don't; some will, some won't. Colored kids today don't need football as much as you all did. Need it, but not as much, you understand. Back then, the thing was to be somebody. Today, it's to get money. Being somebody—that's changed. Money'll make you be somebody. Maybe that's the way it always was. But, when you look at the pros, that's all you see is colored boys, Italian boys, Polish boys. Don't see no Endicott Chub Peabodys the third any more. Never did see that many Jews—course, that Sid Luckman was bad enough to last generations, and Marshall Goldberg, outa Pittsburgh, remember him, you all? Now you sees them Spanish-speaking boys and, God help us, all them crackers!" Chappie paused as the room filled with laughter. "I'm not jokin. You add up all the quarterbacks, all the white runnin backs and linemen, and pro football is filled with crackers—"

Ralph broke in through the laughter. "And the Giants get all the ones with bad knees. Cold weather in the Stadium must make them brittle or something."

Chappie waited, tapping his knife on the tablecloth, until it was almost quiet again. "You see what I'm gettin at? Them that ain't got down there in the pit every week, like in the factories and construction work; the same people, fightin to make a dollar and hopin that dollar will make them be somebody. Oh, it's different now."

"Would you change the way you brought them up, Mr. Davis?" Sandra Dumpson asked. She was pleased to see heads nodding in agreement; hers was a good question.

"No," Chappie said without hesitation. "Wouldn't change a thing. I know I was right, and I know I did the right things for the times. Can't none of us know about tomorrow, you understand. Just do the best we can."

"You know," Bubbles said, not believing it as the words were coming, "maybe you guys gave your kids the feeling of being somebody without them having to get out on the field. Maybe *I* didn't do such a good job." Finished, a shock hit him, as if he'd swallowed ice water too quickly. Could Rick have been ashamed of him because he worked in a foundry—

Onetha saw the stricken look that flashed on his face for a part of a second, then vanished; she'd been his wife long enough to have seen what others could not, and she bristled at the idea that Bubbles had not been the best of fathers; she was angered that, while in the process of trying to make everyone feel better, he had stumbled momentarily into depression himself. She said, thrusting her words into a momentary void in the conversation, "Bubbles, you know Rick and Allison couldn't have had a better father."

"Sure looks like it to me," Ralph said.

"I'm sure, *positive*, that you're all wonderful parents," Simone said. "It is something I feel, yes? In just a short time. We envy you very much."

Ralph wondered how his son—if he'd had one—would've fared. Fathers rarely worried about their sons as much as they fretted over their daughters, or so he had always thought, until tonight. "Besides," he said. "It really isn't any of our business any more what they do or don't do. We've got to turn them loose." He tasted the wine. "Hey, Shurley. This wine is talkin, Jim. Solid on the case."

Clarie was rolling the wine around on his tongue, inhaling with his throat, letting the fluid trickle over his taste buds, and thinking that Shurley really knew his wines when Bubbles rose to his feet.

"Well, here we are, Coach," he said. "Everybody but Moon. We was gonna make this a simple thing, if you can call the banquet simple. But Shurley wanted to have this quiet dinner, just for us. Then the Black Arts Festival people came along and wanted to do their thing, and then there's the big banquet, so it isn't simple any more." He held up his wine glass. "We just wanted to say thanks, Chappie. And me and Shurley and Cudjo and Snake want to thank you guys for coming with your fine-looking people." He paused and said more softly, "Sure is good to see you. To the Junior Bachelor Society and Chappie Davis."

Chappie, weaving a little, got to his feet. Sugar looked out of the kitchen an encouraging smile on his face. Chappie looked around the table. "All my boys but Moon. Yessir. Some of you gone, you know, like Redbones, Greek, and Jake. Gone before their time. Others just fell off the wagon I was trying to pull up the hill. Slick, Ace, Chuck, Moe, and some others. But that's the way it always is. I look around now and I'm proud. We've been through some rough times, good and bad, but at least *we have been* an can say so, stand right here an say so, and that's a lot better than what's happened to a whole lots of people." He waved his hands slowly, as if culling the air for more to say, and finding nothing, sat down.

"Git em, Coach," Henderson said, starting to clap, and they took it up, pounding their palms loudly.

"Eat! Eat! The food gonna get cold!" Sugar, holding a glass of scotch, circled the table patting shoulders and pushing platters.

Shurley raised his chin toward Mickey Mouse as, suddenly, the table became busy with platters being passed back and forth, knives screeching on plates, and with conversation muted by food in the mouth. Then, as if approaching from a long way off, they heard Lionel Hampton's vibraharp. Shurley smiled as he watched them hesitate, forks suspended in mid-air.

"Hamp," Dart said.

"——Benny Goodman——"

"Teddy Wilson——"

"Gene Krupa——"

Puzzled, Simone Foxx looked around.

"'The Man I Love,'" Dart explained. "A tune we used to know when we were kids."

"Ole Hamp," Ralph said. How many times had he seen him in person, leading his band down through the aisles in the rousing finale of a concert with "Flying Home."

Diane slid a glance at her husband and winked. Shurley winked back and peeked up from his food to see what their reaction would be to the next tune. He knew what it was from the opening guitar chords. This used to be everyone's favorite.

"Danny Barker!" Ezzard Jackson shouted. The guitar chords

were immediately followed by big, breathy tenor sax notes, and everyone stilled. "Body and Soul."

"Chu *Berry*," Snake said. To Sandra his voice sounded wistful and she wondered which of the women here he had loved, danced with, thought about.

Chu Berry was still working around the theme and heavy under him, the piano, bass, drums, and guitar.

Jesus, Dart thought. Listen to that rhythm section.

"Work, Big Sid," Snake called out.

"That's Roy Eldridge on trumpet," Onetha said. "But who's the bass?"

"Artie Shapiro," said Shurley. "And Clyde Hart on piano."

"We used to wail on this one, didn't we, poppa?" Evelyn said to Cudjo.

"Tore em up, honey."

Patting the table with his fingers, Chappie said, "Member when Duke Ellington came here the very first time. Played down on the Boulevard. All the dances they done had in this town, colored folks never had their own hall until a few years ago. Always had to rent from somebody else—the Polish Legion Hall, Volinsky's Hall, and finally the Elks got them a hall." Chappie was talking to Sandra and Simone now. "But we had them all here. Basie, Chick Webb, Lunceford, Erskine Hawkins, and these boys would take their little money and buy records every week. Dancinest bunch of little fools you ever did see. They tried to make up dances, put in a straight-arm move or somethin like that. Bet Snake never told you he took up the drums once; and Chops over there, he had him a saxaphone; always wore the cord around his neck so people would know he was a musician, didn't you, Chops? Clarie, now, he thought he was another Herb Jefferies, you understand, and Dart, over there, he had him another kind of music, but music right on, if you like that kind. Ralph's sister, what's her name? Iris! That's it. She got to be a big singer in Europe. Well, her daddy and Ralph's used to be a singer around town here. What, you know her? Is that right?"

Listening to Coleman Hawkins, Roy Eldridge, John Kirby, Sid Catlett, Bernie Addison, and Benny Carter on piano instead of alto playing "I Surrender Dear," Christine Jackson thought, He knows.

When her husband's eyes fell on her they were cold, contemptuous, not unmixed with hurt. But how could he know? By what means could he have come to know? So many people hated him that, even if they knew, they would have cheered for her. Suppose he knows, then what?

Deny it, no matter what. Deny, deny, deny. There are things no man wishes to know. He may see and touch the truth, but he will walk away wanting it to be a mirage, *willing* it to be a mirage.

Onetha Wiggins looked at Christine and thought of a plumpish cat lounging on a sofa in sunlight; her body was hunched in deceptive repose, completely aware of all sight, sound, and movement about her. Onetha had never liked Christine. Her dislike had nothing to do with the way she chased after Bubbles; it had to do with what the kids now called vibrations; they were all bad. Onetha caught the glance that passed between Chris and Ezzard midway through Jimmy Lunceford's "Blues in the Night." Sadly, Onetha turned away to talk to Simone.

Christ, Dart was thinking as the meal moved to its end, only coffee and dessert left. Listen to the *music*. We grew up with so much of it. No wonder these guys nowadays want to be known as musicians, not *jazz* musicians.

BOO WAPPA DO AH, WA-WA

BOO WAPPA DO AH, WA-WA

"C'mon, Bubbles, let's dance," Onetha said. Beat that bitch, Christine, Onetha thought, leading Bubbles to the small dance area.

Cudjo said, "Is that 'Redskin Rhumba' or 'Cherokee'? They both start the same way, right?"

"Umph! That Indian sure had him some soul, didn't he?" Evelyn said, tugging at Cudjo. But Cudjo ignored her. Damned if he was going to throw his back out in front of everyone.

"Goddamn!" Sugar exclaimed as he came up beside the grinning student waiters and Mickey Mouse. "Those Negroes cuttin a rug, ain't they?" His face glowed, and in his hand was another glass of scotch. He started moving in a dance reminiscent of the Black Bottom, and Marvin and Clifford who fancied themselves as the best rock dancers on campus, bent double laughing and slapped palms.

But as they watched, they felt both pride and sadness. Bubbles and Onetha whirling around and around, trying to stay on the beat, popping their fingers and tapping their toes, could have been their parents; their folks Lindying and boogie-woogieing, which was the way they wished them to be. These people sitting at the table and dancing age had not yet captured. Maybe in the morning, but for the moment it was no contest. They wondered if, when they reached fifty, they would be doing this.

". . . You hear the drummer drumm-ing, drumboogie, drumboogie . . ."

"Ella."

"No. Anita O'Day. Sounded like sisters, those chicks. She wailed with her own style, man. Didn't try to copy someone else's like these rock people, always trying to sound black." Chops watched Snake and his wife start dancing.

Snake wanted to cut loose, fling his body and snap it back, move every muscle in time to the music. But Sandra danced another way, just off the beat, always a second late. She'd not improved over the years. Now, Snake ignored it; she'd just have to keep up with him.

Sandra hadn't wanted to dance. She knew she wasn't very good, and had hoped that Ken would lead her in a fast fox trot. She felt intimidated by the black women; she was sure all of them danced extremely well. Ken should've danced with someone else. Sensing his frustration, Sandra grew angry, and in that anger, she began moving faster; her steps and whirls were more decisive, even anticipatory of his moves. She gasped and smiled at her husband. He returned her smile and began shaking his head from side to side, too, cockily; and once he breathed past her ear, "Wail, baby."

When the number was over and "Jumpin at the Woodside" was already up, Ken put his arm around her and led her back to the table. "Let's rest. I haven't moved that fast in a long time. Not even tennis gets to you like these numbers. No wonder we were always in such good shape." He knew that Sandra had hit a peak. He would not push her. For the rest of the night, they'd dance only on the slow pieces.

"How marvelous," Simone said to Sandra, her face beaming, as if at the champion of a people. "You dance so *well*. I myself could never dance those dances; oh, my, I couldn't. So fast and intricate."

Behind the heads of their wives, Dart and Snake winked at each other.

"Let's dance, baby," Chris said to her husband.

"No," he said, and moved the elbow upon which she had rested her fingers as if to disengage himself from her touch.

"What's the matter, baby?" she asked, leaning close to him.

"What isn't?" The note in his pocket seemed to have gathered weight.

"I thought you were having a good time."

"It's all right."

"But better without me, right, honey?"

Ezzard Jackson turned to watch Dart and Simone, dancing on a slow number.

THIRTEEN

Swoop Ferguson was tired. He pushed himself up, hearing their voices echoing up and down the quiet street. He saw them emerging from the Ebenos in a clutch, arm in arm, and move slowly, assuredly, like a band of conquering heroes and heroines, toward their cars. Nearly all the automobiles were driven off in the direction of Cudjo's home. Swoop sat upright, glancing at his watch. He cursed, and drummed his stiffened fingers on the steering wheel. Well, they might not have invited Moon, him being a pimp. That's about the case. Them being big shots and all. Even Bubbles and Cudjo think they shit don't stink. Swoop squinted into the darkness. More than likely that's it. Me and Moon, we're about in the same class; they don't like either one of us. Still, it would be a helluva collar for ole Swoop.

He started his engine and pulled slowly out of the parking lot, the cinders under his tires crackling loudly. He drove slowly past Moon's mother's house, hoping he wouldn't run into a squad car. Not in this city, the force was too small, but in other, larger cities the white cops were steady wiping out black cops—by accident(?)—who looked just like any other Negro in certain situations. Like driving slowly through these streets checking license plates for out-of-town cars. Not finding any on the immediate block, Swoop enlarged his search for three blocks in each direction. Nothing from out of town, and the house itself, like others in the neighborhood, was darkened and silent.

Swoop sighed like a man who has done his job well and looks forward to his rest.

Cudjo and Bubbles could hear their wives upstairs above them, talking under the hum of the dishwasher. They'd all had brandy and coffee while wrapping up the first night's visit with each other. Chappie had fallen asleep in his chair; Shurley had been on the verge of doing the same. Dart had been nervous about his performance tomorrow, and Ralph and Simone had talked intensely about his sister in Barcelona. Chops, Bubbles, Clarie, Snake, and Cudjo had been into what-happened-to-whom, and Sandra, Chris, Evelyn, Onetha, Diane, and Eve had been talking about the women's movement and politics.

They were gone now. Bubbles and Cudjo, cues held in their hands, lightly circled the pool table in the cellar, tall drinks set aside on a nearby table. Cudjo stopped, sighted and tapped a side pocket with his cue stick. "I'ma bank that three-ball right there."

Bubbles yawned. "Man, you haven't made a bank shot in ten years. G'on, fool."

Cudjo sighted down his cue. "Funny," he said. "Ralph and Dart with them beards and Clarie with all that hair."

"Yeah. That's the style. An you know we always was a stylish gang."

Cudjo's cue slid deftly back and forth through his finger bridge; it darted forward, smacking the cue ball sharply, and it hit the three ball, which plunged smartly into the pocket, and then, as if magnetized, the cue ball followed it right in. "Shit," Cudjo said. "I put too much run on the sumbitch."

"You wouldn't know run English if it stomped you, Cudjo." Bubbles studied the balls highlighted on the baize table by the light above. He sipped his drink. He said, "Chops was lookin a little uptight about something."

"Yeah." It was Cudjo's turn to yawn. "Maybe Snake's wife. You see her on that floor, man? I thought her butt was gonna break off, the way she was shakin it."

Bubbles laughed. "For a minute I thought ole Chops was gonna bite it."

"She's a lotta fun, that chick."

Abruptly Bubbles said, "Time I stopped foolin around with you, big man. I'ma run, startin with that eleven ball in that corner." Bubbles bent and sighted.

"Okay, Minnesota Fats. Stop the crap n go."

Bubbles miscued and stared with chagrin as the cue ball rolled limply against a cushion.

"Well, dere, Kingfish, look lak you done blowed de shot,"

Cudjo said. Instead of moving to the table, he racked his cue. "Hey, Bubble, what're we gonna do, man?"

Bubbles slid his cue into the rack and began rolling the balls up and down the table. He picked up his drink again and sipped from it. "Hope the cat don't show up. That's the first thing. I mean, if he ain't clean."

Cudjo took up his own drink. "We're really thinking about the second thing. If he does show up."

"Well, if Swoop was watching us, you can bet there were cops watching his mother's house."

"Yeah?"

Bubbles scowled. "Why? What'd he do?"

Cudjo said, "Enough to have Swoop sittin out there, that's what. Why don't we just ask Swoop what's up?"

Bubbles looked at Cudjo as if that perhaps was the answer; his look turned into a jeer. "When was the last time you spoke to Swoop? Do you think he'd tell us what's going on?"

Cudjo tossed the chalk into the air and caught it. "Okay. Why don't we call Miz Porter again and tell her *if* Moon shows up, he should leave right away?"

Bubbles jerked his head up. "We my ass. *You* call that ole lady and tell her the cops're lookin for Moon. Not we, *you.*"

Cudjo sat down with a sigh. Nearly everyone in town had been involved in the elaborate game of pretending not to know that Moon was a pimp; they'd done it for years, taking their cues from Mrs. Porter: "Oh, Walter's doin just fine in New York. Nice job, sends money all the time." Or, "Walter's been in Chicago so long, you know, and he's been doin so good that he thought he'd try his luck in California." They'd never seen Moon on his rare visits home, but Bubbles and Cudjo heard about them. "Heard Moon was in town driving a hog damn near a block long, two *fine* chicks with him." Or, "Moon came in to see his Momma and his ride was a gold Mark IV, and he looked like he *owned* Hart, Schafner and Marx. He was with some heavy foxes."

It'd been at least ten years since Moon's last visit, but almost every year the women's club at the church had a big send off for Mrs. Porter who was going to visit her boy. Moon, all the old women said, was a good son. Whatever he was, and they were not about to talk about that, he was good to his mother. Let Mrs. Porter go to her grave with her illusions; that was her right.

"Well," Cudjo said. "What else we got?"

"We got tomorrow——" Bubbles glanced at his watch and smiled. "No, *today* and tomorrow, then it'll be over. I mean, no shit'll rub off on anybody if we can take care of business. After tomorrow night's banquet, it's every swingin dick for himself. We're not workin today; why don't we just keep an eye on ole Swoop? If there's somethin shakin, maybe we can talk to him as a last resort——"

Bubbles broke off, hearing the footsteps. Evelyn and Onetha were coming down. "Whatchall talkin about?" Onetha said. "Sandra's big behind, I bet."

"Or maybe Ralph's wife," Evelyn said. "Cute thing. I'll have to tell April."

"If I know April," Bubbles said, "she's been knowing, but she don't have nothin to be upset about. She's a pretty good-lookin woman herself."

"Oooo, but it's late." Evelyn sat down as she spoke. "Yes, indeedy. Late. But, we still want to know what's going on, you guys."

"What do you mean?" Cudjo said.

Speaking at the same time, Bubbles said, "Going on?"

Evelyn and Onetha looked at each other. "Told you," Onetha said. She sat down, too, and patiently folded her hands in her lap. She looked from her husband to Cudjo, waiting.

"Aw, it ain't nothin," Cudjo said.

"Naw. We just talkin about ole times."

"What did ole times tell you on the telephone back at the restaurant?"

"You two Negroes been whispering and pulling at each other's elbows all night. Now, what's going on?"

Bubbles recognized the lines around his wife's mouth and said, "Moon."

"Moon?" Evelyn said.

"Swoop was sittin out there in his car all night," Cudjo said. "Must've been waitin for Moon, because everybody else was there."

"Why Moon?"

"Somethin must've happened. Don't ask us what. But we figure Swoop and the whole police force must have some papers on him, a warrant or something."

"You suppose he's pushin dope too?" Onetha asked. "Well, where is Moon? Didn't Clarie say——"

"Yeah," Bubbles said. "He's supposed to come. But his mother says she hasn't heard from him. She might be lyin; I don't know. Clarie wouldn't lie about meeting him. Wouldn't have no reason to."

"Oh, Lord," Evelyn whispered. Both men turned in her direction, not drawn by the words as much as by her tone. She understood it all and their lifetimes, always more marked by struggle and hope than anything else, were measured by the cadence of the two words; and in her tone too was the submission to forces none of them understood but had always feared, a retributive spirit, perhaps; or one that sought to shear the arrogance from them, an arrogance accumulated in the advance from their childhoods to their precarious presents; and now the name Moon hung before them, like meat set to the smoke, which had rotted in the weather seeping in through a crack in the smokehouse.

Cudjo heard the furnace humm on, and knew the heat was being pushed up into his house; that his bedroom would be warmed precisely to 68 degrees and that daggers of cold could not, as they had in the homes he lived in as a child, stab him. This morning, the thought did not give him comfort.

Bubbles sent a ball rolling softly down the table, aiming it so that it would bounce almost silently against a cushion. Wistfully, he watched the ball, its stripes first blurring against the green and then becoming delineated.

"I've got to believe Clarie," Onetha said. "The man's on his way. Three thousand miles to drop dirt on folks——"

"If Moon knows people are looking for him, he wouldn't come, Neet. I mean, he ain't no dog——"

"I don't care what Moon knows or doesn't know, Bubble. We got these people together. That's unusual for black folks, coming together so they can say to one of them, 'Hey, thanks,' and we've gone and done it, baby. We might set a whole new style. . . . "

She held out her hands, slowly opened them, and seemed surprised to see them empty.

"We're gonna try and keep an eye on Swoop, honey," Bubbles said. "I think, if it gets down to the nitty-gritty, we ought to try to talk to him. We don't know anyone else on the force."

FOURTEEN

Ezzard Jackson struggled up from the headachey, turbulent fog in which he had been uneasily sleeping. His anger had gone through his sleep like lightning fading weakly over the horizon. He hadn't brought up the note; he had been afraid to, and that had caused his anger to gain strength and shift back upon himself, and it burrowed beneath his fear. Tired, drunk, disgusted, he had closed his eyes. But now, motion, a slippery, loving warmth, enveloped him. He came awake in small, the room gray-black with unhurried dawn, knowing the feel; he dully exulted in it, and, wearily, understood the ramifications of it. Yet, he didn't have the strength, perhaps not even the will, to end this motion by speaking, nor with a push of his hands against his wife's head, which was moving rhythmically. He thought about moving his hands to fondle her breasts. He did not do it. He thought about moving with her; he thought hard about it because he wanted to, needed to, almost. But he did not do that either. The loving warmth he knew was schemed. He wished he could shout out that he knew it. A sigh trembled out of his mouth before he could stifle it, and he knew (the feel of her mouth had altered, as if in a grin) it pleased her.

Now Chris raised, shifting her body so that she was above him, drawing her knees up carefully (he heard them gliding into place on the sheet), first one, then the other; he felt her hand encircling him, then guiding him into her. She forced her body down on him, her knees splaying outward. She made a sound; he was familiar with it, and she took a moment to push her hair back out of her eyes. (She'd worn an Afro only a short time; it took too much care.) The movement had silhouetted her straightened body into motionlessness, a figure with the fullness of an Ingres odalisque, and Jackson, shifting his eyes to where their bodies merged, felt the first hint of melting within himself. He clenched the fingers of his right hand into a fist and brought it with all his strength to the point of his wife's chin. She made an abrupt, surprised sound, rose off him slickly with the power of his blow, fell on her side, and lay still. Jackson pushed her with his feet, turned on his side, and went back to sleep.

At 10 A.M. Dart Foxx answered his phone. It was his accompanist, the young man he'd met yesterday. Dart turned on his side away from Simone. "No, it's all right, James. We were just about to get up. Oh, it feels strange, very strange, to be back. It's unreal." Poor James, Dart was thinking. He wanted to get away so badly you could smell it. He wanted to touch and be with anyone who had managed to penetrate this isolation; he could not, on his own, get away. Dart thought of himself, what his life would have been like had it not been for Marcus. And certainly James, Dart knew, hoped he would so impress with his playing that Dart would whip him off to fame and fortune to be the darling of the concert stage, the accompanist who would be introduced, a hand held toward him inviting the swells of applause. A Rubenstein or a Backhaus. Dart smiled. There was already confusion; a pianist was an accompanist or a master, a soloist. James's dilemma was that he would be anything, anything to get out, for however long was necessary. Ripe. A chicken. And now James was suggesting that Dart do an aria from *La Traviata*, the part that Verdi had adapted from Dumas *fils's Camille*, to show the influence of black on white. But Dart wasn't messing around with any operas; he wasn't going out on a limb to satisfy the Uhuru shouting of the local militants. The quickest way to end an already unsteady career was to forget to remember its limits. "I appreciate the suggestion, James, but I think we'll stick to my standards. It's nice of you to think about it, though, but you must have imagined how awfully thin that aria would sound with just a piano and without the woman alternating?"

Simone lay quietly, ears like eyes, hearing as well as imagining undulating, subdued colors, the tones of his voice. James was lean, tense, and eager to please. Good-looking at the right angle. A mediocre pianist, she was sure. There was a difference between being mediocre and having been very nearly great—and then broken. Dart was broken. How much she had not known until they'd arrived in this city yesterday morning. Some cities are like houses: they can charm you as you come upon them, without so much as your putting a foot on the threshold; others chill you, even from a distance. Such was this city. Why, she could not say; it threatened in its very existence. From here Dart had begun to soar. She had pieced it together over the years, and here, too, the breaking process began. One had only to look at his parents and see that they had contributed mightily. The old man with his cunning look and smooth face; the face might have gone well with someone forty years younger, but on Dart's father, it was obscene. And Mama. Still trying to be sexy . . . The old man, Mr. Davis, had tried to equal out that breaking or at least had forced Dart to conceal it. The ends of the circle had joined; the broken man, the broken singer. I hate this city, Simone thought. I should never have come.

"Well, I'll join you at noon. We can rehearse until four, then break. My wife can join us then. Then we'll do a quick run-through and we should be all set for tonight. All right, James?" Hanging up he thought, It would've made more sense if the dummy had suggested Verdi's *Otello*. Ah, but he wanted to im*press* me. Charming. "Darling?" he said.

Simone remained still. And what will *I* do with *my* time from noon until four this afternoon, Simone thought. She made a sudden, almost gay decision to make the very best of it; the whole trip. She recognized within herself the onset of hysteria held in check.

"We thought people who lived in the projects were rich," Ralph was saying. They were driving by the old, empty, flat brick buildings.

The projects had been segregated, but that had not mattered so much then, when they were kids. The apartments were centrally heated. Everything smelled new. The walls weren't layered with cheap paint to conceal cracked plaster. There were lawns in front and back, and space with lines to hang the wash. No coal or wood stoves. Ralph continued. "Maybe we thought they were rich because a couple of black politicians lived in them. Had pull. My mother tried so hard to get us into a spot. She was willing to give an arm and a leg. Maybe that too made us believe they were special."

Eve was listening, trying to imagine what the buildings looked like back then.

"April and I lived not far from here. In the valley. There were times when I looked out the window and saw the hills on every side. Made me think of the opening line from Richard Llewellyn's novel—made a great movie out of it—*How Green Was My Valley*. Something like, 'I am going to leave this valley.' One day I said to myself, 'I must leave this valley.' And I did."

Eve said, "Yes. You did."

Ralph gestured with one hand. "My father used to play touch football in these streets. He taught me to box here. The way they used to box. Classical stuff they don't use any more. No dancing like butterflies. No stinging like bees. What he taught me didn't do much good. You got into a fight and you didn't think about the ole one-two or the hook, jab, and cross, the position of your feet. Whatever worked. Like today, with all this kung fu, karate, and chop suey shit? If a cat whips out a gun on you, forget it."

Eve laughed.

"Some of the girls were badder than the guys. Ole Evelyn there. She was sending people to the dentist every week. Cleaned up the schoolyard with Redbones once, and I guess he never got over it till the day he died. There was a woman named Gladys. Wore caps and suits just like a man. Walk down the street with her ole lady on her arm and dare anybody to look. She whipped a whole bunch of people around here. You talk about dukin? Didn't nobody mess with Gladys.

"Then there was Thompson. Little ole homosexual dude. Gold-rimmed glasses. Lived in a room in somebody's house. Nobody knew where he worked, but he must've had a job. Always wore a suit and tie. Poor cat, every weekend, he be into sitting at the bar, getting stoned, buying drinks, trying to run up on a stranger in town. He'd been better off if he'd been one of those aggressive types. See him staggering along home, two, three in the morning, alone, ain't had no luck again, humming some old sad song to himself."

Ralph took a deep breath and let it out. "Shit," he said. Then, softly, "Jack the Jew. He used to hang out around here. He played cards with all the gamblers. The story was, he was a doctor, but got busted behind an abortion. Everybody went to him for advice, legal, medical, the horses, the numbers, the amount of yeast to put in the beer you were making, how to get on welfare —Funny. Now those days don't seem so bad. Everything was so one-dimensional."

"Age?" Eve said.

"Focus?" Ralph responded. "Innocence, maybe. Probably. Last night I saw that everyone had lost it. Except maybe Bubbles. Yeah. White folks' cliche."

"Bubbles was president?"

Ralph laughed. "Yeah. Oh, yeah. Everybody else was too hip to take on a job like that. We all knew we were jive. Bubbles set about reforming us, making us responsible. Meetings on time, paying dues, helping to decorate for parties. Bubbles took the Boy Scouts very seriously. He stayed in longer than any of us. Ole Bubble."

Big Ralph Joplin opened the door at the first knock and embraced his son and awkwardly shook hands with his daughter-in-law. "Sit down, sit down," he said. "I put on some coffee. Figured it'd help get us rolling."

"How've you been, Dad?" The word was as clumsy in Ralph's mouth as it was to his father's ear.

"Just fine. No complaints. You all getting on good?" Big Ralph was moving from the small living room to the adjoining smaller kitchen as he spoke. He set out the tray on a small side table.

"Ralph sometimes works too hard," Eve said, accepting a cup and saucer with a smile of thanks.

"Oh, is that right?" Big Ralph looked critically at his son, but he was wondering if his life would have been different had Sissie, just once, said that to someone. "Don't let him do that. Don't let his brains bust on him."

Ralph took his cup and waited as his father poured coffee for Eve.

"And Raffy," Big Ralph said. He felt that he shouldn't call her his granddaughter; he wouldn't know her if she walked into the room, he saw her so infrequently.

"Big," Ralph said.

"Eighteen? 19?"

"Nineteen."

Big Ralph looked down into his cup. He and Sissie had married when they were 19. "She's doing okay in school?"

"Sure."

Big Ralph said, "You ever see Bubbles' boy down in New York? He's sure playin some ball, from what I hear."

"No. Haven't been to a game so far this season and only went to a couple last year. The whole thing's changed. I mean the fans," Ralph said. "I think it started to change about the time Jimmy Brown was playing. Going to a game was chic. I can remember hearing people say, when a touchdown was scored, 'Do I cheer now?' and I think that kind of finished it for me—"

"He watches on television, though," Eve said.

"Me too," Big Ralph said. "It's warm. You get that instant replay, but they do too much talking for me."

"I'd rather for him to be home," Eve said, setting down her empty cup.

"Oh, sure," Big Ralph said. Then, looking at his son he said, "Working on another play?"

Ralph nodded.

Slyly his father said, "Lewis and me drove to Rochester and saw *Shadows on the Sun*." He smiled. "I liked it. Lewis said to tell you hello."

"He okay?"

"Same old Lewis, tighter than Dick's hatband."

"He ought to be worth a lot of money, Dad. Never married. Never went anywhere—except to see my play—and never spent a penny on anyone." Ralph cursed to himself. Never should have said that. But it was true.

"I don't know what Lewis' got, son, and I don't care. We're just two old men hanging on."

"Make that three," Ralph said.

"Naw. You're lookin real good." He turned to Eve. "You must take very good care of him, Eve. You like that beard?"

"I love it. He wouldn't be the same without it."

"I guess I'm not used to it," Big Ralph said. This was a stranger who bore his name. Big Ralph sighed.

Hearing it, Ralph said, "Ready?"

"Sure. Just let me get my coat."

Ralph's father was dressed in a shapeless black suit, a white shirt, and a gray tie. He could be going to a cemetery or to perform a thousand ordinary tasks. Perfectly dressed for nothing special. And yet, he knew his father had donned this suit today for the visit to the cemetery and for lunch. Why was it, Ralph wondered, that we still want our fathers to be special and do special things?

The silent car was filled with the smell of flowers, the wreaths held in Eve's small hands, and beneath the steady hum of the engine Ralph thought he heard the sounds of summer, the clatter of roller skates, the heavy breathing of a boy who had skated a long way: *You still won't tell me why you roller-skated nearly five miles every Sunday to sit by your baby sister's grave?* Dr. Bluman! In silence they drove up the hill over the plateau, out along the edges of the city, Eve with the eerie feeling that the car was driving itself, directed only mentally by Ralph; Big Ralph in the back thinking how well his son remembered the city, the way to the cemetery; Ralph thinking of their names each time the car passed over the cracks in the concrete roadbed slabs: *Juanita, Mary Ellen, Robbie, Sissie; Juanita, Mary Ellen, Robbie, Sissie; Juanita, Mary*—Caravans remembered, moving quietly through these streets in greater style than any of them had lived. Sissie would have loved hers. After crawling through the Rockies and gliding past the Great Salt Lake, flashing through the plains, she had arrived to be tenderly moved from the train into Mr. Tompkins' funeral car; Elks, ladies Elks, churchfolk weeping, stretching toward her coffin, murmuring, *Sissie Joplin done come back home, thank the Lord. Rest, Sissie!* Oliver and Big Ralph looking across at each other, then into the cars, the caravan moving, the cop's siren low, leading the way out of the downtown traffic to along this very street. Iris breaking down, finally, in the car in which Oliver, Big Ralph, and he were riding, and sliding down into a grief years deep, perhaps ages, along this very street; and along this very street Oliver and his father had shaken hands silently. There'd been nothing to say. A slow flood of white silk dresses and black suits rose over the little hill where the cars were parked to the graveside, and Ralph remembered someone, a woman who was weeping, starting to sing disconsolately, *Oh, Sissie, don't you weep don't you*

*mourn, O, Sissie, don't you weep, don't you mourn—*and other
voices taking it up, male and female, pushing it to the graveside;
his father's eyes beginning to leak; Oliver stabbing his face with
a new Irish linen handkerchief, Ralph himself letting go, his chin
bobbing on his chest—

The sound of the gravel under the tires brought Ralph back.
He'd turned off the road, under the arch which gave name to the
place.

In her lap Eve shifted the wreaths, looked out at the forlorn
and soiled flags from Veterans Day, the decaying wreaths, the
markers.

Ralph pulled up and parked just below the hill and they
climbed out, holding their coats tightly against them. It pleased
Ralph that his father was guiding his wife to the graves. Suddenly they were there, in a small space where the four of them
lay. Juanita and Mary Ellen had simple markers; Robbie had a
stone and Sissie had a larger headstone. Big Ralph took off his
hat and bowed his head. Eve moved forward and gently placed
a wreath at the head of each grave, on or resting against the
stone. And Ralph sighed, wondering where he would be buried.

This was something that, in passing, he'd found himself thinking about more and more—but just as often dismissing all serious consideration of it. Fuck it. When he was gone, he was gone.
Free at last. However, each time he reached that point in his
thinking, the name sidled into his mind: Raphaella. Raffy. His
daughter. The last of the Joplins. She would become a member
of another family—unless she was strong. No son. She was it.
Why not a son? Eve and he had been agreed, without overmuch
discussion, that they had been too old when they married to
weather the storm created by the presence of a child; too old to
cunningly invest him with the strength that would be necessary
for him to best the life available to him—you couldn't scare him
by telling him it was all sledding on shit out there. No, Raffy was
it, conceived, born into an age of his ignorance (and April's).

There had been days when, pondering, Ralph saw himself in a
heart-to-heart with her, painstakingly explaining every inch of
the family root. Not that there had not been some of those hit-
and-miss, on-the-fly questions asked by her and immediately re-

tracted in manner by her before the onslaught of his eagerness to answer.

No matter. There *was* Raffy. And there was that pride, like so many other things, unspoken, among the JBS, that those who had children managed, or were managing, to give them a better grip on the world than they'd had. A foot up on the ladder. If they didn't make it (make *what?*), they still would have had the chance. That's all anyone could ask for; at least, that was all they could get. It seemed that the time was past when a man or woman could make his own breaks, even with luck, the way they had.

Ralph looked down at the graves again. "Dad," he said, without looking at him. "Where would you want to be buried?"

The movement was sure and strong, as if he'd thought about it a long time. As though studying directions, Ralph glanced down his father's arm until his eyes came to rest, beyond the pointing finger, to the grass on the left of Sissie's grave. "It's paid for already," he said simply. Big Ralph lowered his arm and his smile was slow and warmer than his son ever remembered it being, and said, "You?"

A challenge. The whole family there, or would be. Except Ralph, the first son. *Where will you rest, my son?*

Eve lowered her head against the stiff wind that was making her eyes water. She knew her husband's answer; knew what her father-in-law wished.

"Oh, I thought about cremation. Less space. No space, if you just throw the ashes around for fertilizer."

Big Ralph was startled. "Cremation?"

Ralph felt embarrassed. "I guess. Lots of people burn their dead, you know."

Big Ralph said softly. "Just never thought of it." Iris! Big Ralph thought of his daughter and his mind groaned. So very far away. "And your sister?"

Ralph put his arm around the shoulder of his father and was surprised that it was still so big, so massive. "I don't know, chief. I guess we don't think that much about it."

"Eve," Big Ralph said, turning to her, successfully muting the unexplained panic he felt.

She went to the other side of him and took his arm. "I'd leave the parts of me that are still good to someone. . . . I've already signed the papers."

"It's all right," Big Ralph said. "It's all right."

"Let's go have some lunch," Ralph said.

They turned and walked down the slight hill to the car.

At noon Clarence Henderson who'd left his wife in bed and walked around downtown, trying to find Emma Minding's Bookshop, which was no more, hiked up the hill to the University. He wanted to pick up catalogues to see what courses were being offered in English. The place had grown. New buildings sprawled over areas which once had been occupied by late nineteenth-century brick buildings or World War II quonset huts.

The University had let the city high schools use some of its athletic facilities in the old days—the cinder track around the stadium football field, the board track behind the gym. Now the stadium loomed up before him, renovated, flags flying from the upper stands, cracks in the old walls recemented. Henderson approached one of the tunnel entrances and saw the field being groomed and marked. Game tomorrow, he remembered. He felt a flutter of excitement. Maryland, they're playing. Then he snorted. When they were kids the Hill team used to leave Sidat-Singh behind when it went south to play Maryland. The Terrapins. Ole Jim Crow. That was the rule then: no spades played ball against whites down home.

Henderson walked through the tunnel and stopped. The smell reminded him. He gazed down the track. Of course. Here, right here, they started the hundred-yard dash. You blazed out of your holes (no blocks then), out of this shaded tunnel into the sunlight and up past the stands. Ten and six-tenths seconds. His best time. He walked past the unquestioning groundskeepers to the green and took off his coat and jacket, folded and laid them down. He walked to the track, found a place in the middle, and took up a long-distance stance. He imagined a starter's gun, and he started to run crisply, his tie snapping in the wind. I'm crazy he thought, picking up speed and leaning into the first turn. Coming out of it, he lengthened his stride, conscious of his toes smashing into the cinders. His body told him he'd forgotten

nothing. He heard one of the workers shout encouragement and he fired into the second turn, leaning hard, sucking for air with his mouth wide. Shit, he thought, I'm makin some time and I'm fifty years—his leather soles refused the angle of his lean and he felt himself hurtle through space before he crashed to the ground in a spray of cinders. He rolled over and sat up, his hands braced against the track, and laughed and gasped, and gasped and laughed. I must still be high, he thought, rising now and brushing himself off. He grinned at his foolishness, at an imaginary crowd which shouted, "Yay, Henderson, yay!" Breathing hard he walked to his clothes and put them back on and walked quickly out of the stadium.

Henderson knew why he hadn't gone to school here with Dart, Ralph, and Snake. That is, he knew now. He needed those four years in the postwar South to make himself black, for there he had been afraid to attempt to pass for white. In a way the treatment had worked. He was able to battle the ebb and flow of attraction, to handle it lightly, knowing that his base, his psyche was black, all of it, and that in that blackness lay his reason for existence. Then, he had been drawn to Toomer, the man and the artist, to Toomer's South, Georgia particularly. Had Toomer chosen to be white and a writer of black subjects and topics, he could have walked away with it all; none could touch him; none had the range or the staying power, the mix of Dostoievski, Freud, and half a dozen others. Toomer chafed at his own limitations and so moved to Gurdjieff. Other American writers would venture into mysticism and the occult, seeking new messages, avenues, new ways to bend out form and philosophy. Henderson could understand it, but he was not an artist, and there ended the comparisons of himself with Jean Toomer. His papers had been on Toomer, who else? Doing them for his master's and doctorate had been like examining himself, year by year, experience by experience. But he, Henderson, had not melted away; he had come nearly full circle. That emptiness which must have stretched before Toomer was not there for him. He had the Junior Bachelor Society.

FIFTEEN

At two o'clock, while Papadapoulous was sitting in a corner of the restaurant eating green pea soup which had been cooked with a ham hock, Shurley leaned against the shelves containing rows of whiskey bottles and looked from Bubbles to Cudjo, his apron tail, guided by his slender, restless fingers, whisking into, around, and out of a glass a second, on the average.

Bubbles pretended to look away. Shurley was most upset, he knew, when he was in motion. Like some people wiggled their feet, or tapped them, or ran their fingers through their mustaches.

"Uh, huh," Shurley said to Cudjo. "Uh, huh," he repeated, softly, like a man who had something on his mind. "Okay. I hear you, Cudjo. Uh, huh."

"He's having lunch now. At The White Tower," Bubbles said.

"What do you think, Shurl?" Cudjo asked.

"Looks like some shit, that's what I think," Shurley said, and Bubbles and Cudjo glanced at each other.

"Gee whiz, thanks," Bubbles said.

"Would you talk to Moon's momma?"

"No," Shurley said. "No, I would not. Why do you think I'd do better than you two? Anyway, you said Evelyn was watching his house, so that's covered. And she ain't seen no cop but Swoop cruising through there, right?"

Shurley fixed them with a glare. "Right?"

"Right!"

"Yeah, right! So fuckin what, man?"

"Maybe it's something strictly between Moon and Swoop. Otherwise, wouldn't there be more cops around his house? Wouldn't they have talked to his momma by now, and wouldn't half the town know they'd talked to her because she'd be scared? Right now, she just knows something's up. That's all." Shurley set down the last glass and carefully smoothed out his apron. "I think I know Swoop pretty well."

Bubbles looked at him, waiting.

Shurley untied the apron. "Hey, Mickey Mouse."

The small black man with the big ears came out of the kitchen. "You ready for me to take over, Shurl?"

"Yeah. We gotta go get that plaque from Buonfiglio's. Be back in an hour or so."

"How you fellas after that bash last night?" Mickey Mouse asked.

"Okay, Mick. I wasn't hurtin none then, but this morning, it was a different story," Cudjo said.

"Aw, man," Bubbles said. "I just made up my mind that it's gonna last until tomorrow night, and ain't no while in me trying to get too sober."

"Yeah," Mickey Mouse said. "Y'all put *away* some liquor last night."

"Shit," Shurley said, slipping into a heavy jacket. "You and Sug and Marvin and Clifford, you folks wasn't feelin no pain neither."

"Sure wasn't," Mickey Mouse said.

Bubbles sat in the front beside Shurley; Cudjo rode in the back.

"I've been making pays to Swoop for fifteen years," Shurley said.

There was something about the way he said it that made Bubbles look at Cudjo. "What do you mean, *you've* been making pays?" he asked.

Shurley braked for a red light. "Well, first, I made them for the old man——"

"——shit, man," Cudjo said impatiently. "That's the name of the game in any town in this country. The payoff. Them cocksuckin cops, that's all they been doin since they *was* cops——"

"So, first you made the payoffs for the old man," Bubbles said. He was aware that Cudjo was now leaning over the back of the front seat.

"Then I was making them for myself," Shurley said. He smiled. "It's been my joint for quite a while."

Bubbles lit a cigarette. Cudjo scratched the back of his neck, feeling a sudden itching there.

"It works all right," Shurley said, "having a white man front

for you. And that's between us three until I tell you different, and that shouldn't be too long, okay?"

"Why didn't you tell us before?" Cudjo's voice was plaintive.

"Just figured it was better for everybody to think I was working for the white man. Better for business, since Negroes got their heads all messed up and won't believe we *can* run anything halfway decent. Not that I didn't trust you cats. Do. Always did. Always will. The thing is, maybe I can fuck with Swoop behind him being on the pad, y'dig? Get him to let Moon ease on in and right back out. No hassles. Nobody lookin bad because Moon's in the Bachelor's. Swoop got somethin on Moon and it looks like he wants to pick up all the apples by himself."

"Hey. Let's roll by The White Tower and see if his ride's still out front, then see if Evelyn and Onetha've changed shifts up at Moon's momma's house."

"Okay," Shurley said to Bubbles.

"What's he hittin you for, Shurl?" Cudjo asked.

"Three bills a week."

Swoop Ferguson's car was parked across the street from the restaurant. Shurley turned away and headed uphill toward Moon's mother's house.

"As hard as you can come down on Swoop," Cudjo said carefully, "he can come down on you harder. I mean, it's risky fuckin with them people, Shurl."

"Was gonna do it sooner or later, anyway," Shurley said. Then with a cold anger: "They take you for granted. They think ain't nobody as slick or as bad as they are. Know what? Every time Swoop comes in my store, man, pickin up that bread? Every *time"*—Shurley made a sudden, almost secretive motion, with his right forefinger—"tape recorder goes on."

Bubbles lit another cigarette, although he had just crushed out the previous one. "Hey," he said, turning to Cudjo, but really addressing them both. "Hey." There seemed to be a lilt in his voice. "We're into some shit now, man. You hear me? *Deep* into shit." He laughed softly. "Shurley," he said, "you are sure my stone Negro. My *man."*

Cudjo clapped his hands and leaned back in his seat. "Wheeeew. One minute I was just riding downtown, and the next, I'm about to go upside the whole, motherfuckin police

force. Hey! Gimmee a nickel!!" He stuck his hands palms down over the seat. Bubbles smacked one; Shurley smacked the other; and they laughed.

"I remember that time we was all walking home after a game at the Center, and ran into that Italian man who'd kicked that little colored kid in the ass, and we jumped him. Shit, we were kids ourselves——"

"——it was Shurley who downed the cat first," Bubbles said. "I remember. Tackled the sumbitch. Low. And Redbones came up high with a body block."

"Yeah, whooo!" Cudjo said. "And that was only the start. That cat rounded up every Tally boy for blocks, and we did some dukin, didn't we, man? Right in the middle of the street at Cedar and Almond. Whoo, we was ba-ad."

They pulled up beside Onetha. Bubbles, his window already rolled down, said, "Everything cool, baby?"

"Cool's a fool in an ice cold pool." She grinned. "Nothing."

"We got to run downtown and then me or Cudjo'll be back to send you home." He needed the reassurance, so he asked, "Not a cop, huh?"

"Looks like you're right," Bubles said to Shurley. To Onetha he said, "We're gonna take care of business. We got some stuff for ole Swoop. Everything's gonna be cool."

The store had changed hands many times before Anthony Buonfiglio came to own it. It had always been in the same location, stuck between old, red-brick buildings, although, with each new owner, the walls were painted, new shelves ordered, old ones painted, and the stock orders varied.

Now, cross-country ski equipment was everywhere displayed along with bowling balls, jackets, and shoes. Basketball gear haunted the corners—timing devices, a model of a torso clad in a warm-up jacket, backboard-and-basket sets, colored basketballs. (Bubbles called the green and whites, Irish basketballs; the blue and whites, American; and the red and whites, Russian.) On a wall hung a hockey uniform above rows of skates, golf bags and clubs, tennis rackets of gleaming alloy, and cans of tennis balls seemed to have been grouped in an exclusive section, which had a thick carpet on the floor. For Bubbles it was like re-entering

his youth. Here (when it was Lowe and Campbell) they had purchased, with much scrimping and saving and dollar-a-week payments, their school sweaters upon which to fasten their block letters. The sweaters had been cardinal-red cardigans. (All the JBS preferred them to the pullovers.) The block letters, and often they bought those here, too, because they were better than the ones the coaches handed out, were bold, thick chenille O's which were worn over the heart; upon the O's were embossed the gold-threaded football or basketball or crossed bats and ball or the winged foot—sometimes all four, never less than three for the members of the Junior Bachelor Society. On the upper left sleeve had been the class stripes, in white.

Now the place was Buonfiglio's Sports Centre.

It was strange, Bubbles now thought. You could have been a letterman, but, unless you had a sweater, no one knew about it. What if they'd not been able to buy the sweaters? Was that what made Cadillac and Mercedes-Benz sales soar, that kind of "I want you to know who I am" syndrome?

"Hey, you know where I been since you guys were here last?" Buonfiglio had come rushing from behind a counter, almost knocking over a bowling trophy.

"Italy," he said without waiting. He slapped palms with them, and ignoring the other customers, led them behind the counter into his small office. He pulled open a desk drawer and set a bottle out; then rummaged in another drawer until he found a stack of paper cups. "Dago Red," he said.

"Aw, Tony, I thought you had some dynamite shit this time," Shurley said, taking a cup and pouring.

"Fuck you, Shurley. That *is* dynamite stuff. Say, who's back? Moon coming? He here?"

"Haven't heard from him," Bubbles said, sipping from his cup.

"Uh, uh, that light-skinned fella, uh——"

"Clarie Henderson," Cudjo offered.

"Yeah! Fast as greased shit. That's him."

"You comin to the banquet, man?" Bubbles set down his cup.

"Would I miss somethin like that?" Buonfiglio asked. He was a man of medium height, dark, restless, with blue eyes. He still looked in good shape. Indeed, Anthony Buonfiglio, like Shurley, Bubbles, and Cudjo, still played touch football, handball in the

winter, and an aggressive game of tennis in the summer. After the war he had gone to play for Biggie Munn out at Michigan State, as a running back instead of a quarterback, but he'd been injured the second game of the season and had never recovered full use of his shoulder; not enough to continue playing football.

"Oh, I'll be there. Bringin my kid. They all think they discovered democracy, you know. Like we didn't get along okay when we were kids. Yeah! The plaque!" Buonfiglio turned to a large, flat box and whipped off the cover. Almost reverently he eased aside a black velvet cloth, then held up the plaque which gleamed with new varnish and an inscribed gold-plated rectangle. His posture demanded a second of silence. He shifted his eyes from one to the other, measuring their admiration. Pleased at what he saw, he smiled and eased the plaque back under its velvet and closed the box quietly. He handed it over to Bubbles. "Here, Richie." Only the whites back then had called him Richie. Cudjo slid his hand into his pocket. Buonfiglio's right forefinger zipped back and forth under his nose, then stopped. "Hey," he said. "I didn't know this old guy, Davis. But——" he shrugged his shoulders. "It's like we, you know, this is our place. We had things in common, you know. You know, like, what're people they don't appreciate this kind of, er uh, uh—hey, Shurley—you know what I'm trying to say? *Take* the fuckin thing. From Anthony Buonfiglio. *Tony.*" Now the crooked forefinger raced across his eyes.

"Well, er, ah, we——" Bubbles began. He felt a sudden, palpable, allrightness with things.

"I know," Buonfiglio said. "This is *your* thing. You think I don't know about that shit?" He leaned on his battered, scarred desk. "When Pat McCormick was putting his size twelves in our asses—remember?—and us hating that Irish fuck of a coach—it dawned on me: we had a team, and he didn't give a damn what we were as long as we won and we could not win unless we were together. Now. If Mr. Davis hadn't done whatever the fuck it was he done for you guys, maybe I'd be the poorer. And maybe you'd be the poorer, you see what I'm saying? It all locks together. You can take all the wop power, nigger power, kike power, Polack power you want, but it's gonna take us all to keep

it up or drag it down, and I ain't no fuckin patriot. I'm a god-damn businessman——"

"You a fuckin softheaded wop," Bubbles said. "Gimmee a dime." He held out both hands and Buonfiglio slapped them, and slapped Shurley's and Cudjo's.

"See you Saturday," Buonfiglio said.

For a good five minutes they were silent in the car. The chok-ing laughter then started with Bubbles, now in the rear seat, and spread to Shurley and to Cudjo. Shurley pulled over and slammed the gear into neutral. They laughed and laughed; tears came and they continued to laugh, and then they started to try to talk.

"Where'd he get religion? Coach had to chew him out about not giving the ball to Moon enough——"

"——lookin out for his boy, No-gain Natiello. Couldn't run through a wet paper bag——"

"——locks together——"

"—and if Buonfiglio and the coach *both* hadn't been Catho-lics, Bubble, Natiello would *still* be pickin splinters out of his ass——"

"——and the sumbitch was tryin to cry——"

"——and Bubbles would've been first string——"

"——betcha he can't give that goddamn Dago Red away, ex-cept to——"

"——US!"

"——*take* the fuckin thing. From Anthony Buonfiglio——"

Bubbles was the first to stop laughing. Wiping his eyes he said plaintively, "Maybe he was trying."

Shurley sighed and sat upright. Cudjo rolled down the win-dow and spat out, and said, "Well, he ain't the worst gray boy I ever met."

Shurley put the car back into gear. "Aw, shit," he said. "I won-der if or how much Tony has to pay the cops just for being a businessman? And Tony's been running football and basketball parlays in this town since he got back from Michigan State."

Cudjo glanced back at Bubbles.

"And I don't run a thing in the back of my store, but the

kitchen and the bathrooms," Shurley continued. "But, this being such a small town, the cops work with the health inspectors, the building inspectors, the state liquor commission—shit. They got me just because I'm a businessman, too. A black one." He threw a look over his shoulder at Bubbles. "We'll send Buonfiglio his check. He don't have to give us nothin."

Cudjo shifted in his seat.

Bubbles felt a flash of embarrassment. Covertly, he studied the back of Shurley's head until Shurley's eyes met his in the mirror. Shurley grinned.

"I wanna say somethin, man, okay?"

Shurley nodded.

Bubbles said, "Hey. We been knowin you damn near fifty years—but we haven't known you, see what I mean?"

"Yeah, man," Cudjo said. "Lotsa surprises this afternoon, Shurl. I mean, heavy stuff."

"Not so heavy," Shurley said. "But they're things about a man, good friends and everything, you'll never know, and maybe *don't* want to know."

"I hear you," Cudjo said.

SIXTEEN

"Hello, Momma?"

"Walter! Well . . . who else did you think would answer *my* phone? Where are——"

"I'm okay, Momma. I made a little stop on the way in. Had to do some thinking. I should've called last night——"

"Oh, Walter——"

"Were you worried, girl?"

"Let's just say I was wondering! Richard, Cudjo, and them've been calling——"

"——the things don't start until today——"

"No, no, honey. They started last night, at the place Shurley runs for the Greek."

"I thought today. Well. Listen, Momma, I'll be there tomorrow in time for the banquet. I guess they figure I'm not comin now, so don't tell anybody——"

"No, Walter——"

"——I want to surprise them."

She had been trying to analyze the tone of his voice from the moment she picked up the phone. The watchfulness was gone, now he was sure, maybe even happy. Yes, a mother knew her son. Mrs. Porter's eyes grew wet. Thank God! Recognized the tone, indeed; the triumph tinged with happiness; arithmetic conquered, an entire paragraph in the first reader, making the first teams.

"Son," she said. "You sound—*good.*"

She had never pried into his life, had never asked a single question about the American Express travelers checks he sent her to save, all in denominations of one hundred dollars. Three shoeboxes full of them, packed tight and bound with rubber bands. What you don't know can't hurt you. There had been the rumors, but Walter was a grown man, and knew the consequences of his rumored acts. They had to look out for each other, for there was no one else who would.

"I *am* feelin good, Momma. Pretty good. Now, when I get there tomorrow, I won't be able to stay long. I have to tell you in front. But, when I get settled—I'm movin from the Coast—Momma, I won't be far away——"

"Oh, Walter——"

"——I don't want to get into it now, but we'll be able to see a lot more of each other. An don't you be upset if I have to zip into town and zip right out again, hear?"

"All right, son. And I'm supposed to tell those boys absolutely nothing?"

"That's right."

"I'll be here, waiting, Walter."

"Okay, Momma. You get real dressed up for the banquet. You gonna be my *date* and, Momma——?"

"Huh?"

"Don't you worry about a thing."

Mrs. Porter hung up and looked at her watch. By this time tomorrow, maybe, he'd be here. She'd read yesterday's papers, and holding out the hope that some of the boys and their wives would come by to say hello, she'd made a cake, the kind they'd all liked: rich yellow inside with chocolate layers and frosting. And she'd burrowed through her closets, behind dresses and coats and skirts she'd not worn in years, for the whiskey, and dusted off the bottles and placed them, along with her best glasses, on a silver serving tray. She saw Richard, Cudjo, and Shurley, or their wives, usually in the supermarkets, and once in a while they'd call. She guessed they all felt surrounded by strangers these days, new people who suddenly seemed to have been in town forever and ever. Mrs. Porter had imagined all the old boys and girls gathered in her living room, talking to her son: Sissie and Ralph's boy, Little Ralph. Little? With that big daughter? Clarie and Ezzard and Dart; Christine, Onetha, Evelyn, Diane— Oh, it would've been nice, like the times the boys all came to the house on Saturday mornings before their games, and sat around eating liverwurst and crackers. Maybe, Mrs. Porter thought, maybe tomorrow, although Walter had said he couldn't stay long. In the kitchen now, she lifted the cake cover; she could tell by the sheen of the frosting that the cake was not drying out too fast; that it would still be good tomorrow.

Shortly before noon, perhaps while Clarence Henderson was dashing around the track in the stadium, Simone Foxx entered the Steak and Suds Restaurant on the ground floor of the hotel. She had never got used to eating alone; she felt like one of the lost or abandoned if she did when Dart was on tour. She was glad the place had what the Americans called "atmosphere," which invariably meant a place with dim lights. Yes, she wished to be in shadows.

As she had recognized the onset of hysteria this morning while Dart talked on the phone, she now recognized something else, a rushing through darkness in a sheer gown, her breasts bubbling, her thighs slicking, one past the other, her arms outstretched, her hair flying—seeking an embrace, another body to impact on her own.

"Libiamo, libiamo ne' lieti calici," she'd heard her husband sing in the shower this morning. In fact, she still seemed to hear him: *"Che la bellezza infiora/E la fuggevol, fuggevol ora/S' inebrii a volutta,"* he sang, his voice fuzzed by the streaming water, which also concealed the cracking and straining. Sure, fresh charms to beauty are lending . . . fleeting moments quickly ending, gay pleasures alone should reign. She had sighed deeply, very deeply. The thought was already in his mind, she knew, and the deed would soon follow, dear James, never fear, you and your Verdi, and your Alfredo, with nothing himself, will leave you a duffel of promises, no doubt.

Gratefully, Simone now gripped her martini glass. The scent of the lemon peel wafted past her nostrils. She closed her eyes and opened her lips for the first sip. This was one of the rare good things Americans made. But, she supposed, Americans had to drink them all the time in order to be able to live here. Her eyes still closed, she took a second, longer sip. She was old fashioned, she thought with a smile; you didn't blame the Americans for the way they were anymore, for the simple reason that everyone else was becoming like them, or had already, including the French. Especially the French, she thought, especially the French.

Her eyes opened on Ezzard Jackson, a wan, she thought, smile on his face. She returned the smile. He was much too small, she

reflected, to be rising from his table as ponderously as he was. He sat down with her, placed his drink on the table.

"Morning," he said.

"Hello, is it morning or afternoon?"

"Somewhere in the middle. I may never recover from that party. Where's Dart?"

"Rehearsal. And Christine?"

Jackson did not look at her. "She went to visit relatives." He assumed that. Her bags and clothes were still in the room.

"But don't you have relatives here, too?"

"Only in-laws now," he said.

"And you don't get along too well with them. I remember now from last night. Something you said. Well, does it make you sad to be back, Ezzard? You look——" Simone shrugged.

Jackson laughed. "You don't look so happy yourself, Simone. You don't like America?"

Simone glanced around in mock distress. "This, this is America?"

"Yes," Jackson said. "Yes, it is. This is really America, not New York."

"Maybe that is why I like New York."

They had another drink and ate. When they finished Jackson said, "What're you going to do while Dart's busy, visit his folks?"

Simone wrinkled her nose. "No. What are you going to do? Your wife's away." She felt they were working away at a code not unfamiliar to them.

"Like to see some of the town, what I remember of it?"

"No. No thanks." She smiled at him. She was so quick with the code that she had moved ahead of him several steps. Realizing it, she said, "There must be something better to do."

Jackson's head was throbbing now. The drinks from last night, he thought, overtaking the ones just now; that and recomputing the code. "I guess there is," he said.

They took the elevator together. She pressed the button for her floor; Jackson did not push for his. When Simone walked off, he joined her. She unlocked the door of her room and held it for Jackson. He closed it quietly and slipped on the chain. The room was like theirs. Smelled of soap. Clothes on the backs of chairs. Suitcases on the floor. A certain neutrality palpable in the air, in the furniture, their arrangement. Nothing could remain of the

streams of temporary inhabitants, not flatulence, sperm stains; nothing.

Jackson went to the bottle. Scotch. "When's Dart due back?"

"He won't be back. I'm meeting him at the Civic Center."

"Uh-huh," Jackson said. He wondered if Simone did this all the time, and he felt momentarily sad for Dart. "So you have the afternoon?"

"Yes, and you?" She was leaning back on the bed, her breasts pushed out, and he was trying not to look at them.

"I have time." He handed her a glass of the scotch. "Hey," he said, now looking at her. "That's nice. All of it." He took off his jacket and fitted it to the back of a chair.

With something like relief, for she had read his mind, computed the old loyalties, the thing, whatever it was, with his wife, Simone, too, began to undress.

Good house, Ralph Joplin was thinking as the theater filled up. Many black couples were wearing evening clothes and Ralph smiled. The people were really coming out these days; they were the real factor in the support of plays written by blacks; they had not been before. Ralph loved it when they gave standing ovations; they seemed to have brought them back to theater. There would be standing ovations tonight. The audience was primed for them. Barney Moore had suggested that if blacks supported black book writers the way they did playwrights these days, things sure would be looking up. But books were singular, individual things, engendering none of the mass vibrations such as those encountered in a theater; no mood, like a wind, sweeping all present before it.

Ralph exchanged winks with Snake. Tonight they would gather at his house to wind down the night. On his other side, his father chatted softly with Eve, when Chappie would let him. "Look," Chappie would say. "There's ole so-and-so. Ain't seen him since such-and-such."

Moon's mother, Mrs. Porter, had come in alone and been called to sit beside Dart's mother and father. She'd heard nothing from Moon, no, but she still expected him and had in fact left a note at home telling him where she was. Clarie, with exaggerated charm, kissed her and must've told of seeing Moon on the plane. Oh, he'd show up sometime, she was sure. Bubbles and Cudjo and Shurley, Diane, Evelyn and Onetha leaning in, were conferencing, their eyes taking in Mrs. Porter (whose smile was flashing everywhere, whose hands fluttered about her person in private thrill) with long, oblique glances.

Ralph wondered why Christine was wearing dark glasses, and such large ones at that. He could dig it if she was from New York; but from KC in those oversized specs? Ralph's eyes swept up and down the rows where the JBS sat with family. All there.

"This is some turnout, son," Ralph's father was saying. "Colored folks haven't been together like this ever, outside funerals and Easter Sundays in church."

"Bigger'n a crap game when the trains used to lay over," Chappie said.

Ralph laughed. The buzz and humm of the audience excited him. The parade of spectacularly dressed people kept coming, and he listened with pride to the soft black laughter, and grinned and nudged Eve when the platform-shoed men minced down the aisles clean, their women tipping proudly before them. He wished he were young again, if only to be a part of this parade. *We turn the most ordinary happenings into events*, he thought.

The hum reached a muted crescendo and died as quickly as the lights were dimmed. Ralph grinned to himself in the darkness; this too was theater.

> "They go from these places, taking all with them,
>   tendrils and vines, wisdom and wiles, all but the root."

The voice was a good one, Ralph thought as the darkness began to give way, now lightening, holding, as dawn sometimes seems to do. And he knew then that they were going to do the monologue from his play. He was glad he hadn't, like a playwright, junior or senior, dropped in at rehearsal. He would see the actors after.

> "And they trudge to the far corners of the world,
>   some of them, to labor and linger, and we who
>   stay wonder what it would be like had they remained."

In the still fading darkness, spots struck down on their rows and moved back and forth. Ralph grinned again; they must've fixed the lights this afternoon. Talk about theater!

"Ladies and gentlemen, the Black Arts Festival welcomes and honors the Junior Bachelor Society."

The lights were full up now and the applause was cautious, uncertain, and then two or three people leaped to their feet, pounding their hands with powerful motions that commanded the others to do so as well. The clapping rolled, swelled through the house, swelled larger until the audience was entirely on its feet craning necks to see down into the hole in their ranks where sat the JBS and their families. The dimming lights pushed down the applause, gently, gently, until seats were reclaimed and movement stilled.

In vanishing darkness a note was struck sharply on a piano—a key established—and a spot came on to shine on a young woman who already was singing:

"Lift ev-ery voice and sing
Till earth and heaven ring . . ."

The audience moved to its feet, Ralph thinking of his sister, Iris, and looking at the young woman, he thought, Still another itching with hope, claiming every public opportunity to say HERE I AM, I WANT OUT, AWAY, TO SUCCESS, and he was thinking it as she spread her arms, urging them to sterner, prouder postures, and thinking of the years ahead of her, some to be luckless, fewer to be lucky. She sang with a desperation not quite muted by her regal cool, and clumsily the voices climbed to the pitch. Nearly everyone knew the words to the anthem these days, at least the first verse, Ralph thought. When they were kids, at gatherings, only a few people, usually older, ever stood stiffly at attention and sang out the words; the others mumbled, hummed, slipping and sliding around the notes, the lyrics, and were relieved when the song was over, and its echoes, pitiful, had died.

"Sing a song full of the hope that the dark past has
taught us,
Sing a song full of the hope that the present has
brought us . . ."

Ralph hoped the girl would make it. Surely she would have heard of Dart's "discovery"; a legend like that would live forever in this town. And no doubt, she'd heard of Iris. Two legends, quite enough to inspire every would-be singer in the town forever and ever. There were towns which had no legends at all.

The evening, glittering in green, black, and red costumes, flags and banners, moved ponderously through cute choreography, medleys by the full band, chorus groups—young voices cracked with too many rehearsals, and too many readings from poetry, a militant, foot-stomping, fist-waving rendition of "We Shall Overcome"; the pace was upbeat, furious. Then, as if to reassure the audience that the evening was going to be all right, Dart Foxx came out, a sure presence moving to the lip of the stage. He bowed at his introduction, bowed again, and his eyes swept the house. A presence, Ralph thought. A pro. He'd never seen Dart perform. He glanced at Dart's accompanist and was sure that the young man had never sat straighter; eagerness to achieve was everywhere stamped in his posture. Dart moved lightly to a mike. "I used to sing in church here when I was a kid. One of my favorite songs, one they like very much in Europe, was 'The Old Rugged Cross.' But perhaps now, time having moved inexorably forward, I should sing another spiritual: 'Nearer My God to Thee'—"

A titter ran through the audience. Dart smiled his appreciation. The song was moving in its simplicity. "That boy always could sing," Chappie said through the applause. Dart's mother turned to smile at him.

"Iris Joplin sends you all her love," Dart said, and clapping rose up on the track of his words. Ralph and his father exchanged smiles.

When Dart was through, Ralph thought, Dynamite—for here. He was standing with the others as Dart, taking bow after bow, extended his hand toward his pianist, and he too, bowed like a professional. So now it was time for the finale.

Ralph found himself nervous. There were people in *this* audience who knew the framework upon which he'd built *Shadows on the Sun*, knew which was seasoned and which was uncured or even rotting timber. How far away the play now seemed, like a photograph in a high school yearbook; out of another life.

The curtain opened. Yes, Ralph thought. The monologue where, in his youth it now seemed, he had tried to outdo O'Neill's Hickey in *Iceman;* that period when Barney Moore in his first novel was trying to wipe out Malcom Lowry's performance in *Under the Volcano.* Back then they were Charlie Parkers, taking the standards, "Indiana," "Star Eyes," and creating entire new firmaments.

Ralph had felt his father start as he, too, recognized the scene. The wife could have been his daughter. And I, Ralph wondered, Have I ever been that young?

A tired young couple. You see the weariness in their movements as they undress, article by article, pausing to light cigarettes or to put them out. Little frowns mark their faces; perhaps they've been fighting. In shorts, the young man is cleaning and clipping his toenails. His wife walks in and out of the bathroom, in silence, finally getting into the bed. The man speaks:

Yeah, he would not tolerate no whipped son of his in the house. He'd send you back out in a minute and declare you couldn't get back in until you'd whipped the kid who whipped you. Even if the kid was eight foot eight. No excuses. (pause) I guess all the old folks were like that, though. Toughening you up for survival. But some of us who simply weren't bad enough to be beatin up on giants, just had to get slick, you see. We'd go out, walk around the block, three, four times, mess up our clothes, go on back home and be breathin hard and lookin evil comin through the door! Be talkin about I sure whipped that so-and-so's head. *Good!* That satisfied him and it sure in hell satisfied me. (*The wife shifts in bed, fluffs her pillow and for the first time smiles at her husband. From under the blanket, she sticks out her foot. He takes it and begins clipping her toenails. They smile at each other again.*)
He was a rough man to live with, my father. White men thought at first they might do to him what they tried to do and often did to a lot of other black men in that town: rub his head for good luck, or call him Sunshine, or command him to blow on their dice. They thought

he would snap into a buck-and-wing as soon as they said, "Let's see you dance a little there, boy." They might have said that although standing on their toes they could not have reached his head with their hands; if they thought of calling my father Sunshine, they would have whispered it, and only on a dare, since Jack Johnson then was the shadow that fell across their masculinity, which had been represented by Tommy Burns, Jim Jeffries, and Jess Willard. Jack Dempsey ran from Johnson; didn't want to fight him. And my father was as big as Jack Johnson—and in better shape. White men said nothing. My father gave off those vibes, you know, "Don't fuck with me," and white men thought not twice, but twice times ten, and never lifted hands to rub his head. They didn't call him mister, but they didn't call him Sunshine, either. And when he danced, it was because he was happy and he wanted to, and yes, he could dance, dance his ass off. So they didn't bother him, just left him alone, with his family, his black friends, his black neighborhood, to starve and suffer, wither away. You know a grapevine, honey? It struggles and struggles, gets brown, the shoots curl up and break off, and the leaves get yellow and sick, and you say it's dead, and you stop lookin at it, stop waitin for the grapes to grow. You say, fuck it, ain't gonna be no goddamn grapes. (*He takes her other foot. He works so intently that the clipping becomes an excuse not to look at his wife.*) And then one day, one day when you're walkin past where that old grapevine died— you're just walkin—another summer, maybe, and the sun's really up there, bright and hot—just walkin, not thinkin of anything. Then you stumble—your foot caught on something and you look down, and there's a young tough green vine that's come up out of all that witherin, and you know, you *know*—because, look, you damn near broke your leg on it—that that vine's gonna bear some grapes, with or without your help. It's just not worryin about you; that thing is gonna grow some grapes. He was a tough man to live with. His withering fooled me. It was not a dying. My father had strong, deep-running roots, and I am his fruit. Yea and verily. I am *strong* wine which, when drunk, casts shadows, even shadows on the sun.

Strange, Big Ralph was thinking, how the years had turned that incident around in his son's head. He himself had never forgotten it. With everything else—the situation with Sissie, no work, singing or otherwise—he recalled the incident with utmost fidelity. At the time he'd told himself that kids didn't remember things; that even if his son did understand what the white man had done, really understood the pit into which his touch had cast him, Big Ralph, there was more for him to come to.

Big Ralph had taken his son with him that morning to the large, dull-colored hall which was filled with men whose clothing reeked of too many wearings; and this smell together with the accumulations in the unemptied spittoons, the carbolic-acid moppings, the cigarettes being smoked, the secret, fearful sweatings was an ugliness of which the lines to the counters were but extensions. The men behind the counters, secure in their jobs, calms in the eyes of storms, joked with the men as they shuffled forward, each one hoping that the much-fingered yellow card bearing his name would have a special notation on it this time. A crisp word, a chuckle, a slap on the shoulder, the attempt at bravery, the concealment of resignation or panic or both, then back outside, away from the disease rampant inside.

Big Ralph stood before the man. "Well, before we look, we'd better get us a little luck, hey, boy?" And Big Ralph viscerally understanding the code, this ancient, unaltered code, stiffened to prevent himself from moving his head aside; stiffened to keep his left hand where it was, limp, by his side, signaled silence to its screaming wish to cut through the air and smash the pallid face. But he needed work and so he stiffened and suffered the leisurely, insulting reach, the insinuating rub. "Nothing this week, boy. Next."

But his son, it seemed, did not remember it that way.

Ralph Joplin, Jr., did remember it that way. And something else: the stiffening, the single, massive tremble to impose the will on the wish. He remembered the mashing of his right hand, held by his father, that sudden excruciating deliverance of power commanded through that massive frame down to his own hand at the very moment the white man stretched forward. Ralph understood later (he had not really understood then) that at that moment he had been standing next to and holding hands with a deliverer of death; a man whose vision of a loaf of bread had been stronger than the will, though not the ability, to kill.

Over the years the magic had been simmering, the magic of words which were meant to tell his father the way it really was; to give back his father his image, his wholeness. Magic words: they had created another, better scene than the original. Who had not eaten the shit before the steak?

Father and son looked at each other and smiled as the applause rode over them.

Chilled to the marrow, for he had been standing all evening in the entrance to an empty box, and the upper floors of the center had not been heated as well as downstairs, he lowered his binoculars, glad on the one hand that the Festival was over. On the other hand he was puzzled and disappointed. It was this, not anger, which made Swoop Ferguson utter a low, sibilant, Shit.

Through the curtain he watched as the rows where the JBS had sat with their families emptied, its occupants merging with the streams of handshaking, backslapping people. The JBS would gather somewhere tonight, just as they did last night. Swoop had not bothered to find out where; the information would come to him as John's head on a platter was delivered to Salome. The grapevine. And it did not look as though Moon would be there. After all, his mother had come tonight. All right, another day, one more, he thought. He placed the glasses to his eyes again, thrusting aside the curtain, saw a group of the JBS gathered around Snake Dumpson, and smiled. He didn't have to wait for no grapevine. That grapevine had brought him word that Chops's ole lady was wearing shades because her face was swollen up around the eyes; that Dart and his piano player had spent an hour together in a dressing room. He wondered if the rest of them knew about that, or even suspected. Swoop lowered the glasses. Hear about everything but Moon, he thought.

There'd been no additional fliers on the precinct board, and he'd not requested any more information either; that'd be tipping his hand. Turkey's probably in Algeria right now. Swoop shivered, turned, and went out through a side exit.

Mr. Foxx sat grinning beside the young female actor who had played the wife in Ralph's monologue. She, conscious of Clarence Henderson hovering restlessly by her side, trying to catch her eye, was waiting until she could gracefully slip out of the obligation to be nice to an old man. Across the room Mrs. Foxx sat coyly back in her chair while Chappie, on the edge of his seat, leaned forward talking. Pat Henderson and Dart Foxx, their attitudes those of people talking cultural things, belied the intensity of her conversation at least, which was centered on the possibility of his doing concerts in Los Angeles or, as an alternative, visiting him and his wife, of course, on their next trip to Europe, or even, for there was that possibility too, of seeing him (them, she said she meant) in New York within the next couple of days. The male lead in the monologue stood not far from Ralph. They'd had a conversation, often interrupted, and he was waiting for it to be continued. But he saw Ralph softly studying the female lead and knew it was she, not him, that he wished to talk to. The actor moved away to join other young people who'd been in the show; these were standing in a group to which some older people had been attracted: Big Ralph with Christine's folks and Mrs. Porter; Snake and Sandra, and Onetha, Diane, and Evelyn. Simone Foxx chatted with the piano player who out of the corners of his eyes watched Dart and Pat. Eve Joplin, looking at the female actor, wondered without rancor how many young, showbiz ladies her husband had slept with over the years. Now, Chappie raised his eyes to meet the almost surreptitious approach of Dart's father. Pea-headed sonofabitch, he thought. He's probably already stole something of Snake's. He glanced at Mr. Foxx's pockets and got up saying good-by to Mrs. Foxx and grunting to Mr. Foxx. If things had gone the way they should've, there'd be no pea-headed fools here tonight, Chappie thought.

Coming up on the group of young and old people, Chappie said to Snake, "Somethin about what that man said when the program started tonight. If everybody had come on back and settled down, setting examples for the young people, maybe the place would be different now."

Dumpson said, "Some of us never left Coach, remember, and I can't say the town's any better for our staying."

"Oh we had examples," the male lead said. "Good examples. They showed us that there wasn't anything we could do *here*. The opportunities aren't here. This isn't a theater town, for example. We've got lots of musicians here, but they have to leave here to make good. Did you know Charlie Parker played here once and they threw him in jail?"

"Who's Charlie Parker? Was he a fullback?" Chappie asked, and he laughed. He flung out his hands. "That's just it. Don't nobody stay and try to make it the kind of place where things can happen. They all runnin off for Noo Yawk."

"Well, why'd you do it, why?" Christine Jackson was asking. She sat with her husband in a corner.

"You know why," Jackson said sullenly.

"No I don't. I can't read your mind, Ezzard."

"Forget it."

"You're afraid to tell me. Why are you afraid?"

About to drink from his glass, Jackson stopped. He thought to say something, but the words wouldn't come. He intended to fix her with a hard, menacing look, but when their eyes met, her whites showing through her glasses, her look told him that his look was not menacing as much as it was cowed. He said nothing and turned away.

Christine saw her triumph, felt it, and it had never been so good. She plunged recklessly ahead. "I always believed," she said, moving close to him, hurling the sound of her snarl and the scent of her Calèche toward him, "that a man who'd hit a woman was a coward. Now I know it."

Jackson got the glass to his lips and swallowed. "Yes, I guess I have been afraid. No more."

But she didn't understand. In her righteousness she ignored everything. She had him on the defensive.

All these years he had hoped she'd never say it. Thinking it was all right; saying it was something else. There was no hiding now. The bars of his prison, often comforting, had been ripped away. Her words. He moved away, toward a bar arranged on a table. They had been living on a lower animal level; words were not important. A suddenly exposed throat, a certain shading of a glance and defeat was acknowledged. No words spoken to soil the air, to hinge the memory; no speeches to take back and bury and leave rotting under additional words. But the words had been spoken and his death, of a sort, and his life, after a fashion, were now shaped by the utterance of a single Old French, Middle English adjective. *Afraid* to tell me. No. Afraid of being alone after more than a quarter of a century of being with; afraid to begin new patterns. But no more, at least not so anyone would be able to tell. Sunday morning they'd fly back home. By Sunday night he would be moved out. The kids were big; they'd be all right, and there would be no more notes from people who must have hated Christine as much as they hated him. In the absence of his stated accusation, he had forever consigned Christine to wondering *why*.

Cudjo Evers, their conversation at the dead end where it usually arrived when they discussed what to do about Moon, moved away from Bubbles and Shurley to the bar. His back was a pounding mass of pain. Whooo! Don't let me have a muscle spasm now, he thought. He concentrated on the pain that seemed to be thrashing in the lower area of his back, seeking a place to come to rest. He'd been on the pills half the day; no more. He was tightening with tension, he knew. Moon, Swoop, Shurley, this afternoon's ride now in full focus. Cudjo willed the muscles still. He sighed when he finished his drink, neat. The quicker to get those muscles to relax.

"My man," he said to Jackson who'd just walked to the table. "Some show tonight, huh?"

"Yeah, they really got it together, didn't they? First time I ever heard Dart sing. I mean since we've been grown. Pass me that bourbon, will you?"

Carefully Cudjo stretched across the table. Easy, easy, he said to himself, and got the bottle. Just one more day and maybe it'll ease up. "There you are," he said. "Hey, is Chris doin a number on us with those shades or did you tag her?"

Jackson shrugged. "She digs big dark glasses."

It had been said in the old days that Chops was so in love

with Christine that he'd eat a yard-wide mile of shit to make her happy, and they'd all been comfortable with that assumption. But suddenly Cudjo sensed that things were no longer like that. He placed a hand on Jackson's shoulder, comfortingly, as though he'd missed a key block, as he'd done years ago. "Everything's okay?"

"Sure."

Cudjo watched him walk toward Dart's wife and the piano player. Bubbles and Shurley were now at the table beside him for refills.

"Maybe," Shurley was saying, "he ain't comin, Bubble."

Bubbles poured himself a drink and looked around. "That's what I want to tell myself. But I know that as soon as I do, Moon's gonna show up. I know it."

Shurley said, "Nothin that Miz Porter said made it sound that definite, man. And we've been talkin to her on and off half the night."

"I just got this feelin that he's gonna show," Bubbles insisted.

The thought that had nagged at Cudjo since this afternoon found voice: "Say, Shurl, why don't we just go on over to Swoop's and tell him, man, that we"—he glanced at Bubbles—"that you got him on tape and that if he lets Moon alone, every-thing'll be cool."

Shurley studied the people in the room. This was inevitable; he knew this time and these words, rephrased maybe, would come.

Bubbles looked at Cudjo. They waited.

"Well," Shurley said. He cleared his throat and drank. "It wouldn't be a bad idea, you know. But I don't want to be dealin good cards like that just now."

Cudjo and Bubbles nodded automatically. Cudjo felt his stom-ach sinking.

Shurley glanced from one to the other. "I mean, you don't *have* to be in this, you know." They didn't own any restaurants; they hadn't taped any conversations; the stopper they held for Swoop was *his*, Shurley's stopper, and they had to play when he wanted to, not because they were nervous.

"We in, man," Bubbles said. "We told you."

"Yeah," Cudjo said. A bolt of pain imploded near his spine.

"Look at it this way," Shurley said. 'We go on over to Swoop's and tell him; flash the tapes on him, maybe even play a couple. And then Moon don't show. Hear me? *Moon don't show up.*" Shurley drank. "It ain't only Swoop. You said it in the car, Cudjo. It's the whole goddamn police force. See what I mean?"

"And," Bubbles said, "Moon comin or not, once you tell Swoop you got the shit——"

"Zackly," said Shurley.

SEVENTEEN

The dining room was quiet now. Walter Moon Porter, looking out of the window, saw the additional cars in the driveway, their tops glazed with frost. At the edges of the forest he saw the red-coated hunters, their numbers swollen for the weekend, easing into the tree line. Moon mashed a fork sideways down through his stack of cakes and reflected on how good it was like this, eating cakes and sausages in the woods on cold, crisp mornings. Pan sausages, cooked brown and crunchy, not a drop of fat left in them.

Luck running into this place, he thought, and Heflin; being turned on, turned around. Owning land. "Black people are land people. They jived us into the cities," Heflin had said.

He had said this last night as the new hunters poured in from the cities, lugging their superhigh-powered rifles, the 357s used for killing elephant, the boxes upon boxes of ammunition, their expensive scopes. It all had had the appearance of a company moving up to the line.

"Some of the money folks back in Harlem're payin for rent in those rat nests would easy buy em a five-acre piece for starters," Heflin had said. Heflin had given him so many ideas. Packet upon packet of restaurant-hotel-motel franchise plans upon which he could model a place of his own up in Canada. Tomorrow!

On Thursday when Moon had stopped at Heflin's, he had been wary; if anything, less wary than he'd been in New York. But many of the hunters were cops; they'd bought him drinks; he'd bought them drinks. There was no nation-wide hunt for him, he was convinced. Not like in the Jimmy Cagney days. Killing was as common as having a cold. Cops even killed each other with predictable regularity. No, they didn't know from no Collins, and Moon suspected that given the opportunity, if they hadn't had it already, the way they swaggered around here with their handguns hanging ready, they'd be just the same as Collins.

Poor Momma, he thought. After the banquet he'd have to take her home and head for the border. Be there before daybreak. Dorrie'd be hap-py! Momma would take it hard, but he'd already warned her.

Moon heard a shotgun blast. The sound, echoing through the hills and over the lake, seemed at first constrained, a pushing through a tight place, and then shhfoOOM! SsshhfooOOMM! Moon wondered if the hunter had got the deer, what the deer felt like, what the hunter felt like—ssshhfoOOOM! The *coup de grâce*, the slug ripping through the brown coat a final time, and then silence.

"Sounds like they got one," Heflin said, striding across the room with Moon's bill.

"I thought this was rifle country."

Heflin said, "Shit, man, they use everything around here: cannons, missiles, and hand grenades if they could get away with it. But, I'll tell you one thing. I'd rather them honkies be out there killin deer than killin us."

Laughing, Moon took the bill, scanned it, and dug the money out of his pocket. "Lissen, man. Thanks, hear? I'ma be in touch."

Heflin nodded as if to say, Yeah, I heard that before, but Moon let it ride. Maybe he wouldn't be in touch after all. Heflin said, "Well, you're ready to move on out then."

"I'm all packed. I just got to go back to the cabin and drop somethin. I'm regular that way."

"That's the way to live a long, long time, Coles. Be regular. Ole Louis Armstrong, now. He used to take him somethin called Swiss Kriss, I think, and he was with us for a good while. You take care yourself. I'll see you when I see you." Heflin laid the shake on him and was gone, striding across the floor.

Moon finished breakfast and returned to the cabin. He loved the smell of it: old wood, the heat, even the drafts which crept beneath the door and through the window. When he was finally ready, he put his bag, the attache case packed in it, into the car and got in. He accelerated slowly down to the main road, and turning onto it, gained speed. "One mo time," he said to himself, turning on the radio.

The heat built up in the car and he eased it back down. The music was not quite country, not quite city; somewhere in between, a little of both. The studless snow tires hummed loudly beneath him. He wished the sun would come out. Everything seemed stuck to the gray sky—the dun-black hills and trees, the houses and barns, the towns into which he rushed before realizing it, before slowing down; and then out of the towns again, across chipped concrete bridges, rusting metal bridges spanning turbulent brown streams already swollen with the first winter rains seeping down from the hills.

Now the names of the towns were becoming familiar, remembered with the faces of people who'd moved from them into his city: boys with .22s, girls with long, mannish strides, men with 12-gauge shotguns and worried beagles; towns which sheltered the names of some of the colleges that had played against the team back home during the first Great Depression, colleges which had long since been pushed off the schedule, while the home team went big time, national champs, Cotton Bowl, Orange Bowl, Lambert Trophy.

Moon crept out of the network of county and state roads and gained the U.S. highway, turned left and headed home.

Onetha Wiggins moved briskly from refrigerator to stove to cabinet to table. No wasted motion. A smile played softly on her face. That Bubbles was something else when he had time off. Whew! Thursday night (or, rather, Friday morning), Friday night (last night), and again this morning. She giggled as she flipped a pancake. Three times in two and a half days! That whiskey and all those big-butted women, plus that little juking I put on him myself. Oh, what would the kids say if they could read my mind this morning!

Ummm, she thought as she bit into a sausage. Good. She slipped them into the oven. Crisp them up. She pushed aside the curtains at the window and peered up at the sky and scowled. No sign of blue. No sign of sun.

Turning away she called, "Bubbles? It's on, baby."

She heard his voice and removed the food from the oven, placed the last batch of cakes on top, and set the platters on the table as Bubbles came striding through the house.

"Hey!" he said. "Ummph! Smells like heaven in here."

"Yes, sir," Onetha said, sitting down and pouring the coffee. "I know Chops isn't eating like this, not in the hotel." She snickered. "Maybe not even at home."

Bubbles dug in.

"She looks kind of fat to me."

"Who?" Bubbles said.

"Christine, that's who."

"Christine? I thought you was talking about Chops."

"Chops isn't· a she. You know who I was talking about, Mr. Bubbles. If eyeballs could get drawers, you'd have worn Christine's big behind *out*."

"Yeah? (Chomp chomp chew chaw.) Well, it's true, I *did* look, but not all that much, and when I did I just got to appreciatin what was right here in the house all along (chomp chaw chew chomp) and feelin a little sorry for ole Chops because he wasn't looking any too happy——"

Onetha dismissed his words with a wave of her hand. "Man, if that cow had said let's do it for ole times sake——"

"Wasn't any ole times, Neet, I——"

"Doesn't matter to me if there were ole times or not. Humph! You can do it anytime you want to. Just don't let me catch you!" (Chew chomp chaw chomp.)

Onetha watched his eyes darting from his food to her face, and laughed. "Honey, eat. I'm just teasing you."

"Haw, haw," Bubbles said. "How come you pick the last day to start talking like that? Didn't want to give me any ideas before?"

"Now, Bubbles, you *know* I can't give you ideas in that direction. I got my hands full right now with ole Bumpin Bubbles. Yeeow." She smiled at him fondly. "You playin ball today?"

Bubbles paused and looked at her. He shook his head. "No," he said finally. "No."

"Didn't think so." She sighed and pushed back from the table. "Got to stop sometime, I suppose. You'll never look like Rick again, and I'll never look like Allison."

"Would you want to?" he asked.

"Sometimes. Sometimes, the way I feel, it just wouldn't hurt."

Bubbles snorted. "I sure wouldn't want to get through those times again. Being young."

Young seemed like yesterday, Onetha thought. Just like yesterday. "It's funny," she said. "Everyone looks the same, but different. They act the same, but different; know what I mean? And you think to yourself, they're all grown, but that doesn't make a difference." She thought of women, the way some of them applied new make-up right on top of the old. Like that.

"Sure you don't want to wait until they've all gone and you, Diane, and Evelyn can really wrap it up?"

"Hush, Bubbles. You men are worse than women when it comes to gossip, and that's why you're always talking about how bad *we* are."

Bubbles frowned at her. But he too was thinking about the sameness and the differences; he had, in fact, when she was not around, got out his old scrapbook where the team pictures were slowly and quietly going brown, where the faded and frayed write-ups of their games were. Nine, ten, the faces filled with the fat of innocence; twelve, thirteen, eyes dancing, the fat gone; fifteen, sixteen, seventeen, the faces set in the determination of athletes, smaller copies of Singh, Gregory, Holland, Jefferson, Owens, Peacock, Cooooooool Papa Bell, Gibson, and of the white boys, too; Chappie, ramrod stiff, the last man in line, the only man, centered, coach, scoutmaster, ageless, pin-striped or chalk-striped, settled mustached face, lean hands, long fingers. Yes, the faces were the same, but somehow different. And now, a streak through his nostrils, came the locker room smell of defeat: stale, but sharp, a funk. Strange how sweat had smelled differently after a win. He said, "I thought it would be different."

Her voice was cautious, not quite concealing the coincidence of their thought. "What do you mean?"

Bubbles flung open his hands as if he'd had them clenched too long. "Like, well, if something happened so that we didn't have to go through this thing tonight, I get the feeling that everybody'd be gone in an hour. Like—it doesn't seem to mean what I thought it would mean."

"Yeah." The word came out in a falling breath and she sought to retrieve it. "It's that damned Moon."

"A part of it, yeah, sure. But no one's worried about that but us. I mean, Snake doesn't even know. It's more than Moon. It's the whole goddamn thing."

She watched him rise and wished there was a way she could

help him more. She glanced up at the clock. She was going to have to get the house together. Tonight it was their turn to have everyone. Bubbles would be running back and forth between home and the hotel to see that things went smoothly. Tonight and it would be all over.

Bubbles pulled out of the garage into a gray, sullen morning. He cursed under his breath. It was odd how bad the weather had become during his adult life. When he was a kid, every day, practically, was sunny. Forty-five years of pollution, he thought, by me and everyone else. He drove to Mrs. Porter's neighborhood and circled the nearby blocks several times. Nothing. Suppose he'd flown in and then was flying out? Why hadn't they thought of that before? Not Moon's style, and that was what they'd been working on all this time, Moon's style. Bubbles turned around and drove to Mrs. Porter's. He parked and walked heavily up her steps, to her door, and rang the bell.

He heard her rushing through the house and felt a sudden guilt. Probably thinking it's Moon, he thought. She flung open the door. Her face fell.

"Miz Porter," he said.

"Come in, Richard. What're you doing up so early?"

Bubbles stepped inside. "Er, I ah, always get up early, Miz Porter. I'm at the foundry, you know. But even on Saturdays I get up early. How've you been? Last night was the first time I had a chance to talk to you in quite a while. Sure was good to see you, m'am."

"Richard, Walter isn't here."

"Oh!" Bubbles shuffled. "I just wanted to tell him something."

"Sit down, Richard."

"Oh, I can't stay, Miz Porter. I'm on the way to the hotel to make sure the table arrangements are okay. Things like that." He grinned. "Gonna put you and Moon right with the gang, naturally——"

"What'd you want me to tell him?"

Bubbles said, "Just to call me. Please call me as *soon's* he gets in. Here's my home number and here's the hotel number, okay?"

Mrs. Porter took the paper, stared at the numbers. "You know, Richard, someone's been calling just about every hour asking for Walter. Won't leave his name. You know who that would be?"

"No, m'am." Mrs. Porter was a big woman, imposing, stern.

"You sure, Richard?"

"Yes, m'am."

"Is Walter in some kind of trouble? Richard!"

Bubbles sat down. "Miz Porter, I don't know——"

"Then why's everybody calling and not leaving their name?"

Bubbles leaned forward. "Everybody?"

"Oh, shoots. I mean that one man calling so often."

Bubbles leaned back. "Oh. I don't know m'am."

"Well now I have to tell you, Richard. I'm getting nervous with these goings-on. Now you know I have got to protect my boy."

"You've heard from him." Bubbles moved to the edge of his seat again. He saw that she was caught between wanting to remain silent and wanting to give him a weapon to help protect her son. "Have you?"

Now Mrs. Porter sat down and seemed to shrink. "Richard, please help him." She stared at him. "Please." Nothing about the sandwiches, the kindnesses, the movie money, and yet the eyes were telling him, *Remember, remember, remember.*

Huskily he said, "Yes, m'am. We plan to."

She sprang on the word. "Who is 'we'?" Perhaps this mysterious "we" could help.

"Er—Shurley, Cudjo, and me, Miz Porter——"

She stood quickly. "What's goin on, Bubble? I wanna know what's goin *on!*"

Soothingly Bubbles spread his hands. "We don't know, Miz Porter." Can't tell her about Swoop, she'd shit, Bubbles thought. "Well, there's a guy who thinks Moon was er, ah, you know, with his wife the last time Moon was in town—like that, Miz Porter. I mean there was some talk——"

She was relieved. "Is that all? Shoots, Walter can take care of himself. If the man'd been any kind of man—you sure that's it, Richard?"

"Yes, m'am! But you know people're doin all kinds of crazy things so we just want to make sure all goes well." He rose. "When's he gonna be around?"

She studied him for a moment. There was a plea in her eyes. "He said in time for the banquet."

"Tell you what, Miz Porter. Suppose me and Cudjo come by and pick you up, you and Moon. I'll call you about an hour ahead of time *if* Moon doesn't get in before then. If he does, you make sure he calls me."

She sounded grateful, a weight gone. "All right, Richard. I sure do thank you. It's wonderful the way you boys grew up and got back together again, and are still looking out for each other. Wonderful, wonderful."

"Yes, m'am," Bubbles said at the door, and left.

He called Shurley and Cudjo as soon as he arrived at the hotel, and went to the main banquet room with a curious fluttering in his stomach. He fingered through the cards, forcing his wandering attention back to them. The place was sold out. They had a success. And already people were vacuuming, cleaning, pushing tables and chairs into their places, slapping numbers on them. The workers were all black, and yes, they were evil. Working Saturday morning for a black banquet they had not been invited to. Bubbles felt all this, these strangers grunting and cursing around him ("Man straighten out that goddamn tablecloth!" "Fuck a tablecloth!"), black people he did not know, would never come to know, and he wondered how that had happened in a town where he once knew every black family. Had these strangers no Junior Bachelor Society of their own?

Two hours later in another part of the hotel, Dart was saying into the phone, "I appreciate your staying in New York and trying to land something, but listen, Katya, this thing is *over*. Tomorrow noon we'll be busing down. I want Simone to see something of the countryside. So we'll meet you at the Port Authority like you said."

Simone lay belly down, dressed, her head propped by her hands under the chin.

"Yes, I got the money," Dart said. "How long? I don't know. It's not like we have a heavy schedule back in Europe." He said this accusingly. "No, no. I really want to do something in New York, Katya. Keep trying."

Hanging up, he did not try to conceal his disappointment. "She's still working on a couple of things. Small, but New York."

Simone nodded.

Dart sat down beside her. "Everyone seems to be doing so well, but me. Even Bubbles, Shurley, and Cudjo." He sighed. "They have a settled, sure look about them. No surprises, no disappointments."

"You envy them?"

"I guess I do, but I don't envy their living in this town, thank God."

"Well," she said, "your parents live here, too."

Dart looked at her and thought of the conversation he'd had with Michael about his parents. He shrugged and looked at the floor where the morning paper had fallen. Dart snarled at it. The critic, the same one who'd been covering the arts for the local papers for as long as Dart could remember, had been polite and properly enthusiastic about the "return of the native son," but had supposed that the demanding rigors of singing in Europe had "taken a slight toll on a once magnificent voice."

The rigors of Europe translated to the rigors of age? He wondered if his parents had read the paper.

"My parents," he said finally, thinking of the visits he and Simone had made to their home. Only the colors of the walls seemed to have changed. The furniture could not have been the same, but seemed so. Everything seemed frozen in time, and Dart imagined the voices of the cops in their car calling out softly, "Well, Johnny, can't stay out of trouble." He saw his father going to them, leaning into the window of the car, talking quietly, then coming back into the house to put on his jacket and going back to open the rear door, climb in, close it, and ride off with them.

A visible means of support was lacking. A small chicken, its ghost given up gratefully, lay pathetically, overcooked, in a roasting pan too large. The learning in fragments of words, things seen, that they lived marginally. Social security? Welfare? Food stamps seen in a partially opened kitchen drawer, seen and studied quickly, realization coming even more quickly. Secretly Dart cursed his mother. Chappie would have had her in a mansion. When he looked into his parents' eyes he saw that they'd hoped for him to make it big in Europe; that they'd not said anything about their condition for years in the sad hope that when he returned it would be down Salt Street at the head of a parade of armored cars bearing sacks of gold; he saw that in their eyes and the dismay, crushing, that this was not and never would be the case. He cursed their lack of self-reliance. Not like Ralph's father nor Chappie; not like Christine's mother and stepfather. Dart's parents were just people who all their lives had waited for him to take care of them, and maybe he was as much to blame as they.

He had by implication lied to them, a hint here, one there, and with a scratch of the pen a plain Amsterdam flat had become a reconverted seventeenth-century merchanthouse, a showpiece of the Keizersgracht, the canal of the kings; and yes, checks from time to time, when things were going well; cards and gifts from all over Europe; clippings from the smaller papers with his pictures. The universe it must have seemed to them whose longest trip in life had been no more than eighteen miles away to Butternut Creek in the summer to fill mason jars with sulfur water. These shabby people (who were what he would become), with their plates rattling in their mouths, timidly and quietly but desperately clutching onto a world instead of letting go and allowing themselves to be whirled off into space. No wonder I always lied about them. Made them white. Wealthy. Worldly. Hip for old folks.

His face sank slowly into the crook of his arm. Damn you, Marcus. What could he leave them, he wondered feverishly. A hundred? Two? Three? Slip them something as they sidled past, already mummified, toward their graves. But did he owe them? Involuntarily he gasped and feeling his wife turn toward him, burrowed his face deeper into his arm. Yes. Yes, of course. He could not repay them though, not what they needed, so desperately and obviously needed, which was not love; no, none of those learned intangibles to which pleasing descriptions are attached. Money. Money. Money. For they knew too, now, that his failure could not give them a harder grip on the world, and that oblivion, so much a part of their lives already, would now proceed at an even faster pace. There would be no better life. There would be no more Foxxes. The end of it. Good, Dart thought. Three hundred and fifty dollars. It would look like quite enough; it would allow them to escape.

Dart, averting his face, got up and went to the bathroom.

Simone rolled over and looked at the ceiling. Having seen, she knew. Her own parents had caused her no such problem, nor any other kind. They had disinherited her upon her marriage to Dart, to his surprise. They had cut her off so quickly and cleanly that she had had to conclude that they had been waiting for the opportunity. She had not missed them. Now she thought about them briefly. She stood and smoothed her clothes. Close to the bathroom door she said, "Darling, I'm going to shop for an hour or so."

His voice was muffled. "Okay."

Grateful for her absence, Dart stepped out of the bathroom and lay down. Rest for an hour, he told himself. Feel better. Forty-five minutes later the ringing phone startled him out of his sleep of escape.

"What?" he said sharply.

"Who?" he said weakly, shaken, awhirl in the mystics of happenstance, fearful suddenly of the power of a mentioned name, a thought name. A demon in the room seemed to be grinning at him. She was downstairs in the bar. He hung up, splashed water on his face in the bathroom. He felt a pounding in his head, and now he thought of what he should have said on the phone, but had not. He would kill downstairs. Tear him to pieces, mean, slippery, bloody pieces. Stomp him with raging glee. Dart raced to the elevator and punched the button until it came. He bounded in and leaped off as soon as the doors opened downstairs. Kill. His stride gulped the distance between the elevator and the bar. Kill. Kill. He stoppd in the entrance of the bar, one foot lightly touching the floor, his arms loose at his sides, studying the early Saturday afternoon drinkers.

"Dart."

The voice cut under the hum of drinkers and their sounds, cut through the twenty-five years and unerringly caught his ear. He stiffened, turned and, already moving, saw the arm moving back and forth slowly in a far corner. He moved toward it on legs from which fiber and feeling had almost vanished.

Ash blond. This woman five years older than he? She looked ten years younger. Her clothes were cunningly fitted to show a body thirty years younger than it actually was. He rushed on toward her, reached the table where she sat not with Wilbur

Marcus, but a younger, blockier man. Dart felt as though he'd walked a long way to meet her, and there she was, tanned, oiled, powdered, each wrinkle reflecting a studious pampering, the crowning hair sculpted in its arrangement. Renee Marcus smiled and extended a hand to him. Her body moved pleasurably within itself and the muscular young man noticed and scowled at Dart.

"Ah, Dart," she said, her hand resting long and dryly in his. "How good to see you." Her eyes, slanted now from a face lifting Dart guessed, stroked him tenderly. "This is Rhobert. Rhobert, Dart Foxx."

Glaring at Dart, but not so she could see, the man stood and pumped Dart's hand and dropped it. "Caught your act last night, Mr. Foxx."

Dart speared the man with his eyes, saw him change from young to old, from Rhobert to Wilbur, and he was leaning across the table, reaching, when at the same time he felt her touch, he heard her voice: "Rhobert, go to the bar. I want to talk to Dart alone. Go *on*."

Rhobert rose. Dart straightened and stood in his way, turning his body slowly, guiding Rhobert by with a hand that was gripped viciously in the young man's bicep. "You dumb, end-of-the-line motherfucker," he whispered. "I'll give you an act right now, you so fuckin hip—" and the young man flexed his muscles and attempted to snatch himself away, but could not. He stared dumbly into Dart's grin.

"Rhobert—Dart, let him go."

"G'on, puppy," Dart said.

Renee patted Rhobert's chair and Dart slid into it. "An act," he said.

"He was being nasty. Jealous."

"I know what he was being, Renee. Where's Wilbur?"

"We did see the Festival last night."

"Where's Wilbur? What're you doing here?"

"It was good," she said. "You were good."

"Wilbur must be on the Coast. I thought you got over this kind of thing, Renee. Wilbur didn't like it. It upset him."

"No, he didn't go for it. And I guess you of all people should know."

"Where's he? I want to kill him." He waved to a waiter.

"California."

Dart gave his order to the waiter.

"He's also dead," she said. "He's been dead twelve years."

Dart stared at her.

"Yes," she said.

"Twelve years? I thought——"

"You thought he was still riding you. Poor Dart. He did for a while. He never started a day without dictating a letter or making a long distance phone call about you."

"But——"

"His power was limited, Dart. He didn't do well at the studio. He became an agent, then an independent when everyone else did, but they had more talent, and little by little the bottom dropped out."

"Bring me another," Dart said to the waiter as he seized his drink and downed it in one swallow. "I don't understand," he said.

Her gaze was soft. "Rhobert and I just came back from the Caribbean. I live back here now. For the past five years. Sick father——"

"No," Dart hissed at the thought.

"What is it?"

"Nothing, Renee. You have kids?"

"No. You?"

"No."

"Why do you look that way, Dart?"

"Twelve years. I was thirty-seven then. I could've——"

"Listen, Dart——"

"If I'd known——"

"After the first couple of years no one paid attention to Wilbur. They had it figured out, if they hadn't before."

Dart slapped the table. Heads turned in their direction. "But how come——"

"Your own ghost, Dart."

His head snapped at the words. "But I tell you——" he started, rising halfway out of his chair.

She saw his rage and met it with eyes burning, her head up. "You wanted to believe it. Maybe you *needed* to believe it——"

"No! There were things going on!"

"Not what you think!"

"Then what, woman, *what?*"

She waited until he sat back down and the heads had turned away. "You know," she said. "You know."

Dart felt his head bending toward a truth, and for the first time he saw his fresh drink. Her hand intercepted his as he reached for it and he drew back quickly.

"You really didn't have it, baby," she said. "I'm sorry. You were Wilbur's ego trip, maybe. His way out of guilt for the rotgut he sold in that crummy bar of his in the neighborhood; for the loaded dice and marked cards he used when he gambled there." She leaned toward him. "Didn't they ever wonder why Wilbur *always* won, or were they afraid of him?"

"Even so," Dart said hoarsely. "I would not have been the first person with mediocre talent to have done well. The world's filled with mediocre talent."

"Yes."

Dart finished his drink, placed his elbows on the table and leaning toward her as if engaged in casual conversation said, "Renee. You're fulla shit. I was good and Wilbur did me in because of you. Bitch! *I was good!*" He got to his feet and stalked out.

Swoop Ferguson had started to detach himself from the shadows of the bar at the moment Dart and the young white man had strained at each other, then changed his mind. What they did had nothing to do with him. He was after something else. He didn't know the white woman or the white man, and didn't give a damn about Dart who now was racing out of the bar. Swoop picked up his beer and watched the young man return to the woman. Wonder what that was all about, he thought. Just some of Dart's strange shit.

Earlier he had been upstairs looking over the main ballroom where the banquet would take place, and seen Bubbles huddled over a table fingering cards and writing. He imagined the scene later. The room crowded with people, and Moon appearing. Yeah, not only Moon, but the mayor and all the city council, the bankers and hotshots of the city. Collar him in plain sight?

(Swoop snorted. Oh, no, baby!) But that was what he'd wished to do at first, stretch out that long arm of the law in full view of everybody (SSsswooooOP!) and show those cats, those Junior Bachelors, that they weren't so hot, that they pulled on their pants just like him, pissed like him? Show *all* those snot-nosed Negroes who'd looked down on him and his kind when they came, when he joined the force (which then became the legitimatizing factor in ignoring him); Negroes out there in the foundry, damn it, not as *clean* as him, even; and that Shurley (got that sumbitch good, him an the ole man); and now this faggot Dart, and Snake with his high-actin ways—and they think they're bettern me?

His face half-hidden behind his upraised beer mug, Swoop concluded that he'd have to work something else out. The mayor'd have me up by the balls, fuckin up somethin he was speakin at. Then Swoop put down his mug and left the bar, his great bulk, hamlike legs swinging around each other, his arms whisking in circles from his trunk, and people, as they usually did, moved farther out of his path than they really had to, and he was thinking: I want that Negro so bad I can taste him. Taste him!

EIGHTEEN

By five o'clock the huge room was ready, each table draped with a starched white cloth, the arrangements of baby mums centered, the silver, thick and much used, lined on either side of the plates crested with the hotel's initials. In the front and center of the room, on the face of a podium equipped with a microphone and light was a sign: THE JUNIOR BACHELOR SOCIETY. Head section waiters, already in tuxedos, padded softly around the tables checking the number of places set; they had done this before and would do it several times again. From the kitchen hidden by thick, dark drapes came the voices of the cooks, the bang and clatter of large pots and pans, and, just barely, the odor of food. All was in readiness.

Bubbles, Shurley, and Cudjo sat at a corner table of the Ebenos, looking out at the street. "It's five," Cudjo said.

Bubbles looked at his watch; he'd looked at it only a moment before. "Yeah," he said. "I suppose it's time to go and get dressed. Look at that goddamn rain."

Shurley and Cudjo glanced at their watches. Bubbles smiled tightly. "It's two seconds after five, Cudjo."

"You're sure you don't want me to come?" Shurley said.

Bubbles quickly shook his head. "No. Cudjo, you go on and get dressed. I'll go too. Shurley, when you're ready you pick up the women and get to the hotel. Check out that Swoop from the minute he walks into the place."

"Haven't seen that cat all day," Cudjo said.

"Hey," Shurley said. "Why're we whisperin?"

"Were we?" Bubbles said, his voice louder, close to normal.

Cudjo laughed. "Yeah. Like we were in a funeral parlor or somethin."

"Then I'll come by your crib, Cudjo, after I call Moon, right?"

"Thas it, Bubble."

They rose heavily. Bubbles kept his eyes on the street. He did not want to see Shurley looking around the Ebenos the way he now was, like taking a last look.

Shurley said at last, "Cudjo, you mean they dug up a suit that'd fit you?"

"Turkey," Cudjo said, "if you ain't learned it yet, this man out here can sell you *anything* you need. That's what makes his world go round. You need it, he'll sell it to you. Or rent."

At six, dressed except for his jacket, Bubbles moved stiffly toward the phone. He emptied his glass as he dialed, glancing at Onetha who, facing her mirror, was watching him.

"Miz Porter this is Bu—Richard Wiggins. Moon there? *No?*" Bubbles looked at Onetha again. She was motionless, watching, waiting. "Well, have you *heard* from him? Uh huh." He thought he saw Onetha sigh with relief. "Lissen. Me and Cudjo will come by to get you anyway. Bad night out there. He may show up between now and then. He'd have called if anything came up, I'm sure of it, so don't worry, hear? Why don't you just write a note and leave it for him. Yeah, sure, tell him we're at the hotel." Bubbles turned helplessly toward his wife. "I know he wouldn't want to miss it. 'By."

Bubbles sat on the bed. "Hummm," he said. "Hummm."

Onetha said, "Not yet, I gather."

"No."

"Cheer up, baby. Could be a no-show and we're home free. Just another four hours or so."

"Wooo!" Bubbles said, getting up. "Score's tied and the clock's runnin out and we goin into overtime! I need another drink."

Onetha took his arm. "Even if you do sound like a President of the United States, you lookin mighty fine in that tux, Mr. Bubbles."

He smiled and reached around and hugged her by the buttocks. "I know you don't want me to mess up your face, and I don't want that crap on my shirt. But I loves ya enyway, honey."

"Bring back a big one so I can sip some of yours," she said. She faced the mirror again and thought of when they were kids, before the war, and the semiformal dances they'd had and how Bubbles would come to her house, having walked self-consciously through the streets in a pair of Sunday pants maybe, or anyway, not everyday pants, his rented white dinner jacket and matching bow tie and pocket handkerchief, a matching hat-band around his wide-brimmed Adams hat, a red carnation for his boutonniere, carrying in his hand, as though it were the most valuable package in the world, the inevitable boxed gardenia corsage. Invariably it was spring, or so it now seemed, the night air sweet, and their movements, everyone's movements were a promenade of grace, an exhibition of a youth that would come to know no age, but would move through marriage, motherhood, move through time fixed in penny loafers and bobby sox and double overhanded spins of the Lindy—

"Hey."

She smiled at him and took the glass, swallowed and passed it back. "Oh, Bubbles," she said.

And he, curious at her tone, smiled tenderly at her, puzzled, for there were things he was still discovering about her.

"What is it, Momma?"

"Did I tell you I love you today?"

"No, but thank ya; I sure needs that kinda news."

They grinned at each other and Onetha thought, surprised, that she had suddenly smelled gardenias.

Shurley Walker slipped the recorder and the last two tapes under the front seat of his car. He checked his jacket to make sure he hadn't got any dirt on it, and although he saw nothing, he brushed it anyway. He wondered what he would be doing to-morrow night at this same hour. Sunday night at six. Used to be Young People's Hour at church. He smiled. Just something to keep you off the street. Sunday school in the morning, church until one, except for the first Sunday when the preacher had to lay it on for communion. Rescue Mission until four and back to church at six. The old folks really had it together, at least on Sunday. Not that they didn't work as hard to keep you busy on the other days, too. Homework. Bringing in coal. Cleaning out the stoves. Sifting ashes. And they didn't mind you playing ball. That kept you off the streets, too.

He'd loved the Sunday night walk home, the powdered snow, the ice-cold rain (like now) underfoot, the stop at Okun's Delicatessen for hot chocolate and a salami sandwich, gettin on the girls and making up; loved this time of year sitting up in the living room of some girl's house, no ma'ming and yes ma'ming the mother, yes sirring and no sirring the father in the next room, his finger straining past the edge of panties like a beast with its own mind seeking the place—

Shurley shook his head. His own kids had been into that, he supposed. Gwen and Geoff. They were gone already, to the hotel, Geoff looking like Hollywood had made him in his frilled shirt, belled pants, and pinch-waisted jacket. Gwen. Pretty. Guys were breaking down doors to get to her. Good thing they got the pill these days, Shurley thought. Men, shit, buncha a fuckin rats. He chuckled as he returned to the house. They be steady into gettin into my daughter. Inside, he turned on the television set for the news.

Maybe, he thought, I should have told Diane all of it, the tapes. But she'd have worried, I know. Better this way.

"——society last night at the Civic Center."

Shurley concentrated on the set, saw the film of people moving into the Center, of Dart singing soundlessly while the newscaster talked. They just may have some real news tomorrow, Shurley thought.

Snake Dumpson did not know why he felt something—what, he did not know—whenever he looked across the room and saw his son, Victor, and Dart Foxx, talking animatedly. He had come to the hotel with his wife and children to join Clarie and Pat, Chops and Chris, Ralph and Eve and Dart and Simone for drinks before the banquet. There was, Snake decided, checking his watch, for he was to pick up Chappie and Ralph's father, something clannish about this gathering. All the college men. But Bubbles, Cudjo, and Shurley had not really declined; simply said they'd try to make it, but they had banquet things to check out. In any case they would all gather afterwards at Bubbles' house. Maybe it was Snake's imagination, but it seemed that every time he had looked up the past two days, Bubbles, Cudjo, and Shurley had their heads together. He found himself to be not with them, the Homeboys, and not really with the others; somewhere in the middle; neither/nor.

It did not feel good, being left out, Snake reflected as he made his way to his car.

But later, returning, Ralph's father was asking, "You remember that Colgate game when you was a senior and that big tackle, Muhelhauser, and you had set your mind to running over him in the last quarter?"

Snake smiled.

"I remember that!" Chappie said. "I remember that because—" Because he had been surprised; because he had expected Snake to do what he'd always done, go around instead of through. How could he have forgotten that afternoon? Chappie was feeling good. He was in black tie and he and Ralph had been drinking Canadian Club at his, Chappie's, waiting for Snake, and they talked about old times, swimming in the canal, the way the slick Pullman porters came into town sharp and walked off with the girls; they had not lingered long there. That was too close to Big Ralph, too close. Mostly they talked sports, how Jim Brown as a freshman walked off with all the prizes, and how he'd been an All-American lacrosse player, too. "Yeah," Chappie was musing still. "I remember that. Like Snake decided it was gonna be him and Muhelhauser. Bam! Whooee!"

Snake chuckled deep in his throat. "That boy almost sent me to the hospital, big and bad as he was. You know, I think the pros decided to get tackles just as big as he was from then on."

Big Ralph said, "At first, he was meeting Snake, you know, and layin him right on his back, remember, son? And then Snake was puttin it to him, man. Soon it was that big Muhelhauser on his back. Oh he had Snake all right, but he was goin backwards, and that meant Snake was pickin up three, four yards. Ain't been nothin like it since."

None of the old people had ever indicated that they'd watched him so closely, Snake thought with warmth. He smiled at Ralph's father, who was dressed in a dark suit, the way he'd been every time Snake saw him.

"That was the last time we played Colgate," Snake said. "The very last time."

"Ole Muhelhauser," Big Ralph said.

"Mule shit when Snake got through with him," Chappie said.

"He got killed in Korea," Snake said, and a silence fell

until Snake spoke again. "How you fixed these days, Mr. Joplin? I mean, if you ever run into any housing problems, let me know. I never make promises, but I do the best I can."

"Oh, I'm fine, son. Got a little rat nest over there. Warm and all. But I thank you anyway."

"Coach seems to be doin all right, huh? And listen, I hope this won't be the last time we get a chance to talk."

"Ah, no," Chappie said, feeling warm, feeling fatherly.

"Oh, we'll be talkin, Snake," Big Ralph said. "Maybe too much."

Snake laughed. They'd made him take a double shot of Canadian Club, and on top of what he'd had at the hotel, he was feeling all right. What was it they called CC these days? Like Cadillacs? Oh, yeah, the Nigger-Killer. And Cads were Niggerchines. Mercedes-Benzes too, now.

"Ole Ralph's done pretty good, Mr. Joplin. We're all real proud of him."

"He's worked hard, worked hard," Big Ralph said, shaking his head for emphasis.

Snake said, "I know." These men, perhaps among the last, still believed that hard work brought rewards. Yet Mr. Joplin, whose hard work had brought nothing, still believed. Incredible!

"Whaddaya say, chief?" Ralph said, embracing his father. Big Ralph cupped his hand behind the bulge of his son's head, briefly enjoying its shape covered by soft hair. Black folks sure had that head, he thought, smiling now as he bent to receive a kiss from Eve. "How're you, little lady?"

Chappie moved into the room slowly, grinning, shaking hands, the Canadian Club flowing freely, breaking through the stiffness he felt in his rented tuxedo. He envied Big Ralph his plain suit, but he, Chappie, felt that he couldn't let the boys down. They'd mentioned over and over that the banquet would be black tie, Coach, *black tie*. Big Ralph Joplin, still towering half-a-head taller than anyone else in the room, didn't seem to be bothered by the fact that he was the only man not in black tie. He was having a good time with his son and daughter-in-law. Nothing, nothing, was going to change him.

On the other side of the room Simone Foxx slipped between people until she came to her husband. She slipped her arm through his. Dart was now almost recklessly drunk; she had not seen him so in many years, and he had been talking earnestly, perhaps too earnestly, to Kenneth Dumpson's son. Simone hoped no one had noticed. Applying a pressure the boy could not see, she said, "Mr. Davis just came in darling. Don't you want to say hello to him?"

Dart, feeling the pressure of her arm, hearing the edge in her voice, looked at her, blinked at her warning and patted young Dumpson on the shoulder. Looking a final time into the soft eyes, he let himself be led away.

Clarence Henderson was eying Christine Jackson. She smiled and he smiled. Behind those big, dark glasses, she was missing nothing. He did not really remember how it had felt making love with Christine when they were kids, nor with Diane, nor Onetha, nor with any of the others he'd seen since he'd been back, or would see in a few moments when they went to the banquet. They'd all wanted to give it to him then, touch his skin, play with his hair, and he, not knowing then what it was all about, believed at first it was *him*, the thing he was *inside*, that they wished to be close to. If only they'd shunned him, spat upon him, or meant it when they'd called him names. But no. The way they were opened his eyes, revealed his ability to walk through walls, and he saw them now, the younger women on his campus, in his class, on his travels, heard them in their rages, heard even better the plaintive echoes, like the distant sound of iron bells, and cursed their mutual history. He had been so easy. None of the work, like Moon, just bogarting pussy all over the place, talking up on it, pleading for it (but not really, simply knowing that when the loving was over it would speak for itself); none of those relationships easy with smiles and banter, and that was why he had feared Moon.

Eve Joplin smiled and slid her glance past Ezzard Jackson's sad, intense face to where Pat Henderson had just that moment placed her hand upon Ralph's wrist; and Eve read the flash in her husband's eyes, the quick computation, and she cursed them both. Yes, yes, she told Jackson, she could use another drink.

There was here at almost seven, a kind of time-lapsed panic growing of the budding stage, pistils, stamens, petals, enlarging, taking form, blooming. If someone called out "Orgy!" Eve imagined they would all, including herself, fling themselves together seeking to touch each other in the most basic manner. The last fling or something, for tomorrow evening at this time, they would have gone their separate ways and yet, six of them would be going to New York: Clarence and Pat, Dart and Simone, and she and Ralph. But they would not be going together. Ralph's car would be too crowded with six people and luggage. The Hendersons already had plane reservations. The Foxxes wished to spend a few more hours with Dart's parents before taking the bus. "But, let's get together in the City." They had left it at that and passed on to other conversations. The old home town was special; after it, nothing was.

Jackson passed Eve her drink and raised his.

"What're we toasting now?" Eve asked. A bunch of black Russians; every time you looked around there was a goddamn toast. Ralph now had his arm around Pat.

Jackson pondered. "Bullshit?"

Eve clinked her glass. "You've got it, Ezzard. That I'll drink to."

The bar set up at the corner entrance of the main ballroom was crowded. Big men, slender men, and occasionally a small man greeted each other with great, instant smiles and the yelps of ex-athletes who were still sure that their exploits were achieved in times grimmer than the present. *Offense, and defense, hell. We went both ways; we knew how to play football!* Forgotten for the moment were those differences of race; the triumphs were recalled, the defeats laughed at; they were like old soldiers who gather in their dress blues, who proudly stroke the blood-red infantry stripe on their trousers. Every minute brought a new face, one that openly sought others that would be familiar. The Hill football coach, the former Hill football coach under whom Snake had played, Pat McCormick, the old high school coach, Anthony Buonfiglio and others from the old high school teams, many with sons bigger and wider than their fathers, and these seemed to be wearing on their tuxedos invisible block letters.

You could not tell the difference between the shot putters and the football players, but the men who once had been lean and known the time of Glenn Cunningham in the mile 4:06.7, the western *roll* in the high jump, Cornelius Warmerdam's *bamboo* vaulting pole and the *broad* jump before it became long, these definitely were former trackmen; Jesse Owens' 10.3 100-meter in Berlin, 1936, and Ralph Metcalf's 10.4.

And there came the basketball players, the former stars out of the era of the two-handed set, even after Hank Lusetti, who saw the game change the moment George Mikan stepped on the court for the Lakers, and these smiled and shook their heads when they saw the younger players, reed thin and all better than six three—"small men."

The politicians joined them, shaking hands around, joking, warier than usual, for this was basically a black gathering, and many politicians remembered the sixties, and still harbored the memories of dashiki-dressed black militants who disrupted any and every meeting, who, in fact, couldn't wait to disrupt meetings.

There was, however ethereal, the sense that all had come through something together: hard times, good times, revolution; passed through a sucking maelstrom and emerged in, for the time being anyway, quiet waters, and they were softly amazed and pleased and warmed that they had survived.

When the JBS came down from Henderson's room, the yelps and hoots grew louder, the handshakes and backslaps firmer, the exclamations of surprise and pleasure nearly involuntary, and the coaches and former coaches, the former athletes and athletes called Chappie Coach Davis, and shook hands gently with the wives as the ballroom filled with people, Bubbles and Cudjo escorting Mrs. Porter among them. They eased Mrs. Porter ahead of them and paused to confer quickly with Shurley.

"He didn't come," Bubbles said. "And he didn't call. She left a note."

Cudjo pushed on the pain in his back.

"I saw Swoop a couple of times," Shurley said. "So many people here. He may have gone by now, but I guess he'll be looking in from time to time."

"Terrific turnout," Bubbles said.

"Yeah," Cudjo said sourly. "I wish I could enjoy the motherfucker."

The dark, wet November night had collided with the dun-colored countryside just as Moon felt the wheel rim pound down through the tire to the road without warning. He felt a sudden, gut-dropping glide to the center of the road and he snapped the wheel in that direction, felt the car grow solid beneath him as he guided it, without braking, back on his side of the road and felt it steady and slow to a wobble. The approaching car, with lights blinking in panic, slowed, then rushed on by.

Moon sat in the car when it finally stopped. He turned off the ignition, heard the rain on the roof, and looked up and down the road. Nothing in sight save leaning, weathered houses and barns back off the road. He glanced at his watch. Almost six-thirty. He put the blinkers on, left the headlights on, got out and rummaged in the trunk for the jack and spare. The spare was not a snow tire. Didn't matter, had to get moving. Back inside the car, Moon read the instructions for changing a tire; he'd never changed one in his life. Once in a while through the thickening darkness, he heard a car whining up, saw the probing lights, and then it roared on by. Moon didn't blame them for not stopping; he would not have either. Out again, Moon wrestled with the wheel lugs until he began to sweat, but finally they loosened. It took him longer to fix the jack; he worried that it would slip off and injure him. He worked by feel, and it seemed that he was alone in the world, now filling with mist, the passing cars no more than meteors fluttering through space. "C'mon, baby," he whispered as he fitted the spare. "That's it, just a little bit more. Hawh! Yeh, eassssy, lover. That's it, joog light, honey, uh-huh, ooooo, yessssss. *Yeah!*" Quickly he slipped the lugs back on, tightening them as much as he could with his fingers, then with the wrench.

"YeeeOw!" he shouted into the night when he stood up, finished. He threw the tools and the flat into the trunk, wiped his hands on the trunk floor, got in and drove off. It'd taken him forty-five minutes and he was at least forty-five miles from home. He felt cocky; he'd just finished doing something no one else was there to do for him. He had worked a simple piece of machinery; he had fixed something, made it run again. He turned up the radio and set his foot heavily onto the accelerator. Shit, maybe he could even learn to drive nails straight, and wouldn't that be a bitch!

"I think it's time, man," Cudjo whispered to Bubbles. And Bubbles looked up, his dinner curdling suddenly in his stomach; he glanced around at the hundreds of faces, at the faces at this JBS table, and said to Cudjo, "Oh, shit." Cudjo smiled sympathetically, slapped him on the back, and sighed with secret relief that Bubbles, not him, would have to stand and talk. Bubbles looked over at Onetha and she returned his gaze with steady eyes. The JBS and their wives and families smiled, winked, clenched their fists. Bubbles moved back his chair, took the papers from his pocket, stood and walked to the podium, grasping hands along the way, nodding, concealing his terror. At the podium he adjusted the light and smoothed his papers and cleared his throat.

His voice came out of the amplifiers, big, and he liked the sound of it feeding back across the room, liked the way the faces all turned to him, even the mayor and the men at his table—the big men of the town—Bubbles knew. He spoke on, growing more sure of himself, and then he reached the part where he had to introduce the JBS and each stood, reacting differently to the applause—Snake waving into it, Chops merely nodding at it, Ralph bowing slightly, Cudjo heaving up and back down quickly, Clarie standing stiffly, his hands clasped before him, Dart smiling the way he had last night, Shurley raising both hands.

"We don't know," Bubbles heard his voice echoing back, "what's happened to Walter Porter. He was supposed to be here. In his place, welcome his mother, Mrs. Porter." Flustered, her hands moving about her body, Mrs. Porter stood tall and proudly until at last a smile broke over her face and she sat down.

Bubbles fidgeted until it was quiet and then introduced the mayor and moved aside. The mayor followed him, holding out his hand, smiling, and Bubbles heard the cameras snapping, blinked from the flashes going off. The mayor launched into the history of the city, its first black population before the American Revolution, its abolitionist movement, the work of the Reverend

Samuel May, the Underground Railroad; he spoke of the great black athletes and of the people who had imbued them with that greatness, which did not, he said, begin on the playing fields, but at home, with the love their elders had for them and in the respect they in turn had for those elders.

Chappie Davis was now aware that he would be called upon to say something to all these people. Next. The palms of his hands were already wet. His dinner skipped back and forth across his stomach. He wished for another drink, right now and a big one. He sipped his water. His head seemed to tremble on his neck.

We all know, the mayor was continuing, about the Knute Rocknes, the Lou Littles, the Vince Lombardis, the John Wootens. They receive the molds; all they have to do is burnish them. For every great coach who is well-known, there must be ten greater coaches who've never been heard of. It is only within the past weeks that this city has learned of Coach Charles Chappie Davis. If he worked against odds, he never complained of them; he did not despair. He had a present to shape and, if shaped correctly, it would be adequate to deal with the future. That future has come. The mayor glanced at his table and an aide, holding a laminated plaque, slipped forward and handed it to him. In the name of the people of this city, I am proud to present you with this year's Citizenship Award. "Coach Davis?"

Everyone at the table stood and clapped. People got to their feet, and stood on their toes trying to see Chappie and the mayor, surrounded now by photographers, give Chappie the plaque. They stood and clapped and whistled, and as the mayor made his way back to his seat, Moon Porter in velvet black tie, sweating slightly, slipped into the room, squeezing between standing people and tables until he found the JBS group and moved next to his mother; the people clapped as Bubbles, his arm around Chappie, led him to the mike. "Coach Davis, everybody."

They stood again and clapped.

Moon laughed when his mother turned to see who was clapping so loudly beside her, and then embraced her. He grinned and winked at Pat Henderson who, with mouth open, was staring at his wig.

Chappie grinned at Bubbles and licked his lips. He winked down at Big Ralph. Finally, they began to sit down.

"Uh—I'm supposed to say somethin," he said. "Well, thank you. Thanks a lot. You know I just—I'm not used to talkin in front of people you know. Oh, I can do fine if you give me a bunch of teen-agers——"

They laughed.

"——but now, I'm not so sure." He looked around for Bubbles, and finding him, passed him the mayor's award. "I look out here," he said, "and I think to myself, What did *I* do? That's the truth, you know. When these men were little boys, *they* did all the runnin, I didn't; *they* were gettin the bumps and bruises and gettin so tired they couldn't boogie-woogie, I didn't; *they* wanted to be somebody, otherwise, there wasn't one single thing I could've done for them.

"Some of my boys, you know, didn't make it. Maybe they didn't want to be somebody, not for the world, but for themselves. Maybe they got a little sidetracked." Chappie nervously wiped his forehead. His glance fell on Big Ralph who nodded encouragment.

"But we came a long way; I want you to know that. The mayor was talkin about how far we've come, yes, an I just want you to know that we have gone over, around, and *through* history, and I don't think my boys are done yet; I don't really think so. I was richer than any parent," Chappie said, "because I had em all and they came without my calling them. Times was bad back then, for a whole lotsa people, but they were good for me because I had these boys."

Bubbles saw Moon, raised his chin at him, and smiled. Moon, his Afro sparkling, was shaking hands around the table. Why Clarie and Pat were staring at his head puzzled Bubbles, who now had caught Cudjo's eye and then Shurley's.

"I don't think I can say more than that," Chappie said. "I enjoyed nearly every minute of them and this affair tonight. Thank you." He started to walk away as the applause came up again. Bubbles reached out and caught him by the elbow. He held his hand up for silence and reached under the podium for Buonfiglio's plaque and spoke into the mike. "We can't ever give you what you gave us, Chappie. But, if you ever get tired of watching football on television, we hope you put this on a wall where you can look at it and think of us."

At first everyone thought he was reading it, but, at the same time it seemed, everyone realized that he was crying, holding his head down so the tears would not show. Bubbles put his arm around him and the standing ovation began again. Bubbles saw Cudjo talking quickly, urgently it seemed, to Moon and his mother. They stood and Cudjo guided them from the table. Bubbles looked for Swoop. Chappie made as if to move, and Bubbles holding the first plaque, guided him to his seat, carefully placing the awards in his lap. He returned to the mike to thank the guests, and it was over, the crush gathering at the JBS table. Bubbles hurried down and pulled Shurley aside.

"Where they goin?"

"To your crib."

Head swiveling, Bubbles asked, "You see Swoop?"

"No, did you from up there?"

"Can't see shit, there's so many people. What'd Cudjo tell him?"

"Only that we were gonna party at your place and that they should beat the crowd."

"Uh-huh, uh-huh," Bubbles said, still searching the crowd for Swoop. "What do you think?"

Shurley shrugged. "I don't know, man. I hope it doesn't take too goddamn long to get out of here. Hey! You did okay, Bubble. You'd make a great president for this outfit."

Bubbles, pleased, smiled and said, "Jive turkey, you. Just so I could do all the work. I know about that shit."

"It was okay, really."

Onetha pushed her way through, closely followed by Evelyn and Diane. "Did you see what we saw?"

"Yeah, and you chicks get hoppin right now with Shurley. I got to check with the man for a minute. Get over there quick and keep an eye out for Swoop."

Bubbles moved behind Chappie and the crowd pushed in, the people all smiles, their hands outstretched for shaking or back-slapping, and Chappie grinned back and thanked them by name, his usual cynicism about nearly everyone over fifteen jettisoned for the moment.

Bubbles watched him and thought, He's lovin it, all of it.

Could stay right here until morning. Look at him. He glanced around. I gotta get out of here. Then he heard Snake.

"Can I take some folks over to your house?"

"That would be good. Take as many as you can and we'll manage the rest somehow." The more people Moon was surrounded by, the less chance Swoop would swoop, Bubbles hoped; God, he hoped that would be the way. Gratefully now, he watched the table start to empty. In another hour the place would be empty; in two the people would have stopped talking about Chappie; in three they would be asleep, most of them, and tomorrow everything would be business as usual. But, Bubbles thought, how many men or women had two hours turned over to them so people could say thanks?

Go, Coach.

Cudjo chatting fast and he hoped, merrily, swiftly procured drinks for Moon, his mother, and himself. Where, he wondered, was everybody? He didn't need for Swoop to be kicking in the door right now, when he was holding down the fort all by himself. C'mon people! "Man," he said, pulling himself together and sitting down, "I thought you'd never get here. Been looking for you since Thursday."

"They've been calling and calling, honey," Mrs. Porter said. "But now everybody's together." She squeezed Moon's hand. "Lord," she sighed. "I'm so happy to see you that I don't care about you being bad."

Moon looked at his mother, saw nothing but pleasure in her face, and he turned to Cudjo, saw something there, in shadow, and said to his mother, "What do you mean, 'bad,' Mom?"

Cudjo leaned forward, almost spilling his drink. "Oh, you mean what Bubbles told you this morning, Miz Porter?"

"Of course, son."

"What?" Moon asked.

"Uh—well, you know that guy's wife you were uh—hangin out with the last time you were in town? Well"—Cudjo raised his brows and put on his blandest expression—"he never got over it; said he was gonna get even, so me, Bubbles, and Shurley, we thought we'd sort of keep an eye out for you." Cudjo shrugged. "Probably nothin."

Moon frowned.

His mother laughed. "He's done forgot about that woman already, see?"

Moon forced himself to smile. "Sure have." He cut his eyes hard at Cudjo. Fear clutched at him and slipped off, like lakeweed. He kissed his mother. "Aw, it's nothing, honey. Don't worry. Sure is good to see *you!* Ain't she lookin good, Cudj?"

"Sure is, yes, sir!"

He can't know, Moon thought. He can't. Have to get him alone as soon as I can.

The door banged open. Moon watched Cudjo jump, his eyes widening, then slap a hand to his back, and they were into the room, all of them, their wives, children, and some parents. "Moon! Moon!" they called, closing in around him, the women laughing and kissing him, the men grinning, the youngsters and the old people hanging on the edge, smiling. He'd met them at the table, but their greetings had been restrained. Now there was no public, and they were pummeling him more, cooing, and he was envisioning (that stringy fear for the moment gone) another gathering, in Canada, at his place and Dorrie's; it would be summer, perhaps this summer *coming*, and they'd be near a lake or a river, readying a California-type cookout; Dorrie'd be fluttering in and out of their motel and his mother (as she was now) would be sitting in a comfortable chair, a drink in her hand, her smile warm and bright, pride in him busting all over.

He saw Moon, Shurley, and Cudjo talking.

"Jesus, man," Snake said. "You look like you could still play some ball. Tennis?"

Moon pulled Snake close and whispered, "No. Fucking, that's what does it, Snake. That's exercise, believe it. Jogging, tennis, handball, swimming—nothing's as good exercise as fucking. Tones up the skin too, man." Moon laughed at the uncertain expression on Snake's face.

Snake glanced around. Good thing this was a private party. Glad the table was too full for us to shake hands. . . .

Patricia Artis Henderson looked archly at Moon's wig. "Well, well," she said.

"He's a plant," Henderson whispered just loud enough for Moon to hear. "He grows hair in less than a week."

Moon winked at them.

"Whew!" Dart said, weaving toward Moon who caught and steadied him. "Them's some threads, Moon. Sharp as, sharp as"— he glanced around—"snake shit! S'cuse me, Snake," he hollered to Snake who'd edged away and hadn't even heard. Dart fingered the cloth. "Real velvet. G'on, Moon!"

This cat is some drunk, Moon thought. He did not like drunks. Or junkies.

"You ain't hurtin at all, are you, man?" No, you couldn't trust them, junkies and drunks. He saw Dart's wife pushing toward them, her face wearing an expression of irritation and weariness. Dart grabbed Simone around the waist. "Meet my nigger, honey. Big bad Moon."

"We met at the table, Dart." To Moon she said flatly, "Hello again."

Moon nodded and watched as she led him away.

"They're just so glad to see you, son."

"Be right back, Mom." He eased his way through to where he would intercept Bubbles. "Hey," he said.

He thought Bubbles sighed. "Got yourself settled?" Bubbles asked.

Moon took him by the elbow and led him through. "Hello, Mr. Joplin," he said as they passed.

Big Ralph said, "Say, Moon. You look good, son."

"Thanks, so do you. And ole Ralph over there." To Bubbles he said, "We gotta talk, man."

"Yeah," Bubbles said, and led him to the basement door and downstairs. The loudspeakers were carrying the music Onetha had just put on. She must've seen us, Bubbles thought. Before they reached the bottom step they heard footfalls behind them. Cudjo.

"Saw you cats easing off," he said.

"Why you walkin so funny?" Bubbles asked.

"Back," Cudjo said.

"You ought to get you a pool table, Bubble," Moon said, sauntering around the room.

Back, Bubbles was thinking. First I ever heard of that in a long time. "Cudjo got the pool table," he grunted.

Moon sat down and carefully pulled his pants legs to hold the creases. Something goin on, he told himself, looking at the somber, set faces before him, and it looked like he was smack in the middle of it. "What's that shit you were tellin Mom, Cudj?"

Bubbles sat down. Cudjo looked at him, but Bubbles was looking past Moon somewhere. "That's the story we agreed to tell her. Let me ask you somethin. What the fuck have you done?"

Oh, oh, Moon thought. Bubbles' face still showed nothing. Cudjo waited. Really showing his age, Moon thought. Cudjo did not appear to be comfortable and Moon felt sorry for him. "Just the usual, Cudj. You know my line. That's all. Why?"

Now Bubbles spoke; his words came heavily, loaded with anger and accusation. "You know that Swoop Ferguson nigger, that cop?"

Moon thought. "That heavy boy, quick, that came up after us? I know who he is, yes."

"He's been waiting for you," Bubbles said. "What did you do?" He watched Bubbles pass a hand, wearily, across his face, then focus his eyes on him.

They heard the music, the voices above them, the floors creaking when people walked.

Moon smiled, but the fear held this time. "I don't understand," he said. He held out his hands. "I haven't done anything, man."

"We've been goin since Thursday," Bubbles said. "And every step of the way Swoop's been there, watchin, *spyin*. Nobody else, just Swoop."

Cudjo said, "Hangin out by your mother's, driftin in and out——"

"If it was anybody else he was after, he'd a had them by now," Bubbles said. "So it's gotta be you, Moon."

Moon got up and began to pace. Tell them or not? If he told them and the roof fell in, they'd be involved, and this wasn't any little old thing. Accessories after the fact. He stopped by the door that opened onto the yard and looked out. Why in the hell had he listened to Shurley? He could have followed Cudjo here in his own car. His own car, already packed, the stash in the three shoeboxes crunched under the seat, and in his briefcase. Ready! But the motherfucker was still in the hotel parking lot. For a moment the urge to flee was overpowering. Just reach out, take the doorknob, turn it, and gone. *Gone*. He might have done it; he might have done it, but the sound of glasses made him turn. Shurley was coming down the stairs with a bottle and a bunch of glasses in his fingers. He walked to the center of the room, glancing at everyone and said softly. "Shit, Bubbles, you really ought to get a pool table down here."

"Fuck a pool table," Bubbles said, and the snarl in his voice made them all turn. Avoiding their stares he took a glass and the bottle and poured. "Ole Moon," he said, "was just about to tell us what happened."

"No I wasn't," Moon said, holding out his glass.

"Why not, man?" Cudjo said. "We been puttin out for you——"

"Cause it's bad, that's why," Moon growled.

Oh, shit, Bubbles thought.

Shurley thought, Goddamn.

Uh-uh, Cudjo thought.

"Bad," Bubbles murmured.

"Real bad?" Cudjo asked.

"Superbad," Moon said. "Superbad."

"If it's so bad, why did you show up here?" Bubbles was more curious than angry now.

"I didn't know it was bad until I got to New York and called the Coast. I didn't hear or read anything about it. And I had to come home." He began pacing again. "Wanted to see Mom. You know, I can't understand this nigger, all by himself. He didn't talk to Mom, because she would've said so. And you cats said you didn't see anybody but him——"

"Would he have some papers out on you?" Shurley.

"If he had papers, he wouldn't be runnin around here alone," Moon said. He stopped walking. "Listen. Lemme get outa here. I got plans. I don't see any point in you cats gettin involved, I mean really. It was a mistake. Just one of those things that went bad."

Looking across the room Bubbles sensed that Moon was, in spite of the three of them, alone, with things pressing in, and he remembered one of the first summers at Boy Scout camp when it had been so warm that the earth was hot underfoot, and the water in the river had lowered; playing on the bridge, Bubbles had fallen into the river and not having passed his second-class swimming test of fifty yards, forgot that he could do at least twenty-five; panic accompanied his fall, enlarged with the splash, and all was quiet, brown and warm, the sun a dull glow at the surface; he could not seem to rise; he was alone. Alone, until a bubbled streak of silver split the brown, turned into Moon, he thought, yanking at his arm. And he began to remember to move, that he could move; he kicked and stroked and the brown became less brown, a tan, a beige, an almost gold, the sun and blue sky, the same greening trees, the same corduroyed footbridge, the faces thrust over its ropes, hands somehow connected to those faces reaching down.

They were twelve then.

Swoop Ferguson had circled the block twice and then parked a block away. He heaved himself from the car, felt for his piece, and slammed the door. He walked down the street, feeling the rain pelting upon his hat. Nice, he thought. Nice and quiet. No nigger muggers. No nigger junkies. No niggers whooping and hollering. What you get here is like white folks. Stabbing their husbands, drunk on martinis. Nice, middle-class junkie kids who have the dough to buy the shit. Husbands pleading for pussy from their wives, who ain't about to give up nuthin. Them days gone. Wooo! Didn't matter. He'd made up his mind. Ain't none of this shit for me. He turned up the Wiggins' walk.

On the front porch he heard the music and the voices. He rang the bell, rang it again after a decent interval.

Onetha clapping in time to the music and moving her body. Victor Dumpson and Gwen Walker were doing the Bump. She marveled at the way the youngsters moved their bodies; a whole different style. But, she had noticed, they were starting to touch each other these days, and then the old music, the old dances were coming back. Nostalgia, they called it. "Go, Gwen," she called, and she looked around to see who would be a likely partner, and settled on Ralph. Then the bell rang.

She flung the door open, a grin on her face. When she saw who was standing there, it vanished, then was replaced.

"Evening, Miz Wiggins," Swoop said.

"Oh, hi." The expression on his face was calm, certain. Onetha did not know she'd moved smack into the doorway until he said, "Can I come in? I just wanted to say hello to some of the boys. That was a nice thing tonight."

"Uh, well, it's kind of a private—yeah, sure." What else could she say?

Behind him, the street was empty, slick with rain.

Swoop stepped inside and removed his hat. Looked like a good party. Onetha closed the door behind him. "Let me get Bubbles." Swoop broke off waving and nodding.

"That's all right. Just tell me where he is." He'd already scanned the room and seen that Moon was not there, nor were Shurley, Cudjo, or Bubbles.

"If you don't mind—" Onetha started to say, but Swoop had seen her glance at the basement door off the kitchen and was half a step behind her as she walked toward it.

Her voice came down the stairs high-pitched and tense. "Bubbles!" and they turned. The heavy-set man moved easily down the stairs, studying them each quickly, expressionlessly. To Onetha he said, "Just carry on with the party, Miz Wiggins."

"Go 'head," Bubbles said to her. To Swoop he said, "Swoop——"

Swoop raised his hand placatingly, but his eyes were fixed on Moon. "This is the man I want to see." The hand dropped, dipped into a pocket and reappeared; there was a police badge in it. Just as quickly it was returned. "What say, Moon?"

Aw shit, Moon thought. "Is this the nigger?" Yes, he remembered him; recalled a hefty, big boy who moved swiftly, powerfully, implacably. Clean in starched khakis, home on furlough, his first, like old jocks seeing the old tracks, he'd gone to see the high school football team work out. *This kid is better'n you, Moon*, McCormick had said. And Moon believed him.

"Yeah, I'm the nigger," Swoop said. "And I am also the man." He chuckled as he moved deeper into the room. He passed through them and took a chair. "Sit down gennemens. I've had a long, hard day." He signaled for the bottle and a glass, which were passed to him and he poured.

Moon sat down opposite him.

"You been following us, Swoop," Bubbles said.

Swoop nodded his head toward Moon.

"You got papers on him or something?"

Moon swiveled his head from Bubbles to Swoop, and fixed his glance on the latter when he said, "Oh yes."

Shurley said, "What kinda papers?"

Swoop sipped from the glass and smacked his lips. "Murder papers."

Moon met their glances, each one in turn. He said, "Where's the rest of the force, Swoop, you know, five hundred cops to one black man? How come the house ain't surrounded, or is it? How come no bullhorns and searchlights?"

"Cause I'm so bad I don't need four hundred ninety-nine motherfuckers, that's why."

Moon began to understand.

"What do you mean 'murder'?" Cudjo asked, moving to a position in front of Swoop.

"What say, fat man?" Swoop said. "You know what murder is, don't you? One person kills another."

"Bullshit," Moon said. "He was trying to kill me."

From the top of the stairs Diane called: "Shurley?"

"It's all right. Go on and close the door. Keep things going."

Swoop said, "Ain't no bullshit. Ole bad Moon didn't kill just anybody, you understand. He killed a cop. Didn't you super-jock?"

"Moon?" Bubbles said.

"He was on the take. Heavy——"

"*Move,* fat man," Swoop said, pushing against Cudjo, "so I can see my prisoner." He slipped his hand inside his jacket.

"That shit ain't necessary, Swoop," Shurley said.

"Moon?" Bubbles said again.

"Let this nigger arrest me. Let him make the charge. Lemme hear something," Moon said. He'd play these cards.

In the momentary silence Cudjo, shuffling from one foot to the other, his arms swinging freely, said, "Don't put your hands on me again, Swoop. You got no cause to be so bad in somebody's house without a warrant."

"Sorry, man," Swoop said, smiling. Everybody wanted to keep some face. "I want to talk to Moon alone," he said.

"I'm stayin," Shurley said.

"Me too," Bubbles said.

Cudjo said, "I'm in, too."

Swoop looked around. "Okay, Shurley. That's it. Keep the party moving you two."

Moon thought with a sigh of relief. All these cats is on the take; not a goddamn honest cop in the nation. Well, let's see the tab.

"Call us if you want us," Bubbles said and they started up the stairs. Fuck a Swoop, he was thinking. Him and Cudjo was gonna go right through the house and around the side right to the back door.

They sure want out of this shit, Swoop was thinking.

Moon thought, Why Shurley? Why Shurley?

Onetha sidled up as Bubbles and Cudjo sidestepped through the dancers; Diane craned her neck from across the room, missed Bubbles' motion which sent her away. Snake Dumpson was not so deep in his conversation with Clarence Henderson, which was about the need for new literature textbooks that would include black writers, some folks named Terry, Hammon, and Wheatley, right up to the present, that he did not see Bubbles and Cudjo squeezing through, past and around people, toward a side door. He wondered what was going on. The Ferguson cat was a cop, he knew. With Moon, a pimp? He glanced around the room, quickly noting where the members of his family were. Chappie could have smiled. Just stopped talking with Dart's momma and laughed. Bubbles and Cudjo call themselves slipping out, he thought. Same looks on their faces like when they were kids. The very same. Ain't changed a bit. Serious looks.

Moon had never liked electronic musical instruments; there was no purity in their sounds. Analyzed note by note, they were computers that made sound. Now an electronic bass was reverberating through the basement room. And a Moog Synthesizer.

Shurley sighed and said, "What you got, Swoop?"

"Tell him, Moon."

"You tell him. I'm cool."

"Yeah, you so cool, you killed a vice cop."

"He was taking, man. I didn't even know the man was dead. Until I made a call——"

Shurley very carefully placed his head in his hands.

"——shit," Moon said. "For the sake of argument, let's say you got hold of somethin and you tryin to get over. Just sayin, now. Behind that cracker, nigger-hatin cop. Just sayin. I ain't sayin nothin about you bein here all by yourself; I ain't sayin nothin about how you sent Cudjo and Bubbles away—hey! How come Shurley stays?"

"Shurley's my buddy, ain't you, Shurl?"

Shurley snorted.

"You into this shit, Shurl?" Moon could not believe it.

"Aw, man, don't be no turkey. Just talk to Swoop."

"That's right, baby. You can talk to me."

Moon leaned back and smiled. "That's what I like to hear, Brother."

"You were saying," Swoop reminded him.

Killed somebody, Shurley was thinking. Well, yeah. He supposed that they all, at one time or another, had been ready to do that. If he could have done it and got away with it, he'd have killed a long time ago.

"Yeah, I was sayin—sup*pose* . . . how much would that be worth to you, Brother?" *His* cards are on the table, why not put mine down?

Swoop came forward in his chair, stroking his chin. He cut his eyes toward Shurley. "You can go now, Shurley."

"No," Shurley said, without removing his head from his hands.

"What?"

"You heard me."

"Thought he was your buddy," Moon said, chuckling.

Swoop continued to stroke his chin. "Hollywood," he said. He looked up at Moon. "Big bread in Hollywood, man."

Moon said, "It ain't super." He looked at Shurley who looked back at him.

"Man, go on and deal," Shurley said.

Now Swoop heaved himself backward in his chair. "Well, I guess I got to be a Brother. I'ma help you over for twenty-five."

Moon got up quickly, shaking his head. "Let's go to jail then." He was not about to turn twenty-five biggies over to this hick motherfucker. And Shurley was a witness. "That cracker took my bread, man. You cops're somethin else."

"Well, what you got, turkey? Don't waste my time with no theater."

"I'll give you five. That cat was worth one dollar, Swoop. No more."

They would settle at ten, Shurley guessed. He was facing the door; Moon and Swoop had their backs to it, talking or rather haggling with each other. Shurley saw through the glass, blackness moving on blackness. He felt better knowing they were out there.

"Fifteen," Swoop said, glancing at Shurley.

Moon went into a whine. Without changing his expression, Shurley was startled. How little things had changed. Moon was pretending to cop a plea; he had done it often when they were kids and later he would laugh and painstakingly show them how he'd really won, and what he'd won. Swoop didn't know him.

"I had to split in a hurry, Swoop. I need something to get out of the country. Europe——"

"That ain't my problem."

"Yeah it is. Ten."

Swoop looked down at the floor. He kept their feet within his vision. "Whew," he said. "That's a long walk from twenty-five."

"Well, let's walk then," Moon said.

"Nigger, shut up!" Swoop snarled. For a moment he wished he had carried out his original plan; to swoop him, walk him out handcuffs and all. And this Shurley. He was gonna have to talk to him good. Sitting there taking it all in. But, I'm gonna have to get this bread. Ten big ones don't come easy. Cap the nest egg. Fuck a promotion and a little bigger pension check. Now. Now. "Got the ten?"

It was time to use caution, Moon thought. Only a fool would trust a bent cop. I'll try him. "Give you five and send you five."

Swoop laughed. "I know you can do better than that." He shot a glance toward the head of the stairs. He thought he'd heard something, but nothing moved. It was dark up there.

"I got a problem," Moon said. "I lay this bread on you and then get picked up when I drive away."

"You know you got a witness." Swoop inclined his head toward Shurley.

"Shurley," Moon said, "I feel heat, so I got to say this; I got to go by what I *see*. This nigger said you was his buddy, now what kind of witness for me does that make you?"

Shurley got up and walked down the room and back. Passing the stairs he sensed a presence at their head. Who? he wondered. He passed back.

"Tell you what, Moon. Give me the bread. It's midnight now. I'll give it to Swoop at seven tomorrow morning——"

"Shit! One, I just got through sayin I wasn't sure I could trust *you*. Two, if I could, and you let this turkey go until morning, he could call the cops, cossacks, and coldcockers out and come at seven and get the bread——"

"No. He'll stay right here until then."

Swoop stood. Things seemed to be speeding up. "I ain't stayin nowhere, and I'll take the bread, nigger. Now." He flipped back the edge of his jacket. They all whirled at the sound of feet on the steps, and whirled again when the door opened and Bubbles and Cudjo came in. Chappie came down, eyes wide, as though trying to take in everything. He came on down, holding the rail, walked past them and sat down. "Close the door, it's cool," he said, peering through shadows at Bubbles. Bubbles closed the door. "Sit." He made a motion with his arms and crossed his leg. The pantleg rose up and they saw his skinny shank clad in a silk black sock, gartered to his leg. "Moon," he said. "We ain't had much chance to talk, son."

"No." He turned away from the eyes.

"C'mon, man," Swoop said. "I'll take it."

"Hold it, son," Chappie said. "Sit down I tole you. Everybody."

"Ole man, I don't have no time for sittin."

"Sit down, man," Shurley said.

Swoop looked first at him, with surprise, and then looking at the others, he saw that they were afraid of him. Not physically; they were in good shape. But upstairs, in the head. He was still a cop, with the right to do and be everything and everywhere, almost. This bunching up around him. That was an extreme act for them. They were law-abiding men, and such men are so not because they fear the law as such, but because of what the law can do illegally if it wishes, under the cover of law. Black men understand that very well, Swoop thought. Even Moon, stretching it, worked within, or just a bit outside, the law until that fateful moment. Nothing wrong with running a pimp shop. Then he ran. No, these men would have to step over a barrier of years and habit nearly half a thousand years old; they would not give up all they'd sweated and worked for—reputations, property, careers—all that for *Moon?*

Keep it calm, Swoop thought, and he sat down, frowning at Shurley. "Okay," he said.

Chappie studied Moon again and said, "Tell us what happened."

NINETEEN

They have been down there too damned long, Onetha was thinking; thinking it at the same moment she saw Dart Foxx staggering at her; at the same moment she saw Snake glance covertly at
his watch. It was a moment before Bubbles entered the room, a
moment in which, seeing this movement, Onetha also saw
tomorrow's work: flowered paper plates, upon which half-eaten
food remained, topped tables, teetered upon the arms of chairs,
beckoned from the corners of the floor; empty and half-empty
glasses, like pus-filled pimples, stuck out everywhere; filled ash-
trays, silverware askew. And by now the music did not excite;
it depressed, being so obviously a device which had failed to
draw attention away from the basement and the men in it.
Onetha saw Ralph looking quizzically around, his eyes fastening
upon Bubbles at precisely the same moment she began, with a
quickness which revealed her fears, to walk to her husband.

Bubbles knew at once, closing the basement door behind him,
surprised after all these years at its lightness, that pretense was
over. He felt his wife's hand, cool and trembling on his wrist.
Dart was still lurching forward, another two steps now, and
Ralph was detaching himself, moving toward Bubbles. With all
the movement, Snake's stillness demanded attention, but Bubbles
kept sweeping the room with his eyes. Even with the music playing, there seemed to be silence, a waiting.

Dart's cackling words exploded in fumes of alcohol: "What're
you cats doing down there, having an orgy?" And he writhed
and bent with laughter.

Bubbles felt a long, warm surge of pity, and he tried to smile
as he put his arm around Dart, steadied him. He looked for
Simone, saw her, on her way. Bubbles remained in front of the
door. "Got a kind of a private problem," he said, looking at Dart,
but talking to everyone. No, it hadn't turned out good. "Easy,
man," he said to Dart. Dart was sad drunk, not happy, and Bubbles did not know why.

"Is Walter all right?" Mrs. Porter asked, rising from the cluster of older people, Dart's parents, Big Ralph Joplin.

"Sure, sure."

"Bubbles——" Onetha began.

"Let's all go down," Dart said, rocking against him.

"I'm waiting right here for Walter," Mrs. Porter said.

Ralph was now next to him. Bubbles signaled Snake, who came with pronounced reluctance. "Will you guys see that everyone gets home or to the hotel?"

Snake studied Bubbles. Should he ask questions or just go?

"Bubbles——" Onetha said, close to his ear.

"It's all right, honey. Nothing," he said to Ralph, answering his question. "Everything's cool. Just want to keep it that way." Simone was guiding Dart away, or trying to. Clarie Henderson and Chops were coming forward with their wives. The young people stood to one side, watching, wondering. Bubbles wished Ralph would stay; he hoped Snake would go. All stay but Snake. No, let them all go and get out of this mess, he thought, and then the door bumped his back and he stepped aside to let Chappie into the room, as into the locker room at halftime, the team losing badly.

It was like that. Chappie just walking in, into the center of the room, briefly studying each face, computing with his ancient mind what lay behind it; doing it in silence, forcing every pair of eyes to fix themselves upon him.

He said, "We have had a good time. I thank you. Now, the Bachelors got some business to take care of. Snake, you and Ralph get these folks home."

Funny, Bubbles thought, he picked the same two I did.

Chappie placed both hands on Mrs. Porter's shoulders. "Don't you worry none, May. Your boy's all right. We just got to straighten out a few things——"

"That boy down there's a cop, ain't he Chappie?" Big Ralph's words. Chappie nodded, said nothing.

"Why would a cop be here?" Pat asked. Henderson nudged her.

"*Is* everything all right, Coach?" Snake asked. A final assurance so he could quit the scene gracefully.

"I said it was." Now Chappie moved, shaking hands with Big Ralph, with Dart's parents, the youngsters, doing it with such an air of finality that Ralph, Henderson, and Chops looked at each other quickly, trying to fathom their next move. "C'mon, Snake, Ralph." Herding them toward the door, a look both wistful and disgusted floated to Dart, being led to the porch; the door open, the wet, cold air slicing into the house.

A sense of things and acts being unreal came to Bubbles, time whipped away and out of focus, and even so they were going, *going!* Going to the sound of voices hushed against the outside, car doors opening, engines cranking up; no time for lingering last good-bys, a final taste of something good, promises to meet once again, now that they finally had after so long. Onetha crossed the room and closed the door. Chappie sighed and started for the basement, Bubbles with him. "Guess I'll start to clean up," Onetha said. "And I'll make coffee."

Bubbles paused. The running engines and voices, now muted, but being defined by the closing car doors, possessed a dreamlike finality; where, within the dream and knowing it as such, you tell yourself it is but a dream and that you have a hard grip on reality, but in the morning all parts of it are vivid, but gone, even that reality within the dream, and you wonder and marvel at the swiftness of its passing. And yet he waited, balancing on the balls of his feet. He willed these sounds: engines being cut, doors clacking open, voices once again curling on the night, footsteps upon his porch, the door being flung open—the return of the Bachelors.

He heard the cars drive away and he followed Chappie back down to the basement.

It was quiet in the car. Snake Dumpson's wife and children were cocooned in their own thoughts, impelled to them by the brusque ending of the party. Dumpson felt uncomfortable; some instinct told him that most of their thoughts involved him, and they were negative. He stoked a righteous anger.

They had taken Mrs. Porter home, Sandra spending an inordinate amount of time assuring her that Moon was all right, that she would see him later, and that what was going on was just Bachelor business.

"Then why didn't Kenneth stay? Are you going back, Kenneth?"

Old loyalties in view, as if by magic. Pork chop sandwiches

and movie fare, and a thought of his own mother visiting relatives in Buffalo.

"I guess it's just for those who're there now, Mrs. Porter—" and he began to flounder.

Sandra said, "He'll look back in though, Mrs. Porter, don't worry."

A weary, grayish smile in the midnight dark. Relief.

Now, approaching their home, Sandra felt his anger. Of course he was concerned about the inferences which could be drawn, his being in the company of the man who was a pimp. But, surely, being a pimp in California was not the reason the policeman had come.

"You shouldn't have said that, Sandy." The kids had eased out of the car and gone into the house.

"I know it," she said. "I had to tell her something. All night she talked about how you all stuck together when you were young, and how Bubbles, Cudjo, Shurley, and you—I didn't tell her you hadn't seen them in years—all got together to look after Moon and his problem. She said," and Sandra looked hard at her husband, placing the weight of her own thoughts behind Mrs. Porter's words, "that black people just don't stick together, and that the Bachelors were unusual."

"What do you mean, Moon's problem?"

"Bubbles told her there was a jealous husband after him."

Dumpson was staring at the floodlit lawn, the sculpted privet hedges, and he felt his fear gathering its feet then spring off. He rested his forehead on the steering wheel. God! Is that what this crap's about? Yes, sure, he'd go on back. "I'd better get started so I can get back and go to bed."

Smiling Sandra got out of the car. "Wake me when you come back."

It was with relief that Diane Walker pulled up before the hotel. She had dropped off Dart's parents and with her now was Pat Henderson, Dart, and Simone. It had been plain from the moment Bubbles and Chappie had ordered everyone home, that a third car would be needed. She was anxious now to get back and with Onetha check out what was going on. Evelyn, she knew, would be upstairs asleep; she did that at parties. Simone was shaking Dart. Pat stood indecisively on the sidewalk.

"I cannot wake him," Simone said.

"Well, honey, you just can't leave him there." Diane glanced out of the window and said to Pat. "Girl, give Simone a hand with this man, will you?" She thought of her kids who'd walked home. Rotten weather, too.

Pat leaned inside, exchanged glances with Simone.

"Hold it," Diane said. "Here comes help." She was looking in the rearview mirror, watching Ezzard and Chris emerging from Ralph Joplin's car. Then Ralph's wife. She tapped the horn. Clarie now also seen by Pat, who hastily withdrew from Dart and joined Eve and Chris. Ezzard and Clarie came and peered into the car.

Chops said to Simone, "Just leave him. We're going back. If we leave him in the car, maybe he'll sleep part of it off."

"Back where?" Simone said.

"To Bubbles'." Looking at her, Chops saw how tired she was. Ready to cry. "I'll look after him; don't worry. You better get some rest."

Diane was listening to the tone of his voice, hearing things in it, but she spoke: "You goin' back? Good. Get in." Clarie Henderson, his face drawn, slipped into the seat beside her while Chops helped Simone out.

"And Ralph?" Diane asked.

"He's coming. It was his idea."

"Yes, I could've guessed," Diane said.

"What'd you say?"

"Nothing."

"Uh, darling?" Pat said, leaning inside the window.

"What?"

"It's late. Sure you really want to go?"

Henderson turned away from her in exaggerated impatience. For Diane's benefit. "We won't be long. Don't worry." How could he have got out of it? There was Ralph, driving his father home first, talking about damned if he liked the way things had broken up, and how he hadn't come all this way just to leave when the shit hit the fan, and his father nodding like some big,

old, black wise man, and Ralph saying to Chops, "Let's fall on
back, man, at least get a decent nightcap," and that fool,
scrunched up in the corner like he was trying to get away from
his wife, saying, "Sure, why the hell not," and Ralph saying, a little edge to his voice, "You in, Clarie?"

He knew his wife knew enough about them and the situation
not to raise the kind of hell she might have done under ordinary
circumstances. He took her hand and squeezed it.

Behind them Ralph backed up and pulled out. Diane waved to
the cluster of women still on the walk and eased out into the
street following Ralph. She felt so much better with everyone
coming back.

"What do you suppose is going on, Diane?" Henderson asked.

"Tell you the truth, Clarie, I just don't know." Better not to
scare this cat by telling him as much as she *did* know.

"Wonder why Moon got him a wig," Clarie said.

"If he was as bald as you said," Chops said, "the reason is obvious."

"Yeah, but it could be a disguise, too, man. That's what I'm
saying."

"You didn't *say* that," Diane said. "But that's what you meant."

Henderson grunted. He wished he'd told Ralph, Hell no. I'm
not in.

"Oh, what the fuck does it matter?" Chops Jackson said.

Ezzard had something strange in his voice again, Diane
thought.

It had taken them twenty-five years and more to get back together again, Ralph was reflecting as he drove over the rain-slick
streets; there would not be another twenty-five years for them.
This was it and it had been called, he sensed, by forces from
without which had intruded upon their gathering. No time to
gather without the wives and lie about their exploits over the
years; no time to talk to Chappie, measure the beating time had
laid on him. They had partied, yes, but never got to the talking.
And he was pissed because he felt cheated; something had not
happened. What? Moreover, what right had he to expect something to happen, something good for him? He said aloud in the

car: "This motherfucker *owes* me something good; it was so bad for me."

Yes, he thought, I'm high. We're all high riding a slow streak of lightning; it will strike someplace.

Onetha heard the car door, being cautiously closed, as she climbed the carpeted steps to wake Evelyn. She came back down and was halfway across the living room when she heard a light tapping on the door.

"Snake," she whispered, opening the door. She wanted to embrace him. Tears began to run down her cheeks.

Snaked stepped in and closed the door. He took her in his arms and felt her own around him. "Hey, Neet, hey, there. Have no fear, the Snake is here." He felt her giggling. They both turned at the sound of car brakes squeaking and doors slamming, footsteps on the porch. Snake opened the door before the knock came.

Ralph planted himself in the opening. "We ain't had no nightcap and no chitlins to sleep on, so we came on back, Onetha." He thumbed at Dart. "This nigger here, no booze, just coffee."

"And Di-Gel, and aspirin and Alka-Seltzer, too," Dart said.

Clarie Henderson and Chops Jackson supported him. Diane wriggled around them. "Everything okay?" she said to Onetha and then seeing her wiping her eyes: "They all came back, honey!"

"Why you cryin, baby?" Jackson asked.

"Neet! I say, Neet! Why's it so quiet down there?"

"Who's that?" Ralph said.

"Evelyn."

At the same time Bubbles opened the basement door, his face at first a scowl, then a smile, and then it became filled with uncertainty. "Well, the Bachelors have returned. Dart, how you doin?"

"We came back for the meeting," Clarie said.

"Yeah," Snake said.

"It's heavy," Bubbles said. Onetha turned to him. "Yeah, heavy." He studied them all.

"*How* heavy?" Snake said.

"As heavy as it's ever gonna get."

Henderson said, "Moon?"

Bubbles nodded. "I got to get something out here." He went out closing the door behind him while Onetha searched every face again.

Knew it! Henderson thought. Moon has messed somebody up. Good.

"Well, let's get it on," Ralph said, and he headed for the basement door without looking back.

"Why not, why not indeed?" Jackson said, and he followed.

"Neet?"

"C'mon down and have some coffee, Evelyn," Onetha said, thinking of the heaviest thing she could and dismissing it, only to have it return at once. They closed the door behind them. She could hear voices rising.

"What you doing with Shurley's tape recorder, Bubble?" Diane asked, pointing at the machine.

Bubbles shrugged. "Shurley wants it." He closed the door behind him. Damn, he thought, they don't give you a chance to get in your own house good.

"Aw right, honey," Onetha said. "How heavy is heavy?"

"Killing heavy."

"Oh shit." Diane said it so quickly Bubbles was not sure he'd heard her.

"Who?" Onetha whispered.

"It don't matter now, but it was a cop. But Moon's gonna pay Swoop's price."

"You mean——"

"Yeah. Maybe. Hey. Any sausage around?"

She didn't answer; she was staring at Diane. Bubbles went downstairs.

Evelyn approached. "They *still* down in that basement?"

"Yeah," Onetha said. She sat down.

"Goddamn that Moon," Diane said. "Dragging his dirt here. And you know Shurley, Mr. Jesus Christ, the Saviour. I bet if the shoe was on the other foot, Moon would say 'tough' and go on about his damned business."

"I see the rest of them came back," Evelyn said, yawning.

"Shouldn't have left in the first place." Onetha glanced at her watch. Half-past one. "Help me fix some food, folks. Bubble's talking about some sausage. Next meal may be in the jail." She stood and shook her head. "Killed a cop. Tell you, that Moon is somethin else."

Swoop Ferguson was saying, "Nigger, you somethin else. This ain't no *club* meetin, all your boys come stompin down here. Git these niggers outa here. Now."

"This ain't my house," Moon said.

Looking up at Snake, Dart, Clarie and Chops and Ralph, huddling together at the foot of the stairs, Shurley said, "Well, it surely do *look* like a club meetin."

"Commissioner," Swoop said with a smile and a nod of his head.

His high wearing off, Chappie looked at the faces and nodded approvingly. "What say, boys?"

This, Snake thought to himself, sure did smell like a hell of a lot more than an angry husband. "Coach, what the hell's going on? Why's this police officer here?"

"Commissioner, this doesn't really concern you," Swoop said. "It'd be better if you weren't here." He was looking from the tape recorder to Shurley and back again.

Dumpson felt unaccountably weary. So. This didn't have to do with some woman as Mrs. Porter and Sandra believed. He had wanted to believe that. He felt the eyes of the group upon him. How was he going to react to Swoop's statement? It was like being kids again. All someone had to say was "Oh-oh." The agitator. The spearhead of peer-pressure.

"Officer Ferguson, are you taking a bribe?" Dumpson smiled and sat down. "Are you arresting this man?" He leaned toward Swoop. "What're the charges? Can I see your warrant?"

"Do it, Snake!" Dart.

Dumpson turned to Moon. "What's he taking?"

"Ten, Snake, and don't fuck it up," Moon said.

"Ten," Dumpson said. *"Thousand?"*

"Gimmee that thing," Swoop said to Shurley, reaching for the tape recorder. He heard Cudjo shuffle closer to him.

"You lose again, Swoop," Shurley said. "I ain't giving you shit, nigger."

Swoop nodded his head as if he had reached some decision. He turned to Moon. "You. Gimmee the bread."

"I gotta go get it."

"Like hell. Where's it?"

"My wheels."

Swoop looked around, fixed his eyes on Jackson. "Give him the keys."

"Where's the car?" Jackson said.

"Hotel parking lot."

"Can I get Neet to drive me over, Bubble?"

"Yeah, Chops. Just follow her on back."

Bubbles looked around. He wanted to tell them all how pleased he was that they'd come back; wanted to tell them that this was a terrible thing and he'd tried to spare them. But he was glad they were here. He listened as they talked softly, chuckled, drank; listened again as Moon explained to the others what had happened, and he wondered if Moon, if each of them in turn, would do what they were doing for Moon.

"Why you got that thing, Shurley?" Swoop pointed at the tape recorder. "Don't get foolish now."

Chappie leaned forward yawning. "When I was a young boy, I thought all I'd have to do was swim the river of life and climb the mountain of faith and I'd be all right; I thought I was all through! Now here's another river and another mountain. But I can handle it; I can handle it." He leaned back. "Son," he said to Swoop, "if you'd been three years older, you'd a been one of my boys. But the cards didn't fall that way. I sure woulda made you better than you turned out——"

"Listen, ole man——"

"Let Coach talk, turkey," Cudjo said.

"Yeah, better than you are," Chappie went on. He gestured around the room. "See these boys here? They scared. They got reputations, homes, jobs, families. They are scared. Of you. And they hate Moon, because he done come flying out of the night landing in here with a problem that could destroy all of them and me, too. You hear me, fat boy? You'd be in good shape you took off about seventy-five pounds. Okay, they scared, but they are together. Do you know what that means? That means that as hard as things are outside, no black person should be alone.

Maybe I taught them that. I hope they taught their kids that, talkin about *t'gether*. You, boy, you're alone."

"I'm sorry," Moon said. "I didn't mean to do it. If I thought they'd track me down, I wouldn't have come. I never thought they would. . . ."

"Shit, it's done," Bubbles said.

"Lissen, boy," Chappie said to Swoop. "When Chops gets back, Moon'll give me your bread. And we're gonna sit here until seven in the morning. That'll give Moon time enough to get halfway around the world if he wants to. Moon, I'll talk to your mama."

Moon started to joke: Don't be messin with my mama, Coach, but thought better of it. By seven in the morning, if he left within the next hour, he could be in bed in Montreal.

Chappie looked around. "How's that sound to everybody?"

Snake said, "Ferguson gets the ten thousand and lets Moon get away, and that's all there is to it?"

Moon looked at Swoop. He didn't want to appear anxious. The rest looked at Swoop, who was watching the recorder now resting in Shurley's lap.

"That's the deal. That's all there is to it. I don't want to make it hard on anyone. I just want a little of what everyone else's got, that's all."

"Wooo, listen to that cop whine," Dart said.

"Don't fuck with me, faggot," Swoop said, and a cold sheet of silence poured into the room.

Chappie closed his eyes momentarily, and tried to shut out the words.

Snake swung his eyes slowly from Swoop to Dart.

Cudjo and Bubbles exchanged a glance.

Shurley looked down at the row of red levers on his recorder.

Ralph straightened.

Dart's head cleared quite suddenly, or he thought it did. He walked toward Swoop, stopped and said, "Yeah." He glanced around, meeting every eye. "That's right. I'm a faggot. I've always been. But I bet I'm the baddest faggot you ever met."

All the anger of the day, an even heat, steady, filled him. He faked with his left, a sudden, fanglike movement, as Chappie had taught him, and Swoop jerked aside, and into the path of a right that lifted him partially out of his chair and dropped him back into it. No one moved. They watched Swoop's eyes unglaze; sat motionless as he slowly wiggled his jaw, and Cudjo, closest to him, easily slipped the .38 from his hand when it appeared from under Swoop's jacket, clutched in an unsteady hand.

"Ain't no big thing," Ralph said gently to Dart.

"Shit, I know it ain't," Dart answered, and they laughed.

Swoop felt cornered now, tired and somewhat trapped. He was glad Cudjo had taken the gun, because it sure wouldn't have been cool to blow that Dart nigger away. Had to get that bread. He'd come too far now not to.

"Okay, son," Chappie said. "That's the deal then. That all right with everybody?"

Chops entered through the back door. "Okay. It's here."

Moon stood quickly.

"Hold it," Swoop said, still holding his jaw. "Mr. Davis, you go with him. And both of you come back, so I can count the bread. Then we on the way. Dealin."

Shurley drummed his fingers on the recorder. Bubbles kept shooting glances at him. Chappie and Moon had left the door partially open and a cold, wet breeze came through, carrying the odor of dead leaves.

Moon returned first, Chappie following. He closed the door carefully and bolted it. Moon thought a curse. He had ripped the Mark Cross case getting it from under the seat. He sat down and counted the bills out on the floor.

"Now give it to me," Chappie said. "And you hit the road, son."

"Don't give it to him, Moon."

They all turned to Shurley. "Just keep the money and leave."

Moon shot Swoop a look, then Bubbles, then Shurley, then Chappie.

"Wait a minute, Shurley," Chappie said. "We made a deal."

"*I* didn't make no deal, Coach——"

"Just a fuckin minute," Swoop said, standing.

"*Sappening, Shurley?*"

"*Thing's cool, Swoop.*"

They heard the clinking of glasses in the background.

"*How's the old man, Shurley? Seems like he's turning more and more of the business over to you. Read about the shindig tonight. All the ole boys done come home. The all-stars. The superjocks. The homeboys. Looks like it's gonna be a groovy thing, Shurl."*

"You motherfucker," Swoop hissed.

"Yeah, we gonna try and do it up right. Well, the old man's all right. Gettin on like most of us, but faster."

"What's that?" Moon said, holding the money, pulling it back as Swoop reached out for it. Shurley pressed another button; the machine whirred.

"How come you never count it, Swoop?"

"Because I know Papadapoulous don't be fuckin with the program, that's how come. Tell him thanks. I really appreciate not having any hassles. You all know how to take care of business. Now you take some of those bloods running them dives on the other side of town. They always be wafflin. A hassle to make things go smooth. So don't nobody get bruised. If a white cop had that section, they'd never complain, just go ahead and give up the bread. No, they fuck with me cause I'm a Brother."

"Yeah. Drink, Swoop?"

"No. I got to roll. See you later. Hope you guys have a good time tonight."

Moon stomped with glee. "This cat's been takin the whole world."

Shurley had clicked off the machine. "Keep the bread and go, Moon. Now. Swoop. I want you motherfuckers off my back or this gets to the State investigators——"

"What you mean, *your* back?"

"It's my place, nigger, not the old man's, and I'm tired of you cats stickin it in me. You walk out of here empty-handed."

"No!" Moon said. Then more quietly. "Didn't you listen to the tape? Sounds like the whole police force is on the take. You think they gonna let you get away with this, Shurley?"

Chappie tried to call for attention, but Moon waved him quiet.

"I don't care they ain't fuckin over me no more."

"Man, they don't play by those rules, Shurley."

"We gonna take em on," Bubbles said.

Moon sneered. "Shit. With what? Why you think *I* was running? I know these cats——"

Snake tried to interrupt, but Shurley began shouting at

Swoop: "The trouble with cats like you and the people you work for is that you don't understand that people like me *do* understand. If a man looks all beat up, or even says he quits, you believe it because you have to. Now, I ask you, how in the fuck can a man give up ever, when the shit is so bad, and we're into some deep shit, Swoop. If my rules are crooked, you made them that way."

Moon held his head. "Hold it. HOLD IT! You say I should get my hat and not give this cat the bread. Then what? At seven in the morning, you'll turn him loose, and then you know what? Commissioner, it's gonna be your ass, one way or the other, and Bubbles and Shurley and Cudjo. Because you all live here and you know."

"There're other tapes," Bubbles said stubbornly.

"And they can reach California, Clarie, and to New York, Ralph, and Kansas City, Chops, and Holland, Dart——"

"I know," Dart said. Then he frowned, remembering.

"Look, look," Swoop said. "Just gimme the bread and it'll be cool."

"Cool," Moon said. "What're you gonna tell them? There's a crazy nigger running a club who ain't payin off anymore and that's all there is to it? You gonna tell them about the tapes? Shit, you'll go too, man, dumb as you are, lettin somebody run a tape on you bigmouthing."

Moon looked at the stubborn and frightened faces. Babes in the woods even after all these years. They were right, but dead wrong. "Gimme that," he said, taking Swoop's revolver from Cudjo.

"Moon," Chappie said, "don't be no fool now."

"I'm not the fool, Coach. Unless you come up with something else, Swoop's going part way with me. I thank you for helping me, but you cats need some help, too." He pleaded. "It don't work the way you think it does. It never did, Coach. *This* is the way it happens, and this nigger knows it, and I know it."

"Let me see if I understand," Henderson said. "The ten grand is a moot point now. Whether this cop gets it or not, Shurley has the tapes and will play them for the right people so the cops will leave him alone. What you're saying is that, if we let this man go, the cops'll have their revenge, right?"

"Right."

"Then what do you propose to do with him?"

Swoop said, "Not a goddamn thing."

"Kill him," Moon said.

"No," Bubbles said.

Chappie said, "No. That ain't the way I raised you."

"There's got to be another way," Snake said.

"Well, lay it out then," Moon demanded. "Do you think I *like* this? But you cats ain't in no Boy Scout camp now."

Dart said, "No."

"I'm with Snake," Chops said.

"Don't kill him," Cudjo said. He took another pill.

Moon sighed. "I'ma keep the piece, and I'ma lay the ten on this man, to sweeten him, maybe, to make him think three or four times before he turns the dogs loose on you all. I think you're wrong. I know you're wrong, and I wish I didn't have to say this; I wish things were as great and right as you think they are."

He moved around the room shaking hands. Then he gave the money to Chappie and went out the door, unbolting it quietly and closing it gently behind him.

The odor of cooking sausage and eggs seeped down to the basement and, finally, Diane, Evelyn, and Onetha came down with food on paper plates and coffee in paper cups. They looked around and saw that Moon was gone. They said nothing. They gave Swoop his food and coffee without a word.

And after they'd eaten, the Bachelors, those who did, smoked. Dart snored in a corner. Chops Jackson checked his watch. Snake stared at the pattern in the industrial carpeting. Bubbles, Cudjo, and Shurley huddled together. Chappie riffled the bills as he would a deck of cards. Swoop Ferguson thought of the money, how he would use it, and how they would have to deal with these people. They would have to be dealt with, Moon was right about that. Right about a lot of things.

It stopped raining during the night. They saw the sky barely lightening through the basement door, but no one talked. Through the night they had whispered, passed cigarettes and bottles, and drunk. Now they were tired and limp.

Bubbles could see the sun starting to shine on trees and leaves outside. Color's gone now, he thought, sadly.

Fifteen minutes before seven Snake said, "I think we ought to try to get together again. New York or some place. Not here. What do you think, Bubbles?"

"Yeah, I'd like that."

"I mean, we'd be getting together more, me, you, Cudjo, and Shurley."

Cudjo nodded. The pain was tracking deeper now.

"We ought to try California next time," Clarie said.

"Well, we'll do it someplace," Bubbles said. "If you really want to."

"Better not wait too long or you'll be one short," Chappie said. "No. I mean, two short, one from natural causes."

Shurley slapped him gently on the back. "No, not long."

Jackson said, "I wonder where ole Moon is now."

Each pictured Moon racing to some secret place. Bubbles wondered at the naturalness of his words, his deeds. No, Moon could not be right.

It was seven and Swoop stood and held out his hand for the money. "I'm goin," he said. Chappie gave him the bills. Swoop paused in the back door, the dry, cold morning air blowing around him. "I'ma see you niggers. Real soon."

The import of his words stacked up in the room until Bubbles said, "Look, let's go up and have one more cup of coffee together. Just one."

As they trooped upstairs, Onetha flung open the door. "More coffee on and Evelyn's whipped up a little sweetbread."

At seven Moon raised and peered through his windshield. He ducked back down upon the seat when he saw Swoop walking quickly from behind Bubbles' house. He looked small from that distance. Moon raised again and saw the detective getting into his car. Shit, Moon thought. He was facing in the wrong direction. When Swoop drove by, Moon started his car, pulled into a drive and backed out and followed at a distance. Them cats been to too many movies, he thought. Tape recorder. Trying to save *my* ass.

He lowered the window on the rider's side and took a deep breath of the whipping cold air. The morning was going to be clear, he thought. Make good time.

Fighting sleep, Swoop pulled onto Athens Boulevard. The

thought of the money in his pocket helped to keep him awake. The night seemed to have suddenly lifted part way; the distance was still gray. Street lights still burned. Glancing in the mirror, he wondered why the car behind him was not showing headlights. It wasn't that light, yet. And as he was wondering, the car began to grow bigger in his mirror.

Moon pulled out fast, then slowed as he came up on Swoop. He slowed to match his speed and held the .38 straight out, toward the cop, and felt the gun lurch in his hand, saw yellow, jagged flame lick out again and again, saw, with satisfaction, the surprise in Swoop Ferguson's face, then he mashed down on the gas and sped away as Swoop's car curled toward the shoulder of the road, then down into a ditch and up the other side at a sharp angle. Moon took off his wig and put the gun in it. These would go, one by one, later.

He continued on his way, northward.

Bubbles, sitting at the head of the table, thought he heard a car backfiring way off in the distance; the sound carried clearly through the morning. He looked at the exhausted faces, the limp bodies. Imperceptibly he shook his head. Only his wife saw and understood. She took his hand and squeezed it, and he was squeezing back when he heard, also distantly, sirens. But now they were all pushing back from the table, finished, and Bubbles rose slowly to shake with and embrace each one. He knew they would not do this again, ever.